About Darry Fraser

Darry Fraser's first novel, *Daughter of the Murray*, is set on her beloved River Murray where she spent part of her childhood. She currently lives, works and writes on Kangaroo Island, an awe-inspiring place off the coast of South Australia.

Also by Darry Fraser

Daughter of the Murray

Where the Murray River Runs

DARRY FRASER

mira

First Published 2017
First Australian Paperback Edition 2017
ISBN 9781489248862

WHERE THE MURRAY RIVER RUNS
© 2017 by Darry Fraser
Australian Copyright 2017
New Zealand Copyright 2017

This is a work of fiction. Names, characters, places, and incidents are either the product of the author's imagination or are used fictitiously, and any resemblance to actual persons, living or dead, business establishments, events, or locales is entirely coincidental.

Published by
Mira
An imprint of Harlequin Enterprises (Australia) Pty Ltd.
Level 13, 201 Elizabeth St
SYDNEY NSW 2000
AUSTRALIA

® and TM (apart from those relating to FSC ®) are trademarks of Harlequin Enterprises Limited or its corporate affiliates. Trademarks indicated with ® are registered in Australia, New Zealand and in other countries.

Cataloguing-in-Publication details are available from the National Library of Australia
www.librariesaustralia.nla.gov.au

Printed and bound in Australia by McPherson's Printing Group

Gilda
11.10.1927–07.12.2016
Mum, we miss you every day

One

Bendigo, Victoria, mid–1890s

Linley Seymour stared at the sleeping baby in his crib.

He stirred in his firm swaddling, his sweet face reflecting a happy sleep, a dream floating across his features. His little mouth pouted, ruby-red lips working as if he needed to say a few words.

He is so beautiful.

Something surged deep inside her, shifted in her chest, a force of emotion, and a yawning chasm opened at her feet. She stepped back, the shock of it making her heart race. A moment, a beat later when it slowed, she leaned cautiously over the cradle again.

Solemnly, his wide-open eyes stared back at her. He frowned a moment and let it go, drifting back to sleep.

'You are so beautiful,' she whispered to him. 'And I love you with all my heart.'

But this tiny creature, this serene-looking infant, had, through no fault of his own, created havoc from the moment he was conceived.

She stopped herself short. What was she thinking? Her Aunt CeeCee wouldn't let a thought like that creep in. CeeCee didn't judge anyone. In her work she offered refuge to mothers and babies like this one, not judgement. She wouldn't blame a little child for the sins of his mother.

Or his father.

That was another matter. The bristling needled up Linley's back. She put a hand to her throat as heat crept over her neck, and herded her thoughts back to her aunt. A few townsfolk knew how CeeCee kept herself occupied. Certainly, some did pass judgement, but there were others who were very happy someone offered refuge, just as long as it wasn't asked of them.

Linley rubbed her arms. At times she despaired for CeeCee and their work. Of course it was important, and sometimes dangerous, so it had to be clandestine. The few folk who did know thought they were foolhardy, not brave or enlightened. It kept Linley on her toes to go about their business as quietly as possible.

That meant life with CeeCee was lively and engaging, if a little unsettling at times. Yet it seemed that the nature of her vocation had not had the slightest impact on her aunt's bearing. At just over forty, she was still dark-haired, slim and elegant, vibrant, and certainly not solitary. Linley was none of those things. She often joked that she and Aunt CeeCee were perhaps not related. CeeCee assured her that was not true—they were definitely related by blood: aunt and niece.

Of course, Linley didn't know enough of her father's side to attest to hair colour or any other attributes. She didn't remember him, and he was certainly never spoken of, ever. Perhaps it was all his fault, her freckles and her dark copper hair.

The baby's tuft of black hair caught Linley's eye. Idly, she wondered if her hair colour and her green eyes would appear in a baby of her own if she married a certain black-haired man—

Stop that nonsense right this minute!

She focused. The baby. Concentrate only on the baby in his crib. This beautiful baby … Take a deep breath.

So, now that she had at last decided on a name for him, she should announce it. She was sure that this last month she'd driven everyone mad with her ponderings and musings. Mary Bonner, the baby's mother, had had only a few hours with him before she died, and hadn't given him a name. Yet she had made sure that in the event of her death, Linley would be the one to make that decision, not her husband.

Though why on earth Mary hoped I would take on her child and rear him as my own, I don't know ... Do I?

She'd shied away from that very thought, hour by hour, day by day. Ever since Miss Juno first placed the poor neglected, wretched little soul in her arms at that terrible house. Miss Juno was from the solicitor's office, and had nominated herself to be Linley's agent. The day Mary had died, Miss Juno had accompanied CeeCee and Linley to get the baby from Gareth Wilkin's house.

It was best not to keep wondering why Mary did anything because Linley was only deluding herself. She knew the reason behind Mary's decision, even if the words of it lay unspoken, buried deep in her heart.

Gazing down at the baby, she had a sudden, urgent desire to pick him up, to snuffle into that new-baby smell of him. She puffed involuntarily, resisting the urge until it eased. It was harder than ever to do and lately she'd found herself not resisting one bit. His was a comfortable and familiar weight in her arms these days. She looked forward to it, craved it at times, and it soothed a relentless longing. She'd gotten to love the way her body moved when she held him and quieted him, as if she had, at some other time, been a mother with her own babe and knew what to do.

Very bewildering.

This baby—*oh, for goodness sake, Linley, use his new name ...* how could he possibly be hers to keep? Yet Mary had given him to her. How would she, with her job in the tea-rooms, manage to look after him? But without her job, how would she manage to keep him? Of course she had CeeCee's continued support, but what would everybody think?

What everybody thinks is not a priority, Linley Seymour. She heard CeeCee's voice as clearly as if her aunt was in the room and had spoken to her.

CeeCee was staunch in rallying to the cause. Of course she was. Had she not rallied when Linley herself was a needy child? Besides, the wet nurse would still come for the baby, or Linley would take him to the nurse. At least that sort of feeding was taken care of, although she had no clue how long it would last. She should ask.

The baby stirred again and this time when he looked at her, Ard O'Rourke sprang to mind. A blush warmed her cheeks.

Ard O'Rourke. Had her scalding letter to him blistered his fingers when he read the news, the terrible, *terrible* news of Mary's death? That, and the fact that Linley knew Mary's husband, Gareth Wilkin, wasn't the baby's father.

She pressed a hand to her forehead and squeezed her eyes shut. Time and time again she'd agonised over why she'd rushed to put her furious words on paper. What had possessed her? Why had she marched with one-eyed determination to the post office and mailed the letter? Why had she marched all the way home then instantly, horribly regretted it?

She'd run back to the post office in a desperate fever hoping to retrieve the letter and tear it to bits. Only to see the mail coach charging around the corner, out of reach then out of sight.

———————

Linley called to mind that day of the picnic by Lake Weeroona. The day he left. She remembered clearly. It had started out like she always hoped it would, full of easy laughter with friends, and the chance to finally wander off to be close to Ard. Perhaps today would be the day he'd ask her to let him court her.

Ard, leaning against a tree, as she stood inches in front of him.

Her clothes felt tight. Her voice stuck in her throat, and that peculiar heat pounded through her veins like an exhilarating flutter of a thousand butterflies. And yet … and yet how madly euphoric and exciting the thrill of it.

Those black eyes of his had watched her, a small quirk at his mouth deepening a line in his face. It wasn't a smile, more that a thought had crossed his mind and had vexed him. His dark brows furrowed a little. The beard stubble roughened his cheeks and neck—perhaps two days without a shave—and the blue-black of his wavy hair crept at the back of his collar.

And none of that old-fashioned, silly-looking moustache and stringy beard thing for Ard O'Rourke. One day he had two days' growth and a mop of dusty, sweat-grimed hair, the next he was clean-shaven, with his hair silky-washed and thrust back from his forehead in a long sweep, the loose dense curls waiting for her shaking hands to reach. He had a certain air about him, a leonine grace, as if nothing fazed him or got in his way. A big man, not so tall, but elegant in his movements—

Elegant…?

But he was. Supple. Fluid. And he well knew his worth. Aunt CeeCee had once commented he was more gentlemanly than the gentlemen she'd observed in Melbourne.

Ard had let her gaze trawl over him, his only movement a resting of his shoulders back against the tree trunk.

Then he spoke. 'All I have is some beef jerky.' He held up a ragged piece, then took a bite, a quick clamp and tug of teeth. He held her gaze only a moment then looked away.

Her blush rushed to deepen, and her heartbeat thudded in every pulse point of her body. Something was not right.

She stood, transfixed, waiting. Would he reach out and hold her?

Damn and bother. It didn't appear that he would. After all these years. They were finally adults, and still he would not gather her to him and declare …?

They'd grown up together. For long years they'd glanced furtively at each other, touched hands or fingers, almost as if in a game since they were children. Trailed each other from classroom to paddock to stream, and to their respective families' sitting rooms. Though nothing was formalised between them, Linley had expected that she and Ard would soon step out as a couple, and court, and finally be married. But no, he was so determined to find his way in the world first. Well, she would wait, hard as it was.

She was losing sleep because of him. Going mad because of him, with thoughts and feelings and needs she couldn't explain … Languid, heavy warmth tingled between her legs, softened her. A delicious fear of something she couldn't name rippled inside.

He stood without moving. Her hand rose and rested on the wall of his chest and she felt a muscle jump beneath. A quick glance at his face revealed nothing, just the immoveable stare. Suddenly, he was not all cool and masculine grace, but heat and power and—

She snatched her hand back, but too late. He'd snapped it within his and wouldn't let go, as unbreakable a bond as if she were bound in steel.

But then his bewildering words. They were uttered without so much as a change in his expression—except for a light in his eyes, which, for an instant, were like glistening onyx.

'I'm going away, Linley. To Renmark, where my parents are, to help out there, try to make something of my life. I'll get wages at last, maybe prove I can support a wife. But I don't know when I'll be back. This depression steals everything, and I—' He dropped her hand. 'My uncle Liam can look after the orchard here. Don't wait for me to come back. I can't promise anything.' He'd lowered his head. 'I never could.'

Her face burned anew. Her cheeks would now be as red as her hair—that much her aunt used to tell her.

She snatched her hand away. 'Don't wait?' She began to sputter. 'I don't care how much money you have.'

He pushed off the tree. 'I shouldn't even be here now, Linley. I've no right. I've nothing to offer, nothing to give you. Whatever was there is gone.' His frown was a deep scowl and a dimple in his cheek worked as if by itself. His mouth was downturned, his stare flinty.

'But I—'

'I'll come back, sometime. Sometime when I've made something of myself.' He looked despairing. 'But don't wait for me. I can't give you what you want. I can't be who you need me to be. Not yet.'

Words rushed out. 'That's rubbish, Ard O'Rourke. We can start now, with nothing. I don't mind.'

'I do. I won't be talked around.'

'That's just pride. We could live at the orchard. I could try and ask for more work at Mrs Tilley's shop.'

Ard's frown deepened. 'Aye, a woman supporting a man. I'll not do it, Linley. If I can't support my wife, I'll not be taking a wife.' He straightened abruptly. 'I never courted you properly, Linley, because there was no prospect of ever ...'

Linley gaped at him. 'You've already made up your mind. You never once said that you'd go away.'

He threw the jerky to the ground. 'Things have just got worse and worse here. I can't stay. There's no money, no jobs.'

'But not to discuss anything, just to announce you're going off somewhere?'

'I can't sit around here any longer and wonder if I'll ever earn a living.' He stood so close, seemed so angry.

Linley knew she was losing the fight, knew she wouldn't be able to change his mind. Her life, her hopes of a life with Ard, were slipping away.

She gripped his arms. 'Ard, I could come, too. We could …' She hesitated only a moment, a desperate, pleading moment. 'I don't need to be married if that's what you're—'

He shook off her hands, his black eyes flashing and his mouth set. 'Don't ever say that to me. Ever.' He turned his face away, rubbing his eyes. 'I've already made up my mind. I need to have work. It's been too long already.' He let out a ragged breath. 'I'll go to Renmark.'

'No!'

He leaned in a little and she thought her heart would give way. He only let his cheek warm the air beside hers, a quick touch of his fingers on hers, a sweep of his gaze over her face. And he turned and walked away.

Ard O'Rourke walked away.

Linley could only stand there, staring. If she ran after him, what could she do? He was not a man to change his mind. And she would not beg again.

Ard.

Her cry was silent then, but walking home along the edge of the lake, alone, with not a word to the others at the picnic, she whispered his name over and over.

That had been months and months ago. And now, if she ever saw Ard O'Rourke again she would take him to the authorities. She would brand him a scoundrel and a shirker of his right and proper duty and—

And what? Never talk to him again? Shun him? Refuse to invite him for tea?

As for Mary! Carefree, always with her skirts held high as she ran through the dusty paddocks at the back of the town … Seems like she'd held her skirts high once too often … with Ard O'Rourke.

Linley's blush flared again. She'd warned Mary about being too frivolous and light-hearted with the boys who'd been her childhood friends.

'But we are only friends, Miss Linley,' Mary had said, waving off the well-meaning concerns. 'I've been friends with them all since we were born almost. Do not worry about the prattle and the gossips. I can take care of myself.' There'd been a gleam of high excitement in her eye.

Gleeful in life, she was. Appearing unconcerned about society's mores, she was free with her affections, and with no thought to any consequences. *Silly, silly girl.* Her old aunt had often scolded her, but had always protected her.

Linley shut out Mary's pixie-like face laughing at her from the afterlife. Mary had thought this life was a fun game. However, without a doubt, the end days of her life were nothing like fun at all.

You were a foolish girl, Mary Bonner, but you didn't deserve your type of death.

She checked the baby once more and again he stared at her, wide-eyed, fascinated. He squirmed in the firm swaddle and when she reached out and touched a finger to his cheek, he smiled with a toothless happiness that shot a bolt of pleasure through her.

Her heartbeat thudded in her throat. She reached down and scooped him up, hugging him to her chest. Something familiar stirred, yet not. Something deep inside, but not what she recognised as belonging to her. It was in a place she hardly dared explore.

Ard O'Rourke. He makes me feel hot and melting and sad and bursting with rage …

And I'm holding his baby close to my heart.

Two

1890s Renmark, north-east South Australia

Ard O'Rourke knew he hadn't died because one of his eyes opened. Yet the amount of sly grog he'd consumed last night should've killed him stone dead.

Well, he wasn't dead. So he groaned and rolled over, fighting sleep.

Mary, enticing a man to—to do things he should know best not to do. Mary.

He cranked open his other eye. Shut them both against the buzz of his thoughts and the buzz of a large blowfly about to settle on him. He shook his head to fend them off.

He rolled onto his back. Inhaled.

Linley.

She was in Bendigo, back home in the colony of Victoria. He missed her. He'd missed her all along. Did he have any right now to think she might miss him?

He was here in Renmark, had been for months, trying to earn a quid, trying to help his parents at the same time. Neither was working. The vicious bite of the depression had a big reach, and the new scheme for irrigation on the river was failing fast. Money was almost non-existent, men were being laid off, and he'd been one of them.

He couldn't expect his parents to keep him now he had no job.

Golden light crept high behind the tops of the towering gums. Dawn over the Murray River. A balmy spring promise of summer heat was not far away, and a gentle tide lapped the muddy bank. The spicy, peppery scent of eucalyptus stirred a faint memory.

He exhaled. No pounding head. No vile stomach. Yet.

Linley, forgive me …

Footfalls crunched closer on the leaf litter. Ard eased open his eyes. His father's worn heavy boots landed inches from his nose, puffing fine riverbank dust up his nostrils.

'Here.' A steaming tin mug was thrust just over the large boots, nose level.

'Mornin', Pa.' Ard pushed back the horse blanket wrapped around him and sat up. He palmed his eyes then reached for the mug. He sniffed. Strong, tar-brewed black tea.

'Afternoon, you lazy lump.'

'It's barely light.'

Lorcan O'Rourke squatted beside his son. 'You feel better now?'

'I will.' Ard glanced at his father whose eyes matched his own colour. The cornflower blue was warm this morning, his father's black brows only a little furrowed.

'Was a fine one you threw last night.' Lorcan laid a callused hand on his son's head.

'Seems sly grog isn't all it's cracked up to be. I'm still here.'

His father hunkered down beside him. 'Listen, lad. 'Tis a sad thing, my boy, but Mary was another man's wife, after all. Destroyin' yourself night after night won't change anything.'

Ard lifted a shoulder and shook his head. 'It was fine for her to marry, if she wanted. Just not fine for her to die that way. Birthing.'

'True enough. But it happens. Best to let it take its place.' Lorcan rubbed his chin, the raspy scratch of it loud in Ard's ears. 'Come on, lad. Your ma's got the damper rising and your sister's sent over a joint of mutton. God knows I prefer me fruit first thing in the morn, but Maggie's kind enough to send it.'

'I'll wash the sleep off me and come up directly.' Ard swirled the hot tea in the mug, blew on it to cool a bit then swigged. He watched as his father strode back up the bank to the stone hut he and his mother occupied. It was a caretaker's hut on one of the Chaffey brothers' blocks for the river irrigation project.

George Chaffey, the older brother, had visited not that long ago. His usual vigour and enthusiasm for the scheme to draw water from the Murray had been a little flattened by the 'economic restraints', as he called it. His Yankee drawl was tempered by worry.

Anyone could see now that it wasn't going to work.

The tea soured in Ard's mouth. He tossed it out and threw the mug to the ground. He peeled off his shirt, his undershirt, undid his trouser buttons and let his pants drop. Naked, he waded in a few feet and let the cool water sluice off the last few days' misery. It would only clean off the sweat of first grief, not the deep penetrating seam of guilt that burrowed through him. Inside him was a hard lump. More often than not it was in his throat these days.

Mary Bonner, a childhood friend from his home town, dead, birthing her first child. By the time the news had found him, she'd been dead more than two weeks.

He clenched his teeth until his jaw hurt.

He'd have to face Linley Seymour at some point. She'd sent the news as well, with ill-concealed wrath, palpable in the hastily penned angry letter. It found him only yesterday, just days after Mary's own letter had arrived.

Not a word from Linley before now. Not that he expected it after the way they'd parted. And now this.

Wading back to step on dry land, he brushed off the water and pulled on his pants. He rolled his shoulders, stretched his neck side to side. Bent and picked up his shirt and shrugged into it.

He checked for both letters in the pocket. Safe. Secure.

It wasn't the grog last night that had done him in. It was the bone-gnawing, wearying fatigue of sorrow. The knowledge that Mary had been carrying *his* baby when she lost her life.

Three

Eleanor O'Rourke tidied her long dark hair, removing some pins only to re-pin it more firmly. She patted both sides of her head when done, wiped her hands on her apron and reached for the large wooden spoon fashioned out of a stout stick.

She looked over her shoulder at her tall, black-haired husband as she stirred the simmering fruit. The fragrance of stewing apricots filled the small room and the heat of the fire under the cooking pot broke a sheen of perspiration over her forehead.

'Our lad is sorely tested over poor Mary Bonner,' she said.

'He is at that.' Lorcan wiped a hand over his mouth. 'Don't know what more we can do for it.'

'Naught to be done but to bear it with him.' Eleanor sighed.

'A true thing.' Lorcan nodded. 'I didn't know he carried a torch for her.'

Eleanor shook her head. 'Don't think he did. But something has happened. He feels it deep.' She pulled the spoon through her jam. 'Life is hard enough without more deaths of young people.'

Lorcan nodded again, frowning. 'But you're looking fine this morning, my good wife. I'm a lucky man. It's a pleasure to see your beautiful face.'

Eleanor turned at the smile in his voice and rested the crude stick over the pot. 'Perhaps it's a pair of those spectacles we'll be needing for you, Lorcan O'Rourke. I'm hot and sticky with fruit and looking like one of your old banshees, I'm sure.'

Lorcan flashed her another smile, a dimple deep in both cheeks. 'Not that, my girl.' He sat at the table and lifted a booted foot onto his knee. 'Besides, I don't remember them.'

'And no longer a girl.'

'You're my girl.'

Eleanor's turn to smile. 'I'm lucky to have had a good life so far, Lorc.'

He shrugged. 'But perhaps better had we stayed in Bendigo than risking this venture.' He tapped his large fingers on the table-top. 'You know there's talk the irrigation scheme's failed, that the Chaffeys are in financial trouble.'

Eleanor turned back to the pot with a hand on her back and a stretch upright. 'And who is not, now? You've given it a chance. And Mr Chaffey wanted your expertise in the orchard. He still has to pay your wages.'

'And he has my expertise, such as it is,' Lorcan said. 'But if he can't keep the funds secured, the project fails. No wages. We should head back to Bendigo.' He brushed crumbs from the break-fast damper into his palm. 'Vines do well in the valley at home, and I've an interest to cultivate, but ten acres is not enough land. If we get our last wages, we might have enough to buy more. But without water here, or money …' He spread his hands.

Eleanor followed her husband's gaze out to the enclosed mod-est orchard just beyond the back door. 'It's not far to cart water. Or you could dig another well while we're waiting for the new channel.'

'That would've been my next project, especially if we have Ard for a while. And speaking of Ard …'

Their son filled the doorway. So much like his father in build, in height, his broad chest not yet as deep, his carriage a mimic of Lorcan's, and Lorcan's twin brother Liam, when they were both younger men. Eleanor glanced between the two, and a flutter warmed her belly. Her men. The elder, whose dark hair, laced with silver strands, was still curly and soft at his collar. His intense blue eyes had faded a little and his inner fire had settled. Now its constant warmth glowed, an ever-present beacon.

Ard, her oldest child, made a good-looking young man. It was no wonder the girls went all a-flutter over him. Eleanor hoped he was sensible, but feared perhaps he was not.

Ard looked first to his mother, then to his father. 'Speaking of Ard?'

'We need another well dug. I'm too old for carting the extra water up from the river, it seems.'

'Lorc, you're just too busy with the new project.' Eleanor turned back to the pot and shoved it off the hot plate. She'd have to spoon the mixture into jars in a few minutes.

'Pa, I'm not sure you're clear of high water here. You need to live above that.'

Lorcan lifted his shoulders. 'Took a risk. Not been a flood here for twenty years. We're not living here for long. We'll be gone by the time there's another one.'

Eleanor stared at her husband. 'And how is it you know that, Lorcan O'Rourke?'

'I have an ear to the old men about the place.'

Ard cut in. 'Pa said you had Maggie's mutton. I'll take some and go see if Mr Egge has already pulled in at the wharf. You need stores, Ma?'

Eleanor pointed to a waxed packet in her pantry nook, a small niche in the stone wall. 'Take some damper, too, but eat it quick. In this heat it sets like flint.' She watched Ard tuck the packet under his shirt. 'And if Mr Egge has arrived, bring me some sugar and a packet of darning needles, would you?' She reached up over the stove and ran her fingers along the rough-hewn shelf embedded in the stones to find what she was looking for. She handed him a shilling.

'I will.' Ard pocketed it and turned to his father. 'So if needs be, we should dig that well in the next day or two.'

Startled, Eleanor looked at her husband.

Lorcan raised his eyes. 'And what is your hurry for that?'

'I'll be heading back to our old place soon as I can. I got things to do there.' He doffed a non-existent hat at his mother, glanced at his father, nodded and left.

'Things to do in Bendigo? I thought he wanted to go to Echuca.' Eleanor glanced from the door to her husband. 'Especially now Liam thinks it's a good idea.'

'I haven't heard from Liam lately, not since he said he was going to Swan Hill to live. But he's long said the competition from the Chinamen at home is too strong. Liam liked Echuca.'

'And he was approached by Chinamen wanting to buy the land,' she said, reminding him.

Lorcan reached for the damper, hacked a thick chunk, stood and walked to the cooking pot. 'I reckon this hurry-up for Ard in Bendigo might be something else. Probably whatever's troubling him.' He took the wooden stirrer and dipped it into the stewing pot, then slathered steaming apricots onto the bread. 'As for an offer on the land, nothing yet.' He took a mouthful. 'No reason to bother Ard with it until needs. When it happens, I'll make a decision with Liam about it.'

Eleanor took back the spoon from her husband. 'If what you say about the irrigation settlement here comes to be, we might need the Bendigo land after all. Perhaps it's a good thing to put vines on it. Keep a bit for orchard. We can live on fruit.'

'Ellie, my love. If the Chinese people can cultivate better than I can, and they can work the place better than us with their families and their clans, I'm not about workin' myself to death over ten acres. I'll sell it, move on.' He tucked a loose tendril behind her ear. 'We will buy land elsewhere.'

'How will we manage that?'

'Like we always have. I'm thinking Echuca, too. Liam's fair taken with the area, knows it better than me. Says he might have found an acreage would suit. The land's good, plenty of water, right on the river. And Ard's been there on the river with Mr Egge, says it's the place to be.' He took a look outside then back at her. 'This South Australia colony is too dry by far. And there's not much hereabouts for a bright lass such as yourself.'

Eleanor spread her hands. 'And Ard and Maggie?'

'They can read and write good enough, thanks to you. They can keep themselves. And Maggie has a fine job at Olivewood. Who knows where it will take her?'

'I won't be leaving her on her own, Lorcan O'Rourke. I want her to get over that Sam Taylor.'

Lorc scoffed. 'Sam. The lad needs to grow up. He's a good man, but still likes his mates too much to settle down. She'll get over him.'

Eleanor dipped the spoon back into the pot. 'Well, she's not over him yet. But Ard, without the plot in Bendigo ...'

'He will be fine, my love. A great strapping lad who takes after his father for brawn and his mother for brains.' He chewed and swallowed the last of his bread and jam and sat down at the table. 'Besides, we haven't sold the orchard yet. Might not happen, any of it. But if it does, and your loving husband and your brother-in-law are working on it, don't worry for Ard. My feeling is he'll go for the Echuca idea. He needs to settle down, get his teeth stuck into something. It'll be big enough for all of us to make a good living.'

'Perhaps. He keeps saying over and over lately that he needs to make money, as if he's become desperate. And these last few days he looks worse, beaten down. It's not like him.' She looked at her husband, but he only lifted his shoulders. She shook her head. 'He's twenty-five, so old enough I shouldn't ask, is that it?'

Lorcan laced his hands and looked at his boots. 'You can always ask him, but old enough, that he is. He's grown man enough to do whatever it is he has to do.'

Eleanor looked at her husband. 'At times, he still seems a lad, Lorc.'

He smiled at her. 'A lad who'll find his way. And no worthy journey is ever easy.'

Four

Bendigo

Cecilia Celeste Seymour stood in the doorway watching her niece with the baby boy. From time to time, Linley would reach out to him in his cradle then withdraw her hand. She murmured some, fell silent, shook her head and murmured some more. She hesitated over the cradle, then scooped the baby into her arms, pressed her cheek against his little face and inhaled.

CeeCee smiled. She knew that feeling well, that delightful smell of an infant. It slipped deep into an internal space and brought forward a myriad of warm feelings. 'He looks right where he belongs—in your arms.'

Linley turned with a start then smiled broadly. 'His eyes have not left my face.'

In that instant, CeeCee glimpsed her long-dead sister, Linley's mother. She was so much like her. Even to the way she fashioned her coppery-red hair—the simple winding of a taut plait into a pinned bun at the back of her head. Eliza's mark was well stamped on Linley: the full figure, the straight stance, her strong hands. Her face was open and her smile broad. A smattering of freckles, the colour of Mallee honey, dotted across her nose and cheeks. Her eyes were her father's though, green and moody with flecks of hazel, under well-defined, strong auburn brows. Thankfully, unlike him, Linley was a sunny person.

'He's probably desperate to clutch a great hank of your hair and pull like mad.' CeeCee crossed her arms and leaned on the door-jamb. 'That, or he's concentrating on messing his britches. He's a lovely babe. I'm so glad you haven't given him up.'

'I wouldn't, ever.' Linley shook her head and a bemused frown appeared. 'But I haven't yet worked out how I can provide for him.' Her glance at CeeCee was pained. 'I wanted to keep my job at Mrs Tilley's shop.'

'I know you did.' CeeCee nodded. 'Stop worrying about a job. You have a bigger job now—motherhood. It would've been a juggle to keep up at Mrs Tilley's as well.' She studied her hands a moment. 'Besides, other young women without children need to work. It wouldn't have been fair to keep your job when we can manage without it.'

'It's just that I won't be able to contribute—'

'Nonsense. You've been contributing since you were old enough to walk. How could we possibly have done those things for all our women and children if you had not made a worthy contribution?' CeeCee smiled at her niece.

'You and James didn't ever need me. I only did chores when I was a child. And only lots of hand-holding as I got older.' Linley looked across at her.

'Don't underestimate that.' CeeCee shook a finger. 'And we needed you to keep quiet about our work. That's a very hard thing for a young girl to do, but you did, especially when you understood why. And now you are learning more and more.'

Linley smiled, but it looked sad. 'I still never tell a soul. But I'm sure there are many people here who know what we do without my saying anything.' She gazed at the baby. 'Mary certainly knew to come to you. I didn't tell her about our work, but had I known she needed ...' She stopped.

'Don't feel badly. You didn't know anything about her circumstances at the time. Not your business until she wanted to make it so.' CeeCee came to stand alongside her. 'Perhaps she didn't want to enlist your help.'

'Perhaps.' Linley jiggled the baby, swinging a little.

CeeCee watched a fierce burn redden her niece's cheeks. 'Something the matter?' she asked.

She averted her eyes. 'You never said what Mary told you.'

'All she told me was what you already know.' CeeCee reached around and hugged her niece with one arm, stroking the baby's cheek with her other hand.

'Yes, but how did she know you and James could help?'

CeeCee leaned on the crib and looked over her shoulder. 'She said that she'd heard in the hospital. Probably a kind soul took pity on her rather than shunning her, and let her know to come to us, if she needed to.'

'I don't think she would have told anybody else, do you?'

'Wouldn't matter if she did. As long as we don't attract too much attention, and we don't harbour hardened criminals, the police let us go about our business. It's not the law who comes after us or our poor women, you know that. It's all those too-good folk who believe misfortune will never strike them. Those who believe it's their right to besmirch others. They are the ones their God should help.'

Her niece nodded and rocked the baby some more. His wide-eyed stare never left her face.

So, Linley is worried. Well, I know what that feels like.

Their work had been under some extra pressure lately. James Anderson, CeeCee's beloved of many years and her business partner, believed the suffering economy turned the screws ever more tightly on men already too stretched by their responsibilities. No work, and the city filled with people clamouring for housing.

After the rich had scurried to preserve their cash and holdings once the banks had collapsed, they held tightly to whatever they had. No investment, no spending. The lowest on the socioeconomic scale were the abandoned or widowed women. They came in droves, it seemed, to CeeCee and James in Melbourne. Referred by word of mouth, they found their way to plead for food and lodgings, arriving by stealth at night, with youngsters clutching their ragged skirts, all starving and afraid.

As CeeCee already owned property there, Bendigo had seemed a good place to relocate some of them. Now they owned property in Echuca on the Murray as well, only a short distance away, a few hours on the train.

CeeCee and James had visited Echuca often, had enjoyed the place for the bustle of the busy wharf and the serenity of the river. Identifying a need for their refuge services in that town too, they'd purchased a dwelling to house more unfortunates. Linley had been excited by the new prospect, and a new town. If they decided to relocate there, her help would be invaluable.

Lately, her niece had learned much more of the work she and James undertook. Linley was old enough, and with a young baby in her guardianship she now had first-hand experience of the plight of others not so fortunate as herself. Too many needing—

'In any case, I've finally named him,' Linley announced. 'I'm not ever going to give him up.'

CeeCee straightened up, delighted, and clapped her hands softly, a laugh escaping. 'That's excellent. What have you chosen?' This was more than interesting. Linley was finally declaring herself the baby's parent, even though she was already his guardian in the eyes of the law.

Trying to find a name she was happy with had frustrated all of them, but CeeCee understood. It was a big responsibility to name a child, especially one that wasn't yours, or rather, one that had been given to you to foster. He would carry that name all his life, from infancy to the grave.

Linley looked down at the swaddled bundle in her arms. 'Toby.'

'Toby what?'

She hesitated. 'I haven't got *that* far.'

'Not Mary's husband's name?'

Linley looked aghast. 'Good heavens, no. Not Mary's name either, and for the same reason my surname is not my own father's.'

CeeCee had changed Linley's surname from her birth name of Laurence to hers to prevent Eliza's husband tracking her down. Not that she suspected he could, or would. Once Eliza had come to her, barely alive but in labour, CeeCee had rushed to find a midwife. Once Linley was born, poor Eliza had not lasted long. CeeCee had taken Linley to raise.

Jeffrey Laurence was his own worst enemy, eventually a drunk, using his fists to resolve his problems. He hadn't seemed like that when Eliza married him, but when the baby was first on its way, he seemed to descend into hell.

They'd not seen or heard of him since Eliza's death. Since he'd *caused* Eliza's death. It was as if the land had swallowed him up. And a good thing, too. It was best that Linley's father was well out of her life. She might not have survived had he stayed. CeeCee didn't want to think too long about that.

'You're very decisive about it.' CeeCee squeezed her niece's wrist.

Linley shot her a glance. 'I didn't like Mary's husband, that Wilkin man, from the start. He gave me a nasty feeling, and since, he's just become dirty and odious. I never knew Mary well, but always wondered what she could possibly have thought—' She stopped and shuddered.

'She didn't want her baby born and carrying the name "bastard".' CeeCee watched the colour flush once again over Linley's face.

Whatever is the matter with her? It's not as if she hasn't been exposed to the dark side of people's lives before now.

'Besides,' CeeCee continued. 'She said he wasn't so bad in the beginning, that he'd apparently been sweet-talking her for some time, even before he knew of her aunt's legacy, had seemed quite eager to court her. No sign of any violence or illness of the mind at that time.'

'But why on earth would he agree to marry Mary when he knew her baby wasn't his?' Linley put a hand to her forehead.

How could her blush possibly deepen?

CeeCee frowned. 'Well, once he became aware of the legacy, he clearly thought the inheritance was worth it. Not exactly the right sort of man, after all.'

Linley continued as if she hadn't spoken. 'Then he hands the baby over even before she's cold on her deathbed.'

CeeCee pushed off the doorjamb. 'We'll never really know, but I can guess.' She brushed down her blue cotton day dress. 'Perhaps because he believed the money would come to him anyway. So, no reason to lumber himself with a baby that wasn't his. Indeed, some even desert their very own. Some have to do it, some volunteer it.' She straightened and peered over Linley's shoulder at the baby. 'I just hope for your sake he never comes back.'

'No matter to me.' Linley squared her shoulders. 'He's abandoned him. He handed him over on Mary's wishes. He has no claim on the baby now.'

CeeCee sighed. 'Oh, but he could have, darling Linley. That man's name, Gareth Wilkin, might be on the baby's birth registration as the father. We don't know if your Toby has been registered or not.' She reached across and touched the baby's nose and was rewarded with a wide-eyed gaze and a gummy grin.

Linley bit her lip. 'Wilkin won't be back.'

CeeCee knew Linley was more hopeful of it than sure of it.

'I *won't* give him up, CeeCee. I'll have to have help to keep him, but I won't give him up.'

CeeCee patted her niece's back. 'You won't have to. We'll manage.'

Linley's face was bleak. 'But how?'

'Linley, I do have some expertise.'

'But—'

'And there's still some funds that will see us through the harder times. It got us through the first depression, and if we're careful, we can do it again.' No need for Linley to know the full extent of their resources just yet.

'But it's another mouth to feed, Aunty.'

'Only a small one at this stage.' CeeCee pressed her niece's shoulder. 'You know I would never see an abandoned baby go to anyone not worthy or able.' She peered again at the baby, who switched his gaze from Linley's face to hers. 'And you are both.'

'Some are not so lucky as me to have family like you, CeeCee.'

'True.' She laughed. 'For some there is only forlorn hope, if at all, I know. Mary chose you for her baby. He is lucky his mother thought highly of you.'

Linley gave a short laugh. 'I wonder at that. From what I've heard, Mary was not always so—' She stopped, frowning. 'You and James did so much for her.'

CeeCee held up her hands. 'We did what we were asked to do. We did what we could.'

Offering Mary refuge was exactly the work CeeCee and James had been doing for countless other women—and children—in her situation for years. Even though the perpetrators of the violence might be long gone and never to return to the families they'd abandoned, the colony was not any better at providing for the safety of those left behind. Prospects were bleak, if not nil.

Ordinary people, those who had some little privilege, did almost nothing to assist. And CeeCee understood why. Society was burdened by those who couldn't fend for themselves, this society so full of rules and rarely any of them compassionate. A difference had to be made. Even if under a cloak of secrecy. With-out secrecy, those who were benevolent could be compromised by the unscrupulous. Without secrecy, those who were seeking refuge could bring danger to others.

Not even a marriage could save one from degradation and loss of security. Marriage *so-called* 'law' protected a nasty individual and gave him rights to be cruel and violent.

It wasn't the law at all.

It was well drawn under the British parliament that violence should not be perpetrated on the wife in a marriage. However, a magistrate's 'rule of thumb' a century earlier allowed for common assault to be accepted as lawful. And would a woman question it while at the receiving end of a hard fist? Who would she turn to? It was clear, especially in the far-flung corners of the antipodes, that the local magistrate believed he need not create a precedent.

Once the wife and children sought to flee, sometimes that darkness followed. Those women should not be forced to give up their children, or forced to return to the violence. But the only alternative was the streets and gaol. There was nothing else.

So CeeCee had long ago set about ensuring that there was something else and some*where* else. Her parents had benefitted from their finds in the gold rush of the 1850s and with careful financial planning, had managed to keep and grow their wealth. In their headstrong daughter, Cecilia Celeste (for goodness sake, what a mouthful of a name), they had raised a woman who would not marry until the laws of the land changed and women were given rights and safety. And part of that was now law and enforceable.

CeeCee's parents were dead, her sister Eliza was dead, and now there was only Linley. Eliza had been rejected from care by one of the church houses. She was returned to the man who beat her because she was married to him. She was expected to return to him as his property. CeeCee declared she would make a change, somehow, and do it without the churches. That in itself made the road harder. God-fearing people didn't like someone else showing them up.

Then James and his family had come into her life.

'I know you do a lot,' Linley said. 'I don't fully know how yet.'

CeeCee inclined her head. 'You know mostly how. All to do with good management of finances and some very kind benefactors in James' parents. There's no secret. Suffice for now, we have ways.'

'We have ways,' Linley repeated. 'You always say that. And something always works out, somehow. Is that mostly because of James' parents?' Linley had met them on occasion, but only when she and CeeCee visited James in Melbourne.

'Mostly, but not all. James does quite a lot, too. And I couldn't have done half of what I do if you hadn't been there to help.' CeeCee smiled. 'So you see, it really is down to a few of us. And if you look for magic, you find it.'

'Magic might not fix this.' Linley pressed her lips to the baby's forehead.

'Perhaps it will for "Toby Seymour".'

Linley lay the baby in the cradle, and rocked it until Toby's eyelids drooped. 'He will be Toby, but he won't be a Seymour.'

'Then what will it be?'

Another fierce blush from her niece. 'I'll find him a name. Or—'

'Or perhaps his real father's name. Do we know it?' CeeCee wondered. She knew Mary and Linley had not been close friends, if even friendly at all. So would Linley even know such a secret?

Linley shrugged, a slow lift of both shoulders. She kept her eyes on the baby.

CeeCee slipped her thoughts aside for now. 'He will have to be named something soon if we're to circumvent the trials Mr Wilkin might put upon us. But let's hope there's nothing on earth would bring him back here to cause trouble.'

'I can't imagine what would, Aunty. I just can't imagine.'

CeeCee watched Linley staring at the baby. *Please,* she thought, *let nothing bring Wilkin back.*

Linley leaned away from the cradle and crinkled her nose. 'Oh dear. Not again …'

'All yours, little niece. I had my share of changing a baby's linens when you were that age. I haven't done it since, and not likely to start again.' CeeCee patted her niece's arm. 'You've been doing it so well, so far.' She turned and left the bedroom.

Linley's wail of 'Aunt-ee!' floated down the hall after her.

Five

Renmark

Ard jammed on his hat and stalked past the hitching rail. 'I'm walking today, Ted,' he said to the big dusty gelding tied in front of the caretaker's hut.

The horse nodded.

Bag of sugar, packet of darning needles. Bag of sugar, packet of darning needles.

He rounded the stout stone frontage of his parents' hut, took a one-handed leap over the drywall fence and made his way through Lorcan's trial orchard.

Slim, straight orange saplings were doing well. Four years in the ground now—fruit would come in the next year or two. The apricot trees had already produced, as his mother's stewing pot indicated well. The plum trees were healthy, but Lorcan reported that he hadn't had much success with fruiting.

The few olive trees didn't look as if they were thriving, but they were hardy and cheerful youngsters, perhaps just taking their own time. Ard didn't know much about olives, but if they began to flourish here, he might have to learn. It might be a new market for him if he found he had to stay in Bendigo. Even better, on the river if he made his way there.

He didn't know what he'd meet when he went back to Bendigo, but he'd have to face it. Have to face Linley. Fix the God-awful mess he'd made because he couldn't keep his pants buttoned up. For surely Linley must know.

What hope have I got with Linley now? Still no prospects, no real work and already another ten months down the track.

The row of vines captured his interest and veered his thoughts to the more familiar. Bud-burst had long gone on the vines, and the young clusters of grey-black fruit sat snug against a leafy back-drop. Pa was right. The land here would do well for fruit. Especially for grapes. But only if men could irrigate the flow of Murray water. If only the water would continue to flow.

He clambered over the bottom wall, loped off the track and down the grassy river bank. He stepped onto the foot-worn path and set a pace for half an hour before he detoured atop the bank again to check his bearings.

He would think about his trip back to Bendigo after he had spoken to Mr Egge, captain of the riverboat emporium, the *Murrumbidgee*.

————

John Egge was born a Chinaman on a river Ard had never heard of in a country he would never see, and from where so many of his Bendigo contemporaries had come—though no one else in Bendigo called them his contemporaries.

They were Chinamen, foreigners, and often called worse because of their race and culture. In the gold-rush years they were considered aliens, and an immigration tax of ten pounds was applied to each person if they entered via the Port of Melbourne. They'd arrived in the thousands, landing at Robe in South Australia instead where the tax did not apply. Then they had walked over three hundred miles to the Victorian fields of riches and settled there.

Mr Egge had avoided those masses. In 1853 he boarded the paddle-steamer *Lady Augusta* with his old captain, Francis Cadell, one of the first to navigate the river from Goolwa to Swan Hill. Eventually a river trader in his own right, and very successful, Egge had fought hard to be accepted as a colonial. He often argued with the customs officials about his status on the river, grumbling about the high taxes he had to pay. His was a fine boat laden with goods. Ard liked him, had travelled back and forth on the river with him a few times now. Thanks to those journeys, the river had got to be in Ard's blood.

The silent, moody waterway endured the men, the paddle-steamers and the barges. You had to be sharp, clever to navigate it, for it made man pay the price for folly. In its depths, the fallen giants of red gum would snag an unsuspecting or stupid soul and hold him till his death. Or pierce a boat and trap it fast, delivering it a groaning and pathetic end. Ard had learned every narrow twist and turn in the river in some parts, and wondered in awe at the wide and gently flowing expanse of it in others.

The wharf at Renmark was little more than a tie-up point with a few huge posts driven haphazardly into the water at the bank. Egge's reconstructed steamship, the *Murrumbidgee*, sat alongside, its engine off.

Ard tramped over the dust of the bank and checked for signs of life. 'Mr Egge?' Hearing nothing in reply, he walked to the stern. 'Mr Egge?'

'You don't have to yell.' A white-haired, lean gentleman bobbed out from the wheelhouse. 'That you again, young mister?' Mr Egge squinted in the daylight, wiping his hands on a limp rag.

'Ard O'Rourke, sir. You have space for me to go back with you to Echuca?'

'Might have.' Mr Egge stowed the rag on the wheel and stepped out from the wheelhouse. 'Could use an extra man to help tote some of the stock … Didn't I drop you here some weeks back?'

Ard nodded. 'Mail caught up with me and I have to go home.'

Mr Egge tilted his head, his heavily lidded eyes trained on Ard O'Rourke. 'I need my mahogany showcases polished up.'

'Yes, sir, I'll do that for you but I can also pay my fare.'

Mr Egge stepped to the edge of the boat and peered intensely at Ard. 'Your fare is your elbow grease. This boat has got to be tip-top.'

Ard ducked his head. 'You know I like working the *'Bidgee*, sir.'

Mr Egge made a noise which sounded like a 'hah'. There wasn't a lot in his tone that gave away his homeland accent, but knowing the Chinamen back in Bendigo, Ard knew Mr Egge could sometimes sound like they did. He also knew not to mention that to Mr Egge. He was a naturalised British subject, 'no longer a Chinaman', he'd been heard to say.

'Might be last time, young O'Rourke.'

Startled, Ard simply agreed. 'Yes, sir.'

'Don't "yes" me. Riverboat trade dying. Another drought on its way. All this irrigation settlement worthless then. Might be the last time for the *'Bidgee*. Means we never get a good wharf here at Renmark.' Egge waved his arms and ducked back inside the wheelhouse, then popped back out again. 'You want something off my trading tables?'

Ard had almost forgotten. 'Some sugar and a packet of darning needles for my mother.' He reefed in his pocket for the shilling Eleanor had given him, leaned over the rail and handed it to Mr Egge.

Another 'hah' noise, another brief disappearance and Mr Egge came back with a small packet of sugar and a brown paper envelope. 'Change from one shilling.' He pressed some pennies into

Ard's hand. 'You come back tonight. Goodbye.' And he turned away to the wheelhouse again.

The exchange was over and Ard had his passage. He tramped home the two miles. If Mr Egge was right, and he was a sharp operator, then there was definitely trouble for the irrigation settlers, two of whom were his parents.

———

That afternoon, Ard sat in the tiny kitchen of his parents' hut. 'I'm going back to Bendigo.'

Lorcan nodded. 'You said.' He tamped his pipe.

'Mr Egge's got room on the *'Bidgee* tonight.'

'Good boat, that.'

Ard rubbed his chin. 'He reckons the river trade's dying, and there's drought on the way again.'

His father looked at him. 'We've been hearing that a while now. You think the Misters Chaffey haven't heard it?'

Ard shifted, an uncomfortable tautness between his shoulder blades. 'They've invested here but you—'

'My brother and me haven't let go of the orchard for that very reason. And Liam's been on the place until lately, so it hasn't been neglected. You know we've talked of selling. And that Chinaman Ling has started a conversation. When the time comes, we'll make a decision.' Lorcan continued to tamp, then he lit the tobacco and inhaled in short bursts.

'I'll work the orchard back up again, till you come.' Ard shifted his stance, hung his head then looked at his father. 'I have to go, Pa.'

His father studied him briefly. 'I'm thinkin' that the second well isn't going to get sunk, after all.' Lorcan sucked the smoke back. 'Perhaps that's a good thing. As it turns out, maybe time for us to think about moving back, make a few changes.' He took the pipe from his mouth and tamped the bowl.

Ard looked away. 'Have to make my own way, Pa. A new way. I know that you and Liam managed all the while on the orchard, and I won't be letting you down. I just need to try my hand at different things.'

'You have good experience with the land, Ard.' Lorcan stuck the pipe back in his mouth.

'For growing fruit trees, is all.'

'For *growing*. Don't be putting that down, lad.' Pipe smoke drifted.

'I know it's good work. I just want something more. I'm thinking horses.'

Lorc scratched his head. 'Need a bit more land for horses.'

Ard nodded. At least his father hadn't laughed. Not that he expected he would.

'Still, for now, we got an orchard,' Lorc said. 'We won't starve. We'll eat fruit if the worst comes.'

'That could be years off,' Ard said, but didn't believe it.

Lorcan shook his head. 'Won't be.' He puffed out plumes of aromatic smoke. 'We'll manage, just like before. I'll think on the horses idea, talk to Liam.' He spoke around the stem of the pipe in his mouth. 'Now, do you need some help for this business you have a great burning need to do back home? Might have a pound or two spare.'

Ard looked at his father. 'Maybe extra for the train fare from Echuca. Other than that, I'll be right.'

Lorcan's mouth pulled down over the stem. 'Your mother worries.'

'I know.'

———

Ard took his sleeping mat to the stern, rolled it out, and waved off Mr Egge and his pilot. He slid to the deck. Being under the stars was better than cramped quarters below.

He was tired. Six miles walking in a day in the heat was enough to wear any man out. He stretched and lay prone for a beat or two, then sat up, took off his boots and checked them over. These ones might only just last the journey. Maybe Mr Egge had a new pair for sale on board.

Ard pulled two letters from his old satchel; it was still light enough to read. He held the one from Mary flat between his palms. He looked across to the cement-coloured sandy slopes of the bank beyond. All he saw was Mary's laughing, happy face. All he felt was a rock in his chest.

He looked down at the crisp envelope caught between his hands. He didn't need to read it again; he knew it line by line.

'… *we don't love each other, and it's both our faults for the stupidity …*'

He knew that was true. They had not been lovers before, only friends in childhood. A lifetime ago.

'… *and from that stupidity you and I made a baby, Ard. It is yours, I swear to you.*

'*I had no wish to raise rude suspicions and sully your name by asking after your whereabouts. I care not for myself, I never have. I've lived as I choose and I am aware of others' opinions of me. So for the best at the time, to save my ailing aunt more shame, I found a man who married me quickly, knowing I was with another man's child. I've learned since that he is not a nice man, or good, though I believed him to be, if a bit poorly. He seems to become possessed of some apoplexy at times. But we will be provided for until …*'

Mary had let the line run to nothing. Ard wondered what she meant. She resumed—

'*Miss Linley Seymour has another letter, which I have asked her to keep sealed. We have not been friends, not ever. But she and her aunt are most kind women, and they do good work for women who find themselves in difficult situations. So should something happen to me and my baby while with Gareth Wilkin, Miss Seymour is to open it.*'

One more reason why Ard had to return home. What was in that letter?

He slid Mary's letter back into the satchel and withdrew Linley Seymour's. It near burned his hands. So fierce were her words the pages trembled.

Light was fading. It would do him no good now to try and re-read Linley's blistering accusations as she announced Mary's death. He wondered about Mary's baby, but as Linley had made no mention of a child, he knew it must have died with Mary. A sadness overcame him, and he shied away from everything that brought with it. He tucked the letter into his shirt pocket for the night. In the light of day, he might feel better re-reading it, but he knew not. He just hoped for a sign he could one day approach Linley again. Make it right, somehow.

Linley. Her reddy-copper hair. Her eyes—green … brown? Alive with promises she didn't even know she was making. A woman's body, soft where it should be, he imagined. He'd held her hand, when they thought they'd not be seen, had just glimpsed an ankle when she'd flung herself over a fence. He'd glanced sur-reptitiously at her proud bosom, which had his heart pounding and his thoughts turning to other female parts of her.

Then the last time he saw her, when she reached out and flat-tened her warm hand on his chest, when thunderclaps roared in his ears and lightning bolts flashed in front of him, and love and lust had banged in his gut and his cock … It was all he could do just to hold himself back.

He needed to marry her first, to make her his wife. But he had nothing to offer. No means, no house for her, few prospects. The depression had stripped him and many others of making a mark in the world. The urgency to claw back a living that could sustain a wife and a family had driven him away, and he wouldn't make promises to her he couldn't keep. Many other men had gone mad over it, lost their way. He only had to look at his own father to see what he needed to do to provide.

Ard closed his eyes and shook his head, blew a breath through taut lips. Stretching out on the mat, he gathered the swag under his head and settled back, staring up at the stars.

It had always been Linley. Always Linley.

He clenched his fists. Under the bright night sky, he let out a soundless angry roar. Linley's letter tucked against his chest glowered over his heart, scorched it. And he felt the pain. The hurt he'd inflicted on her had not escaped him. He would have to take what was coming to him. But a life without Linley was not the life he'd planned. He would make amends for the two lives lost. Somehow. And hope to win his Linley back.

He let out a long breath again. No point dwelling on it now. He needed a new plan.

Ard rolled onto his side, folded his arms and shut his eyes against the world. There was sleep to be had.

Six

Bendigo, next day

Gareth Wilkin settled into the large leather chair on the other side of the lawyer's desk.

Bloke feels like a dwarf in this thing.

Tea. He needed a drink of tea. So damn thirsty. Why wasn't the old buzzard offering him any tea? He knew he wouldn't get a drink of rum here. 'I need tea.'

Mr Campbell ignored him.

Might be just as well. Would only have to go take a piss right when he was handing me my money …

His feet couldn't reach the floor. Hated that. So much of this hi-falutin' furniture was made for people who were tall and had money. Otherwise, why would they have furniture so big a body couldn't put its feet on the ground? Because they could pay for more timber and leather and tacks and all the other palaver that went into making a rich, tall person's furniture. That's why their God-blasted furniture was so big.

He shuffled back and allowed his feet to dangle. His left foot's big toe had a bloody great black bruise on it after he'd cut it, kicking the hearth stone the day Mary died. Thing was getting darker, not lighter, and it was creeping up over his foot.

Must be all right, though. Don't feel no pain in it, but stinks for some reason.

Good thing Mr Campbell couldn't see over that desk of his, which was another bloody big lump of timber and leather. Not to mention the fact that the old lawyer himself looked all fancy, what with his nice clobber and clean hands. Bald as an emu's egg, ugly as a bag full of knees, but clearly rich-ugly.

And the rich always had that air about 'em, confident, like they didn't need to worry about nothin'. Well, if you're rich, you don't worry, do you?

And I'm about to be rich.

Mr Campbell was staring at his own hands, large and knotted at the knuckles. Could have been a fighter by the looks of those hands. They rested on some papers.

The lawyer looked up over his spectacles. 'I note the time you chose to send for me was immediately after my client passed away.'

Gareth nodded. 'It were in her papers I do that.'

'Yes. Though perhaps unseemly inside the very half hour it occurred.'

Gareth frowned. 'Eh?'

'The good doctor reported Mrs Wilkin was still warm, and the baby appeared to be feeding.'

Gareth stared back at the lawyer. His guts churned. 'I waited till she was dead. She didn't want no cart ride to the hospital. Besides, the brat was still latched on. Weren't moving nothin' and be blamed for killing 'em.'

Mr Campbell waited a beat. 'Quite.'

Gareth shuffled under the unblinking scrutiny. 'Weren't expecting no troops of folk to come back with the doctor, neither.'

'Ah, well. I thought it best to relieve you of any burden at that sad time in case, in your grief, you forgot to hand over the child.'

Gareth levelled a glare at the lawyer. 'It was me wife, dead. 'Course I was sad.'

'Of course,' Mr Campbell said. He glanced at a rectangular flat envelope, official-like stamps and scrawls on it, on the desk beside his left hand. 'Your wife had made a will, Mr Wilkin.'

Gareth's legs stopped dangling. 'Meaning whatever was hers is mine now.' He licked his lips. Dry as a chip. A man should be able to get tea ...

Mr Campbell adjusted his spectacles and stared over the thin rims. 'She has written her wishes and the law deems those wishes to be lawful. She didn't stipulate anything for you.'

Gareth Wilkin started uneasily. ''Course she did.' A creep of heat clawed its way up his chest into his throat.

'She didn't. In fact, her will stipulates very clearly that whatever worldly goods she possessed she bequeathed to Miss Linley Seymour.'

Gareth shifted in the seat, tried to scuff his feet on the floor. 'Then that amounts to a big fat *bequeath* of nothin'.'

Mr Campbell inhaled and exhaled loudly. 'That might not be so.'

Gareth felt his neck start to sweat at the collar. Why'd she done that? Hadn't he taken her in and saved her from the gossips? Promised to give her kid a home ... Least she could have done was given him the favours he'd asked for. He knew she would've come around, eventually ... knew she would've been nice to him, sooner or later, if she knew what was good for her. It was only that one night he got riled up. Or two nights, perhaps. Her fault, anyways, and so she goes and wills it all past his reach.

He scoffed. 'She can't give it to someone else. She married me and what's hers is mine now she's dead. I married her so that her bastard kid could have a name—'

Mr Campbell held up his hand. 'And on that point, she also made arrangements for her child to be placed under the guardianship of the same Miss Seymour should anything …' He looked down at the paperwork. '… untoward happen to her.'

'I gave Mary Bonner a roof over her head so she could have a life with her brat.'

'And such a pleasant place it was, too.' Mr Campbell frowned. 'I have her letter here, which tells me what she forfeited for that privilege, Mr Wilkin.' He tapped the paper. 'She does say that she agreed to marry for the reason you have just stated, but that you only agreed to it on the promise of the inheritance from her aunt, Edith Bending.'

Gareth shrugged, made a face. 'So I am the rightful—'

The lawyer held up a large hand again. 'Please stop, Mr Wilkin.'

You smarmy bastard. Gareth's jaw locked and he shuffled forward in his seat. What the hell else was in those papers? What had that bitch said?

Mr Campbell pushed back in his chair. He removed his glasses and rubbed his nose as if it pained him. He blinked reddened eyes at Gareth. 'I'm reading here that your wife, despite her belief that marriage to you would at least be civil, thought it was nothing but a sorry and degrading experience for her, despite the bargain made.'

'She *what?*'

'I don't purport to understand what people do and don't do in their private dealings, but what I am reading in Mrs Wilkin's letter is astounding.' He stopped a moment. 'Shocking. Perhaps criminal.' He tapped Mary's paperwork with a stout, firm finger.

Gareth leapt out of the chair and pointed across the desk. 'I was cured of all that before I married her. She made me go crazy with her whining and her brat squallin''—' He swallowed down the urge to lash out, and forced himself to clamber back into his seat. 'I didn't come here to have no trumped-up law person look down his nose at me.'

Mr Campbell harrumphed. 'I have no doubt of that. However, you entered a bargain. Mrs Wilkin entered a marriage contract with you in exchange for her child's security. You were also to receive a part of the inheritance her aunt left her should you have acted in accordance with the marriage agreement.'

'I did that.' Gareth sprang up again. 'Now she's dead I have—'

'No need to shout at me, Mr Wilkin,' he said. 'She maintains here that you did not deliver your end of the bargain.'

'She's *dead* and I—'

'Stop!' Mr Campbell waved a slim, folded document. 'This is Mrs Wilkin's Last Will and Testament, and as I said, you, sir, do not feature in it.'

'—I'm entitled to that money, all two hundred pounds of it!'

Mr Campbell's eyes widened, then narrowed just as quickly.

Old codger looks like a bloody old boot.

'What was hers is now mine.' Gareth could feel the spit dried in his mouth.

'Not so, Mr Wilkin. A woman who has property before she enters a marriage is entitled to keep that property and administer it as she sees fit in accordance with the law.'

Gareth smacked an open palm on to the desk. 'Never heard of such a thing.'

Mr Campbell continued. 'As to the inheritance, my instructions read that the funds will be kept in trust for use by the child's guardian for the upkeep and security of the child.'

Gareth felt his chin pucker, the rage burning the sense from his brain. He couldn't think. He couldn't grasp anything that would make sense of what he was hearing. He squinted, waving a contemptuous hand. 'When did she write this new will?'

'Two months before her death.'

Gareth blinked. *Two months?* She wasn't ill then. She was all right, confined of course, heavy, but he'd been careful and hadn't broken any bones—

'And what was the point of that question, Mr Wilkin?'

Colour surged in his face, his mouth flattened to prevent speech escaping. He withdrew into the seat, his shoulders hunching. *The bitch thought I was going to kill her so she ...* He darted a glance at Campbell and imagined that he could read his thoughts.

His breath came short. 'What else does she say?'

Mr Campbell nodded. 'It would be wise to wonder, sir. Despite her fall from grace prior to your marriage, these papers are very damning of you and your treatment of a woman heavily with child.'

Gareth bared his teeth. 'Her bastard has my name on his birth papers. *I'm* his guardian.'

'I don't believe the child's birth has been registered yet.'

Breath exploded out of Gareth's mouth, but no words came. His wits were lost.

'You handed the child over to Miss Seymour's agent.'

His wits flooded back. 'But I didn't sign no paper to that!'

Mr Campbell shrugged lightly. 'It's well known you are not the baby's natural father, even by your own admission. You clearly had agreed to Mrs Wilkin's request about appointing guardianship elsewhere. Actions, et cetera, Mr Wilkin.'

'Speak louder than words, do they, now?' Gareth thrust upright, a hot surge of fury propelling him. Behind the seething mist that clouded his sanity, he grasped a thought before it darted past him. 'So, these wills. They don't come for free. They don't come cheap. Who paid for the new will? I didn't. I know her ancient old aunt wasn't dead yet either, so there was no money from her. So it can't be legal.'

'That's privileged information and I assure you it is all very legal.' Mr Campbell's eyes widened as he stared at Gareth. 'But it does make a person wonder if Mrs Wilkin set her affairs in order because she foresaw her fate.'

The heat in Gareth's chest whisked away. A cold slide of dread cut across his gut and he felt his features slacken. 'What are you sayin'?'

The lawyer laced his hands and rested them on the desk. 'Only that my advice to you, *Mr* Wilkin, is to walk away. Your wife is dead and buried, but her letter, her will and its content, all give rise to her testament. Her express wishes will stand up in court.' Mr Campbell sat forward. 'Walk away. There is nothing for you here.'

Gareth Wilkin sprang out of his seat, his face burned, the flare surging from his chest to his cheeks. He leaned heavily on the desk, his face not far from the implacable lawyer. '*Mr* Campbell. That inheritance money is *my* property. And I am gonna have it.'

Seven

On the river to Echuca

Ard stood at the stern as the '*Bidgee* raced for the wharf at Echuca. He'd had scarce to do on Mr Egge's boat other than helping heft some wool bales on board at Wentworth. Then a bit of packing up and unpacking the merchandise to secure it from stop to stop.

Plain, gentle river sailing. From time to time they idled, waiting as snagging steamers ahead tackled and winched fallen trees from the water. Snags were impossible to see. They threatened to block clear access through the muddy water, and the danger of holing a boat was all too real.

Wherever the boat docked, Ard tossed his swag onto the bank high above the working parties and slept under the stars. Money was so tight he didn't part with any for food. He needed what he had for the train fare from Echuca to Bendigo. Mr Egge would see him some beef jerky for the ride home. He'd also handed him the sturdy pair of boots Ard had tried to purchase, waving away Ard's offer of payment.

By the time they reached Swan Hill, Mr Egge's stock was much reduced thanks to good sales. The ride to Echuca was a light and fast affair. More cloudless, still days, the sunlight reflecting low banks and tall trees in the calm waters.

It was a relief going back upstream. A homecoming to set right his affairs. With each turn of the side-wheel, with each throbbing chug of the steam engine, with each step closer to home, his heart grew heavier. Linley had to be faced.

Burdened by the deaths of Mary and the child, saddened to his bones, he bore a guilt he couldn't name. Not that it could've changed anything. Besides, Mary had seen right through him.

She'd laughed him off as she adjusted her clothes. 'You don't need to be sorry around me. Your heart's with someone else, any fool can see it, so don't make this something it's not. I just wanted to cheer you up, have a bit of fun. I'm not hankering after you. I don't "love" you. Don't need you.'

She'd certainly made that clear, not telling him about the baby until after she'd married someone else. But why didn't she scream that it was his baby? No family other than her ailing old aunt, her parents dead, no siblings anyone knew of … Why hadn't she come after him?

Don't need you. Was that it, so simply put?

Sad? He was sad, yes, about Mary's lost life and the life of the baby. And yes, he admitted to himself, he was also relieved in a sense, for sure. That sat uneasy in his gut. They'd been lost, both of them … and he hadn't owned to either.

You're pathetic, man.

Guilt. *Guilt.* And more *damn* guilt. He shook his head, a quick flick to try to dislodge the weight of it. He was unused to it. Never thought himself a man to shirk his duty.

Had he known it!

Angry? More than he'd ever experienced … The frustrated, defenceless type of anger where the only relief came from lashing out and hurting something. Something other than a dead woman who hadn't thought he was worth telling of his responsibility. Hurting something, even if it meant crunching his own knuckles into the granite-like trunk of a red gum.

But this anger, this pain, went deeper, and he had no name for it. He couldn't reach into its black hole, grasp it by the throat and choke the life out of it.

And what would Linley have made of all of this? His actions would have hurt her, deeply, even though there had been no formal promise between them.

And why would that make a difference, O'Rourke? He knew how this would have hurt her. He knew.

He tasted bitterness then, a bile that rose and pressed on his tongue, gagging him. He pitched over the stern rail and spat into the water. He wiped his mouth on the back of his hand and bent back over the rail. It wasn't Mary's fault. She and the baby were dead. He didn't even know whether it was a boy or a girl—Linley hadn't mentioned. She hadn't mentioned the baby at all.

Linley.

His chest hurt to think of what he had done to her. He sniffed hard, palmed both hands to his eyes to wipe off the moisture. Truth was, if Mary was going to die in childbirth it would have happened whether he'd been married to her or not. Babies were dangerous creatures, at least the birthing of them was. No place for a man—nothing a man could do to prevent that ...

Except not let your cock rule your head in the first place.

He spat the loose saliva over the stern again.

'You keep that up, there'll be a flood downstream.' Mr Egge stood at his shoulder.

Ard nodded, palmed his eyes one last time. 'Reckon it's time to muscle our way in?' He lifted his chin towards the wharf.

'Reckon it's time. There's a crane swinging free just now.' The old man's eyes crinkled shut as he looked skywards, then back at the wharf, blinking as the midafternoon sun watered his eyes. He leaned on the rail beside Ard. 'Reckon it's time I put this old *'Bidgee* out for a rest. Look to life by the river, not on it.'

Ard thought about that. It was good advice. He'd like to live by the river, too, but couldn't see it for the foreseeable future. He was still tied to the family land at Bendigo.

They both watched the dock for a long moment, then Mr Egge pushed himself off the rail and headed back towards the wheel-house, tugging at his waistcoat before rolling up his sleeves.

'Gun her up a bit, Maxy, take her in at four knots.'

Ard set aside his thoughts, let nothing else into his head other than getting the boat docked and the freight lifted off as quickly as possible. Once it was off, the merchants would pay up. Once they paid up, Mr Egge would be on his way home, back downstream to Wentworth.

Ard would head for the train station. He wouldn't dally atop the wharf, never had. He would only just be in time to purchase a ticket to Bendigo and get on board that train.

And right now, that's all that mattered.

Eight

Bendigo

CeeCee folded the letter and tucked it up her sleeve again. Always the same for her when letters came from James. She didn't want them far from her reach, but not so tucked up against her person that they should irritate if they were snug against her breast.

James was at hand, she told herself, not at her heart. The dull pound of her pulse brought a lie to that. He was always at her heart. She just rarely let it be said.

The front door clicked shut and from the parlour window she watched Linley carry the baby down the path to the gate at the street front, the soft carry bag under him, a bundle on which Toby rested. Linley would walk the three blocks to Mrs Lovell's house, leave Toby to be fed, return, then she would trudge back again and pick him up. It wouldn't be for too much longer—perhaps two or three months—and then he could be fed by their own hands.

She had to admire Linley's tenacity. Not too many unmarried girls would take up another woman's orphan baby and bring it up, caring for it as if it were her own.

What an odd thing to think, Cecilia Celeste. You did it yourself with Linley.

Linley was her blood, her own niece. And CeeCee's liaison with James Anderson had given her the freedom to continue to do so. Of course James was at her heart.

Long ago, around the time Linley had come to her, CeeCee had funded homes in Melbourne and Bendigo with James Anderson. Now that the Bendigo Benevolent Asylum had been closed for some years, the plight of the homeless and disadvantaged was so much more acute, especially for women disadvantaged by abandonment, poverty and illness.

Not that CeeCee had thought too highly of the local asylum when it was operating. It was a horrible place where the inmates, though given a roof over their heads, were subject to overcrowding and despair. The workhouse a dismal, fearful place. The children there had been orphaned, or given up to the asylum because of family hardship, or simply because they'd been deserted by their parents. The place had been all too foreboding, as if being lost in this world was some crime committed by the lost themselves.

CeeCee wanted to see a home where mothers who could not support themselves and their children—for whatever reason— would be looked after, and found work if possible. Or, if they wished, the opportunity to marry, or marry again. It was a timely project. It had achieved some success, and it had been a very busy few years for CeeCee and James. James, who wanted to marry her, even still, after twenty years.

She watched as her niece walked out of sight, then sat at her desk, a new sheet of writing paper ready and awaiting her quill. Words did not come.

Outside, a breeze nudged clouds out of the way. Light spread across the window she'd just left, spilling into the parlour, a small room fitted with a lumpy settee, a large lounge chair and a foot stool by the empty fireplace. The cradle, waiting for its tiny occupant to be returned, stood in a corner behind the settee.

Another warm day coming. Another day with no rain in sight. CeeCee let out a long breath. She should never have written to James in the mood she had been in the last few days. He would worry.

She got up from the desk and went back to the window, dragged the heavy drapes further to one side and returned. Sunlight illuminated the worn carpets and the dust atop the mantelpiece. But her desk was spotless. A pristine workspace. These days, when the baby wasn't squawking or snuffling for a meal or some coddling, she would compose her letters to parliamentarians regarding the petitions of the day. Letters of support for Miss Vida Goldstein and for the suffragist movement would go to newspapers in both the Victorian and the South Australian colonies. She had communicated with Mrs Lawson in New South Wales on her efforts to enfranchise women. CeeCee fully intended to be voting in elections when Federation finally arrived—or she just might have to shift to South Australia, where women were about to get the vote.

She laughed to herself at that. Another depression was looming so her finances needed careful tending. There was the upkeep of her home here in Bendigo with Linley, and the home in Melbourne she owned with James Anderson. There were now two other premises in the mix of things so all that would keep her firmly grounded in the colony of Victoria for some time.

As she lifted the quill from its tray and dipped it into the inkwell, James' letter slipped out of her sleeve to the floor. With a patient sigh, she put the quill down, picked up the envelope and lay it on the desk. Another sigh, and she slid the letter out, unfolded it and re-read. This letter had arrived the day she'd posted her last letter to him.

Darling girl,

I trust you are well and that your new charge is healthy and happy. I am sure with your excellent credentials the baby will thrive. I hope Linley has risen to the task as admirably as you expected.

CeeCee smiled at that.

We have had such an influx of souls lately that we are turning people away, not the worst of them, but those we can see would fare better than others.

He went on to tell her about the house and its occupants, the workers and their charges. It was to the bottom of his letter that she skimmed. In his powerful script he wrote,

'*Until such time as I see your face, I will miss you every minute of the day. When I see you again, my heart will be filled to the brim.*

I await your next visit to Melbourne. I beg you to let me know when that will be.

Yours with the greatest affection, James.'

CeeCee's heart danced again and she smoothed the paper with both hands and let it rest before her. She closed her eyes and James' face appeared, his merry brown eyes crinkling at the corners as he smiled at her, his wide, happy mouth flashing white teeth, his lips daring her to kiss.

A little intake of breath as she tilted her head, remembering his fingers lightly at her throat, their feather-like glide to the swell of her breasts a sweet memory from months ago. Then his mouth on her neck, his whiskers scratchy, and the shivers of delight sped through her all over again.

In his bed they had loved and loved, and there was nothing about his big muscled body, sun-scarred and tanned from years of work on the railways, that she did not crave, did not hanker after, even in her sleep. She clasped her hands, laced her fingers. Memories lingered over her body. She knew she was lucky to be loved by such a man.

CeeCee leaned back in the chair, the memory still vivid.

'Aunty, how do you know if you love a man?'

Truth to tell, it startled her. Her foster baby, her niece was growing up. 'Oh. Well, it becomes a feeling inside. And you just know.' Even to her own ears that answer sounded half-baked and a little dismissive.

Linley had frowned. 'What does it *feel* like?'

CeeCee frowned as well. How *did* one describe that? 'Like nothing you've ever experienced before.'

'And, and how do you know when to … to …' And her furious blush had given her away.

CeeCee wasn't about to be a hypocrite. But Linley had never had a gentleman caller, and as far as she knew, still didn't have one. In that light, perhaps the conversation was a little worrying. 'Who is it you have in mind?'

'Nobody, Aunty. Nobody.'

Which CeeCee didn't believe was true. How could she begin to explain …? Perhaps she simply needed to relate her feelings for James. How she had known when it was right *'to … to …'*.

———•———

James Anderson, and that day of the Chinese street procession in Bendigo, all those years ago.

They'd agreed to meet there after he'd arrived from Melbourne earlier that day. He'd had an appointment with a land agent to keep but after that he would be free. She knew she would take him to her bed right from the moment she met him at the Bendigo train station.

In the main street later, beside him and watching the colourful procession, she knew that was the day she would love him. He lifted her hand and kissed it.

A couple of matrons beside glanced her up and down.

Didn't matter. CeeCee knew what she was about to do. And all it took was to slip her hand into his and tug him away from the celebration. When they finally stood at the entrance to her house, the little weatherboard she lived in, he stilled.

'I would like nothing better than to be in your bed, my dear CeeCee. So you see, my intentions are not gentlemanly.' A lock of fiery red hair fell over one eye and he brushed it aside with a flick of a finger.

'And neither are mine,' she'd replied.

Except for the talk of some of the women whose lives she'd helped put back together, she had no clue what to expect and was eager to feel for herself what being with a man would be like. Most of the women thought highly of that private side of their lives until things went badly wrong.

She remembered the delicious slide of anticipation in her belly, warming her deep inside. Gripping his arms, she felt the solid muscles tense under his shirt-sleeves and then relax as he wrapped them around her and held her close. Heat pooled low and deep between her legs and an exquisite throb there distracted her.

He shook his head a little; his voice sounded strained in his throat. 'We should marry.'

'No, no, I don't want to marry. I want to work, and fight for rights for women. I've told you, I want to be with you, but the shackles of marriage ...' She hesitated.

He frowned down at her. 'They don't have to be shackles.'

'The law of the land ...'

His voice rose. 'I am not the law of the land. You will—*we* will continue to fight your fight.'

'You would tell me anything at this moment.'

'Yes. But I only have my truth to tell.'

He had hold of her shoulders and she touched his hands. 'Come inside, James. Linley is at school for another couple of hours.'

He didn't hesitate further.

In her parlour, she removed her hat, gloves and jacket. His gaze warmed her blood, but it never left her face. She reached over and placed her hand flat on his broad chest and felt his heartbeat thud against her palm. Then she pressed her lips hard against his.

Citrus, light and spiced with cinnamon or nutmeg, tingled her senses as she breathed him in. When he broke away and buried his face in her neck, its scratchy rasp against her throat, her breathless cry let something go in him.

He clutched at her skirts, bunched them higher over boot-clad ankle, over dimpled knee and firm thigh. She slid her hand to his trousers. The smooth feel of well-worn fabric enticed her hand over his erect penis, and then over the buttons she hoped she'd be able to open.

Her breath stopped. The silk of his fingers on her bare skin caressed her thighs and his throaty moan was deep in her hair. She fumbled some more at his buttons then breathed a word in his ear. 'Please …' she said, and she guided his hand.

He flicked open his fly and pulled her against him. Silk again, strong, warm and hard against her bare leg, nudged open her knickers. His penis brushed the bush of her pubic hair and she felt a slip of moisture against her skin.

'Wait.' CeeCee hooked her foot under the little stool close by and stood on it to better reach him.

He grinned, wolfish, hungry and hot, and slid between her legs. He pushed carefully into her until she gasped. Her hands clutched his shoulders and her eyes widened with wonder.

'Deeper,' she breathed.

And he obliged. And when he lifted her off the stool and settled her on the floor under him, some sort of molten magic occurred as he thrust again and again.

And now at her little desk, CeeCee shifted in her seat. A little heat warmed her blood again just then as she remembered her first time, with James. She longed for him now, for his presence, his body, his love.

How do you know if you love a man? Linley had sat there, a hopeful, inquisitive expression on her face, waiting.

CeeCee had squeezed her niece's hands. 'It is the point when he's answered all your questions, and linked all your dreams with those of his own. It is when you trust ...'

Linley frowned. 'How long would *that* take?'

CeeCee shook her head. 'You've been listening to too many of our ladies. It's when you know you can no longer resist ... when you can't resist him, his ideals, his honour, his body ... When you go there of your own free will and with the knowledge and the responsibility that there is no point of return.'

It had taken all of CeeCee's strength to put it so.

Linley frowned again as she digested this information. 'And when do the babies come?'

James and CeeCee had been lucky there. No babies from that first unprotected encounter. Other happy escapades were marred only by a short break in proceedings until James could fit himself with a sheath, ungainly as they were. Many a time they'd thought to abandon the horrible things and deal with the aftermath, but they hadn't allowed that to happen.

'When they're supposed to,' CeeCee said with a nod. 'When you are old enough. When you have found the one to bear with you the duties and the obligations of parenthood.' She thought to finish the conversation there, feeling the perspiration creep onto her neck.

Linley had looked up, and her eyes seemed to shine. 'I will know.'

And CeeCee had felt for her in that moment. 'I most certainly hope you do, though many have been fooled before.'

Now, back in the present again, she rested her hands on James' letter only for a moment more. Then she folded it and replaced it in the envelope.

James. If only she would give in to herself ...

But not yet. Still more work to do.

She sat absorbed in her thoughts before she opened her eyes, took a deep breath and reached for the quill once again.

Dearest James,

I must apologise that my last letter was so needy—

Before she had a chance to write another word, the light insistent tap of a knock sounded at the front door. Clearly she was not meant to be writing a letter today.

She blotted the few words and slid it under the rest of the incoming mail. Patting stray hairs back into her simple French twist, she headed for the door.

'Good afternoon, Miss Juno.' She gave a friendly smile to the girl on the stoop. 'I am delighted to see you.'

'Miss Seymour, forgive this intrusion.' The girl was slightly built with dark hair and a pretty face that made one think of a Grecian artwork. She darted a glance over her shoulder.

CeeCee followed her glance to a carriage she hadn't seen arrive. She saw Mr Campbell's face peer out from behind the dropped shades, and his hand come up in a greeting. CeeCee nodded at him and turned her attention back to the young woman, perplexed.

'Won't you and Mr Campbell come inside?'

'Thank you, no. Mr Campbell has asked me to give this to you.' She thrust an envelope into CeeCee's hand and backed down a step. 'Mr Campbell didn't want anyone watching to recognise him.' She took another step down. 'No one will recognise me, not even after the day at that house belonging to Mr Wilkin.'

'Oh.' CeeCee glanced at the carriage again and the windows still had the shades down. 'Thank you, Miss Juno. And thank Mr Campbell. I will write to him in due course.'

Miss Juno nodded. 'Good day.' She took the last step to the pavement, and climbed unaided back into the waiting carriage. The driver took off after a couple of thumps on the ceiling from within.

A flutter scurried through CeeCee's chest as she turned back inside and closed the door.

Nine

Bendigo

One thing: Ard needed his own horse. Lorcan and Liam had a couple of good work horses on the family place, mainly to pull a cart laden with produce for the markets. But Ard wanted a steed. A swift beast with strength and courage to take him—

A clunk, a screech of steel on rail, a thud. An overhead bag dropped on his head and shocked him out of his train-travel doze. He leapt off the seat with a yelp and muttered an expletive under his breath. It didn't go unnoticed by the two ladies opposite.

'Beg pardon, ladies.' He bent to retrieve the fallen bag.

The young lady—pouty and pretty, about nineteen, all bosom and hip—smiled her thanks as she lowered her lashes. The old lady, bigger bosomed and bigger hipped, was neither pouty nor pretty. Her scowl soured the invite of the younger girl's smile.

Ard bent in a slight bow. 'May I carry your bag off the train for you?' he asked the matron.

'No, you may not.'

Ard inclined his head and handed her the bag. He stood back and both ladies swished past him, the younger behind the older, still smiling. She only glanced his way, a quick flick of her eyes at him, nothing more. Then she whispered, 'Thank you, Ard O'Rourke,' as she moved by.

He stared after them as they left the carriage. No clue who she was. She gave one last look once she was on the station, but her guardian tapped her shoulder and then she was gone.

Ard slung his swag across his back and fastened the worn strap, his new boots dangling off it. He headed out onto the wooden landing of the train station and dodged families waiting to greet loved ones. He nodded at those he knew, and sidestepped those he didn't.

Through the ticket stalls and out into the concourse, he checked for someone in a buggy who might be going out past his place, but he didn't see anyone. He'd have to walk. Another fine reason to get himself a horse. If he was going to be here for a while, he'd need a horse for transport. He didn't intend to be walking to and from the town daily and still get his work done. One way was nearly four miles.

He shrugged. People walked everywhere because horses did not come cheap, and good paying work was not plentiful. But once he had a horse, he knew he could look after it, feed it cheaply enough. If Liam was home in the cottage, he'd speak to him about it. A horse was essential if Ard was to find other means to keep himself.

By now, the family had been competing with the Chinese market gardeners for years, eking out an existence and finding work elsewhere whenever possible. With Lorc and Eleanor away working for the brothers Chaffey, and Liam riding off to God knows where, Ard had to do something.

The railway had been finished to Swan Hill, so no work there. How many of those men would already be looking for other jobs? And railway freight and passenger travel meant the river trade would die; everyone talked of that.

There had to be another venture. Something that would work with both the railways and the river.

Drought was coming again. How would he manage for water? There were times the channel running by their orchard got pretty shallow. Everyone had to be on their guard against water hoarding …

Was it even a good idea, returning to this place?

That thought stopped him up short. Maybe he could plough the orchard into the ground and start again. Start with something no one had thought of introducing. He'd think on that.

Perhaps not. How much time would it take before he could produce enough to live on? Not to mention how his father and mother would take the news that he'd razed the orchard to the ground before there were other means of sustenance in place.

He trudged through the town, switching the swag to his other shoulder. The place seemed bigger than he remembered. It wouldn't have grown anything much in six or seven months … He was just bone-weary, was all. Seemed like bloody ten miles back to the plot, not four.

He rounded B Street, but he hadn't meant to. His steps faltered. This was the street where Linley lived.

He wouldn't have to go past her house if he didn't want to, he could turn around and take the—

No, *goddammit*.

He stood for a moment and eyed the length of dusty road until he could make out the plain, tidy house of her aunt's down the right-hand side. It'd be dusk soon. He shifted his weight, and juggled the swag, then dumped it at his feet, flexing his fingers. She wouldn't be expecting him. He wouldn't even be welcome; he understood that much from her letter.

So … So send a note and make an appointment later to call on her and—

No. *No!*

He rolled his shoulders, picked up the swag and slung it over his back. No time like the present. Get it over with. Bugger the niceties.

Ard O'Rourke inhaled deep into his gut, stood tall, and began to stalk the road to Linley's door. Head down, eyes on the dust beneath his feet, his heart hammered.

Linley. There's never been anyone else.

'O'Rourke. Ard!' The gleeful shout from behind was followed by a rush of hooves as horse and rider pulled up ahead of him. 'Thought it was you, man. You've been gone so long.'

The rider slid off a robust, molasses-coloured gelding, and grinned out from under a mop of straw-coloured hair swept back off his face. He threw his arms wide.

Ard hadn't time to dump his swag. Hauled into a bear hug, the breath was squeezed out of his lungs. 'Sam,' he rasped. His best friend.

'How the bloody hell are you, laddie?' Sam Taylor didn't wait for an answer. He peered at Ard, holding him at arm's length. 'Not too good, I reckon. You're going the wrong way home. It's back this way.'

Ard pushed his friend off. 'And where were you going?'

'Just come from the emporium. Ma wanted some fancy spice or other. Got it here somewhere.' He patted a couple of well-worn pockets in his waistcoat and gave up. 'Doesn't matter. I got it somewhere.' Sam used both hands to scratch his head, knotting the already rough shock of dirty-blond hair. He thudded Ard on the shoulder and steered him back the way he came. 'Here, throw the swag on ol' Pie and I'll walk to your place with you. Come on, tell me all about it. I hear it's a grand adventure up there on the river.'

'Uh ...' Ard looked over his shoulder in the direction of Linley's aunt's house. Perhaps it was just as well. Tomorrow he could—

'Come on, out with it. I might even have rum in my saddle-bags for the walk.' As the horse walked, Sam rifled through his saddlebags and sprung a bottle. 'We'll keep it under cover, but a swig or two won't hurt. God Almighty, Ard, it's good to see you.' He popped the stopper, took a swig and handed it over. 'Here. Now tell.'

Ard took a mouthful. The brew brought tears to his eyes as it scratched and burned its way down his throat. 'Jesus,' he hissed.

'Me da can still brew up a beauty, can't he? Rough as swallerin' rocks, but it does the trick. Now talk while we walk.'

An hour or so later, north-east and past the old gold diggings, Ard could make out the stone hut on the family's orchard. Sam was blathering on about his job at the blacksmith's, and how he knew of something at the cooper's, if Ard was interested.

Only about half an hour to go. Ard would head for the pump and stick his head under cool water to wash off the walk and the rum. Thankfully, Sam did not have a full quart jug with him, but his dry head was beginning to thud all the same.

Then he would lay his body on the cot in the house and sleep till morning. That is, if Sam ever shut up. He could talk the leg off a chair.

As they got closer to the house, three figures stepped out, the shade of the house sheltering them from the sun now low in the sky. Dusk was not far off.

'There's Chinamen,' Sam said, and tugged the reins. The horse stopped in his tracks.

Ard recognised them. One, a slim person, hat on his head, hair still in a long plait but his clothes the same as every other white man's in Bendigo—baggy trousers, a long-sleeved shirt and a waistcoat.

'It's Mr Ling and his sons.' Ard's mind was working. No one knew he was coming home. What were they doing here?

The sons separated a little from their father. As Ard and Sam came closer, the three gave slight nods in greeting.

Ard returned the greeting, first to Mr Ling and then he nodded to the sons. They were cheerful, black-haired lads in their late teens who only spoke halting English. Ard spoke none of their language.

Sam stood swaying by his side. 'Should I be scared?'

'If your shadow jumps up.'

'Funny bugger.' Sam scowled. 'Think I'll sit over here.' He wobbled towards a lone golden wattle and sank, sprawling under its shade.

'Mister Ard.' Mr Ling glanced at Sam and returned his calm regard to Ard. 'Your father and your uncle speak to me of selling this land.'

Ard thought it was the other way around. No matter. 'They have told me of it, Mr Ling.'

Mr Ling had long ago dropped the custom of skirting the main business at hand with polite small talk. And no one expected it of him.

'My offer is seventy pound. You tell them.'

Ard kept his expression bland. Seventy pound. Just over half of what his neighbour got a year ago. 'Thank you, Mr Ling. I will write my father of your offer.'

'He like that offer.'

Ard didn't think so. 'A letter will take a week to get to him, Mr Ling. I will write tomorrow.'

'You telegram Swan Hill to your uncle.' Mr Ling lifted his chin.

Ard decided the conversation was closed. He nodded. 'I will. Good day.'

Mr Ling stiffened. 'Good day.' He flicked a glance at his two sons, and the three walked back behind the house and over the paddocks lined with Lorcan's fruit trees.

Clearly, they'd been checking over the place. Why else would they have been on the property?

Ard watched them take their time. Seventy pounds. But the bargaining had begun. The pressure would now be constant, perhaps weekly for a short time, then twice a week. All the time the original offer still being made.

He felt his blood race. Perhaps life here was coming to a close after all.

Sam rose to his feet, holding on to a tree branch. 'He's an old terror, that one.' Pie stood patiently alongside, his head dipping to nip green shoots at his feet until Sam reached for the reins.

Ard looked over at Sam. 'Come on. Getting too dark for you to find your way home now.' He waited as Pie led his friend to the door of the hut. Sam tied the horse to a post, wobbled a bit and pressed his forehead to the horse's head.

Ard patted Pie's sturdy neck. He was a good horse and he knew his master well. He untied the swag and dropped it to the ground. He ran his hand down Pie's solid flank then loosened the girth and removed the saddle. He took it and the swag inside with him.

Sam was worse for his father's grog than Ard was. He followed, staggered inside the hut and lay on the floor. 'I'll be right in a minute.'

Ard stepped over him to set the saddle in a corner and dropped the swag on top. He grabbed an old blanket and a piece of worn old shirt fabric, stepped over Sam again and went outside to Pie. After a swift rub down, he threw the blanket over the animal, and grabbed the milk pail by the door. He filled it with river water from the channel pump, and set it by the horse. 'Faithful boy.' He kissed the horse's muzzle then headed back inside.

Ard stepped over Sam once more and went to the fireplace. The rule was that whoever was last to leave the hut left fixings for the fire ready to go. He felt along the rough stone mantelpiece for the book of matches—a small, treasured flip-top little fold of stiff paper, kept dry at all costs. He scraped a match with a flick along the stone. A lick of flame crackled and brightened the room. He touched it to the leaves and twigs and old papers in the fireplace. Ard had no clue how long it had been set—Liam could have been gone weeks or months—but the flames grew steadily. He waited a bit before loading on the heavier sticks, and finally with enough logs to burn through the night.

By the time it had well and truly caught, Sam was snoring. Ard looked about the hut. No food to be seen, no tins of bully beef, no jerky wrapped in paper.

Sleep.

He pulled off his old boots and examined them. Still good for a few more wears before he wore in his new pair. He emptied his pockets and stashed the letters on the mantel. He flopped on the single bunk—a low narrow timber frame with rawhide strips stretched under piles of wool skins.

He was hungry, dirty and stinking, but nothing had felt so good in days.

Ten

Bendigo

Linley opened the creaking gate to her front yard and trudged the path to climb the step to the front door. She did have her key, but three trips today already with baby Toby to Mrs Lovell were wearing thin and she couldn't be bothered fumbling for it inside her pinafore pocket. She knocked instead and imagined she heard CeeCee's swishing skirts coming down the hallway.

Some bread and cheese would be waiting for her. Then both she and CeeCee would make the evening journey on foot to pick up the baby and bring him home to settle in for, hopefully, an uneventful night.

The door was thrown open and CeeCee ushered her inside. 'You look a bit worn around the edges.'

'I am.' Linley walked ahead down the small passage past the parlour, out the back door and into the tiny kitchen room. Simply furnished with a table and two chairs, a cooking fire and utensils, it was a haven. She checked the teapot for heat and poured a pannikin for herself, lifting it in offer to CeeCee.

'Yes, please, but I think perhaps something a little stronger, Lin.'

CeeCee had followed her inside after shutting the back door to the main house. She was still in her day dress, a pale green muslin that fell neatly over her compact frame, its cheerful simplicity a reminder of CeeCee's casual grace. She turned and shut the kitchen door, the warmth in the room snug around them. She pushed her hands into her pinny pocket.

Linley pulled a face. 'If we had anything, which we do not. But Madeira would be nice.'

'Indeed it would. Perhaps a tiny splash of rum in our tea, just this once.' CeeCee produced a tiny flask from her apron and poured a nip each into their tea mugs.

'Aunty.'

'Dreadful, I know. But I have something to talk to you about, and we might need fortification.'

'What is it?'

CeeCee pulled a letter from her deep pocket. 'Sit down with me, Lin, then we can finish up and go and fetch Toby home.' She pulled the single page from its envelope and spread it over the table. 'This is a note come from Mr Campbell's office today.'

A shiver raced down Linley's spine, as if cool fingertips had feathered a trace along it. She sat opposite her aunt at the little table. 'Mr Campbell, Mary's solicitor?'

CeeCee let a beat pass. 'Yes.' She smoothed the letter once more. 'He says that Mr Wilkin visited him today.'

Linley frowned at her aunt. 'But you said that Mr Campbell's letter arrived here today.'

'Hand-delivered, no less, by Miss Juno, so that tells me Mr Campbell has grave concerns. It appears Mr Wilkin was most upset that Mary had not made provision for him in her will.'

'I don't understand. Mary made a will and excluded the horrible man. That should be the end to it.'

'If only it were so. Mr Campbell simply says we should be on our guard about Mr Wilkin's behaviour. He says he doesn't believe the man has any claim, but if he finds a sympathetic law person, or finds some money, he might just put up a fight. He also thinks the man has addled wits.'

Linley looked at her hands, clenching and releasing as if on their own accord. She dropped them to her lap. 'I don't believe he has any money to fight for anything. We know he was hoping for Mary's inheritance. She told you that.'

'Well, we know Mary bequeathed it to a trust for her child instead.' CeeCee had her hands around her mug of tea. 'As Mary's solicitor, Mr Campbell is well aware of you as her choice of guardian for Toby.' She folded the letter and replaced it in her pocket. 'So I think he is warning us. We should take some measures of sorts.'

Linley jolted at that. 'What measures? For what?'

CeeCee poured another wee nip into her tea and offered it to Linley, who shook her head. 'I think we should be vigilant, as Mr Campbell suggests. Perhaps at no time should we leave the baby with only just one of us. We should both take him to Mrs Lovell's and we should both be present here in the house at all times. We should both go to market. Those sorts of things.'

'What about the police? We should inform them.'

CeeCee took a sip and set down the mug, her hands enclosing it once again. 'The police.' She looked to the ceiling and back. 'The police do not like women residing anywhere without a male family member alongside. The police might actually take Mr Wilkin's side if he approached them about the baby.' She looked at Linley. 'Here we are, two unmarried women taking on another's baby. A baby who is, by all accounts, a bastard, except for said man's marriage certificate.' She sighed. 'I would venture there are those who would prefer to place the baby with Mr Wilkin.'

Heat crawled up Linley's neck. 'Surely we would never allow that man—'

'Surely. But if it were said that we were not taking great care of the baby, it could go against us.' CeeCee tapped the table. 'There are malicious gossipers all around.'

'My blood boils at all of that.'

'Which is why we do what we do as quietly as possible. Now we might have to do it for ourselves.'

Linley fiddled with the cuff of one sleeve, picking at a slight fray. She might be in need of another day dress soon. She would wait a bit longer before mentioning it to CeeCee. 'Mr Campbell knows that Wilkin handed Toby over to my care. Wilkin practically threw the poor babe at Miss Juno.'

'I am certainly grateful to Miss Juno for acting as your agent. She is a brave girl.' CeeCee nodded. 'Wilkin thought, no doubt, that his marriage to Mary was all he needed to secure her inheritance.' She held up the letter. 'Mr Campbell also says that the baby is not yet registered and that Wilkin was informed of that.'

'What?' Linley's gaze snapped back to her aunt.

'Probably has no clue that's what's supposed to happen.'

The scoff burst from Linley's throat. 'Even if it was his, he would not want him.' She felt the colour rise again and looked away. 'I will register Toby to me and—'

CeeCee interrupted. 'Except now he gets no money unless he's the guardian.' She reached over and patted her niece's hand. 'Lin, you must try and harden your sensibilities a little. You are by far too … ladylike in this business.' She sat back, withdrawing her hand. 'He might now believe he is better served by having the baby …' Her voice drifted off.

'That *cannot* happen.' Linley glared at her aunt.

CeeCee studied her for a moment. 'And you are sure the baby's real father knows nothing of him? Is there no chance he might suddenly appear and—'

'No. No chance of that. He doesn't know about the baby.' Linley's face burned and she knew without looking that her aunt would know she was hiding something.

CeeCee let a few moments pass. 'Clearly you know who the father is, Linley, and that is going to be a great burden for you to carry as you bring up little Toby.'

Linley hesitated. 'You would not think very highly of him if you knew.'

'My dear, it hardly matters to me who he is. Why would it? Except for your having to carry the weight of it all alone.'

Linley pressed her lips shut in case she said something she didn't want to. It was bad enough she knew the identity of the baby's father, she didn't want to add to her own anguish by having to tell CeeCee that the man she'd loved since childhood had—

'And you're sure Mary didn't tell the baby's father she was with child?' CeeCee tilted her head to catch Linley's downcast glare.

'If she did, he clearly hasn't bothered to step up,' Linley burst.

CeeCee sighed. 'A sore point for you and exactly what I mean.' She tapped the table again. 'But what if Mary *did* tell him?'

'He should've married her then,' Linley snapped then huffed out a loud breath. 'We have been over this.' She had to calm herself. Somehow. *Breathe. Take deep breaths.*

'We have. And I'm only trying to help, to find any solutions to the situation.'

'I will take Toby away.' Linley couldn't help the shrill in her voice. 'I could go to your place in Echuca. I will go there with him and no one will know.'

CeeCee nodded her approval. 'Glad you think that way. I've been thinking for some time it might have to come to that, and I know exactly what we can do.'

Linley started. *What?* CeeCee had showed no surprise … 'Do you know something more? Something I should be aware of?'

'No, no, my dear girl.' Another pat to Linley's hand. 'Just be aware. If you feel you have to run, we have to have a plan. Oh, now, I can see by your face I've frightened you.'

'Well, I—what plan?' Her heart pounded, and a throbbing began behind her eyes.

CeeCee sat back in her chair, nursing her tea. 'From here, there are only two places. Melbourne, of course, or Echuca as you say.'

'And go to whom? I have no money except what you provide. I would have to call myself a widow, and masquerade to avoid—'

'We don't need quite the melodrama just yet.'

'But where?'

'Let's not talk of that right now,' CeeCee insisted. 'We should go and get our baby before the night is any more gone.'

'CeeCee …'

'No more just yet.' Her aunt stood, opened the kitchen door and poured out her tea onto the dirt. 'Come along. You'll need a shawl.'

Linley watched as her aunt headed back into the main house. What on earth could she mean? And such a mystery—either Melbourne or Echuca. Did she mean to the shelters?

Oh my lord—have I just become a woman in need of shelter?

She was staring at the open door of the main house when CeeCee's sharp command jolted her out of her thoughts.

'And be sure to lock that kitchen door after you.'

Linley swept from the room, slammed the door, turned the key in the clumsy lock, and clutched it until she was inside. She slung it onto the dresser in the hallway and picked her shawl off the umbrella stand.

CeeCee was at the door, her own shawl wrapped around her. 'Hurry along, miss, we have a baby to fetch. And we will not talk of this as we walk. There are gossips listening everywhere.'

———

CeeCee paid Mrs Lovell for her care of Toby and only once he was sleeping in Linley's arms did they decide it was time to take the walk home.

'And Miss Seymour ...' Mrs Lovell reached across the kitchen table and handed CeeCee a small cooking pot. 'Thank you for the loan of the pot, but my big girl has worked for one. Mrs Lee at the bakery found herself with more than she needs, so my lass was able to buy it. So, this is yours back, scrubbed clean and all. No marks from the cooking fire.'

CeeCee took the long-handled pot. 'If you're sure, Mrs Lovell. But could you not use a second pot, especially now with another little one?'

Mrs Lovell appeared to bristle. 'Quite sure, thank you. You see there, we have our own now.' She lifted her chin in the direction of the hearth and the pot hanging from its handle underneath the mantelpiece.

'Very good.' CeeCee let the pot dangle from her hand as there was no other way to carry it home. Had she overstepped the mark? Oh well, it was just a pot. 'We should be off then.'

Mrs Lovell stood up, her stature made more stout by her buxom, bountiful bosom, and held up a hand. 'Wait, Miss Seymour. My lass enquired further about something I overheard at the market.'

Linley cradled the baby and swayed to and fro as she stood. 'Oh, yes?'

'Well, it might put me out of a job, but it would make things a bit easier all around, I'd reckon.' Her bright blue eyes crinkled almost closed as she smiled down at the sleeping baby.

'In that case, we're all ears, Mrs Lovell.' CeeCee stood at Linley's shoulder, but she was impatient to leave for the walk home.

'It's that tinned milk for babes, Miss Seymour. Been around a while. It is in Bendigo and your baby has had a good start with mother's milk.' She pressed her lips together and moistened them. 'I can't afford the tinned stuff, mind, but neither do I need it.' She looked down at her ample chest. 'My own baby needs me.' She lifted her chin towards the cot in the corner of the room. 'But it might interest you ladies, for Toby, because, well, to save you here and there. You know, for feeding him.'

Ah. It seemed Mrs Lovell wanted to finish up feeding Toby.

CeeCee glanced at Linley who coloured flaming red again. *What is it with that girl?* 'Thank you, Mrs Lovell. Of course we're interested to hear about it.'

'It's called—' She turned her head and yelled over her shoulder. 'What's that milk called, Nellie?'

A flat young female voice answered from somewhere else in the house. 'Condensed Milk. Gold Medal.'

Mrs Lovell turned back. 'Condensed milk, Miss Seymour.'

'Ah. Yes, I know of it.' CeeCee wrapped her shawl a little tighter, and clutching the cooking pot, turned for the door. 'I'm sure Mr Wallace will have some at his shop.'

'Yes, he does, miss.'

'Thank you, Mrs Lovell. And thank you again for looking after Toby. We couldn't have saved him without you.' CeeCee edged towards the door to let herself out. 'We will certainly look into purchasing the milk.'

'Um, yes, thank you again, Mrs Lovell,' Linley said.

CeeCee heard Linley offer her bewildered thanks, and abruptly turned back. 'And Mrs Lovell, if I can ever do anything for you, at any time, would you be sure to let me know?' She reached out and took the woman's hand.

Mrs Lovell stopped in her tracks, her hand seemed imprisoned in CeeCee's. 'I am only too glad to—'

'You've done us a great service, Mrs Lovell, so if at any time …' CeeCee pressed.

Mrs Lovell nodded, reddened and was about to bob.

'And please, don't do that. We are just extremely grateful.'

'Yes, Miss Seymour.' Mrs Lovell dipped her head.

CeeCee smiled and nodded, and sailed past Linley who sailed after her.

'What was that all about? The poor woman looked mortified.' Linley wrapped the baby inside her shawl, hugging him to her chest as she trotted alongside her aunt.

'We don't thank people enough, Linley. Without people like her, Toby would be dead.' CeeCee's pace picked up.

'I know, but what was it about the pot, and the milk and all the "thank yous"? She only had to—'

'Mrs Lovell is a proud woman working for a living and she has every right to be proud.' CeeCee felt the swell in her chest cramp her breathing as she thought of the hardship Mrs Lovell and others like her had endured since time began. Why, if the law, and the men who made the law had any clue …

Oh, some changes had been made, just not nearly enough. She gathered more speed. 'And there but for the grace of—'

'God?' Linley finished for her, trying to keep up. 'Slow down, Aunty. You seem to have upset yourself. Swing that pot any higher and it might fly from your hands.'

'God has a lot to answer for. And God was not of whom I was thinking.' CeeCee still kept her pace, but slowed the swinging pot to rest it against her thigh.

Linley skipped a little to keep up and looked down at her bundle. 'Indeed.'

But for the grace of her hard-working, thrifty, gold-mining parents who left the digging fields of Ballarat when CeeCee was barely four years old, her lot in life might well be the same as Mrs Lovell's.

Time spent with these women propelled her forward once more to push for better lives for women and girls. She must write another letter to James. She must get back to business. Especially after the letter from Mr Campbell. What if she needed to get Linley out of Bendigo in a hurry? She should advise James that it could be imminent …

'Slow down, CeeCee. I can barely see my feet as it is. I don't want to fall into a pothole as big as China.'

… And she really needed to extract from Linley exactly who was the father of this baby. If it was not Wilkin—which everyone agreed, including the insidious twerp himself—then perhaps some other man would try and make a claim once word got out about Mary's inheritance.

The baby squawked and Linley hushed him and cooed, rocking as she skipped. 'Aunty!'

'Sorry. Sorry, Linley.' CeeCee forced herself to slow down. 'You know how agitated I get when I think of the lack of help for these poor women, and their families, the little children—'

'Please get agitated after we've had a pleasant walk home.' Linley hummed a tune and Toby settled. 'And I don't know why you do. You help everyone you come across.'

As they rounded the corner and headed down the street to their cottage, the last of dusk had all but fallen away and the cloak of night spread across the sky. The air cooled quickly and they hurried the last few yards, the warmth of the kitchen fire on CeeCee's mind.

'I will be heartily glad of home tonight.' CeeCee looped her arm through Linley's and hugged her close. 'I am most times

somewhat unsettled at Mrs Lovell's. I am always glad to see home.'
She reached across Linley to lift the latch on the little gate.

'I will be glad to put this little man to—'

A growl from a beast behind the gate interrupted Linley. A
rush of prickles scurried up CeeCee's arm. Her hand tightened
around the handle of the pot and then the little house gate swung
violently against her. Her breath knocked out in two loud grunts
and she staggered back heavily against Linley and the baby.

A wiry forearm crunched her cheekbone and drove her further
back towards the fence, Linley caught behind her.

'Out of my way, you *slut* of a woman.' The voice squeezed from
clenched teeth, his arm a solid rod, the fingers of his other hand
trying to grip her shoulder.

Linley let out a cry and the baby let out a yell. CeeCee lurched
forward into the spittle and stink of the man who tried to get
himself between her and Linley. Her breath rushed in, force-
filling lungs stunned by the gate, her voice hoarse as air screeched
back through her mouth. In her own ears she sounded like the
devil's mistress shrieking her fury.

The man reeled. 'Wha'?'

His violence ignited a scorching flame in her. Double-handed
grip on the pot, she threw her weight against his arm and shoved
the gate back with her hip, and left all the space CeeCee needed
to swing the pot up in one move and *thwack* him under the chin.

His teeth crunched. Drops of warm liquid fell on her face. Still
her lungs sucked air and her laboured voice sounded hoarse and
maniacal in her throat. Dimly she heard a baby wail, and Linley
scream for help.

The man lurched back, yowled, and dived quickly to avoid the
next wild swing of the pot. Caught on the side of the head, he
yowled again, his hands flung up to ward off another attack. He
stood, bent a moment, swayed—

CeeCee swung the pot again. It pounded the man's chest from under his ribs. Her hands and arms shuddered against the force of it.

He toppled, fell on his backside and scrambled back like a crab until he found enough purchase to get up and stumble away.

Aware that Linley still screamed, CeeCee dropped the pot and reeled around to grip her niece's shoulders. Still labouring for breath, she checked every detail of Linley and the baby. She tried to speak.

'Ha … he …'

'He's gone. He's gone.' Linley sobbed into the baby's outraged face and shushed and shushed his shrieking. 'We're all right. We're all right.'

CeeCee sagged against them both, pressing them back to the safety of the picket fence behind. Crying, sobbing, heaving for air and waiting for her airways to clear, she fell against the fence and retched.

'Aunty. CeeCee …'

'I'm all right.' She sucked in air. 'Inside. Quickly.' She huffed small breaths in rapid succession as she poked and prodded Linley inside the yard and up the step to the front door. She only touched it and it swung open. She cried aloud, hoarse, throaty and anguished.

The wreckage inside was all too obvious.

The women crept into the hallway and then CeeCee slammed the front door shut. She bent, whispered for Linley to find matches and a lamp, hoisted herself up on the parlour's doorway and held a hand to her cheek.

Linley ran past her, hugging the crying baby and hush-hushing him as she went. She crossed straight to the mantelpiece, crunching over broken crystal and furniture. She jiggled Toby arm to arm as she searched along the timber shelf for the matchbook.

She rushed it back to CeeCee who clung to the doorway, holding her middle. 'Find a lamp, or a wick. Something …'

Linley stood for a moment, flustered.

CeeCee waved her off. 'Don't trust me to hold Toby, I'll concentrate on holding myself, just find something to light.'

'Where?'

CeeCee's lungs expanded and a cool breath of air found its way easily inside. Relief waved across her abdomen. 'My desk. The drawer.' She tried to straighten.

Linley rushed to the desk, the baby bouncing in her arms. He, too, had quietened, but a gurgle brought a splash of his dinner up over Linley's shoulder.

Tugging at the drawer, she thrust her hand inside. She raced back to CeeCee, candles in her grip. She put the baby on the floor in a clean space between her feet and thrust the candles at CeeCee. She scratched a match and lit them.

'Find the cot. Hope the bastard didn't wreck that.'

Linley scooped up Toby, took a candle from CeeCee and crunched her way back into the parlour. The cot stood in the corner completely free of the carnage around it.

'Check it for glass or broken china,' CeeCee ordered from the door.

Linley swiped her hand quickly, lightly over its covers. 'It's clean, not been touched at all.' She lowered the baby and tucked him in, cooed some nonsense and rocked the cradle. 'It's all right, it's all right.'

It was far from all right. CeeCee felt her knees go, and she slipped a little in the doorway. Her face pounded where the man's forearm had slammed her, her stomach pained with a bruise waiting to come out and her arms ached from the weight of her pot throwing.

The pot.

'Linley, go back outside and get the pot.'

'What?'

'Go.'

'But you're—'

'Get the pot. It's a weapon.' She turned to face the front door, dipping her head in its direction.

Linley stepped around her aunt, laid her hand briefly, softly on her shoulder and rushed to the front door. She pulled it open ready to run through.

A large form loomed in the doorway, a hand raised at the level of her head.

Linley screamed. The baby's enraged squeal emitted from the parlour.

CeeCee turned too quickly to stop the gasp of agony as she focused on who stood in the doorway.

She finally let go and slid to the floor.

Eleven

CeeCee rested in one of the chairs in the kitchen room. She tucked in her chin, made eye contact, and lowered her voice to a whisper. 'You will promise to remain calm while you listen.'

James Anderson gave a curt nod, but his pinched nostrils were a giveaway. 'I will. But I will get him.'

'I know. Just. Please. For now, don't do anything.' CeeCee held his brown-eyed stare a moment. His fiery-red hair had darkened a little … perhaps he wasn't spending so much time outside any more. A few threads of silver glittered above his ears and wove the length of it down to his collar.

Why don't I know if he's spending less time outside? When did the silver in his hair arrive?

Startled, a flutter skipped through her. She *should* know. She *would* know…

Hot water whistled in the kettle on the old wood-burning iron stove. A bowl of cool water and a damp cloth sat just beyond her hands, resting on the tabletop.

Linley leaned over the cot, now moved into the kitchen. She stared at the sleeping baby. 'He's finally nodded off, poor little man.'

CeeCee had a hand against her face. 'We'd better get some of that tinned milk tomorrow, Lin.'

Linley glanced between her aunt and James. 'Yes. I'll go in the morning and wait for the store to open.'

CeeCee opened her mouth to protest.

James held up his hand. 'I doubt the low bugger will try anything in broad daylight. And you'll need some travelling supplies, the sooner the better.'

He sounded terse, but CeeCee knew he was holding his temper.

She glanced at her niece. 'Linley, you know James has a business in Melbourne and also in Echuca. He—'

'Cecilia.' James lifted his eyebrows.

She took up the cloth, dipped it in the cool water, squeezed out the excess and placed it on her burning cheek. Her eye was watery and she knew the swelling would come out. 'We've still so much to tell you, Linley, but no time now. Because of this attack, we will need to take you to one of those places. Melbourne or Echuca.'

Linley frowned. 'Yes. But we don't know for sure that—'

'You know as well as I do. It was Gareth Wilkin.'

'It was so dark, Aunty.'

'Come now, the man's stink is all a person needs to identify him.'

James drummed his fingers on the table. 'You need some medical care, CeeCee.'

'Nothing's broken.'

'At least draught for pain,' he said between clenched teeth.

'A good toddy will do.' CeeCee let out a long breath, dipped the cloth again and rinsed, replacing it against her cheek. 'You will have to find lodgings tonight.' She looked at James and felt the apology creep across her features.

His mouth set. 'My lodgings will be here tonight, with you both. As usual.' James looked at her, a scowl beginning. 'It's either the slightest risk of gossip, against keeping you all safe in this house.'

Linley looked away, set to rocking the cradle madly until she took a deep breath and stopped herself. 'I know you've always stayed before, many times. I welcome it.' Her gaze settled on the floor. 'It doesn't matter to me about any gossip.'

CeeCee closed her eyes at that, and a moment passed. 'Wilkin will not return. He's a coward.' She pressed the cloth to her throbbing cheek.

'Aye, a coward who had a woman wallop him.' James' brows furrowed, the drumming fingers louder. 'He waited till you went out then he sacked the place. What was he looking for?'

CeeCee lifted a shoulder. 'He is the widower of this baby's mother. Perhaps he came for the baby, or to find papers and the like.'

James stopped the drumming. 'But he's not the father of the baby, is he?'

'No.' Linley stepped forward, then embarrassed, stepped back to the cot. She gave it a couple of small swings.

CeeCee flexed her jaw then decided it wasn't a good idea. 'No. He married Mary, the baby's mother, to save her reputation. She was with child to another. But he had the promise of an inheritance to sweeten the arrangement.'

James shook his head. 'And something went wrong.'

Linley's voice rose. 'We know that he beat her. He kicked her. He did unspeakable things—'

'Linley.' CeeCee reached out a hand to her niece. 'Don't get upset.' She looked at James. 'Mary used the promise of an inheritance from an ailing aunt of hers to attract the man to marriage—'

'Horrible, despicable, smelly, *poxy* little toad.' Linley squared her shoulders.

'—and he did marry her. We understand by Mary's letters to the solicitor we engaged for her, that he did indeed beat her. So badly in fact I believe that the effort of birth killed her. She died after the baby was born.'

James shook his head again. 'But before it was born she'd already asked for Linley to take the baby.'

CeeCee nodded, holding her face against an ache. 'She is the one I wrote you about. She asked for Linley's guardianship of her baby. Clearly, we believed Mary knew what might well befall her.'

She hadn't told him everything else before; it was too much to commit to a letter and too prevalent an occurrence for a number of women to be anything but commonplace.

James scratched his head. 'And we engaged the solicitor for her.'

'Mary wanted a will drawn up. And that's why she came to me.' CeeCee inhaled carefully. 'She said she knew I helped many unhappy women. I don't know how she knew. Perhaps our work is not unnoticed, James, after all. So, six months and more with child, her eyes blackened, one closed, her only dress crudely sewn back together for modesty ...' CeeCee glanced at Linley, who stood woodenly over the baby's cradle. 'I paid Mr Campbell to help. He is also following through with the succession for Toby from the aunt's estate. We should learn of its extent shortly.'

James looked at her. 'So the old lady has died. But the widower ...'

'Mary's will expressly denies him the inheritance. She states the funds are to go to the child's guardian. She named Linley as that guardian. After his first beating of her she drafted a legal will.' CeeCee almost felt Linley's wince.

'The court might view the husband as the rightful—'

'The new laws, James. Mary's property before she married is hers to administer. He got away with beating her, but he can't get away with property. Not any longer.'

James frowned. 'I know the laws have changed, but I hope the court will not award him the inheritance. It did come to her after she married.'

'I think it will stand because it was bequeathed to her *before* her marriage.' She frowned, felt the pain shoot into her eye. 'I don't believe he's entitled. And he doesn't have access to the will.' The cool cloth was no longer doing its job. She rinsed it again and pressed it back to her cheek.

James steepled his fingers, tapping them together. 'I don't know what to make of all that, and I was a lawyer in training.'

'Ha. You mean, what a *judge* would make of that,' CeeCee said.

Linley looked up sharply and CeeCee caught her glance. She smiled at her niece, hoping to allay any fears, though one side of her face couldn't cope with it. Tears smarted. 'We should make you an appointment with Mr Campbell, James, so you hear it directly from the solicitor. But that is not our issue at present.'

James shifted in his chair, leaned forward and laced his fingers. 'Of course not.' He tilted his head. 'Which way to go, CeeCee? To Melbourne or to Echuca?'

She stretched her fingers to reach his hands. 'Melbourne, I think. Anonymity would be better there.'

'Echuca,' Linley blurted. She looked at James. 'If you have already bought a house there for us. I would ... I—I have always wanted to be by the river. Melbourne is such a foul and smelly place by all accounts.'

A scorching flush rose in her niece's cheeks. It was true enough, CeeCee knew. She shifted a glance to James.

'We have a house available in Echuca, if you'd prefer.' He'd spoken to Linley then looked at CeeCee.

'I would.' Linley's chin lifted.

CeeCee let out a long sigh, and withdrew one hand to tug her earlobe. 'Echuca it is.'

———•———

They decided to lock Linley and the baby inside the kitchen room by the fire. CeeCee leaned on James' arm as they went back into the main house. They took a lamp, dodging the mess strewn about the hallway.

One of the bedrooms, Linley's, had barely been touched, and CeeCee thought she could sleep in there. James sat her down on the bed and moved a lamp to the little bedside table. With his foot, he swept aside shards of glass on the floor. Bottles of this and that, which must have been on Linley's dresser, had been broken.

He pulled a chair close to the bed. 'I'll pack you a bag of things to take, CeeCee.'

She shook her head. 'I want nothing from here he might have put his filthy hands on. We'll take immediate essentials, and our box of family treasures, and let that be that. If you telegraph me some funds from the account, I will purchase clothes once we arrive. Linley can do the shopping.' She tugged in a sharp breath as she tried to lift her legs onto the bed.

James slipped his arm under her, swept aside the covers and tucked her under the bedclothes. 'I can go for the doctor tonight—'

'No. Please don't, James. Please don't leave for any reason.'

He frowned. 'I'll not leave your side, Cecilia Celeste.' He picked up her hand and pressed its palm to his lips.

'James.'

He looked at her, fine wrinkles at the corner of his eyes more pronounced than she had ever noticed them.

'James, I know you go after these men.'

His stare never wavered.

She squeezed his fingers. 'I don't want to know what happens. But I want it to stop now.'

'My love, I—'

'If there is to be anything for us, with each other, going into the future, it must stop now.'

'Cecilia, these men are the vilest of creatures. The law does not punish them. Someone has to.'

Was his a madness of sorts as well? It didn't matter to her. What mattered to her was that this work didn't kill him, or kill both of them.

'I want it to stop so that you and I have a future. So this affliction that we know is in some men will no longer reach us.' Fear had risen in her, and it was a new awareness. It had been a long time since she'd felt the tentacles of this particular evil.

'I would do anything for you, CeeCee.' He kissed her hand again, and the smile reached his eyes. 'But stopping my work won't stop it reaching us.'

'I mean it, James. I could not bear to be without you. If you were ever—'

'I promise you, CeeCee. I promise. After this one. Now, no more of that talk.'

She sighed. It was enough that she had said it. There was no reason to press her point, she knew it. She tried to smile, though when her faced creased it felt misshapen.

His lips on her hand sent a warm glow through her. 'So, why did you come up from Melbourne? This wasn't a scheduled visit.'

He covered her hands in his. 'Your last letter sounded forlorn. Out of hope. Most unusual. I needed to see you were all right.'

Her last letter. It had been a sad state. 'I'm sorry. I had intended to write—' She winced as she moved.

'CeeCee. I want nothing more than to be where you are.' He lowered his head again to her hands. 'And I am so very glad I came. It terrifies me that you are at the mercy of people like him.'

She scoffed, but knew she hadn't sounded convincing. 'I'm not. We're not.' She tried to sit up. 'This is an isolated case, far from—'

'It's not.' James shook his head. 'You are too knowledgeable about this sort of violence. This is the very thing we have striven to prevent, or to stem, for as long as we've known each other. This is exactly your sister's life all over again.'

CeeCee closed her eyes and eased back to the pillows. 'Would you prop me up with cushions?'

He slipped extras from his chair and plumped them behind her back. Then he sat beside her on the narrow bed, and carefully cradled her.

'Thank you.' She sank against him. 'My sister. I had hoped it would never follow Linley. Have I brought this on her?' Her right eye was closing rapidly, and it felt squashy when she blinked. 'By helping Mary, did I open the door for this to stain my niece? The very thing ...'

'The very thing we do is what you did for Mary. But it has led this bastard and his violence to your door. We've been careful in the past to ensure that his type never get close.' James kissed her forehead.

CeeCee let out a long, careful breath. 'You mustn't leave the house. Promise me you won't leave the house if I go to sleep.'

'I will not leave you alone tonight.' He edged a little off the bed. 'But I cannot sleep in this cot you have here. I will bring in the other bed and sleep beside you.' He stood up.

CeeCee looked at him, saw love in his dark eyes. She could look beyond that and see the burning, barely contained wrath that drove the darker side of his nature.

'I wish we had your big bed.' She hoped to soothe the turbulence she saw in his eyes. 'I wish I had the energy ...'

'My love.' He bent and kissed her forehead again. 'For tonight, it's more than enough that you are safe.'

CeeCee watched him leave. Heard him crunching over shattered glass, heard him drag ruined furniture out of his way, listened as he hefted the mattress and saw him haul it through her door.

He laid it by her bed, its bedcovers still intact. He dropped to his knees on it, rested his elbows on her bed, his chin in his hands. 'This unfortunate incident has, of course, brought my favourite subject to the fore once again.' He regarded her face. 'Though I would prefer you don't look quite like this when you marry me.'

She sank back against the pillows, her right eye now shut. 'I would also prefer to have two eyes on you at all times, James Anderson.' She felt the energy leach out of her body and she sighed, winced and gave a slight groan. 'I have to sleep now, James.'

'I'm right here, my sweet.' He reached across and doused the lamp, settled back on the floor. 'I've thought of this night for many long hours, but didn't quite have these sleeping arrangements in mind.'

'Goodnight, my love.' CeeCee's good eye drooped as fatigue set in. She listened to James' breathing, his own deep sleep not far off.

One of her last thoughts before she dozed was how she loved James. How she should come to terms with that, set aside some of her more stringent objections to marriage and take up his offer.

And the other thought was of how, despite his promise, James would go to great lengths to kill Gareth Wilkin unless she could stop him.

———

Linley stretched out under the thick covers on her mattress, thrown onto the kitchen floor.

Earlier, James had taken it outside to shake off any broken glass and dust, and once satisfied he carried it to the kitchen room, along with clean linen for her and the cot. He'd stoked the fire and ordered her not to move closer to it. The last thing he wanted was an out-of-control fire in the middle of the night.

Toby had settled once again and was sleeping soundly. His little snuffles and gurgles kept Linley smiling despite the shaking up they'd all had.

She plumped her pillow a couple of times, hoped there'd be no roaches crawling on her in the night, then conceded there'd been worse things occur only hours before. She closed her eyes and the warmth of the fire, the covers and fatigue crept over her.

Yet Ard O'Rourke kept her from her sleep.

Ard O'Rourke, I am so angry at you ...

Her belly twirled a little dance, and further down contracted sweetly. Feelings and emotions she could not name coursed through her. That day at the picnic, she'd longed to reach out and stroke his face, run her finger along the line of his jaw and press soft kisses over his mouth. Their fingers had touched and the surge of heat in her cheeks at the time still flamed through her now. She had a ... a longing; yes, that was it—a longing for Ard. A need, deep in her, she could barely explain.

She squeezed her eyes shut and hugged herself as she tried to imagine Ard's arm's around her, his hands on her. Those depthless blue eyes and his black wavy hair ... a Celt from long ago, perhaps. A fiery warrior for his tribe. And that was odd, for she had the dark auburn hair and the pale skin tone of the Irish, and he had the black hair and olive skin of the Mediterranean people.

Intriguing. Romantic ... Intense.

She shivered.

A glimpse of black chest hair, the unmistakeable power of his thighs, the lean hips and flat belly. A strong broad chest. She'd seen him heft bales of hay and sacks of flour, the muscles in his arms and back flexing with supine grace, the sheen of sweat healthy and primal.

Then the last time she saw him, that bewildering afternoon when he declared himself leaving and going off to God knew where …

Of course, now she knew *why* he decided to leave.

With a huff, she dragged the covers over her head but it did no good. The deep pull between her legs throbbed and she knew if she put her fingers there, under the thin fabric of her skirt, she would shatter into splinters and wildly call his name. She turned on her side and smartly turned back again. Her private place was insistent.

She was still angry with him. Angry that he should betray her feelings and father a child with Mary … She bunched the covers over her eyes and stifled a cry.

And she was angry at Mary. Angry and baffled. She'd never given Mary any reason to spite her. So why?

Why, when you could see I wanted Ard? When you knew I loved him so?

But her last thought before sleep was not of Mary, or of Ard, but of the second letter from Mary she had yet to open.

She would do that soon. Yes, she would. Perhaps then she would learn why.

She wasn't sure she wanted to.

Twelve

Bendigo, next morning

Ard lifted his head and stars of pain burst into his eye sockets the moment dawn pierced his eyelids. 'Jesus.'

'No Jesus here.' A voice drifted across the floor. 'Even the devil wouldn't want to be here.'

'You're alive then, Sam?'

'I don't think so.'

'Not surprised.' Ard massaged his temples. 'There's got to be a cure for this.'

Sam shuffled into a sitting position on the floor. 'It's called abstaining from my da's poison.' He tried to sit up. 'Or having more of it to do the job properly.' He pushed himself up with one hand, crossed his legs and held his head. 'I don't think I want to be alive. I need to take a piss but I reckon my dick has dried up.'

Ard rubbed at the sleep grit in his eyes. His tongue felt swollen and his throat was parched. 'I didn't have that much. Is your father trying to kill us?'

'Probably before I get to drink it all.'

'Bloody rotten stuff.' Ard pressed his head with both hands.

'You didn't test as much as I did.'

'Thank Christ.' Ard swallowed a belch, waited a beat to see if his gut would rebel. It settled. He let out a breath. He honestly did not think he'd had that much.

Sam, on the other hand, had drunk enough to down a draught horse. On cue, he let out a groan. 'More sleep.' He fell back to the earthen floor and sprawled with his arm over his face.

'No more sleep.' Ard reached out and pushed Sam's shoulder. 'I got things to do.'

'I haven't.' Sam didn't move.

Ard rolled his eyes and lifted a forearm to wipe the sweat breaking on his brow. His nose crinkled at the armpit odour. 'I'm going down to the channel to wash. Come on. You too.'

'You go. I'm all right.'

Ard shook his head. 'You stink.'

'*You* stink. *You* go.'

Ard swung his legs off the cot, and waited to see if his guts held together. He waited another beat. 'I've got to go back into town. I've got to find Linley.'

Sam cranked an eye open. 'Why?'

'And I've got to telegram my uncle, post a letter to my father. Mr Ling is about the last thing I remember.'

'Old Ling? Was he here?'

'So, I'm busy.' Ard stood up. No roiling guts. That was good. 'Come on, Sam. Get sobered up.'

'You go to the wash-up first and I'll come directly.'

Ard stepped over to a niche in the rock wall. He felt around for the split bar of greyed soap, slipped it in his pocket and headed for the door.

He pushed it open and stepped outside. 'Mornin', Pie.'

The horse nodded, blurted, tossed his head.

'I'll just take a piss, have a wash and I'll get you some breakfast.'
Ard checked the water pail on his way past before unbuttoning his
pants. He stood a little way off to empty his bladder, then started
out across the orchard and down to the channel.

His head throbbed, his mouth tasted like poorly tanned leather
stank, and he needed to do more than just empty his bladder. He
headed for the privy.

God's sake, no more of the rotgut.

Done with ablutions, he headed for the channel, stripped naked
and stepped into the slow-flowing water. He sank with his back
against one wall and let the flow cool him off.

Remembering the soap, he stretched back to his clothes, groping
around until he found the hard cake. And then he set to, trying to
make a decent lather. Some long minutes later and after a frustrated
scrubbing, he climbed out of the water, shook the drops off and slicked
down his limbs to shuck the excess. He eyed the pile of dirty clothes.
Climbing back into those filthy garments didn't sit right with him.

He bent, rolled them into a ball and threw them into the channel. Back in he went and lathered them like he'd seen his mother
wash clothes. He used the concrete channel walls as a washboard
and when satisfied, climbed out again, wiped down his wet body
and with the clean, wet clothes slung over his shoulder, headed
back to the hut, naked.

Pie accused him with one look.

'Sorry, horse. You want food.' Ard strung his clothes over the rail
that served as a clothes line. Then he lifted the lid on a barrel and
dunked an empty tin can into it, drawing up enough oats to give Pie
a meal. He dumped the contents on the ground at the horse's hooves.

'Good lad.' Ard patted Pie's neck then stepped back inside.

Sam sat on the floor holding his head. He looked up, then in
mock horror, slapped his hands over his face. 'Jesus, Ard. You're
bare-arsed naked. If I was a lassie you'd be arrested.'

'If you were a lassie, you'd be arrested.'

'My reputation would be ruined.'

Ard fell silent on the joke. *Mary.*

Sam looked up. 'What?'

Ard shook his head, headed for the corner of the hut and a small wooden trunk. He opened it, and a faint, fragrant waft escaped, some sort of herbs his mother had put in the chest to ward off the mites. Lavender, he knew, but couldn't identify any others. Out came a pair of pants, and a shirt. Then he rummaged some more and shook out a waistcoat.

'You'll smell like a lassie, too, Ard. Good thing you don't look like one, all that black hair. It's everywhere, boyo, swear to God.'

'Only where it should be.' Ard squatted, heard Sam mutter, 'Jesus, get some pants on', reefed an arm under the cot and dragged out his old boots. If he was going to walk back to town, he didn't want to do it in the new boots and risk raw blisters weeping their misery into his thin socks.

He stood, grabbed the pants and pulled them on, threw the shirt over his head and shrugged into the waistcoat. He thrust his feet into socks, then the boots, stood up straight and headed for the mantelpiece. The letters went into his shirt pocket. 'I'm going back into town. Come on.'

'Me head's not right yet.'

'That's not new. Come *on.*' He waved an arm. 'And I want to talk to your father about Pie. I want to buy him.'

'You can borrow him, Ard. But I'm riding him into town while you walk.'

—•—

Ard left Sam to go home on Pie while he plodded on to the telegraph office.

He wrote a telegram to Liam in Swan Hill. *Ling offered seventy pounds for orchard. Please send note downriver to Pa care Olivewood Renmark. Advise. Your nephew, Ard.*

The telegraph operator popped his brows and glanced at Ard, but never said a word. Not that it made any difference. What should have been confidential never was.

He wondered suddenly if his dalliance with Mary had been confidential and a groan beset him. Stalking from the counter to the bench, he reached for a blank sheet of paper and used the dull quill lying over the ink pot.

Pa, trust you and Ma are well. I am. Mr Ling has offered seventy pounds for the orchard. I have telegraphed Liam. What are your thoughts? Loving son, Ard O'Rourke.

He addressed it to his parents, care of Olivewood, Renmark. It would get to them via that address, but it would take weeks longer than if Liam sent a note downriver. Right now, he wasn't in a hurry. Plenty of work on the plot. If he stayed.

Things looked in reasonable condition at the orchard so Liam couldn't have left all that long ago to go to Swan Hill. Now was the time to cart water again, and to keep the weeds down. He needed to tend carefully for the summer. If he stayed.

Linley.

He stepped outside the office and checked up and down the street. Busy this morning. Carriages sped past. Pedestrians took brisk walks to the stores and the post office. Occasional riders on horseback cantered by. It was a thriving place, Bendigo, despite a depression looming again and a drought already in the north of the colony.

No matter—he had lodgings, and food he produced himself. He'd barter for mutton and beef, build a coop for chickens. Maybe. He fancied poultry once in a while. Would be good to have eggs every day too. If he stayed.

Ard looked at his boots.

Linley.

Looking up and down the street again, he knew which direction to take. A mile at most to her place. The sun hovered in the midmorning sky. The cool evening had made way for a balmy day and he felt the air warm around him as he began his walk.

What will I say to her? What to ask of her?

How could he say anything, ask anything?

A childhood friend was dead, and he'd been the cause of that.

Thirteen

Echuca

The train rattled and clanged and shook. Linley held the baby close and tried to shield him from the banging and clanging as best she could. But Toby slept the sleep of the oblivious. She needn't have worried about him. It wasn't the baby she was most concerned about.

She glanced across at CeeCee, who rested her head against the cushioned upholstery of the cabin. It was a wonderful thing that James had secured a private space for them. It was also wonderful that the bruise on CeeCee's face was covered with a light dusting of laundry starch that could be readily reapplied when needed.

CeeCee appeared to be sleeping, but Linley was unsure of that. The night had been taxing for all of them. Linley's nerves were strung. CeeCee said that James's presence last night had calmed her a little, but for Linley, every puff of wind, every creak of a door hinge put her on edge.

Toby had squawked and whimpered before he settled and Linley fretted about having to feed him. Thankfully, he hadn't woken in the night. She'd fetched the tinned milk as early as she could and prepared a little for Toby before they left for the train. He'd sucked it down greedily without issue and seemed content.

Linley looked down at him, wondered what colour his eyes would be, eventually. Right now, they were sort of a bluey colour, almost eerie. Would Toby have Ard's blue eyes or the brown eyes of his mother? Baby's eyes changed colour, she knew that, but couldn't remember if she'd been told just when.

His hair was the silky jet black thatch of his father's, but not yet curly. The button nose didn't look too much like Ard's, but his dark eyebrows, now in a little frown, and the tiny dimple in his left cheek were indelibly O'Rourke.

Her belly fluttered and rushed a little heat to her cheeks. *Ard O'Rourke.* How could he still make her long for him and yet want to belt him on the head at the same time?

It was useless to think of him any more, she was going so far away. Well, only to Echuca, but no one could know. Stupid to close her eyes and see his flashing smile, or the lock of hair that fell over his forehead as he talked … the way his large, callused hands reached up to grip hers as she stepped from CeeCee's carriage on Sundays. Or the intense blue of his stare as her gaze stealthily met his.

Stupid to imagine he thought of her at all, especially now she knew he had … um, lain with Mary.

Linley glanced at CeeCee, her face hot as thoughts of Ard's quick smile—all for her and not Mary—crammed her thoughts. She squeezed her eyes shut for long moments, and when she opened them her aunt was looking at her.

'Something you ate?' CeeCee raised her eyebrows.

Linley muffled a snort of laughter. She floundered for an answer a moment. 'I was wondering what Wilkin's face looked like when he realised that pot was coming for him.'

CeeCee gave a short laugh too, then groaned. 'I wonder. And I wonder what he looks like now.' She closed her eyes again.

Linley knew she was just resting, not asleep. 'Aunty?'

'Mm?'

'James?' He was the only father figure Linley had known. Always kind, always strong.

'No need to worry. He will be on the next train.'

Linley rocked the baby some more, and glanced down at the glossy little head, his cherry-red lips set in a moue. Blissfully unaware of the life roiling around him, he just lay there, tranquil, in her arms, safe from the death and destruction around him.

This baby had a father. Ard O'Rourke.

Linley looked back at CeeCee again, her aunt's eyes still closed, her face composed, calm. Nothing about her current demeanour told of the horrible moments of last night.

'We are lucky to have James, aren't we, Aunty?'

CeeCee took a deep breath, frowned a little, smiled a little, her eyes still closed. 'Yes, we are.'

Fourteen

Bendigo

Ard swung open CeeCee's little garden gate. The morning sun beat down on him as he stood, feet planted.

He wiped his hands on his pants, breathed against the hammer of his heart on his ribcage, and hoped he hadn't sweated up a stink to crinkle delicate noses. Head down, he marched up the path.

A rough voice stopped him short. 'Who're you?'

On the stoop stood a small man, his face battered, recently it seemed: split lips still bleeding, angry lumps on his forehead, an eye swollen shut. The man held an arm over his chest.

'Ard O'Rourke. Who might you be?' He straightened up.

The man hesitated, halting puffs of breath pushed through thickened lips. His eyes narrowed in a squint and his mouth curled in a snarl. 'O'Rourke. Whaddya want here?'

'Naught to do with you.' Ard advanced. 'I'll see for myself that my friends are—'

'*Friends*, is it? Get back off the step or I'll yell for the coppers.'

'Ballocks to that.' A curl of heat crawled up Ard's neck.

'I'm warning yer, don't come up them steps—'

Ard leapt to the top step and bumped the little man aside. He shoved his way into the house and stopped, stunned at the damage inside CeeCee's hallway. At first not comprehending, he stared at the destruction, the wilful damage of CeeCee's furniture. Pictures had been flung off the wall, frames awry and photographs torn. A vase shattered, the flowers lay wilted on the floorboards, the dark pool of spilled water seeping around them. Ard had only called on the ladies here once, but he knew how … He spun around.

The man lunged. 'You mongrel—'

Ard thrust out an arm. The man barrelled into it, bounced to the floor, his breath knocked out in a grunt as if he'd been dropped from a great height.

Ard bent down to get a closer look. 'You didn't say who you are.' He poked the heaving chest with his forefinger. 'A mongrel yourself, perhaps, because there's no resemblance to the fine ladies who live here. You're not family.' He poked again, harder this time. 'Looks to me like you might have run into some heavy objects recently.'

The man scrambled back beyond Ard's long reach. Wheezing and clutching a shoulder, he managed to get into a squat. 'They have something of mine.' It was a teeth-bared snarl. Drops of blood oozed. 'Property that belongs to me. I saw the door open—'

'Stay there, where you are.' Ard's gaze swept back over the hallway. 'Seems to me there's not much here worth having now.'

The man lifted his chin to the doorway just beyond where Ard squatted. 'A bag of letters. In the parlour room there.' He didn't make another move, just stared malevolently.

Ard took two steps into the parlour. The room was just as broken up as the hallway. Someone had gone on a frenzy, wild with rage it looked like, upending the few pieces of furniture, and smashing what was available to be smashed. He couldn't see any bag in here.

What's that in the corner, untouched … A crib?

Footfalls behind him. He heard the crack on his head before he felt it. Pain exploded in his ears—

———

Ard's nose woke up first. Smoke, acrid …

Then his ears woke. Voices, some close to him, urging, urgent. Some further away, murmuring, angry, or crying.

His eyes refused to wake up and he shook his head, tried to pry his lids open. Too exhausting. Vomit bounced into his throat and he lurched over and spewed onto the dusty earth under him. He rolled back, and groaned as his stomach pitched again.

'… Not so, Constable …' A low male voice filtered through. A hand touched Ard's shoulder, and a cool wet cloth was applied to his forehead. 'Lie still, lad.' A soothing voice, muffled, an older man.

Another muffled voice. 'Mr Anderson, we have a witness who says otherwise.' Gruff, no nonsense.

'Constable—?'

'Albert Griffin.'

'Constable Griffin, your other *witness* just happens to be the man who perpetrated these crimes, the wrecking of Miss Seymour's house, the bashing of this man here and the setting fire to the place.'

'And you know that how, sir?' Still gruff.

'Because when I arrived here, this man was out cold on the floor inside and your *other witness* was limping from the place dragging a flaming tinder.'

'We don't know who wrecked the place.' Gruff again.

Ard thought his stomach had settled. He tried to sit up. His head clanged and oddly, he wished he'd drunk more of Sam's grog. Upright, he put his hands to his head.

'You're O'Rourke's son.' The gruff voice had softened a little.

Ard lifted his head and carefully opened his eyes. He squinted. 'Ard.' He nodded once at the policeman, who had a wide kerchief at his mouth.

Grey smoke hung around Constable Griffin's head like a cloud of doom. 'I'm not happy, O'Rourke.'

'Neither am I.' Ard leaned to his side again and up came more bile.

The policeman stepped back.

'He might need a doctor, constable.' All Ard saw were boots of fine leather, well kept but dusty.

'And I need his side of the story.' Griffin again.

Ard slumped back onto the ground. 'I got here some time in the morning to call on Miss Seymour.'

'Which Miss Seymour?'

Ard let his breath go. 'Miss Linley.'

'And?'

'And what?' Ard frowned, then focused on the man hunkered down beside him. The stranger with the boots.

'I saw another man leave the place, torching as he went. I didn't chase him, I decided to check the premises instead, and there you were.' Anderson held his kerchief close to his mouth, but looked back over his shoulder across the street. 'Glad *I* didn't kill you dragging you out.'

The constable bent low. 'Are you sayin', Mr Anderson, that you saw the man try to kill O'Rourke?'

'He cracked him on the head with something and left him for dead in a burning building.'

'You *saw* that?'

'No. I just took one look at a man dragging a lit torch, at this man's bleeding head, caught the flames around me and made an educated guess.'

The police officer harrumphed. 'Not good enough for a charge of attempted murder, I'm afraid.'

Ard looked across the street. 'Jesus.' His voice was hoarse to his own ears. Some parts of the little wooden cottage still flamed, but mostly it was a smouldering wreck. A crack rent the air and the roof caved in. Firefighting men darted out of the way.

'Went up too quick, lad,' Griffin said, following Ard's stare. 'Lucky we got the water cart here before it caught the neighbouring houses.'

Ard craned his neck to check the groups of people hugging each other on the other corner.

Dizzy.

The constable squatted beside him. 'Mr Anderson said you was out cold when he went in. He reckons you weren't the one who wrecked the place. But have you got someone to verify where you were early on?'

Ard coughed and felt four different parts of him split. He held his head again. 'Sam Taylor and I were at my orchard last night. We came back into town early, waiting for the telegraph office to open.'

Griffin nodded. 'That'll do it if it stands.'

'It will.'

'I'll get a hold of Sam Taylor. You'll come to the station if you know what's good for you. Hear me, young fella?'

Ard nodded.

James Anderson stood up. 'Do you know who the little bastard is?'

Griffin lifted his shoulders. 'Could be a man named Wilkin, going by a neighbour's description. Conniving shit of a man, by all accounts. Slippery, you know? Hard to pin down. And why he would want to want to burn down Miss Seymour's house, I don't know.' He stabbed a forefinger at Ard. 'Station, soon as you're able.'

Ard nodded again but his attention was on the name. Wilkin. Was it familiar?

Griffin turned to Anderson. 'From Melbourne, you say?' He took a little notebook from inside his jacket and opened it, licked a stubby pencil and made some notes.

'I'm here to look at a couple of properties for sale. I was on my way to an appointment when ...' James waved his hand towards the smoking cottage.

'We'll need your account too, Mr Anderson.'

'Of course.'

'You right, lad?' Griffin leaned over Ard.

'Soon as my head stops swimming.'

Griffin headed off towards his men and Ard looked up at Anderson. 'Thanks,' he said. 'So you just walked past, saw the bastard, and marched in there to drag me out.'

Anderson squatted alongside Ard. 'You know him if you saw him again?'

'I might.' Ard tried to sit. The sickening rush in his guts subsided. 'Can't place him, though the name is familiar.' He brought himself to his knees. 'Better get to the police station.'

Anderson stood and outstretched his arm. 'Here.' Together they got Ard to his feet. 'That's my carriage over there. Why don't I drive you?'

'I'd appreciate it.'

Anderson ducked his shoulder under Ard's arm. 'Come on. I'll make sure you get there in one piece. Name's James Anderson, by the way.'

'Ard O'Rourke.'

'Interesting first name.'

'Old Gaelic. Irish,' he said.

They hobbled to the carriage. Ard steadied himself and with a leg-up managed to seat himself comfortably enough. Anderson jumped up beside him, took the reins and turned the horse. As they drove by, Ard stared at the charred ruin. Thick plumes of grey smoke still poured off the place, billowing into the clear blue sky.

Linley's house, gone. And I've got no clue where she is.

He sagged, letting out a grunt as his head clanged some more.

Anderson looked across at him. 'With your friend's statement, and mine, the bastard hasn't got a leg to stand on. And I'll get him, any which way.'

Ard glanced at him. He felt heat coming off the man in waves, palpable and fierce. There was something else, something he couldn't put his finger on. 'Griffin said you reckoned the fella wrecked the place. I got there after it was wrecked.'

'Was just about to go in and get him when you came along.' A sidelong glance, a wry note in the voice.

'And you didn't?'

'Happened too quick.'

'And you were just walking by?' Ard pressed.

'Good thing I was.' Anderson stared ahead. 'I'll testify in all honesty, if it comes to that. But it might not.' He clucked the reins and they sped up. 'How well do you know Miss Linley Seymour?'

The hairs on the back of Ard's neck stood on end. 'Why you asking me that?'

'Ease up, man. I'm on your side.' Anderson flicked the reins again and the horse stepped up the pace.

Ard faltered but didn't have a reason not to respond. 'I've known Miss Linley since we were kids. But I've been away these last months, up South Australia, on the river. I ... we ... 'course, now we're grown up, we don't ...'

Anderson glanced over, frowning. 'You courting her?'

'Doubt she'll let me.' Ard heard the grumble in his voice. 'Especially now.'

'She's a strong, brave girl, that one.'

Ard shot a look at the other man. 'And you know her how?'

'The younger Miss Seymour, by watching her grow up since she was a baby. And I know the older Miss Seymour very well. Miss Linley is a lot like her aunt. You'd better be a very patient man if you are going to court her.'

Ard blinked at that. His head felt fuzzy enough. 'So you weren't just walking on past the place.'

James glanced at Ard. 'I know you didn't break in and go on a frenzy in there. It was done in the early evening last night. I know that for a fact. I also know it was Wilkin, for a fact.' His eyes narrowed. 'And you and I need to have a watertight story about all of that.'

Ard shielded his eyes from the sunlight. His head pounded and the motion of the carriage roiled up his guts again. He held on to it, belched quietly, relieving the pressure a little.

'And where are the Seymour ladies, Mr Anderson?'

'That I won't tell you, Ard.'

'Why not?' The world tilted a little again.

'Not until I get word that they're safe and right where I know I can protect them.' He stabbed a forefinger in the air. 'I don't want anybody knowing.'

Ard's stomach dipped again. 'I have to speak to Linley.' He thought of the letters.

The letters! A panic gripped him. He flattened both hands on his chest until he felt the crinkle of the envelopes. His breathing steadied.

'You all right?' Anderson said.

'I will be.' Ard pressed his lips into a line and wished his throbbing head would just fall off. 'You haven't told me anything.'

Anderson clicked the reins and took the next left into G Street. 'I might, if I knew anything about you. But I don't, so as we take our time getting to the station, why don't you tell me why you were looking to speak to Miss Linley?'

Ard closed his eyes. He was on his way to the police station to make a statement about what happened and why he was at the Misses Seymour's house, driven by a man he didn't know who knew Linley and Miss CeeCee well.

Or so he said he did.

Ard decided he didn't have to say a damned thing.

———

Gareth Wilkin watched the carriage pull out of sight and away from the smouldering house. His jaw still ached like a bastard where that bitch had clobbered him with the pan. His teeth hurt at the gums and he knew he'd lose a couple unless he could keep them rooted in his head.

He slicked his lips with a sore tongue, raspy and split, hardly able to drum up enough spit for the job. Just drawing breath pained him where the pan had almost flattened his chest.

The women had run, he knew, but he hadn't seen them leave nor had he heard where they'd run. The smart-mouthed lad was the key. But he was built like a bare-knuckle boxer, that Ard O'Rourke. Oh yes, he well remembered the name from Mary's confession … Ard O'Rourke, father of her bastard. Gareth hadn't reckoned on him turning up to the Seymour place for a social call in the early morning.

Chasing down Mary's inheritance, too? Then you got no chance, boyo.

Still, Gareth had crept back to the women's house the night before to grab the kid. He was going to head for the police station, screaming that the baby was his, so therefore the inheritance was his. He'd forgotten about the birth registration, but that wouldn't take much if he had the kid … But he didn't have the kid.

That brawny lad was the key. He'd come looking for one of the women, the younger no doubt, the one who had the kid. The older one was too feisty for any reasonable man to handle. The younger one, this Linley Seymour, was the one his whore of a wife had given her bastard to. Must find that lad. Give him the once over. Leave him for dead somewhere, no claim to be made.

And then there was that stranger. That big redhead fella who caught him in the act with the torch. Scary thing. He never made a move. Just stood there. Looked like he was burning up, as well, looked fit to burst a seam before he went in for the lad.

Why'd he just stand there lookin' at me? The place was going up like a box of dry kindling.

Gareth's mouth pulled down at the edges. A rock plummeted in his gut.

So he'd be sure to recognise me next time.

Fifteen

Echuca

Linley looked out of the railway carriage. It rattled over grassy plains that stopped abruptly at dense scrub some hundreds of yards away. Dry. The land here was parched. Crackling. She imagined she could hear the snapping stalks of grass as the wind made by the train flattened them in its wake.

The baby snuffled in her arms. She wondered if he was too hot, but a look at his serene sleeping face told her he was comfortable.

She glanced at CeeCee. 'Is it much longer to go, do you think?'

CeeCee opened her eyes and took in the view. 'Hard to know, but shouldn't be too far now. We've been travelling a couple of hours.' She peered into the distance. 'I'd say that high tree line would be on the banks of the river.'

The Murray. Linley's heartbeat quickened. The Murray was excitement, still busy with riverboat trade, and farmers and ...

The railway, and the shearer's strike. The drought. Another depression forecast.

Her shoulders slumped and she caught CeeCee's look. 'I don't suppose I could get my job back at the tea rooms.'

CeeCee gave a bleak smile. 'I asked James to tell Mrs Tilley that you had to leave quickly for Toby's health. And you're right. No more job at Mrs Tilley's. We have left Bendigo behind, my dear.'

'Oh.'

CeeCee eased herself upright in the seat, flexed her shoulders and rubbed a hand across her neck. 'I'm getting a bit stiff. But better than not being able to move at all.' She reached across for the small bag on the seat beside her. The catch snapped open and she felt around the inside. Linley saw a small velvet-covered box emerge.

CeeCee opened it with a quick flick of its lid. 'Here.' Her out-stretched hand had two gold bands resting in its palm.

'What on earth ...?'

CeeCee gave her hand a little shake. 'The larger one is yours. Now slip it on your wedding finger.'

Linley stared at her.

'Come along. We are two ladies newly arrived and we have a baby with us. If we mean to live here we must have husbands who will support us.'

Linley's mouth dropped open.

'Well,' CeeCee continued, her hand nearly under Linley's nose. 'I should say, I will have a husband, but you, my poor unfortu-nate niece, have just lost yours to some dreadful disease and now you must rely on relatives to help. Especially with a young baby.' CeeCee smiled sadly. 'It would not have missed your notice, Lin-ley, how badly women who have lost family are treated in this world.'

Linley shook her head but reached across and took the larger ring. She slipped it on her wedding finger and the surge of a fierce blush heated her cheeks. 'And have you chosen my married name for me?'

'Oh, you can still be Seymour, if you like. But I will be Anderson.'

Linley still stared open-mouthed. 'Will James be visiting us here?'

CeeCee nodded. 'But he will have business in Melbourne to attend quite regularly. He has had to shift his dear wife to cleaner climes for her health and Echuca suits us both perfectly. Of course, it's also very handy because his wife's niece is in need of family and so they will be wonderful company for each other.' CeeCee smiled brightly.

'I don't understand.' Linley looked down as a tiny fist found its way out of the blanket and beat softly at her chest. He couldn't be hungry? No, he was dreaming, still asleep. His little features puckered, lips moving as if he were talking to someone.

'What don't you understand?'

Was CeeCee just a little short with her? Linley looked at her aunt. 'You and he have a house in Echuca.'

'Yes. It houses women who've fallen on hard times. You do know we do that sort of work. But you and I, however, will eventually be purchasing a new house.'

Linley frowned and stared down at the ring on her finger. 'This has all happened very quickly.'

CeeCee let out a long breath. 'Not so quickly. We talked of buying another house as we expand …' She sucked in a quick gulp.

'What's the matter?'

'I think the gate might have bruised or perhaps cracked a rib. I will check with a doctor when we settle.'

'Aunty!'

'Naught to do for a cracked rib or otherwise, Linley. It will wait.' CeeCee shifted a little, grunting as she moved. 'James found a small house which can easily be built on to. It has a large kitchen room already, and three rooms inside, so perhaps we can build a separate dwelling at the back with extra sleeping quarters, and build a small bath house as well.'

Linley wasn't surprised by that. 'James is so very generous, isn't he?'

CeeCee lifted her shoulders. 'After all this time you can't have missed that.'

'I never really thought about it. He's been around us so long, back and forth, that I hadn't ever really taken too much notice.'

'We will talk more of all of that after we settle. First, we need to get from the station to the house. I hope James remembered to telegraph for a carriage to pick us up.'

A carriage! Linley suddenly had too many questions to ask of her aunt. They'd never seemed to have much money. CeeCee had begun to teach Linley her letters at home before sending her to the Camp Hill school in Bendigo. Like other girls her age, she never had many dresses. They kept a sewing box at home of course, visited the markets and the stores and shopped frugally. They cooked, but laughed at their creations. Neither of them were proficient cooks.

James appeared regularly over the years for as long back as she could remember. He had not always stayed at their house, which of course was right and proper. But as she had grown up, Linley began to see it had only been for her benefit, her sensibilities. He probably stayed more times than she would ever know, and she knew of a great many times.

And now, a carriage was to be booked. How could CeeCee afford all this? A house in Bendigo and a house in Melbourne … goodness, the expense! A house in Echuca, and care for a niece for the last eighteen years or so, and … and—

'Are you already married to James?' she blurted.

CeeCee met her niece's stare evenly. 'I have not consented to be his wife.'

'But you will, won't you?'

'Don't sound so aghast, Linley. Perhaps I will, perhaps I won't. James and I have a number of issues between us, most of all is my independence.'

'What has independence got to do with becoming a married woman?'

'Precisely. But Linley, don't be obtuse.' CeeCee shifted uncomfortably again. 'You know my avid interest in the suffragist movement—'

'But you are not a rampant suffragette!'

'Suffragist, Linley. And you're right, nothing rampant about it. But women must have a franchise, a vote.' She sucked in a deep breath and paused before she continued. 'Thanks to the new laws, while what I own before marriage belongs to me even if I marry, I am not allowed to work as a married woman. And work I must.'

'But you don't work now.'

'Don't I just? Not formally, you're right, because society looks down upon the working woman. A husband should provide, et cetera, and if you have no husband ...'

Linley closed her mouth. Of course, a husband should provide ... Toby moved against her breast as if reminding her that Mary's husband did no such thing. Well, a father should provide ...

Her colour flared. *Ard O'Rourke.* This baby's father. Though Ard did not know Toby existed.

What had she done by not telling him? Her letter was full of vitriol and scorn as she informed him only of Mary's passing. She hadn't told him he had a son. How would Ard have reacted had she told him? With derision? Disbelief?

No, not Ard. Of course he wouldn't. He isn't a horrible person.

Oh, what had she done by not telling him? Was it too late?

No. Not too late. She suddenly knew what she would do.

A little cry escaped.

'What is it?' CeeCee sat forward, a frown creasing her brow, deepened by the effort.

Linley swallowed down the sudden anxiety. 'Aunty, the world is a very confusing place.'

CeeCee let out a relieved laugh. 'Yes, Linley, it is, and mostly we all just bob along in it as best we can.'

Linley frowned and rocked the baby as he snuffled again. She gazed at the ring on her finger. 'I know what to tell people of my … husband.'

'Whatever it is, we need to tell the same story, so out with it.'

Linley swallowed. 'We will tell people that he has gone to work in another colony.'

CeeCee's brows rose. 'So, you will not be a widow?'

She shook her head as she watched Ard O'Rourke's son. 'No. He will come for us. That is our story.' As she looked up at her aunt, her heart beat a wild tattoo.

Ard was far away. He might not have even received her letter. And even if he had, why should she think or hope or believe—

'Will he be Mr Seymour, this husband of yours?' CeeCee prompted.

'No. Um, Mister …' Linley pretended to flounder for a name. 'O'Rourke.'

'O'Rourke?' CeeCee looked as if she were mulling it over. 'Fine Irish name. I seem to remember an acquaintance of yours by the same name … Ard O'Rourke, wasn't it? Though he moved away, I believe.'

'Mm, yes, but a common enough surname. I think it's a good story to tell.' Linley fussed at the baby's blanket. 'I must register Toby's birth.'

'Much as I dislike to, we will go to the churches as soon as possible and ask if any of them will help. I know we have to register with the government, get a paper to fill in. Perhaps the church men will have something.' CeeCee waved a hand in the air. 'Failing that, I'll write James and ask him to find out.'

Linley knew CeeCee did not like any clergy, remembering how the churches had abandoned Eliza, Linley's mother, in her need. But to register Toby's birth in Mary's name and the name of his real father was the only way the baby could escape Gareth Wilkin's clutches.

Linley would declare Toby's real father on the register. What would that mean for Ard? She had no clue. But she would see it done. Past caring about the glow of society's pleasure, she still wouldn't deliberately hasten society's ire.

She traced her finger along Toby's face, moving the blanket away from his nose and mouth. A letter tucked into her underclothes crinkled against her skin as she moved. Mary's unopened letter. The one Linley had promised never to open unless something happened to Mary.

Now she felt too superstitious to open it. But she would. As soon as they were settled in Echuca, in CeeCee's new house, she would. Whatever was in the letter, she would undertake, or do whatever else was necessary. She would.

Mary, from long-ago childhood, who'd done a bad thing and had come to Linley's aunt for help ...

Linley looked down at the sleeping settled baby in her arms. Not so bad, not such a bad thing, this beautiful baby.

Heat surged through Linley again. Nothing would harm this child. No sins would be visited on his head because of his two stupid parents. She would bring him up, she would fight for him, she would be his mother.

She felt the shift in the train's momentum and looked out the window. Sure enough, the tree-lined river wove in and out of the vista. A few little buildings popped into view and all of a sudden Linley was aware she was about to take a new road.

Her eyes widened at that. Yes, she had CeeCee by her side, and James, of course. Without them, Linley herself would be destitute and as plainly on the street as the others she'd seen. If she had lived long enough.

She felt the press of Mary's letter against her breast once more, and looked down at her sleeping baby.

Ard. Ard O'Rourke. If I ever find you again …

——•——

CeeCee closed her eyes. Her head throbbed dully now, more so if she moved too quickly. The train's chug had bothered her at first. Now she was calmed by it.

So. O'Rourke. Linley would give the baby his surname.

Little doubt, then. Though the babe's black hair and eye colour might change, Linley's all-too-fierce blush had given the game away.

Ard O'Rourke has a son, and he is lying safe and content in my niece's arms.

Sixteen

Bendigo

Ard was grateful for the cushioned seat at Constable Griffin's desk at the police station. But he couldn't sit up straight. His eyes were blurry, his speech was fuzzy, and each time he blinked the room spun.

James Anderson had waited with him.

'A blow to the head like that one you copped will keep you out of action for a while, son.' Constable Griffin sat opposite Ard, tapping his forefinger on the record book open on his desk.

'What the hell did he hit me with?' Ard blinked again, then decided to keep his eyes shut.

'Something heavy, that's for sure.' Griffin tapped again. 'Now, why had you gone to Miss Seymour's house?'

Ard pried an eye open and stared at Anderson, then back at the constable. 'I was hoping to make an appointment to call on her.'

'To call on her for what?'

'To—to call on her.'

Griffin rolled his eyes. 'You haven't said how you know her.'

'Known her for years. Knew her when we were kids. All growing up, going to Camp Hill school, same classes ...'

'You're turning green again, boyo. I—'

'Might be timely, constable, for me to take him either to the infirmary or to his home.' Anderson sat forward, but kept his gaze on the policeman.

'Home,' Ard croaked. All he wanted was his rawhide pallet and darkness.

Griffin tut-tutted. 'We haven't seen Sam Taylor yet.'

Anderson stood up. 'Constable, if you need a guarantee for Ard O'Rourke, I'll deposit it.' He moved his chair back another few feet. 'Now, let me get the man home. As for Mr Taylor, I'm sure your men will find him in due course.'

Griffin nodded. 'They will. And I don't want O'Rourke going anywhere—'

'If he could walk, constable, that might be an issue.'

'—until we can get some sense out of him.'

'My guarantee, I said.' Anderson stalked around to Ard, gripped his elbow and encouraged him to stand. 'Up you get.'

'Sign off when you leave,' Griffin said.

Ard stood, and once steady on his feet, he followed Anderson out to the front desk.

At the carriage, Ard lost whatever was left in his stomach. Heaving exhausted him, and sweat popped out on his forehead.

As he leaned over the wheel, Anderson patted his back. 'Hospital.'

'Mr Anderson, I just want to go home. To sleep.'

He kept his hand on Ard's shoulder. 'After a visit to the hospital. If it's what I think it is, you can't stay on your own tonight.'

Ard groaned and swallowed down another surge. Anderson helped him up into the carriage, leapt up to the driver's seat then turned the horse for L Street.

———

James waited patiently at the telegraph office while the short, bespectacled operator sifted through a few telegrams.

'Ah yes, here it is.' Ink-stained fingers held out a crisp fold of paper.

James took it and unfolded it quickly. *Arrived safe sound. In situ. Do not worry. CCS.*

James' shoulders relaxed. CeeCee and Linley, with the baby, had found their new home and were settled. He thought for a moment. They'd need money. He'd wire funds into an account CeeCee could withdraw from in Echuca, make the necessary arrangements with the bank here.

First, he would see to Ard O'Rourke. Then he would find a birth registration form. Perhaps there was one at the hospital. There usually was. All the other times he'd needed to register the births of the women in his care, the form was either at the hospital or at the church. After that, the bank.

Then he would pay a visit to Gareth Wilkin.

———

'I'm feeling good, Mr Anderson. I can get home all right.' Ard felt better than he had in the last day or two. A few days lying flat on his back in the hospital had done the world of good. His head was no longer giddy when he moved, and his stomach had settled. He swung his legs to the floor, and waited on the bed for a bit longer before standing.

'It's James, and it's no trouble. Save your strength a bit longer.'

Ard would be glad of the ride home. He needed to get back out there and get water on to the orchard. God knows how long it had been since Liam was there. He should perhaps check at the telegraph office for a reply from his uncle, but he reasoned it would still be too early. Leave that for another day or two. Or three.

'Thank you.' He pulled on his strides, tucked his shirt—which had become a nightshirt—into his pants, shrugged into the waistcoat and buttoned up. He nodded at James again. 'Ready when you are.'

———

On the road, incessant flies buzzed around. Ard and James were brushing them out of mouth and nose all morning. Ard remembered plenty of hot November days and the flies never sleeping in the sunlight.

'Straight up this road, past the old diggings,' he directed, swatting anew. 'You can drop me at the gate. Not far after that.'

'Do you have a horse to get yourself around the place?'

'Only for the fields. I want to get one for myself but they're expensive.' Ard stared ahead, the dusty road as familiar to him as the lines on his hands. Only a mile or so, now. Suddenly it meant everything to get back there and check the trees, the water trough, to set fixings for the fire …

He puffed out a breath, his heartbeat wild for a few seconds.

James glanced sideways. 'Still sore?'

'Only an ache here and there. Head's all right.' He sat quiet a moment. 'Why you helping me?'

'Because you know Linley. And she is very important to her aunt. To both of us.'

'And how is it you know Miss Seymour? Miss CeeCee?'

James chucked the horse some more and the pace picked up. 'Ah. Miss Cecilia Celeste Seymour.' He looked ahead, a small smile on his face. 'Now, that is a story. Miss CeeCee was in the courthouse in Bendigo one day when my father came, a visiting magistrate.'

Ard's brows rose. Son of a magistrate. He shifted on the seat. Magistrates, policemen and the law were suspicious bedfellows at times. 'Miss CeeCee was in court?'

James nodded. 'She was. I'd just walked in to take up my job as a clerk when I heard my father, using his sternest voice, berating some poor individual about the proper protocols for court. I turned to see who the poor man was, only to find a very feminine person with a very outraged voice arguing back.'

Ard glanced at James. 'Miss Seymour, arguing with a magistrate?'

'Correct. I know you don't find it hard to believe.' He gave a grin.

'Arguing about what?'

'As it turns out, about how the law treats womankind. CeeCee had followed some poor beggarly woman into court. She'd been dragged from gaol pending a hearing as to her behaviour in the street weeks before.'

Ard guessed at the behaviour. 'She was working on the street.'

James lifted his shoulders. 'I don't make assumptions any longer. In the work CeeCee and I do, I have seen such great anomalies in the law's treatment of females that I refuse to let the law cloud my judgment.' He turned and looked at Ard. 'If you follow me.'

'And Miss CeeCee and your father?'

'My father shut her down, citing contempt, and ordered that she be escorted from the room. He also ordered his clerk—that was me—to sit with her in the corridor outside and await his further instructions.' James gee-upped past the old diggings. 'I introduced myself to a very prickly woman, who was still berating the legal system for its imperfections.'

'How long ago?'

'Twenty years. Perhaps a little longer. And she's still berating the system.' James slowed near a gate attached to a post by a rope. 'Is this it?'

'Next one, maybe a mile along.' Ard pointed further down the road.

The horse and carriage resumed a steady pace.

'You said about the work you and Miss CeeCee do. I didn't know she worked. I thought she was a lady who brought up her niece, that she had some means of her own.'

'She is, she does, and her niece is the reason for her passion and her ire. More like, truth to tell, the treatment CeeCee's sister Eliza received at the hands of her husband.'

Ard glanced at James who'd fallen silent as he negotiated the last mile before the turn-off. 'Eliza. Linley never mentioned her mother by name.'

James' mouth was a grim line. 'She was beaten and close to death at the hands of her husband when Linley was only a baby. CeeCee took in her sister and the baby, only to have her sister die of her injuries some months later.'

Ard stared out into the brown and wasted paddocks, then back to James. 'And the husband?'

'He was apprehended. Not dealt with properly in my opinion, and CeeCee's, of course. When he was released, he went to where CeeCee lived and threatened her. Then he disappeared. Never heard of again.' James clicked the reins. 'CeeCee badly missed her sister, felt she hadn't ever done enough. So she declared it her business to defend the rights of women who have been beaten and left destitute by their husbands or their families, or by the law.'

Ard shifted uncomfortably. 'A few men beat their wives, I know.'

James glanced over, a wry twist on his mouth. 'There's a line of thought that asserts it's a man's right. But by the laws of Great Britain, it is not. I heard one man in Melbourne was not dealt with properly until after he'd beaten his wife on twelve separate occasions.'

'Twelve?' Ard's father had never laid a finger on his mother. His father might not survive it if he ever tried. Not that he would.

James continued, nodding. 'We condemn it, but have no success deterring it because we turn a blind eye to it,' he scoffed. 'A woman-beater is a coward. What does that make the rest of us ignoring that it happens? And it rarely receives the punishment the crime deserves.'

Ard had given it no thought before now. What was the fate of those women who befell a heavy hand, or lost their place in their home?

'Unless the women have sympathetic families,' said James, 'they are very nearly always condemned to the streets on a perpetual wheel of misfortune. Most often returned after their time in gaol to the men who put them out in the first place.'

'But a woman cannot possibly survive on her own without a man to—'

James cut him short. 'Not lawfully, anyway. Even if she does, on only the *presumption* she is surviving unlawfully, she will meet the wrath of the law. And her children are awarded to the husband, who most probably bashes them too. Sometimes they're awarded to the state. And I don't know which is worse.' He clicked the reins. 'I've seen it all.'

Ard's head was foggy. 'This is a whole different world for me. So how was CeeCee able to—'

'Independence, by way of her father's diligence. It seemed he had secreted his wealth earned on the gold fields and had taught his eldest child, Cecilia Celeste, to be wise and frugal.'

Ard waved his hand towards an upcoming gate and James slowed the horse to make a turn. 'That the law even allows her to carry on this work—'

'Indeed. The law, and society.' James tilted his head.

'And afterwards, did you continue in law?'

'I did, for a while. Now, I no longer practise.' He glanced at Ard. 'I had to spend some long years helping to build the railway to Swan Hill.'

Ard looked sideways at James.

'Let's say I took the law into my own hands at one point and uh, needed a distraction from my indiscretion.' Anderson stretched his fingers holding the reins.

Ard noted the knotted knuckles. A bent ring finger.

James continued. 'But back to the main tale. I was enamoured of CeeCee from that very first meeting and I championed her with my knowledge of law, and still do. My father and mother in Melbourne are also her champions, though from a discreet distance. She has bought herself respectability. It's the only way at present. Society is very slow to advance and the law is even slower.'

'Your parents must be very ...' Ard couldn't find the right words. 'New world, new order?'

James looked at Ard with a glint in his eye. 'If you knew my mother.'

Ard's laugh burst out. 'And mine. My father credits her with my upbringing, me and my sister.'

'She's done a good job. You are well spoken, Ard.'

'I have my letters. I went to school, but mostly I read and write thanks to my ma.'

'Ah, education. CeeCee believes therein lies the answer to all this.' James nodded at Ard. 'But I don't know. How do you educate thugs? I think there is only one way.'

Ard felt he was in over his head. He needed time to sift through this new knowledge, this advancing of ideas.

James went on. 'My mother is all for the vote for women.'

'Mine, too,' Ard said. 'But my father draws the line at them entering the parliament.'

James scoffed. 'Not frightened he'll lose his privileges like some would think?'

Ard was startled by that. 'Not by a long shot. He reckons women wouldn't stoop to entering parliament. And either way, he says, "if a man has to go fishing, a man has to go fishing. Ain't no one going to stop me". Don't reckon he was bothered by losing any privileges.'

'He might be right. Women will vote in South Australia next election. I don't see any mention there of fishing coming to a halt.'

Ard laughed at that. 'My mother, she casts a line herself.'

'Aha!' James looked at Ard. 'Interesting we met, don't you think? Interesting our folk think alike.'

Ard wondered about that. Clearly, James Anderson's family's circumstances were vastly different to his own, yet here they were, relating similar ideals.

The horse and carriage had taken a full turn and now faced back the way it had come.

Ard pointed at the stone cottage to the left in the near distance. 'Home.' He held out his hand and James gripped it. 'Thank you. If I was able to offer hospitality, I would. I've naught but water from the channel well.' He dusted himself off and felt a rush of heat burn his face.

I have naught but water …

James tugged on the reins and turned the horse through the gate. 'Sounds good to me on this fine morning. Let me see what enterprise you have here.'

Seventeen

Echuca

James had organised Mr Jenkins, his sometime employee and carriage driver in Echuca, to meet Linley and CeeCee at the station to take them to the house. As he drove, Mr Jenkins informed them that a Mrs Rutherford would be around directly. For the baby, he added.

Linley sat in the sparsely furnished front room of their new house as Mrs Rutherford nursed Toby. Fascinated yet uneasy, she couldn't work out whether to stare at the full, bare breast with its engorged nipple thrust into the baby's mouth and the clutching little hands, or stare at Mrs Rutherford's face, and hope to make intelligent conversation.

Now Mrs Rutherford, her youthful features serene despite a slight frown, appeared to be in a world of her own.

If only it were me feeding Ard's baby.

Linley's own needy longing confused her. She sat quietly, allowing the hot rush of embarrassment to subside. She was glad no one could see her innermost yearnings. Mrs Rutherford rocked back and forth as the baby suckled. Both were oblivious to Linley, and a pang of jealousy stung as she grappled with her tilt at motherhood.

She let her mind drift. She should go and check on CeeCee. Her aunt had taken to her room the moment they'd arrived at the little house. A cool damp cloth and a tumbler of drinking water was all she said she required. As soon as Mrs Rutherford was done, Linley would ask her for the name of a doctor and visit his rooms to request a house call.

The baby popped off the breast and snuffled and gurgled until Mrs Rutherford changed him from one side to the other, tucking one large breast under her bodice and presenting the other for the baby. He latched on greedily.

'Hungry little one,' Mrs Rutherford said, her toothy smile relaxed, her eyes half closed as she continued her rocking. Her hair, the colour of butterscotch, was parted in the middle and pulled into a bun at the back of her head.

'I don't know if I fed him enough tinned milk,' Linley offered.

'I'll help you with how much when we're finished here. 'Tis a shame you can't feed him yourself, Mrs O'Rourke.' She leaned back in the chair.

A burning rush of heat prickled across Linley's face. 'Mm.'

The woman smoothed a hand over Toby's fluffy little head and rocked some more. 'But he's a bonny boy, and I can see he's much loved.'

The pang of jealousy spiralled all the way to Linley's middle where its sting softened, and a warm glow replaced it. Her belly felt heavy and happy, and a peculiar anticipation threaded though it.

What are these feelings?

She squirmed in her seat and unable to sit any longer, rose quickly. 'I will check on my aunt and be back shortly.'

Mrs Rutherford looked up. 'We'll be about ten minutes more.'

Linley nodded and fled the room. She opened the door to CeeCee's room to see her aunt dangling a cloth over her eyes.

'Let me help,' she said and crossed to the bed.

'I think I'm quite fine, Lin. I must look worse than I feel. My head has cleared, and this cool rag has lightened the load on my eyes.'

Linley took the cloth and pressed it gently on her aunt's face. 'I will go for a doctor as soon as Toby is bedded down.'

CeeCee nodded wearily. 'I think that is a good idea, just to be safe.' She leaned back against the pillows.

Linley took a start. CeeCee agreeing to see a doctor was grave. Her heartbeat sped. 'Oh dear. A new town, new people. Two women on their own with a baby who needs nursing ...'

Her aunt was looking at her. 'Linley, this all requires calm and measured thinking. We do not get into a tizz. Do you understand me?'

Linley huffed out a breath. 'Yes, Aunt.'

'Drop your shoulders and straighten up, and take some deep breaths.'

Linley complied. 'How will we ...?'

'As we always have done, Linley. We discuss it, then we implement it.' CeeCee took a deep, careful breath. 'We will need some bread and some meat, milk and eggs. So you will have to go to the town when Mrs Rutherford is finished. Perhaps you could walk down with her.'

'Yes, Aunty. But you—'

'I am quite well now we are out of that infernal iron claptrap. A sleeping draught would be good if you would spare the time to fetch it for me.'

Linley rose to her aunt's bag by the bed, rummaging a bit before she came up with the packet of powders. There wasn't a pitcher of water yet, so she left her aunt in search of a container.

She found an earthenware jug, then the pump, and splashed water into it. She swilled it and turfed it out onto the dusty patch of ground that served as a frontage to the property before she refilled it. When she ducked back inside she saw Mrs Rutherford laying Toby into the borrowed crib.

'I'll be right back, Mrs Rutherford.'

CeeCee had nodded off again, so she filled a tumbler and left the pitcher of water. Assured Toby would be well enough for thirty minutes, Linley, a carry basket on her arm, accompanied Mrs Rutherford back to her house.

'Not my house, Mrs O'Rourke. It's the house Mr Anderson provides for us.' Mrs Rutherford set a good pace as she headed home. 'Don't know where me and mine would be without him. You are very lucky to have him in the family. There's not too many like him, to help women like me.'

'And you help women like—like me, Mrs Rutherford.' Linley skipped a little to keep up with her. 'How is it you know Mr Anderson?'

'It were through Mrs Anderson.' Mrs Rutherford set her lips and Linley immediately felt she'd overstepped the mark. But then she continued. 'I was down on me luck, beaten in the face by the back of a hand, and clobbered by a four by two after that. I crawled to a hospital near where I was in the city, one little one under me arm, the other still in me belly. It's him I'm feeding along with your Toby.' She hastened her step. 'I must've fainted dead away, and when I woke up, there was an angel of a lady holding my Jane. Seems the lady was Mr James' mama, and Miss CeeCee was there too, shouting at one of the doctors.'

Linley's mouth dropped open. 'Oh my lord, I am sorry you had to go—'

'Don't say it, Mrs O'Rourke, though it well meant, I know. We want none of that at this house.' Mrs Rutherford straightened her shoulders as she walked, a brisk determined step to match her tone. 'I work for Mr Anderson, and Mrs Anderson—' She jabbed a thumb over her shoulder back towards the house they'd left, '—when she's in town, bless her.'

Linley remembered odd times when CeeCee travelled to Echuca and to Melbourne with her in tow. It seemed a very clandestine affair, but very adventurous nonetheless.

Now disconcerting. She was sure there must have been a great many other women helped by CeeCee and James. More than she could remember. She listened as Mrs Rutherford continued.

'I remember hiding in a carriage coming out of North Melbourne,' Mrs Rutherford said. 'Though it were Hotham when I was growing up. My little one was tucked in alongside me, too scared to speak, or cry. We'd been hid by Mr Anderson at this house somewhere, once I were discharged, and then along came this carriage. He told us to get in.' She blew out between thin lips. 'We rattled in that old claptrap until Woodend, got to the train station. We were terrified someone would stop us. Me husband, for one. But that didn't happen. Mrs Anderson was there, waiting. She must have come up before us. I never been so glad to see a lady in all me days. She sat with us all the way to Echuca here on that train. Bravest woman I know.'

A lump in Linley's throat choked her, and a sob escaped. They were all brave, these women and children.

'Then when the time came for me baby, she was back. Came up from Bendigo. Stayed with me until I was birthed of him. That were William.'

Linley couldn't remember what time that would have been. There were many times she and CeeCee travelled, and many women and children. It was the norm for Linley. Not many memories stood out. The last time was not even six months ago. They had booked rooms at a boarding house, a quiet place somewhere. Perhaps that time was for this woman and her baby.

Mrs Rutherford directed her march into a street on their right and the second house along, neat, sparse and clean, was where they stopped.

'We only want our dignity and this here is how we get it. When we find work, we help make room for others in trouble.'

'But people don't find work easily.'

Mrs Rutherford stared at her. 'No. 'Specially women like us.' She turned and took the front steps, then turned back. 'And women like us are just women put out by men who're tired of them. Or too lazy to work for them and the children. Or too drunk. I was lucky he didn't get hold of me children, for sure as anything, I'da lost them to the Destitute.'

Linley's heart dropped. Oh dear God, if she lost Toby—

'Then there's women who like to be lost and on the streets, if you get my drift. But that ain't us, Mrs O'Rourke.'

'No, it isn't,' Linley said. 'You're not lost.'

Mrs Rutherford softened then and rapped a couple of knocks on the door. It swung open as she replied, 'Thanks to Mrs Anderson, your aunty.' She nodded at the woman who answered the door. 'Mrs Cooke, this is Mrs O'Rourke who's stayin' with Mrs Anderson.'

Mrs Cooke, a thin woman, had a smile missing a few teeth, and coarse pale red hair pulled back from her face. She nodded. 'I'm Millie. And cranky old *Mrs Rutherford* here is Annie.'

'I only feel old.' Annie Rutherford beckoned Linley up the steps. 'Now, a word of warning.'

Linley frowned but came closer.

'There's a house across the street, got gloomy windows. You see it? Old biddy Bailey lives there and she swears we are all fallen women. Don't get too close to her. She'll try to beat you.'

'Beat—? What? Biddy Bailey, you said?'

'She's an old biddy. I call her that instead of calling her a bitch—
I don't want to do a good dog down. I think her real name's
Esther or something.'

Millie Cooke laughed. 'It's true. And she's a nasty one, too.
Has the coppers calling in on us whenever she feels like it.'

Linley burned crimson. *Oh no.*

'Yes, and she calls herself a Christian.' Mrs Rutherford dropped
her chin. 'Should be something good about her then, though she
never lets on. She's a widder. Yer wonder why her nose is always
upturned. Not like she looks any different to us overly much.'

'Reckon she's just stupid. Most clever folk would keep their
mouth shut about other folk.' Millie stepped aside in the doorway.
'But then, no cure for stupid,' she said and raised her eyebrows.

Linley laughed, swore she'd remember that.

Mrs Rutherford brushed herself off. 'She's already looking
through her window at our new friend. God knows what will
happen here tomorrow. Come in, Mrs O'Rourke—'

'Linley,' Linley said. She glanced over her shoulder but couldn't
see Mrs Bailey.

'We need to get your baby sorted.'

A little later, armed with information about feeding Toby in
between visits from Mrs Rutherford, Linley had secured the name
of a doctor from the women and was directed to his rooms. Once
there, after ten minutes' walk, his wife said he would be able to
attend the next day, and that it would be a pleasure to see her aunt,
Mrs Anderson, again.

From there, her directions to the general store were clear
enough, and another ten-minute walk took her along High Street
in the opposite direction. In her basket now was a wrap of day-old
bread (she was told), six eggs, and a packet of tea. Milk would be
delivered to their house early the next morning—'so have a pail

ready'—along with fresh bread and a slab of beef, which Linley
hoped would cook well enough. As for vegetables, she had been
spoiled for choice in Bendigo but here her basket was empty. She
was told to return in a day or two.

It seemed she'd walked one end of the street to the other and back
again. It left her wanting to see more, especially as she glimpsed
the wharf, and some odd craft towing barges stacked with wool
bales. The rattle and hum and chug, the faint whoosh-whoosh of
paddles and the voices at the cranes barking commands ...

Another day indeed and she would walk here, perhaps with
Toby if they could find a perambulator to borrow. She should ask
Mrs Rutherford.

Linley headed home. She was eager to be there, to ask CeeCee
a million questions and to sink into this strange new world of
being Mrs O'Rourke.

Eighteen

Bendigo

Ard kicked at the dirt, his boot scuffing up the dust and bits of dried grass. 'Doesn't look so good now, but I might have caught it in time. Bit of water on it again, good as new.'

James looked out over the rows of fruit trees and pointed. 'What trees are they?'

Ard looked across and with a wave of his hand said, 'There's apples and pears. Over this side is the citrus. Lemons, oranges and mandarins.'

'Impressive.'

'It has been.'

James turned. 'You don't sound as if your heart's in it.'

Ard shrugged. 'Drought's coming again, and the Chinamen are strong in the market. My uncle has left and I don't know he'll be back.'

'Your uncle?'

'He and my father own this place. My uncle's in Swan Hill and my parents are in Renmark. If the irrigation scheme fails there, my parents will be back.' He looked around him, the fruit trees thirsty, the sky a relentless blue. 'But to what? We have to think of something else. We've been offered a sum. It might be best to leave.'

James considered that. 'Perhaps. What did you have in mind?'

'I like the river. The Murray. The trade. The future's there.'

James shook his head. 'Not with the rail gone through now. Talk is trade is on the wane. Lots of boats are left where they moor, or founder. Men walking away.'

Ard nodded. 'Trade *on* the river, yes. But if we irrigate, the land can grow anything. Fruit, vegetables. I even hear there's talk of wheat being sown. Acres of it.' Ard felt his spirits rise. Then sag again. 'Don't mistake me, I've loved it here, but there's no future for a white man in fruit and vegetables in this area when the Chinamen do it so much better.' He kicked the dirt again and bent down to scratch up a handful. He let the dry soil drop. 'I'm waiting for my father's answer to the offer. And my uncle's.'

'And what work is it you hope to get if you go to Renmark?'

Ard looked up. 'Not Renmark, I'm not going there. I reckon the irrigation scheme there will fail, and that's already the talk. The Chaffeys don't know the land or the weather. The drought will kill it. You only have to check levels on the river in some places now.' He looked past the orchard, into a place he couldn't really see. 'I came upstream not long ago, lucky to be on board a boat whose captain knows what he's doing. I don't want Renmark. I'm thinking I'd like Echuca. The place is crying out for produce. Only got one orchard there.'

James nodded and remained silent. He, too, scuffed the dirt at his feet. 'Echuca. Big plans,' he finally said.

'If we sell here. Any which way, long term I don't think I'll stay.' Ard's gaze swept past the tired trees, the dried weeds at their bases, the new leaves of spring cracked and brown at the tips. 'I do have to find Miss Linley. But first I'd like to set myself up and make something of it. Somewhere.'

James nodded again, and still looked at his feet. 'She's important to you.'

'James, I'm grateful to you for pulling me out of that burning house. I was calling on Miss Linley for a reason but now she's gone. You know where she's gone.'

James looked at Ard. 'I know they are safe. I just don't know who they are safe from. I will get a message to Linley, if that helps you.'

Ard's shoulders dropped again. 'I will find her.'

'Write her a letter for me to take.'

Ard shook his head. ''Tis too big for words on paper.'

James slapped a hand on Ard's shoulder. 'Then you must be eloquent. Write a good letter. Write a brave letter, tell her how you feel. Then show her.'

Show her.

Horse's hooves sounded on the track and both men turned to see a rider bearing down on them and leading a spare horse.

'Yon, Ard!'

Sam Taylor galloped down the home track, bellowing on the back of a roan. He was trying to keep abreast of Pie, who was saddle-less, stretching the reins in Sam's hands, and with his eyes on the prize.

'Whoa!' Ard and James jumped out of the way as Sam reined in.

He slid from the saddle. 'I was hoping to beat you back here. Beg pardon for intruding.' He flashed a grin at James Anderson and flung out his hand. 'Samuel Taylor. Not an esquire.'

James' lips twitched. 'James Anderson, same.'

Sam turned to Ard who had his hand on Pie, settling the horse with crooning words. 'Heard you were a guest of the coppers.'

'The quacks, with only a visit from the coppers.'

Sam shuffled from foot to foot. 'Nothing to do with the grog then?' He chanced a glance at James, who raised an eyebrow.

Ard shook his head. 'Least of my worries. Went visiting Miss Linley and got myself in the way of an iron bar or something.'

'Ballocks to that.' Sam grabbed Ard by the shoulder and turned him this way and that. 'But she didn't do much of a job—you still look all right.'

James laughed aloud.

Ard snorted and threw off Sam's hand. 'A rotten headache, a few bruises, but not from Miss Linley. Mr Anderson here helped me out. Not before Miss Linley's house was torched, though.'

Sam nodded. 'I heard of the fire. What have you got yourself into, O'Rourke?'

'Not me.'

Sam held his hands up. 'Right. Well, naught to be said but that I've brought vittles and a—' He looked at Anderson.

'A drink?' James supplied. 'Good. We've only got channel water here, apparently.'

Sam's guard dropped. 'A drink. That's it. Ard, me man, and Mr Anderson, let's get out of the heat and flies and get into yonder hut so I can hear you tell the tale.' He rummaged around in the bulging saddlebags and hauled out a couple of cumbersome parcels. He nodded towards the hut. 'Good to meet you, Mr Anderson. After you.'

Inside, they sat on Ard's upturned fruit boxes at Eleanor's red gum table. The door remained open and the window boards were let swing as the breeze, if any, took them.

Sam glanced from Ard to James. 'So, go on. Tell.'

Ard's fingers drummed the table. 'Coppers want a word with you, Sam.'

'What?'

'Verifying Ard's activities night before last,' James qualified.

'We were here, all night. Drunk as monkeys. Or I was.' Sam looked at Ard. 'You didn't sneak off anywhere, did you?'

Ard grunted. 'Four mile from the town in the dead of night, on foot and no bloody moon. I don't think so.'

'Pie was outside. You coulda taken him.'

Ard threw his hands in the air. 'You believe I went into town?'

'No, no. You just wouldn'a been on foot if you did go.'

'Jesus.'

'Sam,' James intervened, 'if the police come for you about Ard's whereabouts, you'll vouch for him?'

''Course.' Sam unwrapped a parcel on the upended boxes. 'Ma's pickled pork, some apricot jam and a slab of bread.' He scratched his thatch of hair, shoved it back behind his ears and unwrapped the packet. 'Board. Knife,' he ordered, and Ard brought both from the hearth shelf. 'You said you needed a horse and I said Pa would lend you Pie. Well, here he is.'

Ard blew out a breath and glanced at James, but addressed his friend. 'Thanks. I'll look after him.'

'You will or you'll die me da's slave, heavin' dung for a living.' Sam turned his dark gaze to James. 'And you, James, mate, what's in this for you?'

James returned Ard's glance. 'A stout friend you have, Ard.'

'Stout between the ears.'

James sat back on his seat and folded his arms. 'I have ladies to look after. I have to protect their interests, which pan across the personal and the financial. And I must deliver a letter to one of them that Ard will write.'

Sam tore off a chunk of bread and carved a thick slice of pickled pork. He used the knife to cut through the wax seal on the pot of jam, dipping his finger to wipe a smear on the bread. 'That so, Ard? You best tell me all.'

'Tell you nothing, except that I'm thinking of leaving.' Ard swiped the knife and dipped his own chunk of bread in the jam.

'In that case, I'll have to come with you.' Sam smirked at James, saluted him with a chunk of bread and jam and shoved the lot into his mouth.

'You don't.'

'I do.' Sam munched down in gulps. 'Coppers did come around home last night.'

Ard gave a start. 'And?'

'Seems Griffin isn't entirely sure of your story.'

Ard scowled. 'I had nothing to do with the fire.'

Sam lifted his chin. 'So you said.'

'You're a daft bugger.' Ard stared at Sam.

'I say we leave and let the copper work it out for himself.' Sam licked the jam off his fingers.

'Why would you want to leave? You had nothing to do with it.'

'The adventure. We'll join a mob of bushrangers. More money in that than the jobs we got.' Sam shoved in another mouthful of bread and jam.

'Ballocks,' Ard said.

James laughed at that and Sam grinned.

Ard glanced at James. 'My friend Sam here makes it sound as if he's got nothing between his ears, and no money in his pockets. He works with his father, who builds houses, fences and the like. He also works with a local smithy. Sam'd just rather have the life of an adventurer. Or a no-hoper.' He looked at Sam. 'If I go anywhere, I'll go to Echuca. It's not far away, but a good place to start again.'

James dropped his chin and frowned.

Sam looked from one to the other. 'Echuca. Heard it's a nice place, lots of pubs. When do we leave?'

———

James wheeled the carriage around and headed down Ard's track to the gate. He pulled onto the road and drove back to Bendigo. He'd be back well before dusk.

So, Ard thought he'd go to Echuca. No mention he knew Linley was there. No mention of a baby either. Perhaps he didn't know Linley had a baby with her.

He wondered what Ard was so keen on seeing Linley about. Sam had turned up at the wrong time, though he certainly provided light relief.

And the Ard and Linley relationship bemused him. CeeCee had never mentioned there was any connection between Linley and a young man, so he was caught unawares.

He'd telegram CeeCee but leave telling her about the fire until he arrived.

Right now, he needed to attend to the second thing on his list before he did anything else.

Nineteen

Bendigo

No moon. Low light by the stars.

Good. And bad. How was a body to see where he was goin' if he couldn't see where he was goin'?

Mr Campbell's offices. In darkness. Front door locked, of course. No street lights left on anywhere so no chance of anyone seeing him, either. Gareth Wilkin flattened himself against the door, then turned and twisted the door knob one more time. No give. He shouldered the thing as a test, then drew back and charged it—

Breath whumped out of him. Shuddering reverberation …

He got nothing but a banged-up shoulder and slowly slid down the door, his eyeballs rattling. He couldn't really give it a good charge, as his foot dragged. He couldn't see a thing when he looked around, and believed he was alone in the street. He stood up, drew back and charged again, full tilt. This time his foot kept up.

The door splintered open with a massive *craaack*. He followed it inside at the speed of light, skidding in the hallway, and went down on his face. Blustering, he fumbled to his knees and scrambled towards the door, slamming it closed from where he knelt.

He pressed his forehead to the doorknob and dragged in agonised breaths.

Jesus Mary Joseph Christ on the cross.

He waited a moment. No noise. No alarmed voices.

He was in.

He spun around on his hands and knees, facing, he hoped, where he knew Campbell's office to be. Second on the right if memory served correctly.

His sight adjusted to the darkness, and with little to guide him but his recollection, he found the door knob. No lock this time. He shoved it open, caught it before it hit the wall and closed it softly behind him.

Musty. Old wood. Old papers. Some sort of lemon scent.

There was the bloody chair he'd dangled from the other day like a damn dwarf on an elephant. Gareth patted down his pockets, and located the note he'd written earlier. That should save the coppers going any further than the smart young buck who thought he was a brick wall.

Now. The desk. Find files, papers… or something. Something with the bitch's name on it. Something which tells me where the brat got taken …

Gawd, this could take all night without a light.

He crawled to a window and peered out. Down on the street he saw no movement. Hard to tell but …

He'd risk it.

He took a matchbook from his pocket and struck one from the fold. A quick flicker of light, enough to show him the desk top. Carefully guarding the flame, he swept the folders atop the desk down to the floor. Cross-legged, holding the flickering match steady, he scanned what he had.

Nothing.

The match went out. He struck another, sifted past what he'd already discarded. Still nothing.

No damn file.

He sat up and banged his head on the edge of the desk. *Fuuuck!* Heat surged in his chest and he beat down the urge to burst out and break something, tear it apart with his bare hands ...

He rubbed his head instead, the dull throb breaking the mood. *Christ almighty that hurt.*

The little flicker of light died. He scrabbled out from under the desk. Eyesight adjusted, he made out another small table on which sat piles of folders.

Aha!

He swiped them down to the floor and struck another match, crawled back under the desk, keen to keep the light hidden.

And there it was. *Mary Bonner.* Not Mrs Gareth Wilkin. Oh, no. Ungrateful bitch had kept up her notion that she belonged only to herself.

He pored over it. Could hardly decipher the legal jargon, but when it came to the part about her inheritance going to the guardian of her baby for its upbringing, he knew he had his hands on gold.

There were letters in the file from Mary to the solicitor... *all that ballocks about me 'mistreating' her—she were me wife, weren't she? 'Sides, if she hadn't whinged all the bloody time I wouldn'a had to thrash her ...* He would destroy those as soon as he was somewhere hidden and safe. And if the letters disappeared nothing could harm his claim. His marriage licence made his claim legitimate. He had that. Somewhere.

If the letters disappeared ...

Hah! Outwitted her.

He took the folder and stuffed the lot down his shirt front. Too late he saw the glow of light fill the room.

'Who's there?'

A lantern's shimmer shielded its bearer, but the voice was male and gruff. Campbell? He lived here? *Jesus!*

Gareth's eyes darted to the door he'd come through, the one now behind him. There was only one chance, one slim opportunity for him to get out with the folder ...

What would it mean to kill a solicitor?

No ... no. Don't kill him. Just get the hell out.

Bursting up from the floor, he shoved the man out of his way, and lurched for the door. Papers sprang from the folder. He cursed, snatched them back to him, then charged for the door, scrunching the files to his chest. Something hit him on the back of the head and for a moment, a star burst over his eyes. Something burned, singed, and a pungent odour swept past him. Heat on his neck, his collar. Stink. Burning ...

Lor' lummy, shit, I'm on fire!

He tumbled forward, out the door, scrambled down the hallway, out through the front door and onto the street. Crabbing his way around the corner, puffing wildly, clasping the files with one hand, he beat himself up and down with the other hand. He dropped the files, stamped his foot on them and wrenched out of his waistcoat, beating himself with it to put out the embers latched in his clothing.

A flapping buffoon!

What's that *smell*? His scalp was hot, his eyes watered ...

Then he heard the voice bellowing for help. Saw the faint glow reach him from around the corner. Heard glass popping and crashing to the street. More yells as people came out of the buildings.

Oh shit, oh shit, oh shit ... the old bastard's torched the place. Oh shit.

Gareth rubbed his face with one hand, picked up and clutched the papers to his chest again, and limped in the opposite direction.

Keep calm. Calm.

Nobody had seen him. It's just a little fire … And if the place burned to the ground, so what? He had *the* file!

He limped in a happy hurry. *I have her will. I have her will!*

A sudden thought trapped him, gripped him by the throat as if he were in the hangman's noose. He clutched the file desperately.

If the place burns to the ground, I will never be able to produce the bloody thing to prove me right!

Oh shit.

He stood stock still, turned and let the file fall to the road. Then he resumed his hurry away, no longer happy.

———

Constable Albert Griffin leaned down to the older man sitting on the curb in his pyjama suit and shaving coat. 'Mr Campbell, you all right?'

'Thank you, constable. A bit shaken, a bit singed, but altogether all right.'

'The doctor is on his way.'

'Good fellow. But I doubt he needed to be pulled from his bed.'

'Better safe than not, Mr Campbell.' Griffin straightened up. 'You were lucky, sir.'

By the light of hand-held lanterns they looked towards a cluster of bed-clothed folk who carried buckets and wet towels with them, in and out of Mr Campbell's offices.

'I'm luckier I have a good set of lungs to bellow and alert my neighbours.'

'Seems you got it under control quick enough with the water urn, and dropping that heavy curtain.' Griffin held his lantern up and the light wavered around them. 'My men are checking a couple of laneways here. You said you hit the man on the head? We'll get him if he's down.'

Mr Campbell coughed. 'My cricket arm is still good. I tossed a beauty—my ashtray, solid brass. Cracked him on the back of the head.'

The constable winced. 'Certainly give him a headache. And you didn't see his face?'

'I did not.'

Griffin heaved in a sigh and exhaled loudly. 'Second fire this week. Hope it doesn't continue.'

Mr Campbell nodded. 'Indeed.'

Griffin glanced over at two figures hurrying towards them. Young police officers—one with a lantern, the other carried a paper file in one hand and held a piece of clothing aloft in the other. 'Sir, we found these. Still smoking a bit.'

Griffin set his lamp down and grabbed the waistcoat, peered at it, swiped at the smoulders. 'Good work. And the file—is this one of yours, Mr Campbell?'

Joseph Campbell nodded as he read its title. 'Yes.'

'Stop hopping, Roberts.'

Roberts, fresh faced, pointed. 'Sir, there's a note in the pocket.'

Griffin poked fingers into the pocket and came out with a crumpled envelope. Bending to the lamplight, he read aloud, 'To Ard O'Rourke, Post Office, Bendigo.' He pulled the note from inside it. 'My wife's papers are safe from you. Leave me alone or I will go to the coppers.' He turned the note over but there was nothing to see on the other side. 'Do you make anything of that, Mr Campbell?'

Muffling a groan, Joseph waved his hand as if to say he had no clue.

Twenty

Bendigo, next day

James Anderson stood in Joseph Campbell's office. His gut turned. He felt his mouth curl at the destruction. Minor, but its nascent threat, all too obvious, had taken hold. CeeCee's little house was testament.

His jaw clenched.

'Only slightly frizzled, James, just like me.' The elderly lawyer held up his right arm. His hand and forearm had been bandaged.

The curtain Mr Campbell had used to smother the flames still lay crumpled on the floor. The desktop had scorch marks on it. Under the desk the lacquer had peeled off the floor boards and curled atop blackened soot. A warm breeze ruffled the remaining curtain through the hole where windows had been.

James inhaled deeply a couple of times before speaking. 'It's beyond belief nothing more was damaged.'

Mr Campbell nodded. 'He dropped a match when he leapt up at me and that's what started it off. My own lantern I set aside, thank God. I'd got most of the flames covered with the curtain.'

'You were quick. And the window?' James leaned out to check the rubble below.

'I tossed the contents of the water urn once and went back for a second shot when it came right out of my hands.' Mr Campbell laughed. 'Felt a right fool.'

'Pity it didn't land on his head and kill him.'

'Pity. But he will have a sore head.' Mr Campbell picked up his brass ashtray. 'Hit him for a six.'

James turned to look at the heavy object in Mr Campbell's hand. 'Good God. That would down an elephant.'

'As for what he took, it seems to be only Mrs Wilkin's files.'

'You think it was her husband?' James asked.

'I do. I did not see his face, as I told the constable.'

James nodded, shrugged, a feeble attempt to curb his ire. 'Ah well.'

'But there is no mistaking the stench of the man. I know it to be him. And of course, the bastard was only about this high.' He held his good arm at chest level. 'The man stinks these days as if he rolls in dead carcasses. I'm not a medical man, but I've smelled that before. First a long time ago, when some lads came back from the Crimea, and since, after accidents on the goldfields, untreated injuries over the years. Some with the sugar disease get it. It's gangrene. One of his limbs would be rotting.'

'Good God, the man needs it taken off. Should be in hospital, not running around the countryside committing arson.'

'It has probably sent him mad. It happens fast. He'd been acting more strangely since his wife died.'

James shook his head. 'It's a wonder someone hasn't taken him away for his own good. You're sure it couldn't have been anyone else?'

Mr Campbell looked for his chair and sat heavily, holding his injured arm away from his body. 'I am sure. There is no possible way it was another man.'

'And you know where to find him?'

Mr Campbell nodded. 'His address is in the file. He and Mary lived in a little dwelling at the entrance to town on the Melbourne side. N Street. I forget if it had a number, but it's the middle house in a row of three.'

'I will pay a visit.'

'Be careful, James.' Mr Campbell frowned. 'I warned Cecilia about him. It seems Wilkin does his best work in the dead of night.'

'A coward.' James flexed his shoulders. He recognised the heat building in his gut, the sweat breaking on his brow. Anger rolled through him as unrelenting as waves to the shore.

'And a nasty one at that. As you know, his treatment of Mary was appalling. The law would not have stepped in, I am ashamed to say, because she came to me too late. Thank God for CeeCee. And you, James. But it was just too late for Mary.'

'We will get her justice, Mr Campbell.'

'Hmm. It might be best to get justice for this Ard O'Rourke fellow first. I don't know what to make of that note. A clumsy attempt, at best, to distract the police, but they might not view it that way.' Mr Campbell sucked in a breath and raised his injured arm again. 'If you need me to represent him at any stage …'

James nodded. 'Thank you. I hope it won't come to that.' He waved his hand at the mess. 'Have you organised a cleaner? Can I help you at all with anything?'

'Miss Juno will be along shortly. I'll let her deal with it, engage the right people.'

'In that case, I'll take my leave and get on with some pressing tasks.' He headed for the door, shaking out his flexing hands. 'Thank you, Mr Campbell.'

Relax yourself. Relax.

'James.' Mr Campbell stopped him with a hand, palm out. 'Wilkin might be a coward, but he's not stupid. Watch your every step. He might have friends, and there are many others who don't like the work you and Miss Seymour undertake. Be careful.'

James Anderson nodded. 'I will. I'll be very careful. I always am. Good day.'

He left Mr Campbell at his desk and headed outside. Looking up to the sky, he realised heat was building in the day. He climbed into his carriage and snapped the reins.

N Street, I'm coming to check your housing properties.

Twenty-One

Bendigo, three days later

Ard glanced at Sam. 'You're serious.'

He lifted the axe and it landed with a *thunk* into a sawn-off tree limb. Thank God his head felt better than it had the last few days. It felt good to be doing hard work. Sweat dripped down his back and snaked down his chest to his pants.

Sam scowled. 'I'm serious. We've got Pie, and now Bolter, and I say we should go in the next day or so.'

'I can't go yet. This place—the orchard. Haven't heard from my father or Liam.' Ard swung the axe again and the thick log split with a crack.

Sam stepped clear of the shower of splinters. 'They're trees, Ard, you water 'em a bit and they look after themselves.'

Ard shook his head, and bent to stack the cut logs. 'Not this time. Neither of the brothers are here to look after the place. And don't forget,' Ard said, swinging again, 'Mr Ling is on the trail. I don't dare leave the place empty.' The axe thwacked, a log split.

Sam swiped a hand through his hair. He leaned on his axe, settled on the handle while the iron wedge sunk into the sandy loam. 'You've come back different Ard. You used to have fun.'

Ard rolled another log over, stood it up, lined it up and brought the axe around with a whistle. *Thunnk*. He did the same with another, and then one more. He dropped the axe, gathered up the kindling and the bigger cuts and threw them piece by piece to the stack. He wiped a forearm over his face, reached across to his shirt flung over a tree branch and swiped the dust and sweat off his chest.

'I heard about Mary, Sam. I only had a letter from her just days before I got one from Linley telling me she died. It cuts me deep. Her dying ...'

'Yeah, Mary, poor bugger.' Sam kicked at the dirt at his feet. 'But her—'

Ard cut him off. 'It made me think. I got things to do, and no time to waste anymore. Got things to do. I reckon time for fun's over for now.' He ignored the deepening frown creasing his mate's brow. 'Things to tidy up. Make something of myself. Find work, or make work, squeeze every last drop out of this depression.'

'You can't force it to happen, Ard. My pa's got me on half wages, work is so slow, I'm not even at the smithy's anymore. And I know Pa's paying me and not himself. He's getting paid in meat and eggs, if that.' Sam shook his head. 'Work's hard to come by here.'

Ard shrugged into the shirt, grabbed the axe and headed back to the stone hut. 'And I have to see Linley,' he said over his shoulder.

Sam threw his hands in the air. 'Linley? Well, all right then.'

Inside, Ard went to a pitcher and downed a mug of cool water taken from the channel earlier in the morning. Sam hadn't known anything of Ard's dalliance with Mary, no one had, and he'd keep it that way. 'I'll go to town and check at the telegraph office. I don't expect to hear from Pa any time yet, but Liam for sure.'

'And what'll that give you—half an answer? You'll still want to wait.'

'Liam can get a message to Pa downriver from Swan Hill quicker than I can get a letter back. He might have both answers already.'

Sam leaned on the table. 'Reckon they'll sell to the Chinaman?'

Ard shrugged. 'Perhaps. If the price is right.' He grabbed a clean shirt hanging on a nail above his cot. 'You coming?'

———

Midafternoon and James pulled up at the corner of N Street. The dirt road, pocked with old holes wearing away to bulldust, was a hazard to carriages. He'd get out and walk, see if he could locate the house.

Mr Campbell couldn't give a number of the house, but he'd said Wilkin's was in a row of three. House were singles, or clusters, not more than eight altogether. It shouldn't be hard to find.

He changed his mind about walking. He was easy to remember. His height, above average at six foot two, his bright red hair and big build gave nosey neighbours reason to remember him. He sat a while, loosened his hands on the reins, surveyed the road just ahead. He could navigate around the holes, ease the carriage along and have plenty of time to guide the horse around any trouble. Looping the reins once more in his hands, he gee-upped the horse, tugged his hat a little lower and idled the carriage down the street.

There, on the left. Three scummy-looking tiny houses, and the one in the middle the worse for wear. Slowing right up, he took a long look at the boarded-up windows, and the proximity to its neighbours. Barely three foot each side. Stripped logs weighed

down old iron sheets that served as a roof. The precarious verandah hardly looked safe to stand under. A door at the front, not
two paces from the road, had a cross beam on it, preventing access
from the street. The place could have been abandoned.

There would be a back door ... As he drove past he saw no
signs anybody still lived there. A sour churn in his gut had bile rise
to the back of his throat. How could the occupants of the other
dwellings not help but hear Mary's screams for help? If she could
indeed scream.

He drove on, careful not to slow too much, or to stop, or to
openly study. Dusk was still a few hours off, darkness not long
after that. There was still time to do what he needed to do.

He would be back.

————

Gareth Wilkin flattened himself inside his cart, fumbling for something under the hessian sacks in the back. He was at the turn-off
to the old diggings, not far from where he knew the O'Rourke
orchard to be.

*And be buggered if that isn't O'Rourke itself riding off to God-knows-
where with a mate. Shit. Thought he'd still be a guest of the coppers.*

Luck was on his side; he hadn't been seen. No doubt his fate
would have been a great blow to the face with a clenched fist had
O'Rourke spotted him. Perhaps worse.

Squeamish, he heaved himself gingerly back into the driver's
seat and settled as comfortably as possible, scorched bits aside. His
scalp was raw under the singed loss of hair and weeping burns
irritated his neck at his collar. Melted shirt buttons left their print
in suppurating sores down his chest. Butter was the thing he was
told, though he couldn't bear to touch the wounds. Salt baths
someone had said, but it stung like a bugger when he'd tried it on
his arm, so he wasn't doing that again.

Watching the two men on horses canter back towards town, he straightened up in the seat of the cart and flicked the reins. The scraggly beast pulling his cart moved forward as if he'd momentarily forgotten what he was supposed to do. Over his shoulder, Gareth watched the disappearing riders and then glanced at the bunches of kindling in the back. The tin of Evening Star kerosene sat close by. Not a full tin, mind, but enough for the job.

His head was flaming, and his throat dry, but he pressed on. He needed a drink of hot tea, laced with some rum, but he'd see the job done. He'd burn the bastard out of house and home just like he'd done to the stupid bitches who decided to get in his way. Then he'd go after that other bloke, the big redheaded bastard. Whatever his name was.

In the driveway now, he flicked the reins again, hard. The horse and cart jolted forward but refused to work any harder. Frustrated, sore and blurry-eyed, he hauled the cart around the back of the hut, sure to be unseen from the road. Sliding carefully off the seat, he stood for a moment, sparing his left foot, while the dizzy spell abated. Then he reached into the back and drew out a couple of bundles of kindling.

Limping, his shirt chafing the raw burns, he carried the two bundles to the nearest fruit trees. He limped back and carried two more, placing them further down the rows. Another two and more agonised steps later, he returned for the tin of kerosene.

Intent on opening it, he stopped and looked out over the trees. He hadn't thought clearly. He stood at the cart, worrying a hand over his face. How was he going to light the fire and get out without being seen? As soon as flames lit up, someone somewhere would see—and see him.

Oh shit.

But he had to do it. He'd come this far. He'd wipe that boy off the face of the earth.

Squinting skywards, he reckoned the afternoon sun gave him about an hour. Time enough to stack a few bundles of kindling further down the orchard. There was another track down yonder; the Chinamen used it to service their own blocks, and it trailed past this one. So he could pick it up and get back to town without too much notice.

That's what he'd do. Take the cart down the block, amble on by as if he'd just wandered off track.

The breeze was slight but visible in the foliage, and heading north. It would work. It was a good idea he just had. The burns chafed anew as he climbed back into the driver's seat. He took out the makings for a smoke, rolled a clumsy one, and went to light it.

Shit, fella! Your brains are porridge. Kerosene.

He shook his head, tucked the unlit smoke behind his ear, picked up the reins and headed into the orchard. Splashing fuel on each pile of kindling he dropped, then trailing a little from tree to tree, he made it to the last row before the liquid finally ran out. He slung the empty tin into the back of the cart and stopped on the dirt track that ran along the bottom of O'Rourke's patch.

Over paddocks of cabbage and some other leafy green good-for-nothing-but-pigs food, he could just make out people in the far distance. He didn't see anyone giving him any interest. Sweat beaded on his forehead and trickled down his chest and back, stinging like a bastard in the seeping scrapes. Easing the cart a few yards along at a leisurely pace, he stopped, carefully climbed out of the wagon and staggered over to the trees to take a piss. Or that's what he hoped it looked like if anyone was watching.

Shaking hands fumbled with the matchbook, and he squatted awkwardly to strike a match. He put its tiny flame to the trickle of kero snaking a skinny little track from one bundle to the next. He stumbled back. He had a bit of time, kero could be slow to take ...

But it wasn't.

Gareth just managed to make it back to the cart and pull himself up to the seat. He gee-upped the skittish horse and heard a crackle of leaves. A look over his shoulder and he saw smoke rising from the foot of a tree, and then watched as licks of low flame travelled to the next. He glanced about. Still nobody around. He kept his drive steady.

I've done it.

Twenty-Two

Bendigo

Ard sat on the steps out the front of the telegraph office, Liam's reply in his hands. The thin paper crackled, the handwritten transcript very clear.

Sam leaned on the post, tipped back his hat and stared into the afternoon sky. 'They look like rain clouds, but I'd lay a bet they're not.'

Ard glanced up. 'You're right. No rain yet.'

'And that looks like Mrs Green over there talking to old Mr Thomas.'

Ard lifted a chin. 'Yeah. Neighbours.' He read the note again.

'Wouldn't mind getting one of them ice-making machines.'

'What would you use an ice machine for?'

Sam scuffed the boards underfoot. 'They're interesting, is all.' He sat beside Ard. 'You gonna tell me what your uncle said or do I have to keep making conversation?'

Ard drew in a breath. He waved the telegram. 'Liam says they'll talk it over, and if the offer's still good, we can sell.'

Sam folded his arms. 'Mr Ling might take his time with that.'

Ard's boot heel tapped out an impatient beat. 'I can't wait that long.'

'Why do you have to wait before you see Linley? She's only—'

'She's gone somewhere. With Miss CeeCee. I don't know where.'

Sam frowned. 'Hadn't heard they'd gone.'

'Only left last few days.'

'So what's the hurry? If you don't know where she is …'

'There's something I have to do. To say.'

Sam stayed silent for a few moments, his frown deepening. 'You going to marry her?'

'No.' Ard shook his head, exasperated. 'Yes. No. She won't have me.'

Sam scratched his neck. 'I knew you were sweet on her—'

'Ballocks you knew.'

'And not only me, O'Rourke. Half the flamin' town knows you're sweet on her. Known since you were eight years old.'

'Yeah, you're right,' Ard conceded. 'But now I'm serious about it. And I can't find her. She's angry at me, I know that much.'

'No point chasing a woman who's mad at you.' Sam tapped a fist to Ard's shoulder.

'If you're talking about my sister, all I can say is Maggie saw sense leaving you behind to go to Renmark with Ma and Pa.'

Sam's brows nearly met in the middle. 'I wasn't talking about Maggie.' He waited a bit, then, 'But if you've got a message for me from her …'

'I haven't.' Ard had not pressed either Maggie about Sam, nor Sam about Maggie. Their trouble to work out. He had his own. But the look on Sam's face was woeful. The last time Ard had seen his sister she'd been none too happy either. He reached out and gripped his friend's shoulder. 'Sorry, mate. Write her a letter.'

'Yeah.' Then Sam lightened up again. 'Come on. We need a rum. Let's head down by the pub, see who's around.'

'I have to go back to the orchard. I need to get water on the trees. If I have to stay until Mr Ling ups his offer, I may as well work.' Ard stood up and slapped his hat against his leg before he flattened it on his head.

Sam sighed and pushed off the post. 'What about just one drink?'

Ard hesitated. He had a lot to think about, a lot to do. A lot of plans to put into place. But one drink wouldn't hurt. He could be well back by late afternoon and turn on the pumps then. 'One. But it's never just one rum. Maybe ale.'

'Good lad.' Sam stepped off the boardwalk. 'Might try the Boundary again. See if they'll let us in.'

At the Boundary Hotel, they tied the horses at the post and headed into the bar. Sam jiggled coins in his pocket and tabled them. Ard added his share.

Sam peered at what they had. 'No gold rush here, mate, but there's enough for three ales. In an emergency, I've got me ma's pound note tucked in me boot.'

Ard shrugged. 'No emergency. One's all I'll have then.'

'One and a half.'

Side by side at the long counter, Sam chugged down his beer.

Ard took long swallows then set it aside. 'You know, Sam, Linley and Miss CeeCee ran off because of that little son-of-a-bitch who lit up their house.'

'He's an evil one, for sure.'

Ard glanced across at Sam. 'You know him?'

'Gareth Wilkin, everyone said. He's a crook. Straightened out a bit for years, then ...' Sam shrugged, took another swallow. 'He's the arsehole Mary got herself married to. When Griffin came to my house he asked if I knew him.'

Ard felt the chill slide in his gut. *Wilkin*. The name in her letter. He automatically touched his shirtfront and felt the crinkle of the two letters there, tucked between his shirt and his waistcoat.

'The shit is a real piece of work.' Sam wrapped his hands around his mug of ale. 'Mary was always so happy … You remember her at school—she kept skiving off with who knows who, but nothing would do her down, you know? Always laughing and happy. We were all kids together, and then we grew up, and now I don't know what to make of it.' Sam shook his head. 'Died, after birthing a kid.'

Ard stared at him, then abruptly looked away. 'I know.' His heart thudded. He took his hands from the beer and flexed his fingers.

'I can sort of understand why she went with Wilkin, a kid on the way and all, and him making the offer. He didn't seem so bad then, by all accounts. Had straightened up, they said.' Sam pursed his lips. 'You wouldn't have heard, being away, but he got back to being a bastard pretty quick after they got married, and with his fists on her—'

'I heard.' Mary's letter heated up against his chest.

'Some reckon she died of it.'

Ard nodded, felt a great hot boulder where his heart should be, his blood boiling at the same time.

'Ma says it woulda been more of a right mess except for Miss Linley.'

Ard blinked hard. 'Miss Linley?'

'Here, drink up, mate.' Sam pushed Ard's mug closer to him. 'You sound a bit dry.'

Ard swigged, straightened in his seat. Sweat trickled between his eyes and he raised his forearm to wipe it off. 'You were saying?'

'I only know what ma told me. If Mary hadn't made a legal paper for Linley, her kid would have gone to some asylum, or died, poor little bugger.'

Ard froze. *Kid.*

'And not like it was Wilkin's kid, everyone knew that, even Wilkin. But because he laid in with the fists, when Mary birthed her kid, she gave it to Linley, legal-like. For safe-keeping, I reckon.'

Gave it to Linley.

Sam slugged down the last of his beer and beckoned the publican for another. He pushed the last of their collective coin across the counter. 'Yeah. Linley is the little bloke's guardian.'

Ard's world tilted. *'What?'*

Sam glanced across. 'Forgetting you were away for all this.' He kept on. 'Caused a stir. But legal is legal, Ma says. So Linley's got Mary's little tacker and Wilkin looks like he's got his balls in a knot over it.' Sam took another look at Ard's face. 'You all right, mate?'

Twenty-Three

Echuca

The baby was finally quiet; a squawky couple of hours had gone by after Linley topped him up with some tinned milk. He was taking a little time to adjust.

She held the bottle for him again. His wide-eyed gaze spread that glow in her belly, and her thoughts once more turned to Ard. She wondered where he might be, and if he ever thought of her ...

Stupid girl! Mary must have had his heart after all.

The baby kept his eyes open as he sucked and snuffled and swallowed. The tuft of his black hair stood straight out from his forehead, and Linley had a sense that perhaps his eyes were changing colour already. Could that be?

A little crease appeared between his soft barely-there brows. A slight tilt of his head, so like his—

Ard.

He would be somewhere downriver—Renmark she last heard, which is where she'd sent her letter after Mary died.

Did he even get the letter? And if he did, she wondered if he'd sat on a log, his back to a tree, his skin bronzed from the sun and

166

had opened his mail. Did he curse at the news? Did he despair? Did he yell?

Not Ard. Lowering his head, he'd think on it a long time. He would drag fingers through his hair until it scraped back from his face and settled on his shoulders, black and glossy and wavy. And his shoulders would hunch a little, then he would let his hands dangle over his knees.

Those eyes of his that mirrored the sky would look up and he'd shake his head. He would lean back, eyes now closed, his beautiful mouth taut, pain across his face ...

Linley's heartbeat quickened and a breath puffed out of her. Her belly was warm and lower down tingled and wanted. She closed her eyes and let the feeling embrace her as she swayed in her seat—

Startled, she sat upright. *Think no more of Ard O'Rourke right now.*

The baby pushed the bottle away. She lifted him to her shoulder, let him make space for his meal, then she stood and walked him around the room. Toby gurgled, and gurgled some more, and when he stopped she rocked him in her arms. She hushed and cooed until at last his little eyelids drooped then she settled him in his cradle, snugly swaddled.

CeeCee called out from her room. 'Come sit with me a while, Lin.'

When Linley popped her head inside, CeeCee was struggling to get comfortable. 'Let me help.' She plumped the pillows behind her aunt and sat by the bed. 'Are you feeling well?'

'Well enough, but I'm not used to being so laid up.' She swiped wisps of hair from her face. 'I feel agitated, as if by resting up I am not achieving anything. I have more letters to write—'

'I'll do your hair, Aunt. You'll feel better.' Linley reached for the small valise under the bed and withdrew a brush and combs. 'At least we have these little things to give us some comfort.'

CeeCee murmured assent. 'We must call for our possessions to be carted up. We must get ourselves back to normal as soon as we can.' She hitched a breath and let it go.

She indeed seemed agitated. Linley reached over and loosened her aunt's plait. The thick dark hair looked relieved as it sprang from the restraints of the ribbon. 'I've not much to call for. Our box of treasures is here.' Her fingers combed out the long waves and then she set to with the brush. 'Besides, it's rest you need right now in order to have the energy to continue working later.'

CeeCee tut-tutted. 'I miss my journals, and Mrs Lawson's newspaper. We will have to notify her of our new address so our subscription for *The Dawn* will find us again. I have kept every edition.'

'I will write to her. Don't worry yourself now.' The brush stroked rhythmically in Linley's hands. 'From what I read last time, things are getting very exciting, or very dangerous, which-ever way you like to look at it.'

CeeCee winced a little and eyed Linley, nodding. 'There are still those who oppose freedom for women, rights for wives within the marriage. We need to educate young women about their rights. Thank goodness our petition for the age of consent to be raised has been successful.'

'We don't know when it will become law, though.'

'It has put transgressors on notice. And it has become a topic of discussion, as it should. It's a start.'

'It still seems very young at sixteen.' Linley thought of herself at that age. She had no clue about life then, nor to what she might have been consenting.

'But far better than as it was at fourteen. Or in some colonies, only thirteen years of age.'

Linley stopped the brush strokes a moment. 'That makes me seem so old, Aunt.' No husband, certainly not the one she wanted, and no prospects now with a baby—not her own—in tow. Her shoulders slumped.

'You are old enough to understand many more things than you did at that age. I am pleased for it. You can better guard against transgressions. We see the … unpleasantness because of a lack of knowledge.'

Taking in a deep breath, Linley said, 'I am old enough, much older than some, I know, to understand the unpleasantness we encounter. But I don't understand what you mean. Rights for wives within the marriage? Of course we have rights.'

'Hardly any by law. Not what you would expect in this day and age. Some things have changed, property rights for instance.'

Linley resumed brushing CeeCee's hair. 'I remember our discussion about that some years ago.'

'Women should also have the right to control what happens to their own person within the marriage.'

'Yes?' Linley set down the brush and took up the discarded ribbon.

CeeCee stopped her. 'Linley, many marriages are loveless, but still a wife is expected to … to perform her perceived duty.'

Linley fired bright red. 'But that is so because—'

'Because nothing, my dear niece. That is exactly what we fight every day. Just because she is married, does not mean she is merely a chattel to be used as her husband sees fit. Not as a slave in his bed, nor as a punching bag, nor to be discarded as he pleases. She has her own mind, and should be allowed to exercise her right over it and her body. There is even discussion on divorce over that very thing.'

Linley burned crimson as she fiddled with the ribbon. *Divorce.* When did this become a topic of their conversation? 'That I haven't yet known a marriage, does not mean I haven't understood what some women—'

'You must not be oppressed in your life.'

Linley sat back. 'I will not be. I have no intention of being so oppressed. You are not oppressed with James.'

'We are not married.'

Linley shot her a look. 'What makes it so different?'

'The law.' CeeCee shifted her shoulders and winced again. 'I would be owned by him.'

'You would not,' Linley scoffed. 'James would never look upon you as his possession. He loves you. I know perfectly well that if you married James nothing about your lives together would diminish.'

'It's not James. It's the law.' CeeCee stopped and stared at her niece anew, her good eye wide. 'I know he loves me.'

Startled by CeeCee's vehemence, Linley frowned. 'Why are you so agitated now? What's happened? You've never been quite so adamant. Passionate, yes, but today you seem too intense. I don't see what—'

CeeCee waved a hand. 'The altercation with that man happened,' she said. 'And now with you and little Toby, I feel my life might be changing. Perhaps I haven't done enough. I want to make a mark that will help you, and others … Give you courage. The women we provide refuge for—'

'You do help. We are helping.'

'But at a legal level, and at a social level where we can change the minds and mores of society.' CeeCee pressed forward on her hands. 'Mrs Lawson, and Agnes Benham and Mrs Lee all think the same about what happens when we give away our independence. Legislating is opposed by men who think we wish to curtail male liberty.' She sank on the pillows.

'The only curtailing I see would be that of bad behaviour.' Linley reached across and squeezed CeeCee's arm. 'You've run out of breath, Aunt. Calm yourself before you do some damage. This is no time to run yourself ragged.'

'Do not give away your freedom, Linley.'

'Are you saying I shouldn't marry, Aunt?' She held her breath just a little.

'Just know what you're in for. Be prepared. Have your own money.'

'The law states I must give up work if I marry. I would have no money.'

CeeCee nodded. 'I will see to it that you do.' Her eyes closed. At least, her good eye noticeably closed; the other puffy eye was closed anyway. 'I will organise a stipend for you from my own funds. As soon as I'm on my feet, I will do that. That way, if you marry, it will still be yours afterwards to do with as you wish.'

As quickly as the conversation started, it stopped. CeeCee's chest rose and fell evenly, her features relaxed. 'Forgive the tirade, Lin. I cannot help but be worried.'

'I know.' Linley pressed her aunt's hands again. 'Do not worry. I promise to be strong, CeeCee. But now I have chores to do.'

Linley cooked for them over the small kitchen fire and then declared a cup of tea would finish off her day. CeeCee accepted the bread and slice of beef, and afterwards settled back on her bed. She shut her eyes while the tea cooled in its mug on the floor.

Linley left her asleep. The doctor would come tomorrow. She was sure CeeCee only needed the rest and tomorrow they could begin the rest of this adventure.

———

Linley woke with a start. Bright sunlight streamed through the bare window in the room. Darting little early birds chirruped around the magpies warbling in the trees.

Morning. Already.

The baby's little fists waved in the air from the cradle. Linley unfolded herself from the chair, tugged aside the blanket she'd slept under and sat for a moment, waking up. The night had been peaceful for her; the baby had only woken once. She rubbed her eyes, checked he was all right for a few minutes alone, then headed out to the privy.

Back inside, she first tended to Toby. She removed his soiled night linen, and left him in a fresh cloth in the crib. She'd heard stories about how babes were often left without being washed, or had soiled clothing returned to them, but the new-fashioned way of dealing with ablutions for babies appealed to her much more. Linley herself would not have enjoyed being left in soiled clothing, so why would a baby?

'Much better this way, isn't it?'

Toby opened his mouth wide in a delighted smile. He waved both arms at her.

'Of course you agree. You're a very smart fellow.' She ran a finger down his velvety cheek, desperate for another breath of baby, so she hugged him up and pressed her nose against his. He gurgled more delight, and reached up to grab her nose. 'And you are *my* little man.' That warmed her heart as much as holding him.

Reluctantly, she put him back into the cradle. Back in the kitchen room, she set the fire burning up to a good heat, the coals from the night obligingly turning to flame once again. She brewed tea, warmed a bottle for the baby, and went to fetch him. With Toby tucked under her arm she headed for CeeCee's room, knocked and entered.

Her aunt was awake and sitting, holding her ribs, but she looked brighter than yesterday.

'Good morning, Lin.'

'Morning, Aunty. Did you sleep?'

'As long as I didn't try to move. I do need to move now, though.'

'There's a chamber pot under the bed. I could sit it on the chair here, if—'

'I think I'll manage to get to the outhouse. How's our boy?' CeeCee squinted at the baby.

Linley jiggled Toby in her arm as she fed him the bottle. 'He seems very fine. Slept through the night. Almost.'

'Perhaps as tired as we are.' CeeCee pushed her long plaited hair back over her shoulder and took a couple of shallow breaths. 'Not so bad as yesterday. I might only have bruised ribs. I seem to be much rested despite the off and on sleep.' She flicked a glance at Linley. 'And I am anxious to get on with things.'

'All right. But your face still looks very painful. Your cheek is a deep purple. Can you even see out of that eye?' Linley pointed at the puffy half-closed eyelid.

'I'm sure it looks worse than it is. Wait till it goes green then yellow.' She patted her own cheek gently then carefully stuck out her feet and put them on the floor. 'I've seen many a black eye in my day, Linley. From your mother, to all the women and children James and I have looked after over the years.'

Linley sighed. 'Yes, of course you have.'

'My own black eye won't stop me.' Her aunt settled in an upright position on the bed and then gradually stood, testing her balance. 'Just a bit ginger.' She stretched her toes towards her button-and-laced boots.

'It's a neat path to the outhouse, no stones or burrs. You can go barefoot.' Linley handed her aunt the shawl. There'd been no time to purchase anything, including new clothes or footwear, before they left Bendigo.

James had promised assistance. He would telegraph the emporium in Echuca and have some essentials delivered. Linley didn't know what time or what day that was likely to be, but she hoped it would be soon. He'd pressed a little money into CeeCee's hands before she boarded the train, but that wouldn't last too long. Hopefully an account at the bank would allow CeeCee to withdraw funds, again with James' help, after being telegraphed from Bendigo. If CeeCee was correct, he would be on today's train. Things might then take on some semblance of normalcy.

Linley sighed inwardly as she watched her aunt totter out the bedroom door. She didn't really know what normal was any longer.

Twenty-Four

Bendigo

James Anderson left the Bank of Victoria and stood on the street alongside his carriage. The afternoon had not rushed to dusk as he expected. He'd had plenty of time to telegraph instructions to the bank in Echuca for CeeCee, and to think over his movements of the next couple of days.

For now, he needed to deal with Gareth Wilkin.

He looked about him. Bendigo was a big, thriving town. Not big enough to get lost in, like a city, like Melbourne. It bustled with a freshness he'd forgotten. Certainly smelled better than Melbourne. Carriages and carts drove past him, pedestrians strode across the wide road, children played along the footpaths.

Trade was brisk, but the loom of depression hung in the air. Nobody took any notice of him except a few gents who doffed hats. Women allowed their gaze to glide over him.

Time to be moving. He alighted the carriage, checked the way was clear and moved out onto the road. The sun had already bobbed low on the horizon but last light still lingered. James rode at walking pace along N Street, certain not to attract attention.

He pulled his hat just a little lower, and settled the dark kerchief at his throat further down under the open neck of his shirt. He turned to stare, first to the left then to the right. The street was quiet; it would be a long while before any men would venture home from the pubs.

It was easy to pick his target. The two houses either side had bright lamplight in a front room. The dull glow of a smaller light coming from a window in the middle house gave him his mark. He wondered who lit the lamp in Wilkin's house. Maybe the bloody donkey didn't live there by himself after all. Perhaps some other poor woman was living with his cowardly fists.

That meant his plan had to change somewhat. He didn't want to burn an innocent person, he only wanted to dish out Wilkin's own medicine and sear the flesh off him. So instead he would settle for crushing Wilkin's ribs, and battering his eye till it closed.

Crush him so his chest would cave in. Batter his eye so hard he'd never see out of it again. Maybe he'd break all his fingers so he'd never use his fists again. Or his hands, so that he couldn't dress himself, feed himself, wipe up after a shit. Or hold his cock to take a piss … or otherwise. Far better idea.

His fingers flexed on the reins.

He rode past the house and turned the horse into a backstreet, passing ramshackle huts and yards filled with junkyard collateral—broken timber boxes, burlap sacks with straw spilling, rusty tin drums, bones of an old cart. He saw movement under canvas shelters in one or two places, but no one bothered to call out.

And then he was at the back of the cluster of three houses. He slowed the horse to a plod and surveyed as best he could in the fast-fading light. No dividing fences. The outhouses were in a line across the back of the blocks. No dogs, no chicken coops, no horses. He kept on his circuit, rode back to the corner of N Street again and stopped, listening.

Distant singing by drunken voices, but nothing to alarm him. They might have been in the street behind him. He looked up past the trio of houses. No one about. Not a soul.

The kerchief came up over his face. He knew he didn't need to do it, but long-held disciplines died hard. Still best to be careful. The weakening light would protect him anyway. If he'd had his own horse, the warrior Mars, a robust Waler gelding he'd purchased years ago, he would just push up on the stoop and knock the flimsy door down. Mars did love a challenge.

James eyed the verandah over the door. It was so low he'd knock himself out, much less damage the horse.

Softly, softly approach …

Anticipation curled in his gut. There was only one way to stop men like Wilkin, and that was with men who called them out. Men who valued life and loved ones. Men who valued right from wrong, and then did something about it.

A low burn of anger coiled around his heart. Fight fire with fire. Be damned the excuses and the eye of the law.

He urged the horse another couple of paces and stopped. Then he slid to the ground. Rounding the corner and into the same street, not far from him now, came two men on horseback. One was in full song—if you could call it a song—that pained his ears.

Damn it. He remounted, wheeled around to ride past the meandering duo, clearly drunk and—

'Come on, Ard, you bugger. You're still not singing,' the man slurred out at full voice.

James dropped his kerchief fast and pulled between the pair. A belly laugh threatened to escape him before he realised the gravity of the situation. All three of them were within cooee of Gareth Wilkin's abode, and at least two of them had cause to inflict some damage on the man.

No, no, no. It had to be clandestine, with no witnesses to run to the police.

Jesus.

'Come along now, boys.' James reached over and grabbed the slack reins of Sam's horse, gripping them in one hand with his reins.

Sam Taylor, mid-song, recognised him with a wobbly grin. He flung his hands in the air and sang his lungs out, a forlorn tune if ever there was one, and loud, James thought, though he couldn't place the lyrics. More forlornly, the singer was painfully out of tune.

And Ard O'Rourke, doing his best to support his friend, but unable to retain any control over him. He met James' eyes briefly and shrugged a little.

James' free hand grabbed for Ard's reins. 'Come on, young fella.'

Secured, he led both the horses and the young men comfortably down the street and away from Wilkin's house. A few shouts from a neighbour, clearly not happy with the God-awful carousing, and that was it. No extra light showed at Wilkin's house. No hurried rush of feet on any verandahs nearby.

Steady as she goes.

James coaxed the horses into a trot, careful not to unseat the wailing Sam. He checked on Ard. 'You look like shite, lad.'

'I feel like shite.' The reply was low. 'I need to get home.' Ard tried to take back the reins.

James held tight. 'Let's get your friend home first. Do you know how to get there?'

Ard looked up and squinted. 'Back to the centre of town, then right at the town hall.'

'Can you ride?' James asked.

Ard nodded. 'I'm not as drunk as Sam.'

James considered, then relinquished the reins. 'Then lead on.' He leaned over and slapped Sam on the back. 'More tune, lad, less noise.'

To which Sam sallied forth ever louder.

At Sam's house, his father came out to the noise, a tall lean man with a shock of straw-coloured hair. He stood on his verandah, hands on hips, and squinted at all three in the darkening evening. 'Could be no other than my son with that noise.'

'Sorry, Mr Taylor,' Ard said. 'We went to the pub.'

Mr Taylor grunted as his son fell off the horse and landed in a heap at his feet, still singing. 'Gawd, his yodelling hasn't improved. He's a sorry business of late. I bet his mother's pound note has gone, too.' He bent to lug Sam upright. 'Get along with you, you and your friend,' he said to Ard. 'I can manage from here, as long as he stops the caterwauling.'

Ard hesitated. James turned his horse. 'Come on, Ard.'

'Goodnight, Mr Taylor.' Ard wheeled his horse to follow James. 'Sorry.'

'Look after Pie,' Mr Taylor called after him.

Ard came level with James. 'What were you doing on that street where you found us?'

He glanced across. 'Looking at properties.'

'It was getting on for dark.'

'There's been a lot of properties to see. I'll be leaving town soon, was running out of time.' James gee-upped to a trot and Ard follow suit. 'And what were you two doing on that street? Not the way home for Sam, clearly.'

Ard was silent for some time. He dragged in a breath. 'Sam reckoned he knew where Gareth Wilkin lived.'

'Ah. The evil little bag of cods.'

Ard blurted a laugh. 'That's it.'

'Leave him to the coppers, lad. Come on, I'll get you back to your farm. I might have to avail myself of a swag there, this time of the night, if that's all right with you.'

Ard nudged Pie to keep up. 'I'd be glad for it. God knows I need a quiet night with someone making some sense of all this.'

James didn't question him. 'Sounds like a night for strong tea and a good feed of beef pie.'

'Tea I can provide.'

James leaned over a little to pat a saddle bag. 'And I can provide the beef pie.'

———

It was clear, even long before they turned the horses onto the road bordering the orchard, that a property was well on fire.

Fear stung Ard like white-hot needles in his chest. The closer they rode, the clearer it became, the sharper his mind through the fog of Sam's rotgut.

'It's my place. It's my place,' he shouted, frantic.

He kicked Pie into a gallop, but the horse was reluctant to give it all, to charge into the roar of the flaming orchard.

Men darted from burning tree to burning tree with sacks or blankets beating down the flames as they licked and scorched their way over his trees. At the trough near the hut, Ard pulled up an ever-fearful Pie, jumped off and tied him to the pump. James dismounted on the run, flung his reins over the pump handle and grabbed hold of Ard.

'Blankets? Burlap bags? Anything?'

Ard bolted for the hut and dragged out what he could. Smoke poured from behind him as he threw what he'd grabbed into the trough then dragged it out, all sodden. He charged the first trees and swung and thrashed at the flames eating their way through his family's livelihood. As he thrashed, he knew it was a losing battle. His head knew but his heart kept him beating down those flames.

James swung heavy blankets alongside him. 'Keep going, lad,' he yelled.

The men Ard had seen from a distance were Chinamen, and still they worked and thrashed and beat at the flames. There must have been twenty of them.

Gradually, beaten it into submission, they had it under control. The men seemed to stop simultaneously. Flames died. Soot and smoke swirled around them. The tree tops smouldered and spat and curled against the heat. Landscape, scorched.

His trees were dead. His land devastated.

Each man looked up, looked around. Silence was eerie. Here and there, a few heavy feet stomped out some fiery spurts. A few burlap sacks crushed down a burst of flame. Men left the blackened field to check their own hands and limbs. Some headed towards the water trough and dunked reddened and dirty forearms or blistering fingers into cool water. Others headed for the channel and slid in fully clothed.

James stomped around the base of the tree closest to him.

In the failing light, Ard stared at row after row of charred and blackened branches, at fallen trees, at sooty balls of scorched oranges and shrivelled stone fruit, just little bags of ash and dust. He stared at tired men who trudged, shoulders slumped, back down through the orchard to Mr Ling's plot. He watched them thrash half-heartedly as they walked past smoking piles of tree limbs. A pair of men helped carry a third whose eyes streamed blackened tears. They passed Ard in silence.

The hut! He spun around. Not a mark. Smoke-filled, but saved.

Mr Ling walked out of the smoking ash-covered desolation. 'Mr Ard.' He carried a blackened bag, his face and his clothes streaked with ash, his hair covered in white soot.

Ard glanced at the Chinese man then looked at his own feet. Gratitude welled up in his throat and his eyes. 'Hello, Mr Ling. Thank you, and thanks to your men.' His voice shook.

'It very fast, Mr Ard. Land, trees too dry. Very sorry.' Mr Ling's voice was low and soft.

Ard lifted his head and looked into the older man's eyes. 'Thank you, Mr Ling.'

Mr Ling gave James a slight nod, and he returned the acknowledgement.

Mr Ling pinched his nose. 'Chin Chee Father saw man and cart. Chin Chee First Son say it man with stench of thousand monkeys.'

Ard nodded.

Mr Ling nodded again, and turned and walked back towards his plot, skirting the edge of the decimated orchard as he went.

James beat his trousers with both hands, and soot and ash rose in a small cloud. 'A thousand monkeys, eh? Can only be one person I know smells like that.'

'Aye. But the Chinamen won't talk to the coppers. Mr Ling's only let me know so I can deal with it.' Ard slapped a palm to his forehead, and wiped the sweat and soot and grime over the rest of his face. He looked at his hands, and back at the smoking ruin that was his orchard. 'Must have been alight for a while.'

James stared over the burned ground. 'Was good of Mr Ling to bring all his men.'

Ard nodded. Mr Ling would have been protecting his own fields from the possible spread of fire, as well as his prospective purchase. Would he keep his offer on the table?

Straightening up, Ard looked into the night sky. 'Naught to do now but wait for morning.' The half moon rising was a bright light through the smoke. 'No wind. Should be safe. No rain, though. I'll check it doesn't flare through the night.'

James reached over and pressed his shoulder. 'Let's get some of that beef pie, lad.'

Twenty-Five

Echuca

Linley was very happy. It was an absolute boon to have a walking carriage for Toby.

Mrs Rutherford straightened and pressed a hand to her back. 'That's as best we can come up with. Belonged to one poor dear ... Never mind that. It'll be fit for your son, Mrs O'Rourke. We just need someone to come along and tighten a few pins and things.'

Mrs Cooke stood back. 'Seen better.' Hands on hips and her wiry froth of rusty hair whipping about her face in the stiff breeze, she eyed the baby carriage. 'Seen worse.'

Linley looked it over. A tired old contraption that needed a fair bit of repair. The three women had walked it up and down the street, to and fro out the front of the house, checking for any instability. There hadn't appeared to be any; it just looked as if there might have been.

'I reckon if you have a spare old blanket or two for underneath, he'll be very comfortable.' Mrs Rutherford scrutinised the carriage itself.

'Could do with a scrub up as well,' Mrs Cooke said.

Annie Rutherford glared across the pram. 'Is that right?'

'And some oil for them wheels.'

'We'll likely have to do it ourselves, so we should set about it.' Mrs Rutherford winced as she stood up.

Linley had a flash of fear in case the woman was beginning to feel poorly. 'Is something ailing you, Mrs Rutherford?'

'Good heavens, no. A chill is all.' She rolled her shoulders. 'It eases with work.' She gave the pram another push and pull. 'Now, if you run home and find some extra padding for the base, we should be able to put Toby in for the walk back this afternoon.'

Now, much later, Linley strolled up High Street pushing the perambulator with a snug Toby O'Rourke tucked inside. The street was busy. Pedestrians, carriages and horseback riders populated the wide road. Most people she passed nodded at her, gentlemen tipped their hats.

She pushed on towards the river, not wanting to go home just yet. She didn't want to idle along for she had little interest in the shops, or the banks, and had no business with the survey office. There'd been nothing at the telegraph office for CeeCee from James. Mrs Rutherford had fed Toby. Back home there was a plentiful supply of tinned milk for his next feed when they returned, so time was at her disposal.

Well, a couple of hours at best. That would be enough. Her mind was on the docks. She wanted to see the boats, fancied she could smell the river not far ahead.

Hesitating at Leslie Street, she knew a right turn would get her to the wharf area. A carriage clip–clopped past her, the driver nodding in her direction, and once past, she stepped onto the road. Compacted dirt underfoot eased the push of the perambulator, yet all the same the carriage rattled and clattered across the road. Toby gave a few squawks but settled back to sleep, a faint frown of discontent on his face.

Linley stood at the corner in front of Customs House and looked across the road to the tall trees that lined the river on the other side. From her vantage point all she could see were the sheds and the cranes on this side, sitting on the wharf above the river level. Men issued shouted orders far away, and carriages and riders passed her by. She heard an engine idle somewhere, but she couldn't pinpoint where on the river it might be.

She crossed the road to stand at the edge of the wharf area and stared wide-eyed at what spread before her. The wharf was huge, much bigger and longer than she expected. A great expanse of heavy timbers rising out of the mud-coloured water. The level was low, lapping fully ten yards below where she stood. She edged closer, pushing the pram carefully, hoping not to awaken the baby.

Toby snuffled and let out a yell. Linley leaned over the carriage to check him, but he was soundly asleep. She drew her shawl up over the opening so he was protected from the sun as he slept.

Horse and buggy passed behind her. She turned and followed its progress until it pulled up a little further along the road. The driver dismounted, and tied the horse to a rail. Something familiar about him caught her eye—

'Missus, you're likely to get mown down if you stand around here.' An impatient voice rasped at her back.

Startled, Linley spun the other way and a working man, by the looks of his clothes, stood with a battered hat twisted in his hands, his gaze on her face.

'Am I not meant to be here?' she asked. 'It seems a public thoroughfare.'

'Not that so much as it could get busy, what with traders and merchants and shearers and the like all milling about, unloading and such things.' He kept wringing the hat with his large, gnarled hands. His shirt was dirty with dust and sweat and oil stains, his pants held up with braces, his worn boots muddied.

'I'll be all right,' she said, though she gripped the handrail on the baby carriage more tightly. He peered at her and she backed up a step. 'I just wanted to see the boats.' She waved over her shoulder towards the river.

He looked over and back again. 'Not too many to see right now. We got the *Hero* in, the *Pilot* and her barge. They're at the dock master's over yonder side. *Sweet Georgie*'s just unloaded waitin' fer her captain. Fact is, that'll be him just there.' He lifted his chin towards the dismounted carriage driver. 'See?'

Linley glanced around but the rider was on the other side of his horse. Only his legs were in view as he hunted for something in the saddle bags.

'So, no sightseeing. It's all work around here, no room for spectators. You should get along now.'

'Oh. But I won't be …' She was about to stand her ground when a team of horses pulling a heavy dray and carrying a dozen or so men rounded into the street from where she'd come.

'Get along, now, missus,' the man said. 'The boys will offload here.' He waved his hat at where she stood.

It was a legitimate reason for her to clear the area, albeit somewhat gruff. She pushed the perambulator back over the road and onto the corner. In front of the wharf master's buildings she turned to watch.

The dray pulled in where the man had indicated and the workers clambered off it to disappear over the boards and down, she believed, to the dock area below. They shouted and laughed, strode or slouched, all in a uniform of pale shirts, buttoned trousers, braces and sturdy boots. One or two doffed their caps in her direction as they went.

How she wished she could get to the docks. Perhaps another day, without Toby, she would visit. She could walk at her leisure, explore without putting herself in the way of working men going about their business. On foot, and with no baby with her, she could get down to the water's edge and watch from a distance.

Her gaze drifted. The carriage driver from before caught her eye again.

Her heart leapt in her throat. 'Ard!' His name came out of her mouth as a croak, the shock of seeing him left her almost speechless. He hadn't heard her. Hadn't seen her.

Her chest felt tight. Too many thoughts raced in her head, crowding out the sense and spinning with the nonsense.

It was him, wasn't it? That black hair, the set of his jaw …

Should she stay and confront him here on the street—this busy street with men coming and going? She rubbed her hands together, lacing her fingers, as she paced past the pram a little way, then back again. She glanced at the shawl over the baby; he couldn't be seen. Her heart pounded, her hands wrung on the carriage's rail, her feet planted her where she stood.

The man walked around the horse's rump, his hand gliding over the broad flank. He checked the harness on this side, intent on his business and oblivious to her.

Of course he hadn't seen her. She was twenty or thirty yards away, and now he had his back to her. But was that him? If so, he was leaner than she remembered. He looked taller. She hadn't seen Ard O'Rourke for many months. He might have lost weight working at Renmark …

She blinked hard. Her breath ached in her throat and tears threatened to erupt, but still she stood on the spot, clutching the pram with all her strength.

What was he doing here?

His hat didn't look right. She stared. Stared hard. She squeezed her eyes closed and open, trying desperately to see his face more clearly.

Definitely Ard O'Rourke, how would she ever mistake him?

Then a female voice caught the man's attention and he looked up sharply. A woman, her hair as black as the man's, hung in a thick long plait down her back. As Linley gaped at her, she burned anew. The woman was with child. She could see quite clearly the proud bulge that was her pregnancy. She walked steadily towards the man and lifted her face for his kiss.

Ard!

Linley's heart groaned, sank. Her knees threatened to give way. 'Ard,' she finally said, she thought in a whisper.

Both the man and woman looked in her direction and she froze anew, aghast that she might have been heard. She dragged the pram backwards. Bumped it carelessly over the ruts and the exposed cobbles of the road. When she looked back, the laughing face was Ard's.

But not Ard's.

What is wrong with me? It is Ard O'Rourke. With a woman who's with child. Kissing her, laughing with her.

But it couldn't be Ard.

Linley dared not look back. She took a wide turn with the pram to face it the other way and stumbled, and the carriage faltered with her. Toby let out an indignant yell, the type that heralded a screaming episode. She tried to hush-hush him. She scurried away from the man who was his father, all the while hoping she could get home without having a screaming episode herself.

Toby would not quieten. With every bump in the road, his squalls grew louder and more agitated. His little screwed-up face had reddened and his eyes squeezed shut.

No no no, don't do this now, Toby-boy. Let me get you home before we both have a complete tantrum.

She hurried down the street, not thinking to turn back to find High Street again.

Good Lord, where am I?

Toby bellowed up at her. Deep inside her gut, the gnawing need to stop, to pick him up and hush him was … The squalling was almost too much, but her legs just wouldn't slow down.

A street corner … She turned right, as much to hopefully get back to High Street and to find her way home from there, as it was to get out of sight. The baby carriage wobbled, jumped in her hands, and Toby hit the high notes. Her ears rang.

'Hush, hush,' she crooned raggedly and realised tears ran over her cheeks. She barrelled down the little street, wondering where on earth she was. Surely High Street crossed it at the end … It seemed to be going in the wrong direction.

She passed buildings on either side of the road, but paid no great attention. Outside one, a woman, stooped over to pick something up from the weeds, stood up and stared at her.

Linley barely noticed until the woman shouted at her. 'You want to keep that one quiet around here, missy. We got gemp-mums coming.'

Linley nodded, ducked her head closer to Toby and tried desperately to calm him down with more hushes. He stopped his rage for a second, took one big-eyed look at her crumpled face and then bellowed afresh. She sucked in a breath and kept moving.

There it was. The street she hoped to find. Now that she had her bearings, she needed to turn left and as she did she nearly ran the baby carriage into a stout, fierce-looking matron on the same footpath.

'Young woman!' The affronted lady drew herself up imperiously.

Her severely parted head of hair was dragged back to the nape of her neck. She had a look of old Queen Victoria about her, a hooked nose, beady little eyes and fat cheeks, as though she kept her spare dinner tucked away in there.

'I'm so sorry,' Linley began, sucking in air, trying not to snivel.

'*You!*'

The accusation stopped Linley mid-sob. She stared at the older woman but couldn't place her.

'You visit that despicable house where those two *creatures* pretending to be married women live with their brats.'

Linley had no clue who this woman was. 'What house?'

'And that would be right, you coming out of *that* street,' she said and flicked a sneer at the street out of which Linley had just emerged.

The baby's screeching had reached crescendo. He now waved his clenched fists in the air, outraged.

The woman peered into the pram. 'Another brat without a father, is it? You're shameful.' The woman held herself taller and swept around Linley to carry on, thankfully in the opposite direction to Linley.

Shaking and tearful after sighting Ard O'Rourke, heart wrenched over the inconsolable Toby O'Rourke, and slighted by a stranger in broad daylight, Linley burst into fresh sobs herself and hurried back down High Street.

———

CeeCee tested her stride again down the narrow hallway of the little house.

Linley had headed off to Mrs Rutherford's, so as soon as she felt up to it, CeeCee had taken a few steps to check her stamina. It didn't take many before her side would ache and her breath would shorten. She'd shuffled along the wall with her eye on the doorway to the little sitting room. At least in there was a chair by the window into which she could collapse.

Linley had pulled a face when she'd seen CeeCee's bruises earlier. 'They're turning quickly, Aunty. You're green around your cheek and faded purple further down. At least your eye looks almost normal.'

'I wish I had a mirror.'

'I'm glad you haven't.'

Linley had helped her bathe her face, and stood by as CeeCee took care of the rest of her ablutions over a shallow basin. Then she'd helped her dress.

'At least I feel human in my street clothes.' CeeCee patted down her rumpled skirt. 'But I will be happier to get this one washed and be outfitted in a new one.'

Linley wouldn't be too far away now. Hopefully with news from James with her.

Oh, how many days before I'm feeling normal again?

She made it to the chair by the window and sank gratefully into it. Inhaling as deeply as was possible, she closed her eyes, the squelchy feeling in her blackened eye almost gone.

Of all the rotten things. Being beaten upon by a man, the very likes of whom she'd struggled most of her adult life to avoid. At least she'd stepped in between him and Linley and the baby. A small price to pay, after all. The baby was safe from a life such as his stepfather would damn him to, and for that CeeCee was glad she had taken the brunt of his attack.

She held up her hands. The shaking was there, again. She clenched and unclenched them, and concentrated on stilling the tremors. This was what remained with all who had encountered violence … a physical memory of it. As if it were embedded in the victim somehow.

CeeCee shuddered, remembered her own sister's face from so many, many years ago. Great with child, with Linley, and crawling towards her big sister begging for help …

Eliza had died of internal bleeding, and CeeCee had snatched her newborn niece and run from the sick bed as fast as she could to hide them both away. But her brother-in-law had found them, threatened them and then left, swearing he'd be back for his kid.

She'd never heard from him again. She used to think she would kill him with her bare hands if he ever showed his face. But she knew, now, he never would.

And now she had become a victim of violence too, but not at the hand of a lover. She wrung her hands.

Deep breaths, my dear, when you can. Keep calm, Cecilia Celeste. He is no danger to you now.

How many times had she said that to some poor beaten woman over the years since her sister's death? The only difference now was her own name.

She inhaled as deeply as she could, exhaled slowly. Do not think of the violence. The violence she had never experienced first hand until three days ago.

She closed her eyes. Closed down those thoughts.

They must get that registration paper for Toby and get it lodged as soon as possible. She would put her mind to the repair of her house. For a moment, she couldn't remember who had insured it for damage. She would think harder on that later.

And while she was at it, did she even want to return to Bendigo? Echuca seemed a perfectly reasonable town. It always had. Once she was able to move a bit more freely, she would explore the place to make sure it was where she wanted to be.

That's what she would do.

Perhaps she would ask James to join her here more often. A little further for him to travel, she knew, but he might be open to the idea. It might even be the right time to propose to him. She smiled at the thought.

Twenty-Six

Bendigo

Constable Albert Griffin dismounted and tied his horse to a post at Gareth Wilkin's house. He barely looped the reins into a knot when a side window flung open.

'Why are the coppers calling on me?'

Griffin looked up. Wilkin hung out of the window, a large battered pannikin in his hand. His voice sounded hoarse. From the way he pulled at his collar, even in the last of the afternoon sunlight, Griffin could tell he was hot. Still, the dirty little bugger never washed. He'd probably picked up some disease and had a fever.

'Not too late in the day for you, is it?' Griffin met Wilkin's gaze as he stepped onto the rickety boards of the stoop. He took care to stand well back. 'Not one, not two, but three fires inside a week. All with your special kind of mark on them.'

Wilkin flicked his wrist and the contents of his cup landed with a splat on the boards. 'That so?'

Griffin knew it hadn't landed on his boots. The little bastard wouldn't dare cross him now. 'You were seen by two witnesses at the house fire. The fire at Mr Campbell's was you. And I hear there's been a fire at Ard O'Rourke's orchard, just yesterday.'

Wilkin bared his teeth. Griffin wasn't sure if it was a sneer or something else. The man was shiny, like when a horse sweated after a gallop.

'I wasn't the only one at that house. Lots of useless bastards there.' He picked his shirt away from his chest, giving it a couple of tugs. 'Don't know no Mr Campbell. Don't care about Ard O'Rourke.'

Albert Griffin inhaled theatrically, and exhaled with a long breath through his mouth. 'You do know Mr Campbell. You had an appointment with him not long ago.'

Wilkin grunted. 'Ah. That Mr Campbell.'

'That same one. Night of the fire in his place, he belted an intruder. Hit him on the head with an ashtray.' Griffin would swear he saw Wilkin remember the impact. 'Man should have a great bloody lump on his skull.' He peered closer at the smelly little bastard.

Wilkin remained quiet. He picked his shirt away from his chest again and flapped it a little.

'You sick?' Griffin asked.

'Fever. Got skin blackened on me.'

Griffin beat down the urge to step back. 'Better get yourself to the hospital, then.' He could see fiery red scrapes at the man's collar, but no blackened skin. Perhaps he had a sort of pox and not burns, after all. If so, he wasn't going any closer.

'Be gone in a day or two.'

Griffin doubted it. 'You should do the same, Wilkin. Might get sicker if you stay around here, playing with fire.' He turned and gave a quick look up and down the street. 'I heard that big redheaded bloke is not a nice man when he gets mad.' He glanced back at Wilkin. 'You know who I mean,' he said. 'And Ard

O'Rourke. Well, I've only seen him in a temper once or twice, and it ain't pretty neither.'

Wilkin eyes were bulging. He flapped his shirt faster, as if trying to cool down. 'Dunno why you need to tell me.'

'Friendly visit. You might want to be looking over your shoulder if you stay here.'

Wilkin began to move side to side in the window frame as if he were on one foot.

'You have a relative you can go visit, someone who'll help you get over your … "fever"?' Griffin folded his arms. The warm, rotting stink of the man floated across the verandah. Griffin lifted a hand to pinch his nose. 'Don't want you here, all sick and all.' He frowned. 'And if by chance you're full up with some God-awful pox and not suffering burns for your trouble, you can get the hell out of my home town.'

Wilkin stopped moving. 'Matter of fact,' he said, after a long pause. 'I have a sister.'

'Where?'

'Echuca.'

'Well, go there. Fast as you can. Train leaves in the morning.' Griffin waited till Wilkin nodded. He turned and stepped off the boards. 'And keep away from matches.' He loosened the reins and mounted. 'You might light yourself up.'

Twenty-Seven

Bendigo

Dawn struggled to break through a thick cloud. Ard sat on the dirt with his back against the stone wall of his hut. He could feel humidity in the air, smell it, dense with char. He watched as mist rolled off his scorched orchard.

His nose twitched with each inhale. He took in the trees, blackened and tortured in their denuded state, skeletal and twisted. There was nothing for him here. Their livelihood was gone. He'd telegraph his father and his uncle, but no point waiting for them to arrive, if they were going to.

He needed to find work. He needed to find his way in the world. He needed to find Linley. And his son.

James came from inside the hut. He held out a tin cup with steam coming out of it. 'A man needs sleep as much as he needs food or grog or both. It's only tea. No rum this morning.'

'Thanks.' Ard took the cup. 'Couldn't sleep. That much wood smoke …'

'You'll get the coppers on to Wilkin?'

Ard considered it and shook his head. 'No, I reckon I might take care of it myself. The Chinamen won't talk to the police and there are no other witnesses.'

'Dangerous.' James squatted alongside him.

Ard was silent. If ever there was a man he would enjoy to harm, it was this Gareth Wilkin. First for the fists on Mary. Second for the fire at Miss CeeCee's, and now, the torching of his own property.

But what the hell is he coming after me for?

'I can't make sense of it. Except that my world will look a lot better without him in it.'

'You got a plan?' James asked. 'And I don't mean a murder plan.'

Ard nodded. 'I want to go to the river. To Echuca. There's still work—'

'Not as much as there once was.'

'But enough to get me started again. I might still get work on the boats, there's timber mills still hiring, I've heard.' He shrugged. 'Maybe I could learn to shear sheep.'

James sat on the ground, eased his long legs in front of him. 'Drought's coming again, the rail has gone through to Swan Hill, shearers are striking and losing work. Times are tough. Echuca's much smaller than Bendigo if you're looking to find work.'

Ard glanced at him. 'You know Echuca?'

James shrugged. 'Some.'

Ard stared at his boots, scuffed the dirt underfoot. 'I know a boat captain, a Mr Egge. He's going to retire in Wentworth. If he hasn't got work, he'll know someone who has.'

'And when the work dries up, what then?'

'I'll find someone who's got some land and wants to grow fruit and vegetables. I'll rent land. I'll get chickens and maybe a cow. I've heard the army's looking for horses all the time. Maybe I'll breed horses.'

'Good plan. I like the sound of breeding horses.'

Ard looked at him. 'You know anything about it?'

James shook his head. 'Sadly, no. That means the adventure's all yours.' He stood up. 'I'd better get along. I have to catch the train today. Reckon you'll be right?'

'James. Mr Anderson.' Ard got to his feet and tossed his untouched tea. 'I need to find Linley. I need to find her real bad.'

James nodded. A frown creased his brow. 'Understand you do. Let me find out if she wants to be found, first.' He took a slow breath. 'And I don't believe you've written me a letter to take to her.'

Ard's jaw worked. He clenched his mouth shut as the surge roiled up from his guts. 'A letter won't be good enough,' he said between his teeth.

James gave a little laugh. 'Steady on, lad.' His tone was soft, but stern. 'You've had a nasty couple of days, not much sleep or food.'

'I'll come with you. To see Linley.'

'No.' The frown deepened. 'You will not.'

'I have to—'

James stepped close to Ard. 'Listen to me,' he said quietly. 'I have left CeeCee and Linley vulnerable these last weeks and I will not do that again. I will protect my family from anyone and anything.' His voice was clear, low. 'Do you understand me? From anyone.'

Ard waited a beat, sure that he did not want to tackle James, but stood his ground. 'I'm not a—'

'You are, lad. A threat. To my peace of mind about this.' James took a breath, then stepped back. 'I have a train to catch and business to attend.' He turned for the horses.

Ard stared at his back. 'I know the only train today departs for Echuca.'

James shot a look over his shoulder, his face grim. 'Do not get on that train.'

'It's just …' Ard dropped his shoulders, rolled them back and forth. 'I found out she has my …'

After a moment James prompted, 'She has your …?'

'Son. Linley has my son.'

———

They rode back into town. If James moved quickly, he'd make the train departure. It wouldn't serve any purpose to linger in Bendigo. He'd already transferred funds to CeeCee the day before. He might as well travel to Echuca and withdraw more from his account directly.

At the telegraph office he sent a message to Bill Jenkins, his hired help in Echuca. Bill would pick him up from the station. Three days had already passed, and he'd not got any word to CeeCee. Now, armed with Ard's revelation, he needed to get to both the women. He needed to ensure they were indeed safe.

He hadn't told Ard of Linley's whereabouts. Ard hadn't penned a letter and didn't want James to deliver a verbal message to her. He had accompanied James to the station then took the reins of James' rented horse to return it. The lad had hesitated only for a moment before giving a short 'goodbye' and riding off.

James bought his ticket and embarked. Time had been against him to change clothes, so he found a seat in a back carriage, hopeful nobody would wish to share. His clothes reeked of burned and smoking orchard.

The whistle blew a shriek and the train lurched and scraped and ground forward. Then it stopped, screeching to a shuddering halt before it left the station. He heard the frustrated yell, 'Hurry up and get on board, man,' no doubt bellowed by the driver or the porter.

Moments later, the whistle blew again and the dissipating steam of it flicked high above James' window. Bendigo receded. He leaned back, closed his eyes. Thoughts drifted.

Last night had been long and fraught, and though he'd slept, it was lightly, fearing the worst, late at night, with a flare-up in the orchard. He was aware at times that Ard tossed uneasily on his pallet across the small room of the hut.

The charred wood smoke still in his clothes, James dozed fitfully. Not even the swaying and chuffing of the train lulled him into a deeper sleep. CeeCee was on his mind. He hoped she had found a doctor to attend her, heal her battered body.

Timing had diverted him from his plan to exact retribution on Gareth Wilkin. In due course, he would revisit that. The man would not live out his days into old age.

I promise you, CeeCee.

His pledge jolted him. He would have to stop his work, after this one last time, otherwise his promise was an empty one, a lie. But he had to keep CeeCee safe, her niece secure.

He'd stop. Step up his campaign to marry CeeCee and bring her to Melbourne. There as a married couple, they could move their philanthropy forward and drive their message harder. Finish dealing violently with these men.

I promise you, CeeCee …

He'd slept. Checking the passing terrain, he thought he'd maybe slept an hour. He stood up, stretched, shook off the heavy nap-induced fog in his head and stared out the window.

Need to take a piss. Elmore station can't be much further up the track.

Twenty-Eight

Bendigo

Last night Gareth hadn't thought twice about the copper's warning. But now he jolted awake. Why hadn't he been arrested? Copper knew he'd torched those places. What was he letting him go for? Why did he warn him off? Was something out there waiting for him? Or someone?

He jumped. *Wassat?*

Scratch of rats across the boards of the floor. Birds landed on the roof, claws clack-clacking. Horses' hooves in the street. Street brats, were they staring in the window? Shape-shifting monsters in the shadows of the room ...

He blinked hard to clear his sight, his eyes squelchy.

Get out of here. Get the train. Get to my sister. She's not gonna be happy, but she's kin. Has to look after me. If anyone knows what to do about these burns, Esther will.

Lay low for a while. Get healed up then get the brat back, get the money that's mine from that dead bitch slut, the money from the old dead bitch dragon aunt.

Dunno how, but I will.

Get to the train. Get to my sister.

———•———

He almost missed the train. It was pulling out by the time he'd staggered onto the platform. The idiot at the ticket office had to be convinced he wasn't drunk.

The porter flagged the train to a halt before it got up too much steam, and he pulled open the door on the first cabin. Gareth stepped aboard. The yells of the driver rang in his head but he only thought about yelling back; his energy had gone.

He lurched into the seat. Good. Cabin's empty. *Don't need some brat of a kid staring at me, holding his nose and bawling that I stink.*

He was used to it. But today he hurt, he stank worse than normal and he reckoned he would look like a corpse.

Don't need no kid giving any lip.

The cool leather seats didn't afford much comfort for long. The constant shuddering of the train chafed the weepy patches on his skin. It felt like the newly healed ones had broken open at his neck and the deep sting from loosening scabs made him woozy.

He felt in his pocket for the old flask, took it out and shook it—ah, a drop of tea left. Cold by now, but no matter. He turned the lid, upended it over his mouth and let the dribble of liquid slide down his throat.

Better than nothing.

Now, Echuca. If only he could remember how to get to his sister's.

———•———

The train slowed at Elmore. James only had time to alight, visit the gentlemen's rooms and reboard.

Every cabin seemed to have passengers disembark. One or two compartments remained closed as he passed by back to his own cabin. A few more folk looked ready to embark from Elmore, either on their way to Rochester or to Echuca at the end of the line. The train must nearly be full.

As he pulled the door open to his cabin and stepped inside, he was greeted by another man already seated there.

'Morning.'

James nodded and took his seat. 'Morning.'

'Hope I'm not intruding.' The man pointed at James' hold-all, clearly there before him. 'A carriage further down had a vacant seat but it didn't smell too good in there. The sole occupant looked like he'd had a run-in with a smithy's forge.'

James stared at the man for some moments, then shook himself out of his thoughts. 'I beg your pardon,' he said. 'I was miles away. Of course I don't mind. Who'd have thought the train to be full?'

The other man nodded and slid his stocky frame along the seat towards the door. He drew his hat down over his face and cut any further conversation.

It suited James. He stared out the window, and watched the station buildings disappear from sight. The train chugged on, cut through the plains country, flat and scrubby.

He was sure the little bastard was on this very train.

Twenty-Nine

Bendigo

Ard O'Rourke knew he should wait, at least for his uncle Liam's reply telegram. His father's would take longer, even if his answer came via Liam in Swan Hill.

He *should* wait. Not tear off like some madman ...

He paced outside the telegraph office, looking up at the sun. Near midday, he reckoned. The train would be halfway to Echuca by now.

He was nearly out of money, and his family's credit was thinning. So why stay in Bendigo? Wasn't like he had to keep the orchard secure. Anything worth a penny had all gone up in smoke.

He steered his thoughts away. He could rebuild, though ... if he put aside all other ideas. Ideas about finding Linley.

There'd be more than enough to do. There was nothing much left in the house. Only a few bits of furniture remained. His mother's kitchen table was a prized possession, he knew, built for her by his father. It had been stored in the shed, untouched by the flames. Apart from that, his parents had taken anything valuable with them to Renmark.

He paced some more. He'd need to build everything from scratch. The fences. A new stable. Maybe a verandah for the hut.

All I have to do is make a decision. Think, man. Think.

To stay or to leave.

Stay. Rebuild the orchard, start to clear it. Use the farm horses and the old dray, thankfully saved by the Chinamen, to scrape the dead trees and branches ... He would have to wait before he could start that. The earth underneath had to cool some more, tree roots could still be smouldering. Especially the big eucalypts that bordered the east side.

Or leave. Go to where Linley was. It chewed him up, burned in his gut.

James knew where CeeCee and Linley were. He protected them. He was going to them. To Linley. And she had Mary's ... his ... son with her.

Linley. Prim and proper, yet with some mettle, some fire. Staunch. Blunt in her conversation, proud of her opinions. Yet gentle, intelligent. Her eyes, direct, searching. Her fingers, light, only once on his sleeve as she tried to get his attention.

Linley, who took in his child.

His gut curled as he remembered the stricken look on her face when he'd told her not to wait. He'd walked away, gone home, gone deep into the orchard that afternoon. Mary had followed some time later with a basket of little pies, a quart of rum, and laughter.

Big mistake.

He didn't need to wonder any more. He needed to act. Mounting, he turned Pie for the open road. Pushing the horse harder, he galloped out of town, headed for the orchard.

The rage built in his bones. He would go to Linley. He was sure he knew where she was because James Anderson had taken the train to Echuca that morning, and had ordered Ard not to board.

He slowed Pie. The rage cooled, but his breath came fast and his heartbeat sped up. Echuca. Three days' ride if he was sensible. Did he have three days? He could leave today, travel to dusk, camp out, be on his way just on daybreak. Long days, but he could do it. Pie could do it.

He had water canteens, and a small barrel he could fill and seal tight. Pie would carry it easily. He'd have to get some of Sam's beefy jerky to keep him going. Take some fruit from home … No orchard now. Perhaps not fruit.

Three days was too long. He needed to go by train tomorrow. He'd have to find the fare somehow. There was nothing left in his mother's emergency tin. He wouldn't steal, wouldn't beg. He'd have to sell something. There'd be something of value left in the hut, surely, but he had to hurry. Had to make good with all the time he had left to him.

His boots barely touched the horse as he urged him harder. *His boots.*

The new boots, compliments of Mr Egge. They'd be worth at least part of the fare to Echuca.

Had to hurry. Get to the hut. Grab what he needed, get back to town. Maybe stay at Sam's, that way Pie would be fed and watered. From there, Ard would have an easy walk to catch the next morning's train.

The ride home was gone in a blur. As soon as the charred remains of the orchard came into view, his thoughts sobered. His heart rate slowed with Pie's decreasing stride. Cantering up the driveway, the odour of burned wood reached his nostrils.

The landscape looked different even from the time he departed this morning for town. The stone hut stood at the edge of a blackened paddock, the stricken trees no longer fertile. The future, as it once had been here, had vanished. Now it lay elsewhere. He was right to get moving. He didn't need to stay here.

It no longer looked like home.

Thirty

Echuca

CeeCee felt better. Much better. Surprisingly like her old self. What wonders a doze in a chair could do, the sunlight streaming in.

Goodness. How long had Linley been gone? She was only taking Toby to the town to check at the telegraph office for her.

Patting her face gently with both hands, she determined it felt like her face, the one she knew, not the swollen one. She'd give her right arm for a mirror, but James hadn't thought to purchase one for the house.

She sat up straight. No dizziness. That was good. No erratic heartbeat. That was good.

Taking a couple of deep breaths, she tested her sore ribs. Not so bad. A little bit tender, but clearly only bruised, not cracked as she'd first suspected.

She tested her neck and shoulders. All good there, too.

If it hadn't been some time in the morning she might have reached for the rum bottle to celebrate, if she had one. Or to give her a bit of a bolster.

Standing, slowly, and with a hand ready to steady her should she fall back to the chair, she straightened her legs and breathed deeply again. A few tentative steps and still no adverse reaction from her head or her chest.

Wonderful! Mending nicely.

She stepped carefully to the window and drew aside the light calico curtain. Daylight blazed ever brighter and she squeezed her eyes shut. A little squeamish squelch from her blackened eye, but that was it.

It looked to be about late morning, perhaps even lunch time. Good. That meant Linley wouldn't be too long.

Barefoot, she headed outside. She stood for a minute absorbing the heat of the day then hurried as best she could along the dirt path to the privy, her feet not enjoying the hot ground. *Oh, for some new shoes.*

Once relieved of a full bladder, she returned inside, leaning on the doorjamb to dust off the warm soles of her feet. Not too bad, no shortness of breath, no giddy head.

I am going to venture a walk.

Thirst headed her to the kitchen and she poured a pannikin of water, tossing it back as if it were the rum she'd thought about earlier. She poured another and swallowed, then made her way back carefully, with deliberately calm steps, to her room.

She retrieved her boots, sat on the bed and pulled them on. Sore ribs protested her leaning over to tie the laces, but she only gave in to it once or twice.

Get used to it, my girl. We are healing and that's that. Bloody man won't be stopping me.

The wash cloth hung loosely over the small bowl of water in the corner of the room. She dipped it, wrung it out and rubbed it over her face and neck. It would have to do. Refreshed, and still testing herself, she walked purposefully to the front door. Nothing bad happened.

Good.

She picked up her bag, a small lace and drawstring tote in which she kept her handkerchief and a small purse of coins. Her hat waited on the floor nearby.

We must get on and get some furniture for the place. Where is James?

She scooped up the hat and placed it on her head, tucking wisps of hair under it. Certainly no time to redo her hair properly. Hopefully she was presentable enough for daylight. No matter. A walk in the sunshine was bound to do her wonders, even if it was just to the end of the street.

Stepping outside into the heat of the day, it felt wonderful.

I'm alive!

Deep breaths and aromatic eucalyptus filled her nostrils, warmed her lungs. Making her way down the little path to the gate, she opened it and turned left, taking care to mind where she was walking. Her breathing was even, her steps confident. Mindful not to overdo it, she paced with measure. With every stride she felt better.

This part of town was new to her but she headed for a landmark she recognised—a church, its spire not too distant. She'd know exactly where she was when she got there. It wouldn't take long.

She wasn't a churchgoing woman as such, much to the disgust of people she couldn't care less about, but today it would serve a purpose for her—perhaps she'd be able to obtain a form to register Toby's birth. That is, unless something would smite her pagan self for being anywhere close to such holy ground. Not that she cared much for holy ground, either.

A lovely red brick building stood graciously ahead, its stately spire serenely pointing, she suspected, towards heaven. She swung open the gate, and keenly felt the weight of the last few days drop away.

St. Mary's, the sign said.

She looked up to the clear blue sky and laughed to herself. No smite so far.

She would check that a door was open, and sit in a pew for a few moments to gather her pagan self.

———

James alighted at the Rochester stop and waited in the shadows of the station building. Not all the cabins emptied of their passengers, but those passengers who did disembark hurried to the restrooms.

Wilkin was not among them.

Ladies already on the station with covered baskets sold their wares: cold pies, some fruit, bread and jam in thick slices, some with boiled eggs. James reached into his pocket for a couple of shillings, and lifted his finger to attract the attention of a vendor. The woman, her plain apron over a dull-coloured dress, offered him a heavy-looking paper bag. 'Two fresh mutton pies, still warm from me oven, and two boiled eggs.'

James handed over his shillings and pocketed some pennies as change. He nodded his thanks and returned his gaze to the waiting train carriage.

'And when you're finished, if I could have me bag back, sir?'

He nodded again, opened the bag and grabbed out the eggs, still in their shells. He thrust them into his coat pockets and took out the two pies. Stacking one on the other in one hand, he gave her back her bag.

'There's a bench around here, sir, if you need to sit.'

Wolfing down one pie, he took a seat, from where he could continue to watch any lagging passengers alight.

No one.

The second pie was good. He'd consumed the first one almost without noticing so this one he savoured a little. The thick, strong gravy around rich mutton oozed through a perfect pastry, the likes of which he hadn't tasted for a long time. He licked his fingers clean. A good draught of beer wouldn't go astray, but nobody would be selling beer here. Looking about, he saw a water station not far away, but decided against leaving his position. His thirst for water was second to his thirst for vengeance.

Rubbing his face, the beard stubble of a couple of days was scratchy under his fingers. A bath would do him wonders, as would a shave and some fresh clothes. How long had he been in—

There! A face at the first carriage window and then it was gone. Was it him? It could have been a child peering out …

A whistle shrieked. James glanced at the station master who waved passengers aboard, bellowing as he went. He lingered as long as he could but the face at the window did not reappear. Would he risk being seen entering that cabin?

If Wilkin was in there he'd kill him … But too hard to dispose of the body; it would be seen being chucked off the train. Or— could he stand the stink of the man's body if he kept him in the cabin after he'd despatched him?

No. More chance he'd be found out and witnesses called to bear. Far too risky either way.

I'll wait until the train stops at Echuca to execute my next move.

An interesting choice of words, Anderson.

Thirty-One

Bendigo

Sam looked at him. 'What—tomorrow? Shit, lad, what's the rush?'

Ard snorted. 'I told you, I have to find work, and fast. No good in Bendigo anymore without my fruit trees.' He stood just inside Sam's yard. 'I'll roll out my swag here tonight, if that's all right with your ma.'

Waving a hand in the air, Sam said, 'What happened to our adventure and riding off to join the scallywags and visiting all the pubs in Echuca?'

Ard turned to tie the reins to Sam's gatepost. 'You've got work with your pa. Me, I've got to find work. And creeping around this place waiting for Mr Ling to up his price, or Pa and my uncle to come home, is not for me. No one can steal a burned-out orchard.' He wiped a forearm over his face. 'I don't need to be here and I need work.'

'Didn't you tell me that Mr Anderson said the river is losing trade?'

'But the sawmills are still hiring, and people need fruit and vegetables. I can work a plot.'

'The Chinamen got that worked out,' Sam said.

'Here they've got it worked out, but they're not in Echuca.'

Sam folded his arms. 'How you goin' to get started?'

Ard opened the gate and stepped into the yard, a three-foot strip of dirt from the pickets to the step. 'I'll find work first, and plan from there.'

'There's another depression already on the doorstep.'

Ard nodded. 'Seems.'

Sam's eyes narrowed. 'What're you not telling me, mate?'

'Nothing.' He shrugged. 'What?'

'I could help,' Sam said.

'Maybe come up later.' Ard sat on the stoop. 'Besides, your pa needs you here, too. And you need him, if it comes to that. Another depression, who knows what'll happen.'

Sam sat beside him. 'Bleak prospects.'

Ard nodded. 'Grim.'

'I could—'

'I've got something I need to do, Sam, something I can't tell you about right now. And Pie needs to stay somewhere until I can come get him and buy him from you.'

'You know Pa says to keep him.'

'I know. I'll send you a telegram in a week's time. Let you know what work's around. Maybe if I find work, and they can hire you, too, or maybe we'll work our own plot together, somehow.'

'And maybe you're mad leaving here. Maybe I'm mad thinking I'll go.' Sam looked at his hands. 'Don't leave it too late to let me know.'

Ard rolled his shoulders. 'I won't. I'll write you to bring me some of the stuff still in the shed at the orchard.' Then he shrugged, eyes wide. 'Train doesn't leave until well after sunrise … Got any rum? Night's early. We could just have one.'

Sam perked up. 'Now you're making sense, laddie.'

Thirty-Two

Echuca station, late morning. The train slid the last few yards, the steam whistle shrieking as the carriage clunked and rolled to a stop.

James grabbed his travelling bag, jammed his hat on his head and threw open the carriage door. Sure he would meet Wilkin as he tried to alight, he stepped onto the platform and headed to the first carriage. Dodging the few passengers on the platform, he could see the door of the cabin he aimed for was open. He hesitated only a second and realised no one was emerging.

Level with the open door, he peered inside. If anyone had been in there, they'd gone. Empty, except for the undeniable stink of Gareth Wilkin.

'Mr Anderson!'

He rounded at someone calling his name.

'Mr Anderson! Over here.' Bill Jenkins, only a few yards away, waved a hand. 'Thought I'd missed you, sir. Got the cart waiting out the front.'

'Bill. Good man.' James looked over his head.

'You looking for something, sir?' Bill's thick, gnarled hands grabbed James' bag. He sat his hat back on his head and led the way out to the concourse.

'A short bloke, sores on him. Stinks.'

'Sounds like a pox or something.'

'Burns, I think.' James abandoned his search. Too many people about, including Bill. He slapped him on the shoulder. 'Good God, man,' he said and nodded at the laden cart. 'You have been busy.'

Bill tucked James' bag into a wedge of space in the back of the cart and waved his hand at the load. 'You did telegraph to get whatever household stuff yer money would buy.' He clambered up to sit behind the horses, gathering the reins as James climbed up beside him. 'Had me missus come with me to Mr Egge's boat, and to Mr Thompson's store. Reckon she did orright.'

James studied the load over his shoulder. 'She did at that.'

'Yessir, there's ever'thing there for the ladies, the baby, the kitchen, and all other womenfolk requirements.' He giddy-upped the horses. 'What yer didn't buy I reckon me and the boys could build.'

'Reckon you might be right.' James swung his attention back to the road as Bill steered the cart away from the station. 'Let's get to the house.'

There was no sign of Wilkin, but he was here, James knew it.

His only thought now was of CeeCee and the news he had to tell her.

Thirty-Three

Echuca

Widow Esther Bailey refused to even glance across the road to that house with those women in it. A menace to the wellbeing of all decent womenfolk in the town, they were, those women. Unlawful women. That's what they were. And there was a new one among them. Good Lord. If I see one more slovenly woman with a dirty-nosed child there, I will drag that policeman here by his ear to sort them out once and for all.

They'll attract undesirable types who'll come sniffing around, dragging Lord only knows what with them. They will bring men into this street who use their violence on them and the children. And probably others, should we object to their presence.

Why a Christian woman has to put up with this, I don't know. If only Mr Bailey were still here, he would have them out on the street.

Well, if the truth be known—and she bristled a little as she corrected herself—these particular women hadn't attracted any undesirables so far. Not that she'd seen, anyway. But they would, she was sure.

Only, they'd told her that they had been removed from violence in Melbourne to her quiet street under the protection of a benefactor … Oh, bosh. How likely a story was that? And what was this sort of 'benefactor', hmm?

But at times, Esther caught herself wondering. What would her life have been like if somebody had removed her mother and her from the violence and fear in her own childhood home? How lucky they were then, these women across the street—if it were true, of course.

It was true that there hadn't been any trouble. Unless you called a little child by the name of Jane 'trouble'. It seemed the scallywag had quite taken to Esther, despite her efforts to dissuade the toddler.

She stopped herself smiling, brushed down her white cotton blouse and skirt as if to remove the dirt of their existence. Her boots swept her along her side of the road on the flat dirt pathway, her eyes averted from the offending house opposite, her nose in the air.

It's only a matter of time before the rot sets in. She would have to discourage the women and the children, somehow. She wouldn't be able to stand the sort of violence she'd endured as a child and as a young woman if it visited her again, even if only in close proximity. Those people had to be drummed out of the street before it followed them here. She shouldn't have to be frightened for her life anymore.

She reached her gate. Odd. The latch was unclipped.

She never left it unclipped. Dogs and all sorts of other unwanted presences might appear on her doorstep, including the grubby children from across the road. Even if they were cheerful and cheeky, they belonged to those wretched women.

No sign of the children.

She stepped through the gateway, turned on her path and snapped the latch back in place. A furtive glance about, but she couldn't discern another presence.

Firm in her conviction she had not left the gate unlatched, she stepped to her front door, a hand on her chest, her heartbeat pounding against her palm.

Oh my Lord. The front door is ajar.

Not much, just enough to see that it had been opened and not closed properly.

She stood stock still, her heart hammering. The children had never been so outrageous before. *Oh how ridiculous, Esther.* Why, they were barely able to toddle across the road on their own let alone undo the latch of the gate and open the door to the house.

An intruder, then.

She cast a glance about, turned back to look across the road at that house and saw a curtain drop. *They* would know someone awaited her inside.

Her nose pinched, her head thumped. And *they* would do nothing, not even warn her. *Typical.*

She turned back. Stared at her door. Her gaze darted to her two windows, darkened with thick fabric to keep the view across the road blocked from her sight, and blocked from any beggars and … and neighbours looking in.

Esther heard a voice call out and backed up a step, hand on her thumping heart.

'We saw someone enter your house, Mrs Bailey. You might watch out.'

She turned and looked back across the road. That Mrs Cooke or whatever she called herself, the one with the mess of orange hair, stood at her front gate.

'You should … mind your own business.' Esther stared at the woman but couldn't stop her chin quivering.

Mrs Cooke shrugged. 'That wouldn't be neighbourly in this case.' A child pushed out from behind her thin skirt. 'It were a man, if you want to know. An' he's still in there, lest he's took off out the back way.'

Esther froze. The breath stopped in her throat. She watched Mrs Cooke nod at her, then prod the child back inside the house. She backed up another step. She would go back to the main street and go to the police …

'Here,' a voice called out.

She turned again to see Mrs Cooke marching across the road, a sturdy switch in her hand.

'If you want, I'll come in wi' yer. He's not likely to tackle two of us.'

Esther watched horrified as Mrs Cooke unlatched the gate and came to stand alongside her. She smelled of baking, of sweat, and of some fragrance coming from her hair. Her blotchy freckles had blended in places so that the pigment on her face gave her a sun-browned look.

No one with that colour hair would enjoy too much sun …

'I …'

'Go on,' Mrs Cooke said. 'It's your house. In yer go.'

Caught off guard, Esther took a step or two towards her front door and stopped.

Mrs Cooke stepped around her. 'All right. I'll do it.' She strode to the front door, shoved, and it banged against the inside wall.

They saw a form scuttle down the hallway and duck into a room on the left of the house.

Esther recognised who it was immediately. She closed her eyes a moment. 'It's all right. I know him.'

'Are you sure?' Mrs Cooke asked. 'We women on our own have to look out for each other. God only knows—'

'Yes, yes. I'll be all right,' Esther snapped. 'Please go.'

Mrs Cooke stared at her then thrust the switch into her hand. 'You call out, now, if you need—'

Esther pushed past her and stepped inside, closing the door. She gripped the switch more tightly as she heard Mrs Cooke shut and latch the gate.

There was no doubt in her mind who it was. It was her brother. The only menace that had come to pay a visit was from her own family. Esther was ready for him, though. She had hoped never to see him again. But now he was here, she would do anything to be rid of him.

'Gareth.' Her voice sounded stern despite a little tremor. 'Come out where I can see you.'

As she moved down the hallway, the switch slapped against her skirt.

Thirty-Four

James and Mr Jenkins unloaded the furniture at the new house and set each piece in its tentative place until CeeCee returned from her outing. Mr Jenkins left on foot as she arrived, and would return the following day to check if he was required.

While they were still on the street, James greeted CeeCee with a kiss on both cheeks. Then he proceeded to help her inside despite her exclamation that she was perfectly all right.

'I hope you are, my sweet. Nevertheless.' Gripping her arm lightly, he steered her inside, down the hallway and into the little parlour. 'I have some news.'

CeeCee faced him in the doorway. 'I am a little creaky, and in some places more bruised. But now you're here and we're all alone, I'm really much more interested in something more personal between us.' She laid the palm of her hand on his face and whispered, 'Could your news not wait while we take some time for ourselves?' Leaning in, she wrapped her arms around him and looked up.

He stared down at her. 'I'm not sure it can wait, CeeCee.' His hands slid around her waist. 'Though I'm sorely tempted.' He dipped his head to the nape of her neck. 'Let me—'

'Is it life or death?' she murmured and her hands floated through his hair, her breasts pressed softly against his chest.

James' mouth teased along her skin. 'No ... but not pleasant.'

'Is it something we can fix right now?' Her fingers played down the front of his shirt and on to his trousers. 'Is it dangerous?'

He held his breath. '... No.'

She reached up and kissed his mouth, lingering. 'If we walk this way, you can tell me in my room.' She tugged his hand and with her other hand tugged at the buttons on her dress.

He followed. 'But you've been out walking already. Are you not tired?'

'It was invigorating once I found my rhythm. Such a pleasant day.' At the door to her room, she turned and stroked his face again. 'And I need to feel alive and safe and loved. Please, let's leave your unpleasant news until afterwards.'

He let out a long breath. The news could wait, it could wait. What harm? What was done would not change. His erection hardened as she pressed closer.

The tip of her tongue touched his lips. 'I need you fast and hard and without mercy.'

'Is that right?' he whispered low. 'How can you be so wanton? I would be wary of those bruises, darling girl.' His penis strained at his fly. His hands shifted to her breast and he brushed the nipple until it rose under her light chemise.

Backing into her room, she pulled James through the doorway and locked the door. 'I am wary of the bruises, but I am more sorely in need of you, my handsome man.'

She sat him on her bed, unbuttoned his trousers, brushed her hand along the length of him. Lifted her skirt above her knees. 'You'll have to help. I am breathless for it ... I can't get up on your lap by myself today.'

'It could hurt you …' He was hard and ready. His gaze swept the dark curly patch of hair between the open legs of her drawers, his naked penis strained.

'It won't, but we need to hurry.' She threw her head back. 'James—'

'No sheath …' He slid his hands up, squeezed her soft flesh, felt her muscles tense under his fingers. The thought of throwing her back on the bed, her knees up while he dipped his tongue into sleek—

'We can risk it this time.' She shimmied, her bare knees touching his.

Standing, he lifted her atop him, arms under her backside. Once she was straddling his thighs, he gripped her hips, kissed her, then rubbed his face into the curve of her neck. Words were lost as he nudged between her legs, as he lowered back to the bed.

She gasped as he slid inside.

'Hurt?' He stopped, straining to keep still.

'No…' Breathless. 'Wonderful …'

Her thighs firm, she pushed down and he surged up inside. She rode deeper, cried out, grinding his need. Popping the buttons of her blouse open, she pushed a breast, its nipple taut, into his mouth.

He sucked. At her sob he stopped again, unsure. He'd loved her long and hard before, but—

'Harder. Keep going … hurry,' she pleaded and her fingers dug into his shoulders.

He swelled in her, and the spasms of her own pleasure came quickly. Then he soared, bucking up hard as his seed flew into her.

She teased every last drop from him. As she leaned over his shoulder, he felt her tongue on his back licking little tastes. Lifting her head with a murmur of pleasure as she moved, she pressed kisses to his face. Still together, he lay them down on the narrow bed, and his body slipped from hers, spent.

Soft, warm arms and languid legs still wrapped around him … He closed his eyes. His body was heavy with release. Drowsy. Needed to sleep …

Instead, fighting off sleep, he propped himself up on one arm and out of the tangle of her limbs. He gazed at her. The yellow and blue-black bruises on CeeCee's ribcage and chest as she lay alongside him caught his eye. Her beautiful breasts were marked as well, a long thick line of one bruise due, she'd said, to the top rung of the gate slamming into her.

Slow, roiling anger simmered through him. He crushed it down. Had to. Anger would wait and feed later. He dipped to her nipple and licked.

She smiled a response. 'You see? You didn't hurt me.'

'You should be a little fragile, my love.'

'I missed you, James. I needed you.'

His heart clamped and he kissed her forehead. 'I'll always be here.'

CeeCee shifted a little to make more room for him. 'We don't have much time.' Her fingers tapped through the hair on his chest then her palm rested over his heart.

'You exhaust me, woman. Let's wait for tonight, CeeCee. Plenty of time.'

'Oh, but with Linley and the baby …'

He held up her left hand. 'This ring says I have every right to sleep with my wife.'

'But Linley—'

'Miss Linley knows that we are husband and wife in all but name.' Fingers folded over hers. 'And I will rectify that as soon as I can, too.' He looked down at her, raised his brows. 'What is this? No protest this time?'

Gorgeous dark amber eyes gazed back at him. 'No, James. No protest this time. I'm ready.'

———

CeeCee washed and dressed with James' help. He'd done the best he could for himself in a basin in her room but longed for a bath as soon as possible.

And then, when they sat on new furniture in the little room in the front of the house, a cup of tea each laced with rum, James told her of the news. He relayed the story, the fire at CeeCee's, the fire at Mr Campbell's, and finally the orchard fire.

CeeCee clasped his hands. His grip was strong but as she absorbed Wilkin's crime, her hands flew to her face. 'My house.'

'Houses can be rebuilt and you had it insured. But it is the many things destroyed within that cannot be replaced.' He took her hands back and pressed them between his.

Her mouth twisted. 'The main things were the photographs I had left of my family. We have so few with us. Oh, a few well-loved letters lost, my writing desk, lost.' She sniffed. 'But this violence … it follows us, James. I wish it were over. I wish we could finish.' She stopped. Swallowed. 'Yet we can't finish, I know. There's too much to do.'

'That's true, for now.' He stretched out his long legs. 'And I met an Ard O'Rourke in the days before the fire. I found him unconscious inside your house just after it had been burgled. He seemed to be looking for Linley.'

CeeCee waited a moment. 'Most probably. Not badly hurt, though?'

'Scrapes. A lump on his head. He was lucky.' James blew into his tea, then sipped. 'The fire at his orchard knocked him more, afterward. Probably best he wasn't there at the time.'

She sat back, giving James a despairing glance. 'And Mr Campbell?'

'He's a tough old fellow. Shaken a little, but well enough.' He loaded an extra wee dram of rum into her tea cup, and encouraged her to drink. 'Have a little more of this. I don't think it will lead to your ruin, darling girl. It'll fortify your nerves.'

She laughed a little then, and winced. 'I need fortifying.' She took as deep a breath as she could. 'What a mess.' She put a hand to her chest.

'We will get you a doctor, and we will stop all our shenanigans until then.' He patted her knee.

'If we must.'

James sighed. 'We must, for a little while.' He leaned back. 'At least all of that business in Bendigo puts past the mystery of our Toby's father.'

CeeCee nodded, her hand over her heart, and sipped her tea. 'I have news on that front, too.'

'Tell me.'

She settled the cup on a saucer and it rattled a little. 'I've known Ard for a long time. I've watched him grow up, not close to his family, but I knew them of course. He and Linley, and others, were friends at school. They've known each other for years.' She thought of the younger Ard. The sturdy lad with the intense gaze and the wild black curly hair had grown into a fine man now, it appeared.

'Ah. Of course, since school days.' James sat his tea cup down and laced his fingers over his stomach. 'Ard is of the belief that Toby is his son.'

CeeCee nodded, reached across and squeezed James' hands. 'I guessed that a while ago now.'

James' brows rose. 'Does Linley know he is the father?'

CeeCee nodded. 'I'm positive of it, though she hasn't actually said.' She took another swallow of tea, closed her eyes a moment as its warmth swept through her. 'It seems she might be embarrassed to tell me. The only thing that matters to me is what he does about it, that Linley is not hurt by it. She loves that baby as if he were her own. So if Ard's come looking for her, I hope she can forgive him. She's long carried a torch for him.'

James grunted. 'And he for her, and I believe it's much more than just a torch. I might have pulled rank on him and warned him off.'

She darted a glance at him. 'I don't think we should warn him off. I think we should be encouraging the two of them ...'

At that moment, Linley rushed in the gate with the baby screaming at the top of his lungs from a bouncing perambulator.

'Oh dear.' CeeCee sat forward to look out the window, and winced. 'Perhaps you could get the door, James, before she flies through it. And ... and we might wait a bit before we tell Linley of the fire.'

She heard James at the door, then Linley crying and raging about some person who'd slighted her in the street. How she'd gotten herself lost trying to dodge this awful woman who, as it turned out, only lived two blocks over and she knew that because she'd caught up behind her after finding her way back home and how she'd seen someone at the wharf she knew and—

'My dear girl.' James carried the gurgling and gulping baby in his arms as he herded Linley, red-faced and tear-streaked, and the pram into the room where CeeCee sat. 'Sit there and gather yourself.'

'And I can't stop Toby screaming,' Linley wailed.

'He seems comforted now,' CeeCee said and nodded towards James holding the baby, rocking him in his arms. A warmth spread across her belly, surprising her.

Linley gulped down more sobs and sat in the chair James had vacated. She snatched up the tea cup beside her and swallowed the remaining contents, then spluttered on the rum-flavoured hot tea. She sniffed loudly.

CeeCee withdrew a handkerchief from her skirt pocket and handed it to her niece. 'You have had an adventure, Lin.'

'A horrible day.' Another sniff or two.

James carried the baby back and forth in the room until he settled, burrowed against the broad chest, his chubby fists waving. 'I'll give this little man a few more moments to compose himself then I'll replenish our tea, ladies. I will be back shortly to hear all about this adventure.' He hummed at the bundle in his arms as he left the room.

CeeCee waited until Linley wiped her eyes and blew her nose. 'Well, if we're to wait for James, I'll tell you of my adventure today. I found a church this afternoon.'

Her niece frowned, sniffed some more.

'And a very helpful reverend by the name of Stephen Reville. An Irishman, to boot.'

Linley looked horrified. 'Catholic?'

CeeCee tut-tutted. 'I don't care what persuasion he is, although he did invite me to attend some meetings. It was somewhat awkward.' She laughed at herself. 'But what luck I had. He was able to assist with a birth registration paper. Isn't that wonderful?' From her other pocket, she withdrew a large folded piece of paper. 'It seems all we need to do is fill it in and mail it off to the registrar's office in Melbourne.'

Linley reached across and took the paper.

'Then of course he asked me if I was going to baptise *my* baby.' CeeCee smiled.

Her niece stared at the paper in her hand. Then she glanced up at her aunt. 'What did you just say, Aunty?'

CeeCee faltered. 'Of course, you don't have to baptise or christen him, but it's the done thing, after all.'

'Is it?' Linley sounded as if she'd forgotten.

CeeCee frowned. 'Is there something distracting you about the paper, Linley?'

Wide-eyed, Linley shook her head. 'It's just that I thought I knew whose name to put in the column where it says "father's name".'

'Yes?'

Linley looked back at the paper, then shifted her gaze out the front window. 'Now I'm not so sure I should.'

James stood in the doorway, a sleeping baby in his arms. 'Hard to fill the kettle and put it back on the stove when you've got an armful, but we managed.' He took the quiet baby to the pram and put him in it. 'What's this you're not sure about doing?' he asked Linley.

She glanced across at her aunt and back to James. 'I'm having trouble deciding what to put on the birth registration paper.'

'What part?' James queried. 'Can I help?'

CeeCee sat up. 'She had a name picked out. O'Rourke, wasn't it, Linley, for the father's name?' She glanced at James, who leaned against the mantelpiece.

Linley's cheeks flushed. She nodded.

James raised his eyebrows at CeeCee. 'Then, that should be the name,' he said decisively. Looking about the room, he finally pointed to a small box near the doorway. 'I had Mr Jenkins bring some ink, paper and a couple of quills. I could help you fill it in, Linley.'

'The man whose name it is, Ard O'Rourke,' Linley blurted, 'has a wife, and a baby on the way.' Tears erupted afresh. 'That's what happened today. I saw them.'

'No.' James shot a glance at CeeCee.

'Yes,' Linley declared, her face screwed up. She used the handkerchief again. 'I saw them at the wharf not an hour ago. She was out here.' Linley extended her arm its full length, her cheeks reddened.

'No,' James said again and let a laugh slip. 'No. It wasn't him you saw. It couldn't have been.' He knelt down beside her chair. 'I left Ard O'Rourke in Bendigo this morning. He most certainly was not on the train with me. There's no way on earth you could have seen him on the wharf.' He glanced at CeeCee and gave a little shrug.

Linley gaped at him. 'Ard is in Bendigo?'

'Most definitely, my dear girl. Now then.' James reached across and took the registration paper. 'Let's get this underway and I'll take it to the mail.'

Thirty-Five

Swag slung over his shoulder, Ard boarded the train bound for Echuca. Minus one pair of new boots, he had a little money in his pocket after he'd paid the fare.

Thank you, Mr Taylor, once again. Sam would benefit from his father's purchase of Ard's boots, no doubt about it. And it was a good thing they hadn't got mad drunk last night; he needed a clear head this morning and Mrs Taylor had seen to that. She filled them up on a robust beef dinner with potatoes and thick gravy, then took away the rum jug. And that was that.

If Ard got work again on Mr Egge's boat, or even if he was directed elsewhere, he'd have another new pair of boots in no time. He felt lucky. He felt hopeful.

The swag sat on its end at his feet. Hardly better than a couple of old horse blankets now, but enough for his needs. Sleeping on a sandy bank would do him, used to it as he had been for most of his life.

The train rattled to life and the chug of the engine pulled it reluctantly out of the station. No one else had joined him in the compartment. Ard snatched off his battered hat and threw it across to the other seat. He was on his way to find Linley and to find his son.

His son.

He exhaled loudly. Why hadn't she told him the baby had lived after Mary's death? No clue.

How would he be a father to this baby? How would he hope to support him?

Another thought clanged in his head. Would Linley even allow him to be a father to the baby?

Too may questions. Too many unknowns.

The first unknown was their whereabouts. Echuca, for sure, if that's where James Anderson had indeed finished up. Someone would know where he was. Nobody could miss the big bloke with the bright red hair and the look of a zealot in his eye. Anderson knew Miss CeeCee, and with CeeCee he would find Linley for sure in Echuca. It wasn't that big a town.

Shifting around to get comfortable, he felt the crinkle of the letters in his waistcoat. No need to revisit Mary's letter, he knew it by heart. It was as plain as plain could be. But Linley's letter … had she given him any clues and he'd missed them? He withdrew the two letters, tucked Mary's back and sat with Linley's in his hand.

Addressed to 'Ard O'Rourke, Renmark', it had found him quick enough. The boys at the Renmark wharf had given it to his father once the mail was sorted. From there his life had changed. He hardly knew how to run with it. Shock, grief, loss. Fear. He could consider everything he felt and still not glean a way forward, so he stuffed all that into a room in his head and shut the door on it.

The letter rustled in his hands. He fingered the envelope then gripped the pages within and unfolded them.

She had simply put 'Ard'—not 'my dear friend', or 'Dear Ard', just addressed him as if he was nothing to her.

He couldn't believe he was nothing to her. At the gleam in her eye, he'd felt his own heartbeat race. Freckled cheeks had pinked up whenever she returned his gaze. The furtive touch of hands when they were down the street, jostling others at the market … No. Not nothing.

The picnics they took, as friends, all of them, with simple fare as each could afford. Apples and pears from Ard's place, mutton pies from Sam's mother's kitchen, beef jerky CeeCee had provided for them. Others had brought along jam sandwiches and beef pies and they'd sit, old school friends, on an old blanket provided by some-one's mother. They'd play a game of cricket, rules much modified.

He and Linley would be close, sometimes fingertips would brush. The last time they picnicked, he'd told her that he was going away for a time. When he saw her bewildered face, stricken, a look that nearly brought him undone, he'd walked away. He hadn't misinterpreted her expression.

And so, what did he do? He went home to the orchard, and found that Mary had followed an hour later.

Ard folded the letter again and rested it on his lap. Now this. This business of his baby, whose mother was dead, and whose life was being held by the woman he loved.

Shaking his head, he pressed down the mounting heave of his chest. He squeezed the letter in his hand. The thin paper rustled again and he opened it and read.

Ard, Mary Bonner is dead after childbirth. She told me that it was your baby and that you know it is the truth because she wrote you a letter.

You dallied with her but she married a Gareth Wilkin to give a name to the child she will never hold. I just wanted you to know she's dead.

And I am so angry at you, Ard O'Rourke.

Mr Wilkin turned out to be this awful creature, a man who beat her and harassed her and, finally, it is my belief, killed her.

Two lives have been dashed. I found out too late about you. She told me after it was too late for her. I would have made you marry her. Why didn't you marry her, Ard O'Rourke?'

She'd signed it, 'Linley Seymour'. Nothing else.

He scanned the letter again. He could have been mistaken ear-lier, but he didn't have any clue that the child might have lived. He read 'two lives have been dashed' and assumed she meant Mary's life and the baby's. It wasn't until Sam told him in the pub that he realised Linley had been given Mary's baby.

Was he so thick? Who else could she have meant?

Hers? Linley meant her life?

Vitriol leapt off the page at him again. So fierce were her words, so damning of him as a person, as a man, that he couldn't bear to re-read it. He folded the letter and lowered it to his lap, staring out the window. The train chugged and chortled and rattled over the line sweeping past dry, brittle countryside. And here he was, a man with barely two pennies to rub together, no work and no means likely, trying to find her and the baby.

He would secure work, a place to sleep and eat and get that out of the way. Set about finding Linley. Somehow. He would think of something.

And do what, O'Rourke? And do what?

Be the man I want to be.

Thirty-Six

Echuca

Esther pushed the heavy pannikin across the table to her brother. 'Do I understand correctly, that you did not just light one fire, not two, but three fires?'

Gareth Wilkin took a slurp of strong tea. His lip curled. 'I love me drink of tea, but I need rum in this axle grease.'

'You do not,' she snapped. 'You shouldn't drink at all. You know that.' She stood with her back to the kitchen fire, hands on hips. 'And as soon as the water heats again you'll go back for another bath.'

'Already had one.'

'I can still smell you.'

'It's me foot. A toe's turned black. And I shouldn't bath with all these burns. It's bad.' Wilkin slurped again, his chin barely off the table. As he shifted his scrawny white shoulders, tufts of stringy long hair gathered at odd places along his collarbone. Instead of falling into the strange hairless concave of his chest, they grew over and down his back.

'Some have healed. Some were stuck to your filthy clothes.' Esther pulled out a chair and sat opposite him. 'Some have infection. They must be poulticed.'

Gareth pulled the bed sheet more closely around his middle. 'An' where are me clothes?' he demanded.

'Burned. And much of the stink with them,' said Esther. 'They're gone.'

He started to rise. 'I need clothes.'

'Then you'll wear something of Mr Bailey's.'

'Not wearin' no dead man's clothes.'

'And take that look off your face, brother. You'll not live here stinking. You'll get yourself to a doctor, because it's obvious there's some sort of affliction in that foot.' She sat back, drumming her fingers on the table between them. 'Why did you come here?'

He waved a limp hand at the pink and weepy burns under her salve on his chest. 'I knew you could fix this.'

'Which brings me back to your three fires.' She leaned towards him then thought better of it. 'I thought you learned a long time ago that you and matches are not good companions.'

Gareth gripped the pannikin with two hands, the backs of which wrinkled with new skin growing out from under the drying dead skin. 'I got money coming to me.'

Esther blinked. 'Have you, now? And how has that got anything to do with your affection for fires?'

He sniffed, hawked, then took one look at his sister's face and swallowed it down. 'I married. There's an inheritance.'

Esther felt her eyes pop. 'Married?'

'Yair, me. I married. And she's dead, so the money comin' is mine.'

She pressed an open hand over her heart. 'You were never good with women either, Gareth.' He was good with his fists, and that was all, just like their father. 'You married, and now your wife is dead?'

He glared at her. 'Not my fault.'

Spoken just like their father all over again. Esther felt a weight in her chest, and her breath lagged behind her heartbeat.

He sputtered on. 'And the wife's old aunt died and left a fortune to her.' His gaze shifted about the small kitchen room, then back to her face. 'So now, it's mine.'

Esther watched his lip curl again and a frisson of fear rolled down her back. Not for herself. She would never let Gareth make her afraid again. She closed her hands into fists around the switch, rested it on the table and let the silence grow between them. Her brother shifted, adjusted the sheet again, and rubbed a hand into his hair. His head jerked a little, like he had a sudden twitch.

'How did she die?'

'Old age, I reckon. She musta been a hunnerd and fifty.'

Esther's hands unclenched. 'You know exactly who I mean.'

'And there's a brat.' His gaze riveted back on the tabletop. 'I have to get the brat.'

Shock hit her hard. 'You have a child? You?' Her mouth fell open but then her voice was lost. She closed it again and shook her head, pressing her two hands against a racing heart.

Gareth didn't confirm or deny. And that raised her suspicions. She looked past him out the window to the fading light of the day. The pile of burning rags smoked and spat sparks in the middle of the yard, away from where she pegged her laundry to dry.

She looked back at him and wondered again about the infirmity he suffered, this sickness in his head that would roar louder than God spoke in his heart … Though she doubted he thought of God at all these days.

Her brother seemed about to wreak havoc on her life once again, but this time she would not stand for it. Mr Bailey had shown her kindness, was a stern man, but loving and fair. She'd seen nothing of her father and her brother in him. He'd passed away, God rest his soul, and she would use what he had taught her to thwart her brother's behaviour.

Her brother had a child. She would take it and bring it up as hers, with love. Not with beatings and unspeakable violence. Esther willed herself to remain calm. 'Where is the child, Gareth?'

'Dunno. That's it, you see. I have to have the kid to get the inheritance.'

Esther frowned. 'How did your wife die?'

He didn't hesitate. 'After birthing.' The darting glance was more furtive if that could be so, and his chin rested on the table, the pannikin thrust away from him.

Esther sat back. As usual, he was not telling the truth, or not all of it. She had to glean more information. 'I am sorry to hear that.' Conciliatory. With sympathy.

He grunted. Seemed hardly bothered by the bereavement.

'How long ago was this?' With compassion.

His mouth was downturned, his shoulders hunched. 'Two months. Three months.'

Which was it? Could he not remember when his wife died? 'So, where is your child?'

His palm came down on the table, and the spittle flew from his mouth as he snarled, 'I dunno. I dunno, I told yer, woman. Yer don't think I know what yer doin'?'

Esther thrust her chair back and shot to her feet. The switch came up and slammed down on the tabletop so close to his shaking fingers that he snatched them away. He stared up at her, gaping.

'You will not raise your voice in this house. Not to me, nor in front of me.' Her body shook with a sudden rage. The switch cracked on the table again and she watched as he flinched. 'Our father got away with it, beat our poor mother, and me, but you will not follow his footsteps.'

Gareth tried to shove the chair out from under him but the tea spilled, his arm fell off the table and he nearly lost the chair altogether. 'Too late,' he rasped. He tried to hang on but slid in a crumpled heap to the floor.

Esther's skirt rustled as she came around the table to him, the switch tapping against her side. She leaned down close to him. 'Not while you are in this house or you will be sorry.' She stared him down until his eyes shifted. He crawled over to the hutch to haul himself upright.

'Where is your child, Gareth?' She followed him. 'Is it a boy or a girl?'

'Dunno. Boy.' He gathered the sheet around him and edged back to the table, sitting with a wince.

Esther spread her hands. 'How can you not know where your child is?'

'She gave it to a guardian, a stuck-up woman to bring it up in Bendigo.'

Esther took to her own seat once more. 'This is bewildering.'

'I have to get a birth registration paper.'

'You what?'

Gareth wiped his nose on his forearm. 'He's not registered yet. I have to have me name on the paper. I have to have the kid with me …' He looked up at her puzzled face. 'To claim the money from the old aunt. You can get me that paper, can't yer? You and your churchy friends?'

'I don't understand this. If your son is in Bendigo, you must get back there and—'

'I have to get the paper first and get it to the government registrar.'

She laid the switch on the table between them, tapping her fingers. 'There is much you are not telling me, Gareth Wilkin.'

'Aye. There is.'

Thirty-Seven

The morning sun bathed James Anderson's back as he stood on the front steps of the house Mrs Cooke and Mrs Rutherford occupied. He looked across the road, beyond his horse and cart.

'You mean that house there?' he asked of Mrs Cooke. He nodded towards the shuttered weatherboard, the front windows darkened by heavy curtains.

Millie Cooke stood just inside the doorway. 'Haven't heard any wild screaming, so I doubt there's a problem. Maybe the old biddy has a secret gentleman caller?' She stopped and glanced at James. 'If you'll pardon me, Mr Anderson.'

He gave a laugh. 'Well, until we hear screaming, we'll leave them to it.' He stepped inside. 'Now for that cup of tea, if you will.'

'Annie should be done with young Toby's feed by now. We was firing up the billy for Missus CeeCee so tea won't be too long.' She led the way down the tiny hall.

The house was almost identical to the one CeeCee and Linley now occupied. Two rooms off to one side of the hallway—bedrooms where each woman slept with her children—then the small sitting room and the kitchen room, with a new stove installed. The wash-house and the outhouse were out the back as usual.

CeeCee was sitting in a chair by the wood stove. Annie Rutherford settled Toby in a basket by her feet, and discreetly adjusted her bosom under her blouse.

'Good of yer to give Mrs O'Rourke a little spell,' she said. 'He has a good set of lungs, little Toby, when he has a mind.'

CeeCee looked down at the contented baby in the basket. 'He's certainly got us well trained. Yes, Linley had need of a walk by herself today. She's seen something at the wharf she's interested in.'

'Not sure she should be there by herself. Some of those lads can be rough.' Millie looked from CeeCee to James.

'She said just a short walk by the water, away from where the boats dock,' CeeCee qualified.

Millie nodded. 'All the same,' she said and brushed down her skirts.

James looked outside to where three small children were playing in the dirt, the barren back yard open to the paddocks beyond. 'We must fence this off for you soon,' he said to no one in particular. He would pick up some rails, palings and nails as soon as he could.

'No hurry for that, Mr Anderson.' Annie pulled a large tin from the pantry and prised off the lid. 'Now, we have a tea cake, fresh baked.' She removed the small slightly risen cake and placed it onto a board to serve.

CeeCee leaned forward, holding herself across the middle. 'What are those bits in it, Mrs Rutherford?'

'Them? That's some dried fruit I bought from Mrs Tippett down the road. Her son works on a farm downriver, up Mildura way.'

'They're raisins, Mrs Anderson,' Millie said.

CeeCee accepted the proffered slice. She took a bite. 'Delightful.'

Millie Cooke smiled. 'They add to the sweetness when we can't buy sugar. Thought of it meself.'

'Well done.' James took a slice and stood by the back door. 'You've had no trouble lately, ladies?'

'None, Mr Anderson.'

CeeCee accepted a pannikin of tea. 'Very good. Perhaps some education is all that's needed.'

'Them churchgoing folk like Her Majesty across the road, have their own sort of "education",' said Millie. 'If she doesn't "educate" the coppers on us each time we take a breath, I dunno what.'

'I'll have another word with the constable.' James leaned on the doorjamb.

Annie lugged the big kettle back to the stove, the teapot filled and brewing again. 'She's cranky, all right, but it seems the kids like her. Sometimes I reckon she's blowing her bags just because she can.' She poured herself a pannikin. 'One time I caught her playing with my little lass, but she shooed her back over to me the moment she spied me.'

Millie chortled into her tea. 'Her husband's dead, so that can't be him visiting. Though why you'd have something visiting you that stank like that, I don't know.'

James stilled. 'What's that you said, Mrs Cooke?'

'Well, I didn't see who it was in there. He snuck in before she got home, he weren't real tall, I saw that. When I got over the road to see if I could help her, the place smelled like the back end of a dung heap.' Millie waved her hand in front of her face.

Annie smiled a little in apology to CeeCee, whose gaze was firmly fixed on James. Millie went on, but James didn't hear. He returned CeeCee's gaze.

Annie cut across Millie's chatter. 'What can we help you with, Mrs Anderson? We'll do what we can for you.'

'Er, thank you for seeing us at such short notice.' CeeCee dragged her gaze from James. 'Since my accident and subsequent moving here, my niece and I have found we need some help in the house. Would you both be happy to work a little while for us, until I get on my feet that is?'

'Of course.' Millie nodded.

'We hope to build some extra rooms on our house, and here as well, so your help would be ...'

'Happy to,' Millie said, still nodding.

'And you would continue, Mrs Rutherford, to assist with baby Toby until he transfers completely to tinned milk and solids?'

'Of course, of course,' she answered. 'So Mrs O'Rourke will stay here in town until Mr O'Rourke comes back?'

Lost in thought, CeeCee took a moment before replying. 'It seems she's happy to be by the river.'

'Gets in your blood, the river. I know some who'd die to be away from it.' Millie pushed a hank of ginger hair back into a pin at the side of her head. 'Though to me it looks like it's dying itself. Level's gettin' low.'

'Drought again, they say.' CeeCee nodded, a frown on her face.

'So more men out of work, more trouble on the way,' Annie said. 'Nowt to do about it.'

A tinny wail reached them from the other room.

'That sounds like my William needing his feed now. I'll take myself off and see to him.' She nodded to James and CeeCee as she left the kitchen. 'Good day.'

'Of course. Good day,' CeeCee replied.

James set his pannikin down on the kitchen bench. 'Doom and gloom—it might be a few years off yet. We should hope for that.'

'When do you need us, Mrs Anderson?' Millie asked. 'I could start tomorrow, work in with Annie and Master Toby.'

CeeCee smiled. 'Tomorrow would be wonderful. Mr Anderson has to return to Melbourne on business, so your help would be greatly appreciated.'

'Yes, that's so,' James confirmed. 'We will have another two women to get to the house here from Melbourne. Thankfully only one who has a child. There's no consumption or pox in either and we will try to accommodate them directly. Perhaps in the extra rooms here in due course.' He glanced at Millie. 'One of them has a violent husband who hides in the night and follows her every movement. There is much work to be done to ensure her safety. And having said as much,' he said, going to CeeCee's chair and holding her arm while she stood, 'we should be along, my dear. You still need rest. Just a little venturing out is enough for one day.' He steadied her, then bent to pick up Toby in his basket.

'Where are these women now, Mr Anderson?' Millie asked.

He smiled. 'The same house we had you safe. But I am afraid it might have been compromised now, so our haste is all important. Thank you for your hospitality. Good day.'

James stepped outside and clamped his hat on hard. He doubted it would disguise him much. At the cart, he placed the baby's basket in the middle of the seat and helped CeeCee up to sit beside it. She pinned her hat on her head and lowered the rim as James walked around the horse. He stared a moment at the house opposite.

The drapes barely moved. Nothing gave away the identity of those behind the darkened windows. Nothing stirred but the branches of the trees nearby, and the leaves of the shrubs at the front of the house. It was as still as if no one lived there.

James climbed onto the seat, picked up the reins and gee-upped the horse. They drove in silence out of the street, turning into another that led back to their house.

'It might not be him, James.' CeeCee held onto the basket between them.

'Perhaps a coincidence,' he replied, his tone flat. 'A great big coincidence.'

'You have to get that registration paper mailed so it can be lodged as soon as possible. Then we have to let Mr Campbell know it's done.' CeeCee reached over and placed her hand on his arm. 'You have no time to go after—'

'I know it.' He felt her fingers grip him, understood her urgency for Linley and the baby. 'But if it is him, you are in danger. All of you. How can I leave without knowing for certain that it is *not* him?' He looked across at her. 'How do we know if he's seen us here already? He could have.' His voice was low. 'What are you thinking?'

She shook her head. 'I'm not sure they're thoughts.' She rubbed her arms, then adjusted her hat. 'Just feelings.' She looked down at the sleeping baby. 'I don't want you to do anything, James. The violence must stop. You know it doesn't change anything, instead it perpetuates. Please just stay with us … get us home.'

He grunted and flicked the reins.

Thirty-Eight

Ard found the smithy's shop without looking for it.

He walked the street from the railway station towards the river in the midday heat. His shirt stuck to his back under the swag and he tucked a thumb under its rope to keep it from rubbing his shoulder raw. The rap and clang of hammer on hardened steel, on anvil, signalled a smithy's shop nearby. The thud of molten metal being coaxed and belted into shape, the bellows pumping, and the smell and burn and sizzle of the coals beckoned him. There, around the corner, on a dusty patch of road stood an open shop, stone-built and solid. A soot-blackened figure pounded the thick mallet onto a shape on top of his bench.

As Ard got to the wide doorway, the blast of the forge rushed him headlong. The smithy glanced up, drove a few more blows onto the steel then turfed the mallet across the bench. He wiped a forearm over his forehead, though Ard could see there was no sweat. It was too dry in here for sweat.

'Yer back here again. What can I do yer for today?' He reached for a rag and rubbed the grime from his face.

Ard took a look around. 'Not me. First time here.' The shop was crowded with the paraphernalia of building wheels, shoe horses, cooking pots … jobs finished, jobs half done. A big pile of jobs abandoned, he suspected, piled in the back corner.

The smithy wiped his eyes again. 'Weren't it you in here yest'y? I shoed your big stallion, that MacNamara of your'n.'

Ard shook his head. 'Don't have my own horse. Must have been someone else.'

The blacksmith took a step closer, and squinted at him. 'Be your brother, p'raps?'

Again, Ard shook his head. 'No.'

The man wiped his hands on the rag, tossed it aside and leaned back on the bench, his burly frame relaxed. 'Well, if it weren't you, and weren't your brother, swear you got a dead ringer out there, mate.' He folded his arms.

The shop was stifling. The heat of the day outside was mild compared to the temperature in here. If Ard stood where he was and not a foot further in, he could feel the cooler air on his back.

'Strange thing,' Ard agreed. 'Look, I'm up from Bendigo, looking for work. Reckon you'd know who'd be hiring.'

'And about fifty other fellas looking for work, too.' He ruffled his hair with both hands and flecks of dirt sprayed off. 'Why you asking a smithy? I got no extra work.'

'You shoe horses. Build cart wheels.' Ard waved his hand around. 'Lots of folk must come see you. And boat builders. They all need you. You'd hear a fair bit.'

'Thing's are slowing down now with the railway and all. Reckon the sawmill's still hiring, but …' He flexed his hands, thick and scarred. 'Still, the wharf's yer best bet. Blokes coming and going all the time. How you earned a livin' before?'

Ard lifted his shoulders. 'We owned an orchard down Bendigo. Burned down last week. I've worked the river a bit, with Mr Egge. Can turn my hand to just about anything.'

'Well, then, wharf's best, I reckon. Bound to be something for a young fella like you.' He pushed off the bench.

'Thanks.'

Ard turned to go when the smithy called him back.

'Sure yer name's not MacHenry?'

Ard nodded. 'I'm real sure. It's O'Rourke.'

'Bugger me if you ain't like that fella, yest'y.'

Ard waved and walked back to the street, away from the stifling heat of the forge. The air cooled his back and made the trek down to the river bearable. The swag shifted across his shoulders; he would be glad to be rid of it.

The mighty wharf stretched out before him. Great red-gum planks and hewn trunks lifted the three-tiered construction up from the riverbed in a criss-cross of beams and joists and posts. He'd half expected to see the place abandoned. For an industry people said was dying, it still looked plenty busy to him. Five boats lined up, waiting for the cranes to get to them. Barge after barge, loaded with wool bales stacked high, jostled and sloshed against each other on the low-level muddy water. Men stood on the deck of the wharf, and leaned over to shout orders or jibes at men still on the boats below.

Spectators stood a long way off, leaning over a chain-link rail that looked flimsy to Ard. He could see some ladies, their white dresses puffing slightly from a gentle breeze, stepping back and forward nervously, perhaps afraid of falling into the river below. He stepped carefully onto the wide expanse of the wharf deck. The broad planks of solid timber underfoot, gnarled with tar, were gapped. Some felt loose as he strode the length of it, past a long storage shed and the men who worked there. They nodded at him as he passed. He nodded in return, tipped his hat. He might need to revisit these people to look for work.

'Watch where yer goin'!' A voice bellowed up from below.

Ard stopped in his tracks. A head poked up from beneath the deck, Ard's boots only inches away.

'Yer'd have come down on me head, mate, done yerself an injury, too. Broke a leg, maybe.' The head ducked back under again and Ard heard chortling above and below.

He looked across at an open shed, laden with wool bales. A figure lolled in the doorway, tipped a finger to his hat. 'Need to watch yer step, mate.'

Ard checked his feet again before moving back to a safer path. 'Looking for work on the boats, if you know of any.'

'If a bloke's not going to survive walkin' on the wharf, how'd he survive a boat on the river?'

Ard snorted. 'Was just distracted a moment.'

The man, at least as tall as Ard, was a good deal heavier. Not lardy, but stocky, muscular.

'Easy enough.' He remained leaning on the doorjamb. 'What work you after? All we got is loading and unloading.'

'I worked on the *Murrumbidgee* with Mr Egge a few times. Crewed the way to Renmark and back.'

'Didja now? Nice boat full of nice trinkets and such. Good captain. Good crew. But I don't know of anything going on the river.'

Ard nodded his thanks and moved on. *The 'Bidgee is more than a 'nice' boat, mate.*

A little further on, he leaned over the edge. He spotted the *Hero* tied up at the other end of the dock, smugly sitting away from the cranes. So, too, perhaps the *Clyde*, though he couldn't be sure. Back closer, the old girl *Kelpie* sat in a huff as she waited attention. Closer, almost underfoot and steadying for the cranes, were two splendid boats—the *Lady Mitchell* and the *Lady Good-night*. Ard had heard of them. Hard to miss the river talk of new boats and skippers, all jostling for position and trade up and down the highway they called the River.

They'd have work for sure. Ard leaned further over but couldn't see anyone on either boat. Checking for another manhole to take him down to the next level, he saw the closest was yards away, over by the next crane. No harm to get down there and call out, see if anyone was around. He knew these two boats travelled regularly between Echuca and Swan Hill. If he got work, it wouldn't be a stretch to get a closer look at the terrain, seek out land he could …

Suddenly, a figure caught his eye, over near where the *Hero* was tied alongside a small building. A woman, carefully making her way closer to the water's edge at the foot of a bank studded with lanky gums. Before he could even see her clearly, he knew who it was.

His heart banged against his rib cage. Shading his eyes against the sun, he squinted into the afternoon light and blinked. Dare he believe what his eyes were seeing?

With a quick glance at his feet to be sure he wouldn't step into a hole, he took off. Bounded over the boards. The swag bounced on his back and he ran with nothing else in his mind.

Linley!

—·—

Esther slapped the registration paper down on the table in front of her brother. 'There it is.' She turned to the stove, added a small rough-cut log of wood into the fire and resettled the heavy plate lid. The kettle went back on top, and steam began to rise as it came back to the boil. 'You'll thank me.'

'I do.' Gareth reached across and fingered the corner of it.

'Though what good it'll do you without knowing where the baby is, I don't know.' She glared at him. 'And why you're not so unhappy about that, and more worried about the inheritance—'

'Shut up, Esther.' His chin almost reached the table, he slouched so much.

Two pannikins thumped on the table in front of him. 'I didn't lie to my good pastor to have you tell me to shut up.' Her nose crinkled. 'You need to get back in that bath and scrub yourself again.'

He glanced up. 'Me burns are bad. Me foot's bad. It's what stinks. I almost can't get a boot on.' He pointed at his bandaged foot.

Shaking her head, Esther sallied on. 'And you'll sleep in the laundry room. Heat the boiler. Dress in there, too,' she ordered, and adjusted her apron, smoothing it down. Suddenly she had no interest in her brother or his issues. If, in fact, she ever did. He was like the lid jammed tight on a boiling billy, waiting to burst from the tin can and damage the first thing it came into contact with. And she'd seen too much of it before her marriage to want to see it again.

But if Gareth makes one wrong … No. This will not do.

'What're lookin' at me like that fer?' he growled.

Her mind made up, she pointed at the blank form. 'You do with that paper what you must and then be gone from here.'

He snorted. 'Or you'll what? You have to write it for me, and then I *might* be on my way.' He scanned the room. 'But seems to me ol' Bailey left you a nice little place here. Big enough for two.'

A sinking in her belly sent her gut cold. 'Not big enough for you and me, Gareth.'

'We'll see, after you write on that paper for me,' he said. 'Kettle's boiled. My tea's strong and dark with some of that fine sugar I know you got hid on the shelf.'

'It's not sugar. You're not to touch it. It's—'

'I'll do what I want. I'll have sugar.'

A chill danced through her veins. It wasn't his voice, it wasn't the arrogant slouch, or even the stench coming off him again. It was the threat he represented. The threat of their father appearing night after night on the doorstep, his fist always bunched, his arm swinging and the grunt of his primal thrusts on their mother as she cried out in pain. They'd both witnessed the horror, heard the terror. Yet despite all, her brother had turned out just like their father. Esther would not revisit it again. For anybody. She did not have to save anyone. Least of all her violent brother.

She moved swiftly, her skirt swishing against the rough table. She gripped the switch that Mrs Cooke had given her yesterday and swung it hard. It slashed down on the table, the slap loud in her ears. 'You're a *fool*.'

Gareth fell back, mouth open, legs kicked up as he went down on the floor, the chair thrust out from under him.

'Wha—?'

'This is my house,' Esther hissed at him close to his face. 'One misstep while you're here, Gareth Wilkin, and I'll bury you myself in this very yard.'

He skittered back, pressed up against the cupboard behind him. 'What are yer talkin' about?'

She swept to his side and knelt low, her face just above his. 'And you won't even see it coming.'

When she stood upright, looming over him, he scuttled away out the door and into the yard. She shifted her gaze to the innocuous tin on the shelf over the hearth, the one Gareth thought was sugar, and set her mouth in a grim line. He *was* a fool. She should put that tin elsewhere.

Esther stared at the switch in her right hand. If she wasn't careful, the inner rage she knew was with her would take over. All the years at the hands of her father she'd battened it down, kept it contained, buried it deep.

Would retribution serve her justly? Would God forgive her this?

Naught to forgive. Not retribution, but protecting herself, when no one else would.

All it would take was one wrong move from Gareth. Just one.

———

Jaysus. She was mad. Me own sister, mad as a cut snake.

What happened to the meek and mild quivering little go-for she'd been when they were growing up? He'd have to get his gumption back up and deal with her like their pa dealt with them all.

Gareth crouched in the corner of the washroom. He eyed off the tub, half full of his previous bath water.

Cold. I aren't getting in no cold bath water.

He needed to get Esther to write that paper and get it registered so he could get his hands on that old biddy's money. That's what he needed to do.

Shit. It was back in the kitchen with that madwoman sister of his. Nothing to be done for it but to go back in there and grab it. He stayed crouched for a moment, screwed his face as he checked his thoughts.

So, why am I sat in here for, like some toady coward?

Mindful that his legs poked out from under his dead brother-in-law's shirt, and his feet were in oversized socks, he propelled himself up.

Look ridiculous. A man should be shamed. Well, not me. Them others'll be shamed when I'm a rich man.

Gareth clomped his way unevenly back to the kitchen, his left foot hard to manage. When he got inside, Esther wasn't there. Well, he'd find her and when he did …

Over at the stove, he unwrapped a piece of bread warming in a cloth on a plate, took a bite then tucked the rest up his sleeve. He poked his head out of the room, checked the hallway. He took two steps and looked into the dark parlour room.

Pfft. Women's *fafferies.* Lace and cushions and teacups and what-not. He'd show her who was boss. Inside, he picked up a cushion from the settee and flung it across the room into the heavy drapes. As they parted briefly, he saw a man and a woman at a cart across the road.

He scuttled across and held the curtains shut, allowing only a sliver of light so he could see. Blinking hard, his sight only a bit fuzzy, he focused, his heartbeat like thunder against his ribs. That hurt, still. It pounded in his throat.

It was him. That big redhead bloke. Staring at his sister's house.

And it was her. The guardian girl's aunt. The one who could handle a heavy cooking pot. And that was a brat's carry basket on the seat beside her.

So, they had business at the house across the road, did they?

Thirty-Nine

James settled CeeCee back at their house. He gave her orders to sleep in the chair, and not move too far until he returned, orders he knew would not be taken any notice of at all.

He pulled the cart alongside the post office, stepped down to tie the reins and headed inside. He waited in line and when his turn came, he presented the filled-in birth registration form.

The young desk clerk answered with bright-eyed efficiency. 'Yes, sir, we do know the address of the Births, Deaths and Marriages registrar in Melbourne. I can address it for you, and make sure it's mailed speedily, along with your mail to—' He peered at the other envelope. 'Mr Campbell in Bendigo.'

'I'm also in need of a marriage declaration—'

'Yes, sir, we do have a form for a marriage declaration here. You take it along to your church man and he'll do the rest, or he may even have his own form to give you.' The clerk glanced at James' expression then continued. 'Or you just fill in those few lines and lodge it by mail. I know, sir. I just done it meself. Same registrar's address. Are you going to fill it now, sir?'

James shook his head, aware there was a queue behind him. 'No. I'll take it with me and bring it back directly, once we've filled it in.'

'Absolutely, sir.' The clerk seemed a little overjoyed, which bemused James. 'Bring it back when you're ready. Congratulations, sir!'

James leaned in and spoke quietly. 'No need for congratulations.'

The clerk mimicked James and leaned towards him. 'Well, sir, in that case, there is a pastor here who helps all sorts of people. Pastor McNeill. He doesn't need a church, sir, if you know what I mean.'

James stood upright, finished with this enthusiastic postal dolt. 'When does the mail leave here?'

'Every Tuesday—that would be tomorrow—by Cobb and Co. Oh, we expect it gets to town in three or four days, broken wheels, lame horses and bushrangers aside, if you know what I mean.'

'And the charge?'

'Two shillings will cover it all, with change.'

James headed back out to the cart. The birth registration would make CeeCee and Linley happy, and ultimately would make little Toby happy.

Another couple of stops to make, first to the store for more pots and pans, and a mirror, he had been ordered, and then on to the grocery store where he would buy good Mrs Cooke some sugar.

As for the other form he had tucked in his pocket, he'd keep that hidden away a little while longer. Pastor McNeill, eh? He would seek the man out.

Toby's inheritance would soon be protected by the registration of his birth. It would be in the mail room of the registrar on Friday, and hopefully processed the following week. Mr Campbell would be well pleased with the news.

James wondered about Ard O'Rourke and whether or not it'd make him happy. He wouldn't think too hard about it; it would make no difference to the current circumstances anyway. If Ard ever did find Linley, he'd deal with it then. He caught himself.

Perhaps, Anderson, you need to mind your own business more.

Didn't matter, none of it. Nothing could go wrong now. Because soon he would find the little bastard Wilkin, and make sure of it.

Forty

Ard pounded down the wharf, lost sight of her, caught only glimpses of her dress as it seemed to float behind a group of people, or waft between a stand of trees ...

It was her. It was her. *Sure of it.*

No missing her glorious blaze of copper-coloured hair when the breeze loosened her hat. It had shimmered under the noonday sun before she'd clamped the hat back to her head.

Don't shout, don't shout, you'll frighten her.

He skidded off the boards, slipped on the loose sand underfoot on the bank and went down hard, thudding on the ground. *Christ, that hurt.* His eyes watered. He couldn't see her. He struggled to his feet, rubbing his backside hard. One of his ankles felt tender but still held his weight. He hobbled a few steps then felt it ease under the load.

'Eh, lad!'

Ard glanced over his shoulder, back up the bank.

An older man, sporting a droopy thick salt-and-pepper moustache, headed towards him, his bow legs carrying him smartly to the end of the wharf. A portly belly wobbled in front of him.

'Lad,' he called again. 'The boys up yonder said you asked about work. I got work. I got a load of wool to pick up Koondrook way, not far …' He arrived at the edge of the boards and stopped, doubling over as he caught his breath.

Ard took another look around for the apparition that had been Linley Seymour. Nothing. He slapped his dusty trousers and adjusted the skewed swag. 'Right. I can do that.'

'Good lad. Some of my boys, the fools, are downriver. Shearer's strike, thinking they can lend a hand.' He took a couple of deep breaths. 'So I'm short-handed here. Be grateful. Tom Minton's me name.'

Ard took one last look around, his heart sinking.

Gone. Gone again. But she's here, I've seen her. I have to find her.

But he needed a job. He looked back at the man and took the proffered hand. 'Ard O'Rourke.'

———

Linley had spent all the free time she'd allowed herself.

It was quiet by the river but not as cool as she thought it would be. Besides, there was a lull in the busy-ness of the day, it seemed. The action from boat to wharf and crane, then to cart or dray, had slowed up.

She sighed. Another day, if she could possibly coax CeeCee into taking care of Toby for just a few more hours, she could venture here again. There was a peace about the river. Here she could sort her thoughts about the news James had imparted: the fire at their house in Bendigo. Nothing left of the old life now. The shock had dissipated, the fear had passed, the sadness had crept in and stayed.

At least her only real possession, a tiny photograph of her mother, was still with CeeCee in the treasures box. Her aunt advised that she should mourn for the house but settle those feelings quickly.

They had their new life in Echuca now, and they needed to do all they could to ensure it would be a safe and happy one.

The river. There was an ancient timelessness with every minute lap of a muddy wave. But then there was the trade itself on the water, the industry, the commerce. A chug of engine, a swoosh of paddle, the barges silently gliding behind the steamers. Men shouted greetings to one another, boat to boat. And of the few vessels carrying passengers, the ladies stared silently at the crowded bank, and their children were hardly able to contain chattered excitement.

Linley let out another long sigh. Something magical was here, but she knew she shouldn't linger today. CeeCee was still a bit sore and sorry even though James' appearance had cheered her immensely. And Toby needed feeding. She needed to keep up the introduction of the tinned milk so they could leave Mrs Rutherford in peace.

She made her way up the rough dirt path to the bank, careful to watch that she didn't step into loose pebbles and go sliding down again. She stood for a moment on the main pathway while she caught her breath. Her gaze alighted on a familiar figure, far away on the wharf, almost as far across as he could be, and her breath caught in her throat.

Ard.

Don't be so silly, she chided herself. It's that man from the other day. But oh, how much like Ard he was, even from this far away the resemblance was striking. She stared intently. *So like Ard.*

Her feet took her in that direction a few paces before she stopped and took a vantage point by a large stand of gums. Wouldn't do to make a fool of herself again. Forget about it and get on home.

Still she waited and watched, squinted in the bright sunlight and then when the man disappeared under the top level of the wharf and didn't reappear, she turned away.

Fool. Why on earth would it be Ard O'Rourke? You fool.

Crossing the road, she marched her way home, more annoyed for allowing another sighting of Ard's twin to stir up unruly emotions. And she shouldn't be idling her days away … she should be helping set up the house, and organising some food in the place to cook, and do the washing. And … and …

Oh, how boring.

Perhaps she could arrange with CeeCee to mind Toby while she went and found some work. Though Mrs Cooke and Mrs Rutherford said there wasn't much to be had.

She turned into the road where she'd been accosted by that nasty drudge of a woman the other day. All of a sudden furtive, she hurried that little bit more, her eyes on her feet over the rough path. *Silly.* She should be on the lookout for any ambushes along the way, not the footpath. Head up once again, she charged along.

She would help CeeCee with her correspondence. CeeCee always had so many letters to write offering assistance and support to some group or another. Linley's interest in the suffragette— sorry, CeeCee, *suffragist* movement—would help her do the same kind of work CeeCee did. She could even help develop the refuge houses James had mentioned.

Whatever that entailed. More letter writing, she expected. It would hardly create an income for her, but CeeCee seemed to get the funds to keep them both alive from somewhere. She did wonder where all the money came from to fund the projects she knew CeeCee, and now James, had begun. It was a strange thing for a man of his wealth to undertake.

Well, she presumed he had wealth; he was always impeccably turned out, and certainly able to purchase a household's furniture at a moment's notice. And if a man had that sort wealth, why on earth would he bother with the plight of women, and those of a far lower station than his?

A mystery. Well, mystery to her or not, Aunt CeeCee was very taken with him, clearly had been for years. Easy to see why. He was handsome in that confident, charming sort of way. A very caring person. Linley loved him, too. His was an under-stated presence, where Ard's was right up front, blue eyes blazing hot and cold, a flashing grin or a lopsided smile, high energy just bursting under the surface—

Her stomach dipped. *Ard, again.*

She slowed a pace or two. Perhaps she should go back and check that it really was that other man … She turned around and stood for a moment, heartbeat racing at the possibility.

Oh, how stupid.

She turned back and marched the rest of the way home.

Ard climbed halfway down the ladder that led to the second tier. Then he stopped. The thought struck him so hard he swore he heard his own voice bellow at him. His ears rang.

Go after Linley, man!

Hooked on a jutting beam as he charged back up the rungs, the swag wrenched off his shoulder and plopped into the greasy water below the boards. No time to stop. He shot through the opening and back onto the main deck of the wharf.

Left or right? Left. The direction he'd last seen her. He scrambled to his feet.

'You coming, lad?' A voice drifted past him from below.

'Sorry, Mr Minton, an urgent task I suddenly remembered.'

Five minutes—that's all it could have been. Maybe ten. He could find her. He *would* find her.

As he ran, as he gained momentum on the wharf, a familiar figure bobbed up from a manhole some yards in front of him, and threw a bag ahead of himself.

'Ard, lad. What's the hurry?' A tall, older man, a replica of his father, his twin brother, stood up and brushed himself off.

Ard stumbled to a halt, but his racing heart kept jumping. 'Liam.'

'That's me. Off yon boat below.' He waved down to the new-looking paddle-steamer idling at the second tier before he opened his arms wide. 'Good to see you, boy. Your pa thought you might be here already.'

Ard walked into the big embrace, awkward but resigned. 'Good to see you.' He was engulfed in the hug then pushed out of the powerhouse grip.

'I got news.' Liam brushed a heavy lock of his hair back from his face. The silvery streak in it from the middle of his forehead mirrored that of Ard's father.

Distracted, Ard darted a look over Liam's shoulder but saw nothing of his quarry. 'News?'

'What is it with you, lad? You're all beside yourself.' Liam frowned.

'Someone I need to catch—'

''Less it's life and death, listen up, lad. Me and your pa have agreed to sell the orchard to the Chinaman.' The frown gone, Liam beamed at him. His face creased and the crow's feet at his eyes were pronounced, weathered.

Ard stared at his uncle. 'You have?'

'The place isn't much now its trees have all burned, is it? And we figure it doesn't owe us anything over nigh on forty years. Sad. I've settled with that, but there it is.' Liam picked up his bag. He clapped a hand on Ard's shoulder and steered him along the boards. 'What do you think, lad? I know you had your heart in the place, but with it burned down ...'

Ard shook his head. 'Not for a while, now.'

Liam held him at arm's length. 'You right, lad?'

Ard inhaled deeply. 'I got myself into a stew just then …'

'That so?'

They continued to walk, Ard keeping up the pace as he stared down the main street. He couldn't see any figure in a skirt disappearing around distant corners. 'I was looking for work on the boats, when—'

'Boats are almost done according to those who know.' Liam strode along. 'Might be a few years left in it, is all. Which is why we came to the decision about the orchard.'

Ard frowned. 'Don't follow.'

'Lorc and Eleanor see the writing on the wall at Renmark. The Chaffeys are fighting with the banks and the government already; money, credit, is harder to come by.' Liam stopped a moment and looked back along the river. 'So they'll leave there. Now the Bendigo patch is burned and Mr Ling wants to buy it, Lorc and I can start again.'

Ard shot a glance at his uncle. 'Mr Ling still wants to buy it?'

'So you said in the telegram.'

'That was before it burned.'

Liam thumped Ard's shoulder. 'Land is land, lad. Chances are those boys will plant something different, anyway. And fire is good for this land. It'll be all the better for it. We'll bargain if we have to, but like I said, the plot doesn't owe us anything. We can get ahead before this depression takes a hold again. Get started.' He squeezed Ard's shoulder and released him with a little push. 'So, that brings me to the rest of the news.'

'A lot of news for a few days.' Ard thought of his own news, but let it lie for now.

'It's been brewing a while. You ready for the next bit of news?'

Ard had slowed his pace. Linley was here in Echuca. He'd find her. It just might not be today. 'I'm ready,' he said.

'Well, two things. We—your ma and pa and me—will buy land here, maybe a hundred acres.' Liam's eyebrows rose. 'What do you think o' that?'

'Hundred?' Ard stared at his uncle.

'I got a bit put by, so's your pa. If Mr Ling puts up at least his seventy pounds, we'll be in front. We've found a patch.'

'Where?'

'Hereabouts. Nearer the sale time, we'll go there.' Liam nodded. 'The railway's been through a while now, and through to Swan Hill too, so there'll be people traveling, more people coming to live all along the river. They'll need fresh food, and quicker than they can grow it before they get sorted.'

Ard whistled low. 'Hundred acres is a big job.'

'Us old boys still got a bit of life in us. And there's you.'

Ard snorted a laugh. 'I've got nothing. Not even my old swag.' He thought then he should have gone and retrieved it, sodden and all.

'But you got brains, lad, and muscle.' Liam clapped him on the shoulder.

Ard looked back and forth for traffic before they stepped out and headed to the main street. They crossed together, his eyes focused on the road ahead.

She was long gone.

Thoughts returned to Liam's news. 'It's a good idea. I like it here. I thought I'd find work on the boats, maybe at the sawmills somewhere.'

'We'll need you ourselves when we buy the land.'

'I'd need a wage, Liam.' Ard's thoughts were beginning to fly. 'Maybe I can do both. Land won't sustain all of us until we're established. I'd find some work, somewhere. Find other opportunities.'

Horses.

Liam lengthened his stride again. 'Right now, before our thoughts run away with us, we need to get some food, lad. The pub, perhaps.' He nodded towards the closest hotel. 'The Star's a bit too rowdy. Somewhere quieter. Maybe the Bridge Hotel.'

They passed the Star and headed for the corner.

Ard continued, 'I've been thinking a lot about horses lately. Buying one for myself, and then starting a farm, breeding—'

'Food for thought, lad. First things first. If we get this place, it has the space for all sorts of enterprise. And a couple of houses on it. Might need some repairs on the second place, but that's no worry to us. We'll need new plant stock, equipment.' Liam nudged his nephew. 'We'd have somewhere safe to sit your mother's table.'

Ard agreed with a snort. 'Wouldn't be home without that. When they leaving Renmark?'

'Should be the next week or two. They've not much to bring back, all would fit on their cart.' Liam lengthened his stride. 'You didn't say if the shed burned.'

'It didn't. He didn't get to that, just the trees.'

'They get the bastard?' Liam glanced across at Ard.

'Chinamen saw someone, but we couldn't prove anything with that alone.'

Liam lifted a hand. 'Pity, but perhaps the bastard gave us the shove we needed to get on. We've been thinking about a move for some time.'

Ard looked at his uncle. 'News to me.'

'Well, more's the point, *I've* been thinking of a move for some time. You know I've been wanting to go to Swan Hill.'

'You visit there, I know that.'

'I'll be marrying there, too. Soon, I hope.'

Ard burst out laughing. 'Marrying? Congratulations, uncle. I had no clue you were hiding a lady there.'

At the corner they turned left, the red-brick, double-storey Bridge Hotel in sight.

'Did you not?' Liam gave him a lift of his eyebrows and a small grin. 'Not hiding exactly, but she's been near there about thirty odd years.'

'Don't do anything in a hurry, do you?'

At the entrance to the pub, they pushed open the door and headed in for the bar. Smoke and hops and stale sweat met them, familiar smells. Ordering two pots of ale, they found a table near a window, pushed it open and sat as the warm breeze of the day wafted in.

'I'm not staying here long this visit,' Liam began. He rubbed the black and grey stubble on his chin. 'I'll take the train to Bendigo, meet old Ling and get the sale underway. Got yer digs here yet? Place to stay?'

'Only arrived this morning. Still finding my way around.' Ard felt like his head was spinning. Suddenly, there was so much more to think about.

'We'll get that sorted. Now, I've been *told* by my brother,' he grinned at Ard, 'to organise moving what little is left at the orchard. You can help at this end, soon as the land deal goes through.'

Ard nodded. 'Gladly. But I hadn't expected things to go in this direction. Where to start?' He glanced at his uncle. 'Why would you want to buy here and not in Swan Hill if you're marrying there?'

Liam took a long draught of ale, then looked into his nephew's eyes. 'A good question. It leads me to the other thing I have to tell you. About family.'

Forty-One

Linley had calmed herself by the time she got home. Toby was in his crib after his little outing with CeeCee. Her aunt had taken to her bed to sleep, to regain some energy, she said.

James had taken the cart back into High Street to search for more of CeeCee's requirements. He'd be checking for mail at the post office. He'd purchase the fencing timber he needed for the back yard and, he said, there was also sugar for Millie Cooke. He'd deliver it all himself.

Her aunt had given James such a menacing look as he left, and Linley wondered why. He'd merely smiled at CeeCee, kissed her cheek and departed. CeeCee had sighed quietly and retreated to bed.

Linley rocked the cradle, then widened the open window to let the breeze fan the baby. He looked happy, comfortable. And sleeping soundly, she hoped, with a full stomach, for at least an hour or so. The resemblance to his father brought her thoughts back to Ard. Even in such a tiny baby, his father's stamp was strong. The fine, dark hair had a curl here and there beginning, his tiny dimple a replica of his father's.

Her chest palpitated and she lifted her hands from rocking to clasp them in front of her. It was time to read the letter Mary Bonner had sent. Linley knew Mr Campbell had held on to it until the circumstances Mary predicted had occurred. How long ago now? Two months and two weeks since she'd died.

Linley shuddered at the memory of going to the hovel in which Mary had lived with Gareth Wilkin. Waiting, seated inside a carriage with CeeCee and Mrs Lovell, a wet nurse, at her side. It was the same day Mary had died. The very hour, almost.

Miss Juno had stood on the crude step at the front of Wilkin's house. Her back was straight and her head high, and she looked confident. She had been a quiet strength as they all endured the carriage ride to the house. Linley had decided then and there that she would like to get to know Miss Juno. CeeCee had often talked with Mr Campbell about her own philanthropy and her work for women's rights; perhaps Miss Juno was sympathetic, too.

The doctor had emerged, sidestepped Miss Juno with a nod, and beckoned two men at a cart parked ahead of CeeCee's carriage. They climbed down and took an empty pallet from the back. They would bring out the dead.

Linley watched as Miss Juno stood stoically by the doorway. She hadn't heard what Miss Juno said, her voice too low. Then Wilkin appeared and thrust a bundle at her.

'Here's the brat. He's shat himself again.' Then he slammed the rickety door in her face.

They'd all heard that clearly enough.

The men carrying the pallet thrust the door open and marched inside. Miss Juno rushed back to the carriage and handed the infant up before climbing in. Horrified, Linley rose and reached for the raggedly swathed baby. She staggered back under the stink that followed him inside. With a cry, she clutched the baby to her and sat back heavily.

CeeCee handed her the small coverlet they'd brought with them, then held the baby. Linley, sobbing without tears, unwound the rags and flung them back outside the carriage. She wrapped him up again in the clean cover and cried aloud.

Mrs Lovell hadn't uttered a sound. She opened her bodice, leaned over and took the baby firmly. She pressed him to her breast, a pale milky liquid already seeping. He latched greedily.

CeeCee sighed aloud. Miss Juno tapped vigorously on the carriage roof. It lurched forward.

Mrs Lovell rocked forward and back a little in time with the carriage. 'He's feeding well. He's feeding well,' she said and closed her eyes. 'He's strong.'

Linley could hardly bear to remember what the baby had looked like under the dirty fabric. His little belly button hadn't quite dried off properly. Skin had crusted around it, and the soft baby flesh of his armpits and between his legs looked weakened and sore.

CeeCee had gripped her arm. 'Your work for this little mite begins. Come along, Linley, hold on to yourself. We need to get him home and cleaned up, fed some more and loved.' CeeCee looked over and smiled at the woman with the baby at her breast. 'We are eternally grateful, Mrs Lovell.'

'These little ones are not at fault, Miss Seymour.' Her eyes remained closed as she fed him. 'We must give them their best chance.'

Linley's thoughts were a-jumble, her throat nearly closed with a lump that just wouldn't go away. She sat by CeeCee, her aunt's arm looped through hers.

'First thing we do at home,' CeeCee said, 'is draw him a warm bath. Then we get a doctor.' She turned to the woman beside her. 'And our grateful thanks to you, Miss Juno.'

'It is my pleasure to do it.' She had nodded, given a taut smile as if she were holding on to strong emotion, folded her hands in her lap and turned away to stare out the window.

Now Linley couldn't imagine that same little waif was this bonny baby sleeping contentedly, far away from the hell into which he'd been born.

Ard's baby.

My baby. A rush of love surged in her chest, swelled her heart. She would love this little boy fiercely until the day she died and then into the hereafter.

She sniffed and let her hand trail off the cot. Checking that her aunt's door was closed, she moved silently to her own room, its spartan furniture still alien and unwelcoming. Soon that would change because James would bring back other pieces, or order some more furniture to be delivered.

Under the pillow, she withdrew Mary's two letters and laid the opened one aside. With a deep breath, she sat on her bed and held the unopened one between her palms. Would Mary tell her how to bring up her child? What name to call him? How she was to be remembered to him?

Linley slid a fingernail against the seal of the envelope. It opened easily, as if ready for her. She withdrew the only page inside and took a deep breath.

My dear Miss Seymour ...

Forty-Two

Ard stared at his uncle. 'You have a son?'

Liam nodded. 'A fine man, thanks to his mother, the lady I intend to marry. In fact, it's my son's boat that carried me here. The *Sweet Georgie*.'

Ard blinked. 'I have a cousin. Pa know that?'

''Course he does, known for all time. But not his business to tell.'

Ard lifted his shoulder. True enough, he supposed. 'A cousin.'

'Aye, and you could pass as brothers. He's taller, bit leaner than you, but still clear as family. Only, he has a few years on you, maybe eight or nine.' Liam tilted his ale back and took another swallow. 'Dane MacHenry, he is. He has a sister too, but she's not mine. The family has a station out of Swan Hill.'

Ard opened his mouth but found no words.

Liam looked across. 'Not unheard of, boy,' he grumbled.

'No judgement, uncle. In fact, I've found out that I ...' Ard didn't know how to continue.

'What?' Liam held a hand up for another round of ales.

'Nothing.' Ard shook his head. 'Tell me what happened.'

His uncle shrugged. 'Simple. I saw her one day in the street, long ago in Bendigo. I was barely your age. Captivating, she was. Still is. Jemimah Calthorpe.' He frowned into his ale.

'And?'

'And what, lad? What the hell do you think happened if we had a child?' Liam looked around, as if someone might have heard.

Ard barked a laugh. 'I mean, why were you not with her?'

'Ah.' Liam paid for the ale delivered with a thud to their table. 'Some rubbish to do with the old wars between the English and the Irish. Me parents were not long out of the old country, free Irish immigrants, before the Great Famine. But Jem's brother wouldn't have it, he was English. Neither would my father.' He looked sideways at his nephew. 'My pa was not a man to cross. In any case, her brother, a high-brow, took her in, God bless him and all, then married her off to some poor sod who'd have her. Not an Irish, either. Now he's dead and I'm claiming my girl.'

Ard stared at Liam, at the rawness still on his face, at the grief he thought he could feel still coming off the man.

'I let her go, back then, instead of standing up to be counted. I thought she'd be better off. We should have run away and got married soon as we knew the baby was coming.' He wiped a hand across his mouth. 'I spent every day of thirty years and more regretting that we didn't. I'm not missing out again, and now my son has bairns of his own, and another coming.'

Ard's thoughts ticked over. *Family.*

Liam smiled then and the grief seemed to drop away. 'So, to answer your question, I'll go to Swan Hill, but I can help with my share of the Bendigo land to get this new place going here. Will benefit all of us.' He took another big swallow of ale. 'My son has two other boats, and he'll use them to freight crops and wool from his place to Adelaide and back to Echuca as long as river freight lasts. He'll also back-freight fruit and vegetables from here. Fresh is sorely missed downriver. It'll work well.'

Ard couldn't miss the pride in his uncle's voice.

'Dane and his wife want to breed horses on the station out of Swan Hill, too. Lorc and I'll look into that. No point waiting for a depression to down us when there's opportunity to dig in and be ahead, to look after ourselves.'

Ard's focus sharpened. 'I really like the idea of horses. A depression could wipe us out, though. At one time, I thought sowing wheat would be a good idea, but even that's failing here.'

Liam nodded. 'We'll look at anything, but best to start with what we know we're good at. If we're self-sufficient like we have been, and we live on the river close to water, no matter a drought or a depression, we'll be all right. As family ... all of us, we can survive.'

Family.

'I let her go back then ... every day of thirty years and more regretting ...'

Ard downed his first ale, and gripped the next pot. 'How soon do we know about this hundred acres?'

'Soon as I secure Ling's seventy pounds. I'm to put a holding sum on the place we want here before I get the train.' Liam held his hand up for another round.

'Two houses on it, you say?' Ard's thoughts were coming thick and fast.

'Aye, though I'm not sure of the state of the second one. I'm assured the main cottage is sound.'

'We should have a look at it. Soon.'

'Soon as I get back from Bendigo. Be a week or so, I'm guessing.'

Ard nodded, thinking hard. Then, 'When do you think Pa will get here?'

Liam shrugged. 'Could be any time from now. Lorc wanted to make sure he got what's owing to him, and if that fell short he was leaving straight away. If he can, he'll put the horse and cart on a barge, come here first, get Eleanor settled then head for Bendigo.'

Ard focused hard on his drink. 'There's so much to be done.'

'That there is, lad.'

Ard wasn't thinking of his parents' new land holding.

———

He saw Liam on the four thirty to Bendigo, and stood, one hand clenching the two single pound coins his uncle had given him for lodgings. The train chortled out of the station. Ard watched it go until it disappeared down the line. Leaving the concourse, he headed back to the main street, keen to find somewhere to sleep for the night. Tomorrow he'd walk to where Liam had told him this new patch was. He'd take a look around, get to know the place.

His uncle a-marrying. He had a cousin. Paddle-steamers. Fruit and vegetables. Horses.

Linley. Now it was more important than ever to find Linley.

As he turned into the township he looked up and saw James Anderson on his cart.

Forty-Three

My dear Miss Seymour,

Miss Juno of Mr Campbell's office has kindly assisted me writing this letter. It is my apology to you; it comes from my heart, if you will forgive so familiar a term.

I told you in my first letter that my baby was fathered by Ard O'Rourke and it is true. I was with Ard after a great deal of rum and addled thinking, and that is my only excuse. I cannot hope to soothe the terrible hurt I have inflicted.

I was a selfish person, Miss Seymour.

When I found myself with child, I knew Ard would stand by me if he knew about the baby. But he would be miserable in a marriage to me for I know he loves you. He went away to make something of his life and I knew full well even before we fell together that his life would never be with me.

So I married a man who said he would be good to me despite all. I couldn't have been more wrong.

I am now so far along with child, and now so beaten at the hands of Gareth Wilkin that I fear for my baby even if we both survive the birthing of it. I say so because he will kill me and the baby I am sure, after he has my inheritance.

I know about Miss CeeCee and Mr Anderson both, and that they do good work for those less fortunate in life, such as myself. Miss CeeCee has helped me for I have no family now. If you are reading this letter, you have taken my child because something dreadful has happened to me.

I want you to be my baby's guardian because I know you love Ard. I know that you will forgive him this indiscretion with me for the sake of his baby. I know you are a woman of compassion, perhaps not what I deserve, but certainly what my child deserves. What Ard's child deserves. My actions, and Ard's, are no fault of this child. Perhaps one day you and Ard will have a child together, and be a complete family.

Mr Campbell has my Last Will and Testament and you would by now know its contents. The inheritance from my aunt Edith Bending will be held in Trust for you to use as my child's guardian. Mr Campbell assures me the law will stand by my decision. I fervently hope it is so because to date, I have no reason to trust the law.

I believe you will see this letter, to be sent to you only after my death. From wherever my soul might be at that time, I thank you for your kindness, beg your forgiveness, and, Miss Seymour, beg your further grace—please look after my child, and in the future, let my child know a little of me.

Sincerely

Mary Bonner

CeeCee knocked rapidly on Linley's door. 'Whatever is the matter, Lin?' she implored as she swung it open.

Linley's blotched wet face and dripping nose screwed up in a wordless answer.

'Linley.' CeeCee hastened to sit on the small bed, reached into her pocket and withdrew a handkerchief. She wrapped her niece in a hug. 'Tell me.'

Linley pushed the crumpled letter into her aunt's hands. CeeCee smoothed it out and read quickly, sighing here and there, frowning once or twice.

'Well,' she said. 'That explains it, doesn't it?' She looked at her niece. 'And Ard O'Rourke knows about Toby, doesn't he?'

Linley hiccupped and pressed the handkerchief against her eyes. 'I haven't told him. I just wrote him a letter after Mary died. I don't even know if it got to him.'

CeeCee gave Linley's shoulders a squeeze. 'But you knew Ard was Toby's father?'

Linley nodded, sobbing in ragged breaths. 'Mary told me in an earlier letter.' She patted the older envelope on the bed beside her. 'That's why I put his name as father on the registration certificate. First because he *is* the baby's father and second because I couldn't stand Gareth Wilkin having any claim whatsoever.'

'Oh, Linley.'

'And third because it's *right*.' She hiccupped through the sobs.

CeeCee glanced down at the letter again. 'Are you sure that Mary wouldn't have been with anyone else? That she only *says* Ard O'Rourke is...'

'Oh Aunty, I don't know, I don't know. But you only have to look at Toby to see the likeness of him to—'

'It's all right, Linley. Keep yourself calm. Nothing changes.' CeeCee thought quickly. She hardly knew Ard, but what she did know was he seemed a reasonable lad. And as a lad ... no, what would he be now, twenty-five or -six? Not a lad any longer, but a man.

And the father of the baby. The baby to whom Linley was a guardian.

These young people! What tangles!

And do these two, Ard and Linley, love each other?

CeeCee gazed at the silently sobbing Linley. Her niece hadn't ever said ... Was CeeCee so blind she hadn't noticed ... and yet—

Good lord! All those furious blushes and the embarrassment and the high emotion in Linley since taking the baby ... CeeCee had hoped it was only Linley adjusting. Just the last girlish notions as she grew up and into her motherhood role. But no, it was all for Ard. All Linley's longing for a man of her own.

It was, most likely, her niece's own primal urges. Seeing little Toby at the breast, feeding hungrily, and smelling that peculiar baby-smell that only babes have. Wondering at the strength in the clutch of tiny fingers. At the wide-eyed stare of a month-old babe as it never left your face. Knowing that this baby was the son of the man she loved.

Oh yes, CeeCee remembered her own maternal feelings for Linley when she had been thrust into her keeping. But it was not a road she wanted to travel for herself. Linley was her sister's daughter, and she would look after her niece as best she could, but CeeCee had never wanted a child of her own. When Eliza died, Linley was enough for CeeCee.

Linley must be feeling her own maternal surge with Toby in her arms. CeeCee gripped her hands in hers, patting absently. *Oh dear.*

'I think the best thing we can do now is try to find Ard O'Rourke,' she said to Linley, who blew loudly into the handker-chief, shaking her head.

———

Linley was horrified. 'Oh no, CeeCee. I could never face him now, after all this—'

'How absurd.' CeeCee drew back. 'Linley, I'm surprised at you. Of course we have to find Ard. If only to give him the chance to—'

'No. *No.* What could he do? What reason would I have to ever speak to him again?' Linley stopped. She hadn't meant to say that and she knew CeeCee had caught it.

Her aunt narrowed her gaze. 'What reason? I think you have a very clear reason to speak to him again. You have his son, Linley.' CeeCee's frown deepened.

'He need never know.' She felt the hiccup in her throat. 'Men don't usually want to know these things, do they?'

'Only one way to find out, now, isn't there?'

'No, Aunty. No matter how stern you might sound, I can do this without Ard O'Rourke.'

'You would withhold this information from him?' The frown lifted into raised brows, eyes wide.

'Why would he ever need to know?'

CeeCee inhaled deeply. 'You said yourself the baby has Ard's stamp on him. How would you hide that from all the world?'

Linley could hear a creeping frustration in her aunt's voice. She rubbed her forehead. 'I don't know. I don't know.'

CeeCee took her hands. 'Linley. I can tell you have strong feelings for this man.'

Linley felt the hot surge rush into her cheeks, the tiny pin pricks of heat darting over her face. 'He must know. He must have known.'

'Known what?'

'That I—' The air stuck in her throat.

CeeCee sat back.

'That I have loved him ...' Her voice trailed off and a new flood of heat rushed to her cheeks. 'So how could he ...?' Linley looked at her aunt, despairing.

'Ah. So how could he be with another?'

Linley nodded, unable to speak. Tears squeezed out afresh and dropped onto their still clasped hands.

CeeCee sniffed. She shook her head. 'I can't answer that. Except to say that to us women, it seems men do some stupid things. Sometimes they attach no emotion to the act of ... of love.' CeeCee stopped a moment. 'Or perhaps the stupid dolt didn't know you loved him.'

Linley blurted another sob, half a laugh, half a cry, remembering what Millie had said about there being no cure for stupid. 'I feel so ridiculous.'

'Why on earth?'

'He will think I trapped him.' She sighed and glanced at the ceiling.

'How?'

Linley looked at her aunt. 'That I agreed to take Toby to trap him.'

CeeCee scoffed. 'Mary came to me for help, not you. And afterwards, you agreed to be Toby's guardian, to look after him ...' Her voice trailed off and she focused on Linley.

Silent moments passed. 'Now you understand, don't you?' Linley said sadly. 'I can see you do.' She wrung her hands in her lap. 'Did I agree to take Toby only so that Ard would eventually have to come to me?'

CeeCee frowned more darkly at her and Linley had to look away. It wasn't like that. But it looked like it. She didn't want to trap Ard, certainly didn't want a man who didn't want *her*. Mary had said the same herself. Linley wouldn't have taken care of Toby just to lay a trap for his father. She loved that baby, fiercely. She did. She could look after him, and she would.

'That will be something for you to sort with Ard, Linley, if you choose.' Her aunt looked as if she'd taken pity on her.

'That wasn't the reason, CeeCee, not at all. But it was all sorts of things. Our work. Mary's pleading letter. Yes, it's Ard's baby ...' Fresh tears threatened. 'But not a trap.'

Her aunt tsk-tsked. 'First, the man needs to know you have his son, and better he learns it from you than from the gossips.' CeeCee leaned closer to her niece. 'And second, you need to admit to yourself exactly what it is you want.'

Forty-Four

Millie Cooke blew a dangling wiry ringlet back off her face.

Swear to God the floors get harder to do every day with the little 'uns scampering about now.

She shooed her youngest, Freddy, out the back door with a broom, laughing as he scooted ahead of her. She stood up straight and stretched. Albie, her other boy, and Jane, Annie's oldest, were squatting in the dirt trying to make houses. Satisfied all was well, she turned back down the hallway. She needed a cup of tea. With Annie gone down the street, she was on her own with four youngsters, including baby William in his crib, sleeping soundly after Annie's feeding.

'I'm needing a bucket of tea, not just a cup.'

She'd set the kettle back on the stove as soon as—

Outraged screams rent the air as the back door burst open. She spun around to see Freddy under the arm of a small scrawny man, baring his teeth and on a limped march down the passage. Her heart pounded. Beyond him she could see the other two little children pick themselves up off the ground, screeching in bewildered fury …

At least they were making noises… No blood. No bent limbs.

Her mouth fell open as he advanced. Freddy was trying to reach her, his chubby arms flailing, his voice in full roar, his cheeks an angry red and the tears and snot running in rivulets. Rooted to the spot, Millie saw the man gather the child from under his arm with both hands and then he threw Freddy at her.

She scrambled to catch him, and went down with the heavy child in her arms. She rolled over him, well practised, arching herself to protect him as the bunched fist came down on her side and head.

'Where do they live?' he roared. 'Where do they live, those what just left in the cart?'

The fist came down again and she felt bones break, and from somewhere deep, pain thrust a groan of agony out of her.

Freddy still screamed, squirming in her arms.

'Tell me, you slut! Tell me or I'll break the necks of all these brats,' he snarled.

She looked up and saw the fist again before her eye collapsed under the punch. Her head snapped back as she felt her grasp of Freddy give way, but he wriggled closer, sobbing deep in his throat. He clutched at her, and she pulled him closer into her body, her grip weakening as agony throbbed through her.

Liquid dribbled down … she swallowed blood … Was her nose shattered? She heard a voice. 'B Street,' it said, and it sounded like her own.

'What house?' The mottled face thrust into her fading vision. 'What house?' he screeched again and grabbed her hair, wrenching her head up.

'Four,' she breathed.

The taste of iron on her tongue, sliding down her throat, she watched as the stinking bastard made for the front door, tore open the bolt and disappeared outside. The last thing she heard was the toddlers squawking their horror from where they sat.

Then, blessedly, nothing.

Forty-Five

Ard leaned against James' cart, his arms folded, his mouth tight as he listened to the older man. James had pulled up in the main street and alighted as soon as he'd seen Ard waving him down.

'I can't say it surprises me to see you here. But I told you not to come. I haven't spoken to Linley about your meeting with her. It wouldn't be in anyone's interests to have you land at the house without her knowing you were about to do so,' James said. 'Much less not knowing if she'll even agree to see you.'

Ard kept his voice low. 'I'm desperate for it, James. I can't start all over, here, in the same town, without knowing one way or the other if she's—'

'Have you any work yet?' James demanded.

'No.' Ard kicked at the dirt underfoot. 'I've been to the smithy's, but he hasn't heard of anything. I went to the wharf to look and that's when I saw my uncle. He told me of a new hundred-acre property my family's purchasing, but that's a way off yet.'

James nodded. 'It'll be a big job when it happens. Much to do.'

Ard looked up. 'Just need to get something to keep me going before then.'

James rubbed his forehead, glanced into the back of the cart and blew out a breath. 'All right. I have a small job now, in fact.' He thumbed over his shoulder at the timber in the back. 'A fence for one of my properties. Might only take you two or three days.'

'Gladly.'

'Have you found lodgings? Can't have you sleeping rough.'

Ard shrugged. 'I'm used to it. I'll make a new swag, toss it down somewhere.' The two pounds Liam had given him for accommodation could be put to better use than sleeping in a hotel.

James looked him over. 'Perhaps a new shirt wouldn't go astray, either. Store's there, on the right,' he said, pointing to a shop half-way down the street. 'You'll get the makings for a swag in there, too.' He climbed back on to the cart. 'I'll wait.'

Ard ran down to the shop, made his purchases and lugged them back to the waiting cart.

'Let's get this timber off-loaded at the house.' James released the brake. 'I'll introduce you to the two women there and you can start straight away. I'll ask them to feed you, too.'

Ard climbed aboard. 'Grateful.'

'Tell me about this property you've got your eyes on.' The cart moved off the curb.

'Don't know much. My uncle's given me directions, some-where on the river, close enough to town. Big enough for the family. We'll plant fruit trees and vegetables first, staying with what we know.' Ard looked over the shops of the main street as they left. 'And I'm interested in horses.'

'You said. But in the meantime, I might have more building jobs need doing.' He slapped the reins a little harder and the cart picked up speed. 'Unless you're intent on river work.'

Ard thought back over his little luck on the wharf earlier. 'I would if I knew I could get the work. There might be odd jobs here and there. I don't care so much what I do, I just want steady work, if I can find it. Same as everyone else.'

'True enough.'

They turned out of the town and Ard caught a sidelong glance from James.

'The situation here with the Misses Seymour might be compromised,' he said.

Ard felt a thud in his chest. 'How so?'

'Linley has guardianship of Toby but it appears the baby's mother left a will.'

Ard remembered Mary's written words. He lifted his shoulders. 'Mary wasn't clear in her letter to me about a will, but she did say that Linley had another letter.'

'And in the will, she made her son the beneficiary of a sum of money to be held in trust by his guardian.'

'Linley.'

'Aye. And as long as Linley has the baby in her custody, the money will come to her.' James flicked the reins and the cart lurched a little faster.

Ard shifted in his seat. 'Yes?'

'Mary's husband believes the inheritance is his right, and that it's his right to administer. From the attack on CeeCee and Linley, and the destruction of their goods and chattels, the fires, the attack on you and on their solicitor Mr Campbell's office, it appears the bereaved husband is clearly out to seize the child, or at the very least some legal papers.'

Ard gripped the cart rail. 'But they're here in Echuca, Miss CeeCee and Linley and my boy. You brought them here to be safe.'

'I did. But I have reason to believe that the husband is now in this town, and possibly living not far away.' James glanced at Ard.

'Can he claim my—?'

'We've done everything we can to anticipate a legal challenge on his right to—'

'What do you mean?'

James turned the cart into the street where Annie Rutherford and Millie Cooke lived. 'We've registered the boy's birth, and Wilkin's name is not on the certificate as the father.'

Ard felt a lump in his throat and swallowed hard. He was the father. He believed it wholeheartedly. *His* name should be on the registration.

'Sweet Jesus Christ,' James ground out and the reins flicked hard over the horse's hind. The cart shot forward.

Ard hung on, bewildered, until he followed James' stare. Ahead he saw a woman bent over a crumpled form on the street. Three little children milled about.

James shoved an elbow at him. 'Get out, man, quick, and get those children out of the way of the cart!'

Ard leapt out and scrambled into a run. One little fellow, standing on his own near the two figures, was bellowing at the top of his lungs. The others, a girl and boy, stood in the middle of the road screaming. The shrieks only got louder as Ard pounded down. He could hear the cart not far behind, so he scooped up the boy and girl and rushed them to the path closest to the prone figure.

'Now, mind you stay here out of the way of the horse, do you hear?' Snivels and snorts and gulps and nods met him in answer. 'And look after this other little fellow here, all right?' Ard scooted the other boy into their little circle. 'Hold hands now and let us look after your ma.' He knew nothing about little children.

James pulled on the reins, braked hard and leapt off the cart. 'Out of the way,' he said to the woman kneeling over the unconscious figure on the ground.

He thudded to his knees. 'Millie ...'

The other woman spoke, her eyes wide, her voice reed-thin. 'I can't bring her round. I can't bring her round.' Her pinched face was pale and blotchy. Her hands that had supported Millie's head were bloody.

James pressed his fingers against Millie's neck. 'She's alive. What happened here?' He stared across at the screaming children. 'What the hell happened here?' he shouted at the woman.

'He must have gone over and—'

'Who, for God's sake?' James' face was screwed up.

Ard bent down. 'I'll empty the cart. Let's get her in the back. I'll take her to a doctor—'

'Who did this?' James roared at the woman.

The children broke into fresh wailing and screaming and Ard thought his head would split. He hurried back and knelt with them. 'Quietly, now.' He gathered them close and pressed them to hold on to each other. He looked back over his shoulder at James hovering over the two women.

Who are these people?

'I think it was my brother,' he heard the kneeling woman wail. 'That child, the little girl came over to my house screaming,' she said and lifting a hand, pointed to a house across the road. 'And when I came out to see why she was so upset, this woman was crawling down the path ...'

Ard watched as James stared across at the house, his mouth dropped open. He dragged in air, then glared at Ard, it seemed in terror. 'Two streets back, B Street. Turn right into it, number four.' He paused, breathed raggedly. 'It's CeeCee's house. Hurry.'

Ard was bewildered. 'But this lady—'

'She is my responsibility. I'll stay with her. Just go, go quickly.' James came up on his haunches, scraped his hands under Millie and hoisted her up in his arms. He staggered a little then steadied and turned. 'What's your name?' he asked of the other woman.

'Mrs Bailey.' The woman came up to her feet, her face white.

'Mrs Bailey,' he said between clenched teeth, 'help me inside with these children, then run for the doctor, if you would, and send someone from there for the police.' Then he turned to Ard and shouted, 'Move, lad—get going!'

Ard charged across to the cart.

'On foot, Ard.' James bellowed at him from the doorway, trying to manoeuvre the prone Millie inside. 'And hurry. Number four! Gareth Wilkin might already be there. Go.'

Gareth Wilkin.

Ard bolted down the road and pounded his way past two streets. *Linley.* Skidding east into B Street, he heaved in air, panicking until he found house numbers. Four—across the road and...

He took the wide dirt road in a few bounds.

What if Wilkin wasn't here and CeeCee and Linley were having a bloody cup of tea?

But James was so sure.

No noise. No sound from within the house. He leapt the gate, stomped over the soft dust at the front of the house, swung around the pump at the well and landed on the verandah.

A parlour window. Closed lace curtains. He would be clearly seen if—

'Ard!'

The anguished shriek pierced his confusion. He threw himself at the front door, his body barrelling into it, shoulder first. The jamb gave way and the timber groaned under his onslaught. The door crashed open and he fell inside, stumbling into the hallway. He gained his feet, breath ragged and blood pounding.

A door flung open. Ard spun to face it. Linley charged into the hallway, clutching a bundle in one arm and a large knife in the other. She pointed with the knife to a door opposite. 'He's killed CeeCee, I know it,' she screamed. 'He's killed her!'

Ard stepped towards her, looking down only a moment to the bundle hugged to Linley's chest. Tiny eyes, wide with curiosity, stared back at him. His heartbeat ricocheted around his body.

'*Ard!*'

Linley's urgency jolted him. He spun on his heels, his back to her, shielding her and the baby. The handle of the knife met his fist and he opened his fingers to grip it, staring at the closed door ahead of him.

'Can he get out?' he asked over his shoulder, his voice hoarse, ragged, heartbeat thudding in his temple.

'Only the window, but I don't think he has.' She was crying. 'He's in there with CeeCee …. He just came out of nowhere—'

'Can you run?' he grated.

'*What?*'

'Run to the other house,' he whispered between his teeth. 'James is there.'

'No. *No!* CeeCee—'

'Run, Linley. You have to. Get James to come. Send someone for the police.'

'I'll stay, I'll stay—'

'Not with the baby,' he ground. 'This is no place … James sent me. One of the women has been attacked. Go.'

Linley came out from behind him, a hand covering her mouth. 'My God.'

Compelled, Ard turned, looked down once again at the calm dark eyes staring at him. The little face pouting and mouth moving as if about to speak. 'Go, Linley. Please.' He reached out to touch the button nose and his finger looked huge against the baby wrapped in swaddling. He withdrew hastily. A fear gripped him, a claw clutched his heart and squeezed. Then he grasped her elbow and pushed her towards the door.

'If that man follows …' Linley's voice trembled, but it didn't sound like fear.

Ard pushed her through the shattered doorway. 'He never will. Go.' His voice was rough, scratchy in his throat.

A fleeting moment and she was down the steps. Ard turned for the other door. Fear gripped harder, ragged, vice-like … Fear that he'd sent her on her way, without being by her side. Fear that he might not live to see his son grow, fear he would never be that husband, father …

In a split second he understood loss, real loss. Devastation. An unbearable punch to his gut. He sucked in a painful draught, forcing his lungs to work. Fury boiled up inside. He charged the closed door with all his might.

It banged open, splintered at the hinges. Ard burst into the room, awkwardly gained his feet, stumbling, steadying.

Gareth Wilkin sprang at him.

A snarl and a roar rent the air around him, and Ard went down heavily, the knife flung out of his hand on impact.

Forty-Six

Toby was squeezed tight to Linley's chest. Torn, she waited a split second until she heard the second door give way. She gathered her wits and dashed out through the gate. And ran and ran. Because it was Toby she needed to save. It was Toby she *could* save.

She ran on.

CeeCee.

Ard.

Annie … or Millie.

Each name was a wail in her head, but with each breath she gained strength, with each stride she gained hope.

Toby squawked and wriggled but she didn't lessen her grip. She ran over the first crossroad, checked for coming horses and carts, skirt clutched in one hand.

She rushed past the few houses along the next part of street, her boots thudding as she bore down on the next crossroad. Her lungs pained, her throat had dried. One arm ached with Toby's weight, the other with its fierce clutch on her skirt.

Please God, don't let me turn an ankle …

She found reserves of strength, sprinted into Millie's street and raced to the house.

'James, James!' she yelled, and darted up to the front door. Tears streamed over her face and the air wheezed into her lungs.

Children wailed and sobbed, and wailed and sobbed anew from the floor when they saw her burst inside. Toby started to whimper against her chest and it sounded like the prelude to a full-blown outrage. She slowed and cooed as she scurried in and out of the front room.

No one.

In the second room, she pulled up short. James was sitting in a chair by the bed. Millie lay on it, unconscious. Linley froze in the doorway. James leapt up.

Annie Rutherford squeezed a cloth over a bowl of bloodied water. 'Leave the place for five minutes and all hell breaks loose,' she muttered. Her usually healthy complexion was pale, and a sheen covered her forehead. She dabbed at Millie's face and neck.

Linley was frantic. 'Is she …?'

'Doctor's coming,' Annie said.

James took her free hand, his face ashen. 'Linley?'

She clutched his arm, squeezing hard. 'Please go to our house, James. Please. We need to get the police—'

'They've been sent for, and as quickly as the doctor. Is Toby …?' James glanced at the baby in her arms, who quietened the moment he laid eyes on James.

'He's well, he's well. Please, go help Ard. I'll help Mrs Rutherford here. Hurry.'

'Tell me.' James gripped her shoulders, his dark eyes fierce.

'No! Hurry!'

He pressed his lips to her forehead and sprinted out.

Annie Rutherford stared at her. 'What happened at Miss CeeCee's?'

Linley shook her head and sobbed. 'I don't want to say it. I don't want to say.'

Annie, her face a grim mask, turned back to Millie. 'Then best you tend that baby of yours, and our other children, if you would. I will tend my friend.'

Ard realised he was staring at the ceiling, at a moving ceiling. For moments it looked as if it would fall on him, and then that he was floating up to meet it.

Close your eyes. Too tired to look any more, to make sense of it.

Visions crowded under his eyelids. Teeth bared, stinking breath blasting over him, his skull cracking a thud on the boards as he was flung to the floor. Grappling. Rolling in the clutches of a mad thing. He'd tried to toss it off, to hurl it across the room. Something had slipped across his forehead, a ripping slice and then warm liquid had begun to run into his eyes.

Rolling. The weight on his chest had vanished. Then another thud landed like a hammer-blow and had borne deep in his side. A hissing breath left his body.

Fast-moving footsteps retreating. Then nothing. Blackness.

Now he waited again. Heard nothing. Something sticky bothered his eyes.

He brought up a hand, tried to focus. Fingers. He touched his face, saw blood. Touched again, higher up. More blood. He sucked in a breath as he felt an open wound, raw, squelchy …

Pain was building high up in his back. He couldn't reach it on his side, couldn't find the energy to try to stand. He moved his head and saw a bed. A chair.

He waited some more. Tired.

He focused on a booted female foot. And another. And a pale green dress. As he squinted harder, trying to keep a focus, he recognised the deathly pale face of CeeCee Seymour.

Forty-Seven

Esther Bailey had run as fast as her boots and her stays would let her. She hadn't moved this fast in years, though if truth be known, she still wasn't moving at a run.

She'd picked up her skirts and stumbled over the uneven path, sometimes veering on to the road to avoid other pedestrians. One leg seemed like it couldn't keep up. Her breathing was laboured.

Too many mutton pies and lardy cakes.

Carts and carriages had passed her but she hadn't thought to flag one down until she stopped to heave in her breath. And then a kindly soul stopped for her. Not only did he take her to the doctor's, he promised he'd go on and report to the police, especially with a little help from her sharp tongue. But she cried her thanks and alighted inelegantly at the doctor's rooms. The man had gee-upped his horse and his cart leapt forward, on his way to the coppers, he'd said.

From there things were a blur.

The doctor ordered her to stay in his rooms with his wife. He mounted his own horse and took off to the address she'd given.

But Esther was in a hurry to return home. She insisted the doctor's wife should let her go, promising that a cool drink of water was all she needed, that a calm walk home would soothe her nerves until she could make herself a cup of tea in her own kitchen.

There wasn't much the woman could do but agree, and Esther made a more sedate journey home, but her mind was still in turmoil.

———

Gareth Wilkin lifted the heavy kettle onto the stove. He shoved a log into the fire and watched as it took, the flames reaching through the hole before he clanged the tamp back down on it.

He stared at his hands, still shaking. He hadn't been seen by anyone, coming into the yard by the alley behind the house. But the moment he eased open the back door, his limbs started to shake uncontrollably.

His hands had blood on them. Blood was on his clothes. He lurched back outside and worked the water pump, doused his head and neck then turned his face up to swallow mouthfuls.

Thirsty thirsty.

Tea is what he needed, plenty of sugar in it. That's what he needed. Sugar that Esther kept atop the stove. He staggered to the kitchen, cursing his foot. Boot would have to come off, if he could manage it himself ...

Reaching for a pannikin, shaking, fevered, he knocked other crockery from the shelf. China crashed to the floorboards, splintering, shattering. Bloody stuff in his way. He had to stop the shakes. Once he stopped the shakes he'd think about what to do next.

Had he killed them both? He'd only grabbed the woman by throat and shaken her.

Bloody dark-haired bitch stomped on me foot. Lucky I didn't pass out ... was the only thing stopped me takin' off outta there before that O'Rourke bastard arrived ...

But she'd slipped, banged her head. He hadn't done nothing. If she hadn't tried to rush by him, shouting her head off at the other slut …

Just lucky I got that young bloke by surprise. Left the knife in him, somewhere, bugger it.

And still he didn't have the brat. Even when he'd scampered off, he had no clue where the young bitch had gone. He'd just crabbed his way back to Esther's place, fast as he could.

Sweat popped off him. His tongue felt swollen. He had to piss but—

Coppers coming for me for sure… Should leave, else be hanged as quick as look at yer.

Tea. Rum. Bah! Esther wouldn't have rum. Sugar'd have to do.

He couldn't wait. He needed a brew. He sloshed water from the kettle into the pannikin. The tea looked only lightly steeped but it was just hot enough.

Thirsty thirsty thirsty.

He reached up and dragged down her special tin to the table, then poured straight from the container into his cup, enough to suit his tastes. He stirred it with a finger. He hadn't had sugar for a long time …

A noise at the front door!

He scuttled back out to the laundry room and hunkered down beside the boiler, the warmed cup in his hands. Esther wouldn't come looking for him, and he knew the coppers wouldn't be along yet … there'd been no one to go running for them.

He had a bit of time.

He must be mad. Otherwise why wasn't he running for his life?

Because I still have a chance at grabbing that brat and me two hundred pounds.

Forty-Eight

James charged through the gate of the little house. In three bounds, he landed at the doorway and swung back the unhinged door. It banged against the wall inside.

'CeeCee!' he yelled. 'CeeCee!'

A voice rasped from the second room. 'In here.' Ard, his voice a wheezing breath.

James flew into the bedroom. Ard was on the floor sidling towards CeeCee. Her prone form was partly hidden by him and partly by the bed. He ran to her, collapsed to his knees. Slid in blood. It was everywhere. *Everywhere.* Aghast, he checked her as quickly as he could. His hands came away clean.

'Not hers,' Ard whispered hoarsely. 'My scalp torn, lots of blood ...' He tried to sit with a shoulder propped against the bed, hanging onto his side.

Something clattered to the floor by Ard. A knife.

James eyed the gash on his forehead, the blood still running in streams. 'Jesus, man.' He reefed into his pocket, withdrew a handkerchief and pressed it into Ard's hand. 'Hold this on it—stop the flow.' He tried to see the wound in Ard's side.

Ard brushed his hand off. 'I'm sorry, James. I'm sorry.' His voice was breathy, a gurgly sound.

Christ, no! James tore his glance back to CeeCee.

'I should have got him.'

'Hush yourself.' James stared down at CeeCee's face. She looked serene. Bruises on her neck.

A blow to his gut from within burst the breath from his body. He stilled, couldn't see her chest rising and falling. He reached out a shaky hand and held it under her nose.

Can't tell. Can't tell.

He couldn't feel her breath, her life …

———

'Miss Linley, your baby needs to be fed. Give him here.' Annie walked back into the kitchen.

Linley looked around in a panic. She'd held on to Toby so tightly for so long she didn't know if she could let him go.

'And go and round up them kids of ours and we'll set to with some supper for them. Dr Wilson says Millie will be fine, one day soon.' She wiped her hands down her apron and opened her arms.

'I can't think straight, Annie.' Linley held out Toby.

'You've been thinking straight all along, and we need you to do that a wee bit longer.' Annie took Toby, opened her blouse, and sat down by the stove. 'More wood on the cooker, too, if you please.'

Linley followed orders. She stuffed logs into the stove and then went out the back to gather the three toddlers and brought them inside. Annie told her they could have the remains of the cake, heated up on the stove and dipped in some warm tea. She rocked back and forth in the chair while Toby nuzzled peacefully.

'Keep working is best, Miss Linley.'

'Just Linley, please.' She helped the children onto their little chairs and began to dish up the cake, her hands shaking. 'I'm so very clumsy at the moment.'

'No matter.'

Linley slapped thick slices of cake in front of each delighted child, and splashed warm tea into a dish for them. 'I really should get back around to the other house—'

'You'll do no such thing, Mrs O'Rourke.' The doctor walked into the kitchen, his hat under his arm along with his bag. 'If this woman's attacker is anywhere around, you're to stay put until the police come.' He dusted himself off and put the bag down. He looked over at the three children. 'No injuries there?'

Annie shook her head. 'No, Dr Wilson.'

'Good. Now, Mrs Cooke might have a fractured cheekbone. Naught to do for that. I've put a couple of stitches above her eye and another on top of her head. You know to keep them clean, Mrs Rutherford.'

Annie pressed her lips together and nodded curtly. 'Yes, Dr Wilson.'

'Any suppuration or fever, you're to let me know.' He turned to look at Linley. 'I'll prescribe something for your nerves, young woman.'

'No, thank you. I'm quite fine.' She couldn't keep her voice from shaking.

'I doubt that. I'll leave a powder, for both of you.' He opened his bag, reached in and withdrew an ampoule with a little stopper. 'Only a smidgen in warm water.' He handed it to Linley and walked out of the room.

Hammering blows on the front door gave Linley a start. She darted to the kitchen doorway and peered around the corner into the hall. The doctor pulled open the front door. Police. Three other men in uniform had dismounted and were marching up to the verandah.

'Afternoon, Dr Wilson.' The older man, with grey hair, long droopy moustache and big sideburns, looked around the doctor to Linley. 'Miss, I'm Sergeant Love. We heard the assailant was from one of these houses. Which is it?'

Linley pointed out the door with a shaky finger. 'Straight across.'

He nodded to the troopers, who turned and ran over the road. 'We'll come back here, directly,' he said to Linley, and turned to the doctor. 'If you'd be so good to stay a few minutes longer, doctor.'

'Very well, sergeant.'

'But our other house!' Linley cried.

'In due course,' the older man called back over his shoulder.

'A cup of tea, if you would, Mrs O'Rourke,' the doctor asked, and took Linley gently by the elbow and guided her back into the kitchen.

Linley was shuddering so much she feared she'd scald him, or herself. He had to pour it himself, then he poured her a cup and ordered her to drink.

He set another aside for Annie and took a seat at the kitchen table. 'You should be commended for your good work, Mrs O'Rourke.'

Bewildered, Linley hesitated a moment and looked to Annie.

''Tis Mrs O'Rourke's aunt, Dr Wilson. She and her husband have begun this work.'

Stretched out in the chair, his legs crossed, he was mindful of the children and their sticky cake fingers close by. 'It is a new concept. Not one that is thought of too highly at present, I might add.' He tucked his chin to his chest, his lips in a firm line.

Annie threw Linley a quick look with narrowed eyes, then gazed at the suckling baby at her breast. She turned away to change him over.

Linley's shuddering slowed. Her breathing calmed, vision cleared. With straightened shoulders and a voice still ragged in her throat, she said, 'And I will continue the work, doctor. I don't care if it is highly thought of or not.'

'Good for you.' He seemed not at all slighted by Linley's remark. If anything, he seemed pleased by it.

'We will care well for Millie Cooke.' Linley's voice had steadied.

'I would think nothing less, Mrs O'Rourke.'

A voice called from the front of the house. 'Doctor?'

Dr Wilson marched into the hallway and Linley followed.

Sergeant Love leaned in the doorway. 'No reason to fear anything over the road,' he reported, his eyes on his boots. 'He's not going anywhere, not now.' His face was grey.

The doctor stared at the policeman. 'I should take a quick look, in that case.'

The sergeant shook his head. 'Naught to do. Will need a pallet and a cart before the hour's out.' His voice was rough.

The doctor raised his eyebrows. 'All the same.' He jogged across the road and disappeared into Mrs Bailey's.

Linley wrung her hands. What about CeeCee? *Would he hurry? Would he please hurry?*

Not a minute later, the doctor ran back. 'Quite correct, Sergeant Love, we should waste no more time. I will accompany you gentlemen to the other house immediately. Let's go.'

The sergeant whipped off his hat. 'Mrs O'Rourke, we will need questions answered at a later time.' He tried to clear his throat.

'Get along with you, sergeant.' The doctor ushered the officer back to his horse, the others already mounted and waiting. He turned, plonked his hat on his head and touched the rim briefly. 'Good day,' he said to Linley, who had followed outside.

She wrung her hands. 'Will you let me know as soon—'

'When I have something to tell you, my dear Mrs O'Rourke.' The doctor mounted and wheeled his horse about. 'You are safe here,' he said to her. 'You'll have no trouble from the occupant of that house. But do not venture there for any reason.'

The sergeant urged him to follow them. They rode off, and that relieved Linley only a little. She stared malevolently at the little house across the road, then paced back to the kitchen, her heart a lump inside. Instinct was to go to CeeCee, but her job was to stay with Toby, keep him safe, and help keep these others safe.

She sat with the children, who chattered at their little table.

Annie rocked with her eyes closed, tears trickling out. 'They didn't leave a bloody copper here, though, did they?'

Linley squared her shoulders. 'We don't need a copper here now, Annie. Wilkin won't be back.' She blinked hard to moisten her dry, scratchy eyes. The boulder in her chest weighed on her, and her shoulders rounded in a physical response. It felt like her heart had gone to lead.

'Little you know of this type of man,' Annie said.

Linley knew enough. But she understood what the doctor had said to her—Wilkin was no longer a threat.

Annie reached around and from behind the stacked logs beside the stove, she withdrew a small axe. 'For splitting kindling.' She leaned it against her chair.

Violence was as close as it had always been.

Linley turned her attention to the children, who played a game with their soggy cake.

———

Esther watched in angry confusion as the troopers stormed her home. She clutched at the fence palings of a house at the end of her street, fearful that if she didn't, she'd fall over and pitch face first into the dirt.

What were they looking for?

Holding on to forestall any more lightheadedness, she watched as the three officers stumbled back out of her place minutes later. One of them gagged raucously in her front yard. The closest of his mates grabbed him by the collar and dragged him back to the road where their horses waited. Their constable, or whoever he was, stepped—at first tentatively, then with more resolve—across the road to Mrs Cooke's house. They garnered a fourth man, the doctor, who rushed into her house, only moments later to exit, mount up and ride away.

She waited till they were out of sight, then breathed a deep lungful and walked steadily towards her house. Her feet burned in her boots. Bunions. They'd need a good soaking in some salts.

At the first crossroad, she wondered if she shouldn't go around the back way, deny the sticky-noses any sightings from the front of her house. God alone knew what a mess those troopers had made of Mr Bailey's house ... and to be openly sick in the front yard—disgusting. They needed reporting, the lot of them.

She'd report them, all right.

What *were* they looking for?

Oh no.

Her steps faltered. No, she wouldn't report the police for anything.

You're a fool, Esther. It's your brother who needs reporting, and the sooner the better.

She stood for a moment and stared. Her house stood sentinel over its tiny frontage and the road that passed by it.

Her brother. No wonder she thought of him as an imbecile. He had endured much as a young boy. Their father, a violent, vicious man with dark and vile tendencies ... She shuddered. Had Gareth gone that far in his own madness?

Oh, please, dear God, surely not.

She knew his own memories of that horror would be strong. For herself, she kept her own vigil. No man had touched her since her father. And even if they had, she would have been in no physical shape to accommodate them, such was the brutal legacy of her father's treatment of her. In dear Mr Bailey, she had found a much older man who wanted only affection, as he could not engage in a physical relationship with a woman. A blessing for her, in a way, but she did feel the keen loss of never having borne a child. That overriding sorrow made her reluctant to enjoy anyone else's children.

That was before little Jane had tottered across the road.

She started to walk again. As she came up to her house, she glanced across the road at Mrs Cooke's. It was quiet.

She pushed open the gate at her house and stepped onto the little porch.

Forty-Nine

James stood back at the gateway to Annie and Millie's little house. He leaned over the pickets, his head swimming. It hadn't been that long a walk, but he was exhausted. All he could hear were Dr Wilson's shouted words ringing in his ears at the other house. *'She's not dead, man!'*

Had Ard saved her life? He must have got there in time. Was that how Ard took the stabbing? It looked to be so. What cost to Ard for saving CeeCee?

He rubbed a hand over his face, felt his own tears, hawked back the snot in his throat and spat.

No feebleness now. CeeCee is in good hands.

So is Ard.

At that house, one of the troopers had bolted to the hospital for the ambulance cart, and when it arrived the doctor had ordered James to return to Mrs Rutherford's. He told James that he needn't worry overly much—Mrs Anderson was quite safe. He was not to accompany the ambulance, as his presence would be needed to calm the women at the other house.

After the cart had gone, James' relief had been palpable, almost too enormous to bear. It was a physical walloping that weakened his knees and sent him to the gutter, crying like a baby. He blubbered out his relief, and finally pulled himself to his feet and trudged back to Annie's.

Now he straightened up and pushed off the fence. Felt more himself. In control again. He glanced at Annie's house. No sounds from within. Perhaps no one had seen him. He turned and looked at Mrs Bailey's house, and the rage he recognised came swiftly, boiling his blood and banging in his head.

His jaw clenched, his fists clenched, guts roiled. He stepped onto the road and a few strides found him at her front door. As he shoved it open, the resounding thud echoed down the small hallway. He wouldn't yell out; wouldn't run to it.

I promise you, CeeCee.

Wilkin would be taken like the rabid animal he was and put out of this life forever. Hunted down like James had hunted down Eliza's husband, like he'd hunted down others.

He checked one room, the parlour. In disarray, but no one was there. The next door, a bedroom, dainty in its decorations. Nothing.

The kitchen. A kettle had burned a scorch into the dining table. Shards of glass and crockery crunched under his booted feet. He stopped. Listened for any giveaway sounds, any scrapes of shoes on stone steps, or footfalls behind or in front. Nothing. James turned full circle, slowly. And then he heard it.

A retching, faint but close.

The back door ajar, he saw another room outside. The washhouse. Only two steps and he stood in the doorway. There ahead of him stood the woman from the street, a large switch in her hands. She was looking at a body, slumped against the boiler, not far from her feet. She seemed as cool and calm as if she were reading a pleasant book.

He took another step. 'Mrs Bailey,' he said, and looked beyond her.

She glanced at him. 'This poor wretch is my brother.' She inclined her head.

There was Gareth Wilkin, drool at his mouth and down his shirtfront. A stink of something far more pungent than onions hung in the air. Vomit stained the floor around him and faeces crawled over his ankles from under his trousers.

James grimaced, covering his nose and mouth. 'What has …?'

Mrs Bailey sighed loudly and turfed the switch out the door behind her. 'Seems he mistook rat poison for sugar in his tea. I told him it wasn't sugar. I told him.' She tilted her chin towards the pannikin on its side by Gareth, a tannish stain around it. 'He always so loved his tea.'

James stared at her. The woman seemed hardly affected by the devastation in front of her. That, or she was as mad as her brother.

Wilkin's retching was barely audible, his body's last response to the havoc of arsenic. James' gut ran cold. *To put him out of his misery now would take less than …*

'Go away,' Mrs Bailey said. 'He'll die. It won't be long now and there's nothing to be done for him. I'll stay with him, but you …' She turned to James. '*Go away.*'

In her wide-eyed stare, he believed she knew who he was, deep in his soul, what he'd done. How he'd despatched men like her brother, and without a backwards glance.

For the first time since Eliza's husband, he knew, absolutely, he'd done the last of that work. He knew Wilkin would pass from this life without any help from him. Yet if there was one poor body that needed assistance now, it was Gareth Wilkin.

James backed out of the room, confounded by his thoughts. He reeled through the house, shoving the front door open as he stumbled onto the porch. He gulped great lungs of fresh air and shook the stench of that house from his nostrils. Nothing he had done, nothing he had ever seen was as bad as what was happening to Gareth Wilkin.

He lurched across the road to the house, leaned once more over the picket fence, and coughed up stringy bile. As evil as he thought Wilkin to be, his death was worse than anything James could have inflicted. He would have despatched his prey quickly, with nought but a few words to remind the guilty of his crimes and the reason he was about to lose his life. He'd never have left him to die like Wilkin was dying now.

James waited long minutes until his stomach settled. Hands clasped over the fence, his weight on it, supported by it. His head cleared. It was no longer a concern of his.

And he thanked Mrs Bailey for glaring at him. Had he shown mercy and put the man out of his agony, as sure as James drew breath, the woman would have turned on him. And he would be found guilty of murder and sentenced to death.

He clutched his chest, sucked in the air. Light-headed. He breathed in long, deep draughts and the spinning slowly dissipated. Deliberately, he turned his thoughts.

Linley. Have to tell Linley about CeeCee.

A horse and cart careened into the street followed closely by a horse and rider. The hospital ambulance cart and Dr Wilson. Two men and a woman alighted.

Dr Wilson rode up to James and as he dismounted, said, 'Mrs Anderson is being attended to at the hospital.' He clapped James a couple of times on the shoulder. 'Steady on, Mr Anderson. She is as well as we can make her for the moment. I'll know more later. But for now,' he said and pointed across to Mrs Bailey's house, 'We need to remove that mess in there.'

James nodded. 'He's still alive.'

Wilson's eyes widened. 'Is he now? Surprising. It won't be for long.' He untied his bag from the horse. 'You look like shite. Get some whisky into you if you have any. Rum, if not.' He started across the road.

'And Ard?' James called, but the doctor had disappeared inside Mrs Bailey's house.

Linley rushed out of the house. 'James! What of CeeCee?' Her face was pinched white, her eyes bloodshot and harried.

James held up his hands. 'She's alive, Linley. CeeCee is in the hospital. That's all I know.'

She hurried out the gate and to his side. 'Thank God. And Ard?' She clutched his sleeve. Then she looked in horror at the blood on his clothes. 'Whose is this?'

James took her hands in his. 'Linley.'

Fifty

Three days later

Linley sat alone at CeeCee's hospital bed. The ward was quiet except for a much older woman in the next bed. Her mouth was open, and each time her throat rattled with the chug of a snore, Linley wished she could go over and wake her.

A pair of stained dentures sat in a dish on a little table between the two beds. Linley pulled a face and touched her own teeth with her tongue. She'd been fortunate, having had very few problems with her teeth. Just fortunate altogether, and because of her aunt.

CeeCee, asleep and propped up a little on firm pillows, had been dressed in a new white cotton nightgown, courtesy of James, though at Linley's insistence over the hospital issue ones. Its dainty lace and pintucked yoke was tied in a loose simple bow at her neckline. She looked much like she always had. Well, except for the bruises on her throat and the lump the size of an egg on the back of her head, that was.

The doctor had said her voice was lost, and perhaps it might not return, such had been was the pressure of Wilkin's hands on her throat. Linley's tears threatened again, but she swallowed them down.

Would not do to cry like a baby in here.

She was lucky, they said of CeeCee. All manner of things could have happened. Terrible things. Perhaps he hadn't had her by the throat for long, after all. Linley didn't know. CeeCee had screamed at her to grab a knife and run with Toby the moment she'd seen Wilkin enter by the kitchen door. Linley had swiped a knife off the bench and barricaded herself and Toby into CeeCee's room, the blade her only protection. She wasn't going to leave CeeCee. Not for anything. Not for all their lives. She had to stay. She had the knife and she would've used it.

Toby was safe, still at the house with Annie, who tended Millie and the other children. It had been three days now. At least CeeCee looked brighter each time Linley visited her.

Ard was another matter.

Linley patted her aunt's hand and was pleasantly surprised when, in her sleep, CeeCee murmured and smiled. That surely must be a good sign.

'Well done, Aunty. Come back to us soon.' Linley stood up and leaned over to kiss her forehead. 'I'll come back tomorrow, CeeCee.'

Then she steeled herself and walked out of CeeCee's ward and down to the ward for men. She checked with the sister that she was allowed to visit Ard and after a curt nod, a ward nurse was beckoned to take her.

'You can't stay too long, Mrs O'Rourke,' she was told. 'We need to attend to their baths and their meals.'

She didn't know what to expect, but her heartbeat leapt when she saw him.

Ard's bed was in the middle of six along a wall, only three of which were occupied. One held a child of perhaps twelve whose breathing was laboured, his face shiny with sweat. In the other was a man of about sixty, but it was hard to tell. He was curled up like a baby facing Ard, and appeared to be staring at him, but his eyes were vacant. Linley brought a chair to Ard's other side.

His eyes were on her. 'If you look directly at me, you won't notice his stare so much.' His smile was a little lopsided.

Linley's gaze roved over him. 'Yours is not such a pretty face right now.'

There were stitches in his scalp at the hairline and more stitches travelled down part of his forehead to the top of his left ear. Puckered, it looked sore. They'd snipped away some of his hair, and the stubble poked through. His face was black on that side, purple and deep pink where the blood had run under his skin. In some parts it had already begun to fade off to green and yellow. A swathe of bandages covered his stomach and rib cage, a plump wad of padding sticking out at his right side.

Linley needed to run her hands over the smooth skin of his shoulders and down onto the warm muscles of his chest. Just to feel for herself that he really was all right. She didn't dare. She looked around for a distraction.

A discarded shirt lay rumpled at the end of the bed. She fiddled with it. 'Thank you for being there for my aunt.' Tears threatened again, damn and blast them. She lowered her head a moment. 'She surely would have perished at the hands of that man. Thank you, Ard.' It steadied her, and she looked up.

'I was a moment's distraction.' Both his eyes were closed.

'Nevertheless.'

There was so much she wanted to say to him, the father of the baby she had in her care. But where to start and what to say? The angry words she had written to him months earlier about Mary's death sat heavily on her mind. So, too, did Ard being with Mary.

Linley huffed at herself. She'd had no claim on him. Never did. He was free to go off with someone else. She just hadn't ever thought he would.

Well, why not, Linley, you fool? You weren't engaged to be married or anything even close. He is a man, after all.

She bristled. But how could they both ever—

'How is Miss CeeCee?' He shifted, but grunted and stopped.

Linley caught herself, rolled her shoulders, tried to relax. 'They say they won't know for a while longer.' She looked down at her hands. 'James is distraught.'

'Yes. He would be.' His good eye opened a little.

She smoothed the stretch of linen sheet where it tucked under the mattress. 'How much longer do they say you're to be in here?'

'They reckon the hole in my side closed up pretty quick. No damage to my lung. So now they'll watch for infection. It could be a week.' He shifted again. 'Send me mad.'

'But you're still in pain.'

He grunted again then sighed. 'I'm lucky.'

Lucky. *We were all lucky.* Linley nodded. The doctor had told her the knife had missed all vitals but had plunged deep enough. He would be sore for months, with the ever-present threat of infection hanging over his head.

Ard had his eye on her. 'And how is Toby, Mrs O'Rourke?'

Linley's face warmed. 'He is well enough. Has a good set of lungs on him, and he's always hungry.'

Ard shuffled his legs under the sheet. 'He looked a fine lad when I caught sight of him.'

'He is.' She smiled, felt the light in her voice.

He tried to sit up. 'Linley, when I get out of here …'

The nurse returned and stood by her. 'Time for you to go, if you will, Mrs O'Rourke. We have to get on with our patients.'

Linley glanced at the nurse. 'I'll come back soon, Ard.' She stood up and made no attempt to reach for him.

With his one eye still on her, he smiled crookedly. 'Tomorrow, then.'

She didn't answer.

As she left, she heard him say to the nurse, 'My shirt, please. I need something out of the pockets.'

She heard the nurse give what sounded like a platitude.

The early summer evening made a pleasant walk home, yet even as Linley came up the street to Annie's house, she tried not to glance at Mrs Bailey's.

Three days now since those terrible events. Mrs Bailey had been taken to hospital. They'd said she was in a small room by herself, resting. The police had come to see her, too, but the gossip Annie had gleaned was that she had nothing to say to them. Linley wondered if she even still had her wits.

Gareth Wilkin had died that night, apparently, a most vile and agonising death. She shuddered all over again remembering when Annie related to her the type of death arsenic poisoning would induce. Though how Annie knew was something Linley had yet to discover. And she was in no hurry for that.

Coming up to the gate to the house, she saw James sitting on a kitchen chair pulled out onto the small verandah.

'How are the patients?' he asked, and stood up as she approached.

He indicated she sit in his place, which she did.

'CeeCee is the same. She looks peaceful.' She glanced at him. 'In fact, she smiled just before I left.'

James leaned against the verandah post. 'When she gets out of hospital, Linley, we will be married. I will never unwittingly subject her to a life without some protection—'

'She wouldn't view it like that, James. You know that.'

He shook his head. 'In our line of work now, it is clear to me that she, you, all of us, are not safe. This wouldn't have happened if CeeCee and I had been living together as husband and wife.' He hung his head, the red hair stringy with sweat as it fell onto his forehead. He checked his hands. The fingernails were dirty, skin roughened and torn in places. 'Excuse my state. I have been building a fence to keep myself occupied.'

'You know how CeeCee feels about being married,' Linley said.

'She told me just after you arrived in Echuca that she was ready for it. It gave me great hope.' When he looked at her his red-rimmed eyes were pained.

'Then lucky you, James.' She smiled. She knew how much they loved each other.

James stood straighter. 'Mrs Rutherford has kindly said that I can bathe by the outhouse. Then I will take my leave to the other house.'

Linley started. 'But you said there was a lot of blood—'

'Mr Jenkins and his boy sluiced it out with lye and hot water. He says it's clean as a whistle.'

'Oh.' Linley shuddered. She wasn't sure she ever wanted to go back there.

James looked rueful. 'No matter what happens in this work, Linley, we must continue. No epidemic was ever managed without putting shoulders to the wheel.'

She inhaled deeply. 'And it is an epidemic, isn't it?'

'As much as the influenza, regrettably,' he said. 'Except I don't see it running its course and dying out any time soon.'

Linley rubbed her hands down her crumpled day dress, one Annie had lent her until she could find a seamstress. 'I see it everywhere, where I never used to look before. Almost as if it can't be unseen once I do see it.'

He nodded. 'That's right.'

She started to say something and stopped.

'Go on,' he said.

She spread her hands. 'Why is it you champion the cause, James? A man ...'

He smiled. 'If not a man, or men, then who? We are the per-petrators, after all. We should be the ones to stop it. We should cull the sick ones.'

'But you are alone. I've never seen another man in this work.'

He shook his head. 'Others approach me. More curious, mind you, than anything else. And then it's usually to deride me.' He smiled at her then looked at his hands. 'I'm used to it. We are not reliant on anybody or anything, no agency or parliament to tell us right from wrong, so it doesn't matter what they think.'

'But your finances must suffer.'

'We have benefactors who like to stay very silent. It is not a popular cause.'

'Why must it be so?' Linley cried all of a sudden. 'Why must this violence occur on women and little children?'

'Indeed. And why do we turn a blind eye to it?'

She struggled to breathe, keeping her emotions in check. 'I have no answers.'

'I'm not sure there are any. I only know to keep mine safe from hurt.' Then he coughed and turned his head. 'Or I thought I knew.'

'Oh, James.' Linley stood up to hold his arm. 'You have.'

He patted her hand. 'And our other patient. How is he?'

Linley ducked her head. 'He seems well.'

'That is good.' James smiled a sad smile. 'I will take my leave, my dear Linley, and get to my bath before it's too dark to see the tub.'

A small but loud squawk reached their ears.

'Aha,' James said. 'I do believe that one belongs to you.'

He opened the door for her and followed her to the kitchen. He continued through to the laundry room outside and Linley heard him carting water to heat in the boiler.

Annie Rutherford had just fed her youngest and put him in his crib. She took up Toby and cradled him in her arms. 'One more to feed and then we can all go to bed.' She crinkled her nose. 'But this one is for you to do something about first.'

'Oh dear.' Linley opened her arms for her baby, stinky as he was.

Fifty-One

Two weeks later

Ard waited in the cart while his father and mother alighted. The track had been rougher than he remembered, and his aching side had felt every rock and rut.

'Not enough you let my orchard burn to the ground, son,' Lorc said and rolled his eyes. 'You go and get yourself stabbed by some madman, laid up so you can't take your turn digging up the new plot.' He held out his hand and Eleanor gripped it as she stepped to the ground.

Ard shifted along the seat and eased himself down. *That's not all by half, Pa.*

'Your father is making one of his funny jokes again, Ard.' Eleanor smiled at her son. 'We thank God you're all right.'

Lorcan stood with his hands on his hips and looked towards the river. 'One hundred beautiful acres all around and a mighty river runs by.' He nodded, satisfied. 'Liam did well. What a find.'

The stands of high gums in the distance lined the banks of the Murray. A breeze carried the sounds and smells of summer—warbling magpies, buzzing flies, baked earth and eucalyptus.

Lorcan's broad grin earned him a laugh from his wife. 'But there's some work ahead of us,' Eleanor said. She winked back at Ard. 'And just when I was getting used to all that finery and soft living your pa had for me in Renmark.' She stepped across the uneven ground to the cottage. 'This looks a little worse for wear.'

They knew the previous owner was long gone. No one had maintained the place since. Straggly, parched remnants of some sort of citrus orchard were corralled behind the main house. A fallen-down stable, its timbers rotting, its roof iron rusted thin and brittle, stood beyond that. Ard knew that would have to go. He'd salvage what he could, but an earlier inspection made him think it might only have been good for the campfire.

'At least we got all our owed wages, Ellie. And we'll make this finer than anything in Renmark. Finer than Olivewood, perhaps.'

She peered inside through the window. 'A good thing we did get our wages. We'll need every penny for this place.' She tested the boards of the verandah.

Ard exchanged a glance with his father, and then stepped up beside his mother. He gripped a post and gave it a shake. 'Sturdy enough.' He reached the door and swung it open. 'In you go, Ma. See—it's big enough to fit your table.'

And that earned him another smile.

Eleanor ran her hands along the timber walls of the hallway, poked her head into the first room, then moved across to the room opposite. 'One of these could be our Maggie's room when she comes.'

Lorcan called from the doorway. 'Then we'd all better get a hurry along. When my little tempest arrives, we'll want everything in good working order or we'll hear about it for the next year.'

'And the other room for Liam when he visits.' Eleanor glanced back at her son.

Ard just nodded. He'd told her he wanted to occupy the other house, fifty yards away. He would repair it and outfit it himself. Eleanor hadn't asked why. Ard reckoned she wouldn't ask just yet.

'There'll be room for Liam at whichever house,' Ard said. 'Whichever one has room when he comes back.'

'Good lad.' Lorcan followed his wife inside.

Ard didn't go in after his parents. He took a slow walk to the other cottage. This was the one he would occupy. He and his own family …

He needn't have made the walk; he knew it was a direct copy of the house his parents would live in. But on his first inspection when Liam had returned, he'd realised it was the house in greater need of repair.

He stepped inside, wanting to see what his own fireplace would look like, to envisage a table there, a chair here, new boards over the earthen floor. To walk into rooms where his children would grow up. He stood at the doorway and inhaled deeply. Here he would begin his life again. Here, by the river. Though a depression loomed and another drought already crept over the colony again, with careful considered work he would have an abundant life.

Despite his cautious steps and a dull throb at his temple where the stitches ended, his heart rate sped up. Yes, here he would establish himself. A room on either side of the hallway directly off the verandah, a dining room come parlour, and another room opposite that. Out the back door was the kitchen room, a wash-house and the outhouse further back. A few old orange trees stood skeletal and abandoned beside an old lean-to that was perhaps once a tack room. He wondered what stock the family would decide to plant. The round-table discussions were always robust and lengthy until final decisions were made. Something for him to look forward to.

The Murray River meandered in the near distance, the large stands of gums towering above its banks. In the quiet, standing on the back step, Ard thought he heard the *whoomp* and chug of a steamer, though he couldn't tell from which direction.

A lot to plan, a lot to do. Prepare the land, feed themselves, purchase stock and equipment … He still might have to seek work on the river to help fill the coffers.

Whatever he had to do, he would. It would be a good life. He would make it so.

There was only one other person to convince.

Fifty-Two

James sat at CeeCee's bedside in the hospital ward. Holding one of her hands between his, he massaged absently as he spoke.

'I don't know if you can hear me, my darling girl, but I'll keep talking to you anyway.' He lifted her hand to kiss it. 'Linley and Toby are quite fine, still at Annie's place until I can convince Linley it's safe to go home.' He rested her hand on the bed. 'You'll be pleased to know that I had no need to deal with Wilkin. Without my assistance, he came to his own end, and it was a sorry one at that.' He rubbed her forearm, testing its warmth under the cotton of her nightdress. 'Poor Mrs Bailey is not so fine, but they say she just needs a lot of rest.'

There didn't seem to be any reaction. He kept up the news delivery.

'I received a letter from Mr Campbell yesterday. He is fine, too. And Miss Juno sent one along. I must say she is very interested in what we do. And they both asked after you …' He paused at that and cleared his throat. 'Mr Campbell told me to tell you that all is well with Toby's succession. Probate has come through and there's a tidy sum waiting for Linley to sign for it. He's thinking to travel here to save her going there.'

CeeCee's eyes were closed; her breathing seemed normal, her face serene. The bruises on her neck had faded in the obvious areas, and others were appearing, not as new or angry ones, but ones that were deeper and finally coming to the surface.

The doctor still didn't know if she'd ever come back to him.

It felt like his heart was breaking all over again. 'I promised you, my love,' he whispered. 'I've stopped, and now you must come back, else what was it all for if not for you and me, together?' He lifted her hands to his lips and pressed them to his face.

He sucked in a breath, battling to staunch the emotion squeezing his chest. 'Millie is coming along nicely. She's a brave one, that one. And Annie is bearing up well, looking after the children as well as Millie. That's just as brave, wouldn't you say?' He smiled in case she opened her eyes. 'Linley helps, too. She's feeling very useful. And I'll have you know, she's written to your suffrage ladies about you. I can't remember all their names, but you will know who. It looks like Linley will take up our mantle, darling CeeCee.'

His Cecilia Celeste. She had defended her family almost to the death. Stood and fronted the violence, not once, but twice, with no care for her own safety. Violence was not unknown to her; the chance of it finding them was there every day as she undertook her work. But it hadn't got this close since Jeffrey Laurence.

Long ago, her sister's husband had threatened violence on CeeCee. That was the man's last threat. James had made sure of it and never looked back.

But was it wise to continue their work? Was it something they could bear if the violence came home to them again? They had brought this into their lives, but if they didn't do this work, who would? Who would give those women and children a home, safe from this madness that hid itself behind the so-called sanctity of marriage and the family?

And at what cost to us? I could have lost her this time, lost Linley and Toby as well. I can only be in one place at a time.

His chest expanded uncomfortably at that thought. He hadn't been there for CeeCee then, had sent Ard instead. Yet he felt he'd done the only thing he could. A split-second decision. Millie had been in his care from the moment she'd crawled up the steps of the Melbourne sanctuary and she deserved to be taken care of.

And if Ard *hadn't* been available to be ordered to the other house, to go to CeeCee?

Well, yes. I'd have had to leave Millie. And I would have.

James continued with his report. 'We have another coming to stay soon. Agnes, remember? She doesn't have a child, which is a good thing for her. She is escaping a particularly dire situation.'

Sighing heavily, he leaned back in the seat and laced his fingers. He didn't need to tell CeeCee the particulars right now. She hadn't stirred. She looked tranquil. Did it mean she suffered no pain, that she was just resting after the ordeal, the shock, and that she was only taking time to heal?

Emotion bunched in his throat. He pulled himself together, let her hands lie on the bed, and continued with his news.

'And Ard O'Rourke is on his new block here. Lovely hundred acres with river frontage. His family have come back and they'll be building it up with him. I believe he has a sister who'll return to live and work on the place, too. Fruit and vegetables are their expertise, and now they've some good knowledge of irrigation. But Ard's intent on breeding horses. So he says there's much to learn. Meantime, for wages, he'll find work on the boats, if he can.' He scraped forward in the chair and took her hands. 'I don't know how, but he and Linley need to find each other again. They have a baby to raise.'

Did he see a tiny smile then? No. No, just imagined he did. Wished he did.

'CeeCee, come back,' he whispered, a hoarse cry at the back of this throat. He pressed her hand to his face.

Come back.

Fifty-Three

Ard had been discharged before Linley had come back to see him. Not that he thought she would, but he'd hoped for it.

Over two weeks now. Two weeks of listening to his father boom about the plans for the new block. 'Rivermore' Pa wanted to call it, though Eleanor had her reservations, so as yet the place was still unnamed. Ard thought 'O'Rourke's Run' would be the obvious name, but his mother shrugged and glanced at his father. Liam had come and gone again, stating that he didn't care what it was called as long as he had somewhere to stay when he returned.

They'd ordered root-stock of apricot and peach and olive. Lorcan had visited a Mr Lenne over the way on the Campaspe River, only a few miles away. He'd introduced himself to the orchardist, keen to glean his advice and to strike up a friendship. Mr Lenne's place was remarkably productive and Lorcan had indeed been impressed.

On their new block, vegetable stock of potato, cabbage and cauliflower was already in the ground, and runners had been constructed for peas and beans. Eleanor looked forward to the first crop of her own apricots, though she knew it would be a few years off. She was happily surprised and delighted that Mr Lenne had sent some home with Lorcan for her.

While Ard convalesced, his was the job of measuring up and ordering timbers for the house's flooring. He drove the cart back into Echuca to pick up supplies—his body adjusting to the ride to and fro. He was also to bring back bits and pieces of furniture so they could get by until their own came upriver by boat.

Loading up the last of the stores from the grocer's, he heard a familiar voice call out.

'Ard!'

And there was Sam Taylor, driving a laden cart covered with rope taut across its cargo. Pie was tied to the cart and Bolter was harnessed.

'G'day, Sam,' he called and waved. He had written to Sam as promised, once his parents had arrived. 'I didn't expect you for another week.'

Sam pulled his cart over to the side of the road to tail Ard's. He tied off the reins and leapt off the seat. 'Told you no point staying in Bendigo. Me pa said I could help you out. So here I am. And there might be paid work besides, somewhere.' Dusting himself down, he lifted off his ragged and sweat-stained hat and swiped his forearm over his face.

'If you're lucky.' Ard leaned on his cart, rested a bit. Sometimes the wind just got knocked out of him for no good reason. Didn't last for long, but he wasn't pushing it. He looked past Sam to the cart he'd pulled in. 'What you got in there?'

'Your ma's table, lad, and everything else I could fit on that wasn't burned. Took me four days to get here.' Sam drew up an elbow and knocked Ard's shoulder. Then he balked at Ard's face. 'Oh, your shoulder. Sorry, mate. You said in your letter.'

Ard's eyes watered at the soft thud. Pain shot up his neck and into his face. He knocked off his hat and slid to the ground.

Sam's eyes popped. Dropping to his haunches, he laid a hand on Ard's other shoulder. 'Jesus, look at you. I'm sorry, laddie.'

Sweat broke out on Ard's forehead, and for a moment it felt like his eyeballs were spinning.

'Ard? *Ard!*' A woman's voice rang out.

His gaze widened. He felt Sam slide around beside him to see who was shouting.

A whoosh of feminine skirts and a faint whiff of something flowery wafted up Ard's nose.

'Ard, are you all right?' She dropped beside him and a slender hand gripped his forearm.

He stared at Linley.

Sam stood up. 'Miss Linley. Fancy seeing—'

'Help me, Sam. Help me get him up.'

Sam held his hands out. 'No, no, perhaps he's best on the ground a minute. He took faint or something. He's all right, I reckon.'

Linley stayed where she was, staring at Ard. He tried to focus properly on her.

Linley.

A man from the footpath had a grip on her pram. 'Miss? Your baby carriage … Miss!'

Linley broke away from Ard's side. 'Thank you,' she said to the gentleman. He eased the perambulator off the footpath and handed it over to her. She checked inside at its occupant and breathed a sigh.

Ard swallowed down a curling nausea. Stars in his eyes were fading and his scalp had returned to normal but the aching thud at the back of his shoulder still sucked the voice from him.

Sam turned to her. 'Miss Linley.' He peered into the baby carriage. 'Is this Mary's baby?'

'Yes. Mary's baby.' She ducked back down to Ard. 'Are you all right?' She repeated, gripping his chin. 'Ard?'

He nodded. *Linley. And the baby.* 'Linley,' he croaked. He took her hand and held it at his face.

'What's the matter with you? What happened?' Linley turned to his friend. 'Sam?'

Sam was still looking into the pram, staring hard at the baby. He frowned, looked at Ard, then turned back again. 'I just told him I brought his ma's table.' He looked into the pram again. 'The big sook fainted.'

'He got stabbed in his side, Sam, under his shoulder.'

'Yeah. I forgot that for a moment.'

Ard dropped Linley's hand. 'I'm all right, got my breath back. Give me a hand up.' He waved to Sam.

Sam thrust out his arm and Ard looped it with his. He clawed his way up the cart. Once standing, he rested on it, steadied, and leaned over to look into the pram.

So did Sam. 'Ard, lad.' His voice was low and rough. 'Have you got something to tell your best mate?'

Ard inhaled, ignoring Sam. He felt Linley bristle beside him. 'Linley, please, let me call on you.' He took her hands in his. They seemed dwarfed against his callused fingers and big-boned knuckles.

Sam moved fast. 'I'm going to, uh, get old Bolter here a drink,' he said and climbed back into his seat. 'I'll wait for you over there, Ard.' He pointed to the horse trough down the street. 'And we'll take this stuff to your place,' he called over his shoulder.

Ard looked back at Linley and the still-sleeping baby.

She rocked the pram a little. 'I would have thought you too busy now, Ard O'Rourke, to come calling.' The pram rocked some more.

'Busy, yes. We are.' Ard just knew she was going to try and get away quickly. He swallowed down the urge to babble. 'Building up the orchard. I've still got the floors to do in my cottage.' He thumbed at the timber in the back of his cart. 'I've got to—'

'Very interesting.' The pram rocked and rocked.

He looked down at Toby again, his heartbeat thudding in his throat. 'He looks very fine, Linley.'

She rocked and rocked some more. 'He is very fine. He is well looked after.'

Had her voice softened just a little? He couldn't let her go, not without a promise to let him call on her. 'I'm sure of that.' He glanced into the pram. 'And, um, Miss CeeCee, is she improving?'

He watched the bloom of colour diffuse her cheeks. A small shake of her head. 'Neither improves nor deteriorates.'

Ard nodded. ''Tis not a bad thing, then.'

She lifted her chin. 'True enough. Now, we must get on with our errands.'

Ard stepped away from the cart. 'Can I help?'

'No.' She pushed the pram past him.

'Linley.' He had to stop her.

'Good day, Ard.'

Her coppery-red hair shone as it peeked out from under her hat. 'Linley, I have a house on the property, I'm repairing it. I have prospects again. I'll work hard.'

'You do that, Ard O'Rourke.' She kept going, past the horse tied to his cart.

He followed. 'I won't give up.'

She stopped then. His heart hammered and that sent an ache back through his head.

'You already did that.' She glanced at the baby in the pram.

'I didn't give up. I didn't *know* about the baby. I swear, if I'd have known—'

'You *must* have known. Isn't that why you left?' Her voice was anguished, low, and her eyes darted about the street. Then she checked herself, and moved on.

He followed. 'I *swear* I didn't know.' He fell in alongside her, patting his shirt pocket. 'I still have Mary's letter to me, the one where she told me—'

'I have to get stores. Excuse me.' She pushed away again in a hurry.

Ard stopped. His voice rose. 'Tell me when I can call, Linley?' Then he realised there were startled looks from passers-by.

She didn't answer. He watched as she pushed the pram back onto the footpath again and stalked into the grocer's shop.

Fight rose in him like a whirling dust devil. His throat dried. Mindful of his aching side, he turned and strode back to the cart, picked up his hat and climbed into the driver's seat. Checking his clearance, he pulled out onto the road and drove towards where Sam had parked.

He pulled behind the water trough. 'Mind my cart, Sam.' He eased to the ground, tethered the reins, then began to cross the street.

Sam stepped alongside. 'Ard, take it from me—don't go chasing an angry woman.'

Ard pushed past him.

'I mean it.' Sam stepped in front and held out his hand in Ard's way. 'Besides, you're in the street, man,' he growled. 'You'll embarrass her more than you'll do yourself any good. End up shooting off your own foot.'

Ard stopped. Sam was very rarely serious, but when he was …

His head still hurt, and the blood still pounded through him. He had to stop, or he'd fall in his tracks. He glanced at Sam, and nodded.

Sam nodded in return. 'Let's get you and me back to your block. I got these things to deliver to your ma. And on the way, we'll stop and you can tell this whole story to your old mate here.'

'Nothing to tell, Sam.'

'That so, Ard? I reckon there might be. Mary's boy is in that baby cart with Miss Linley, and he's got the O'Rourke stamp on him, no mistake.'

———

They drove in single file out of town, Ard's cart in front of Sam's. A couple of miles down, Ard pulled over under the shade of a huge stand of gums on his left.

'You want rum?' Sam called as he hauled his cart to halt.

'No.' Ard alighted carefully, and sat on the ground amid the leaf litter and dry twigs. Shade was good. He had his water flask and swigged from that, then drew up a knee and rested his arm on it.

Sam sat beside him, his own water flask in his hands. 'Mary Bonner,' he said. 'She always did have her skirts ready to go up for you.'

'Ballocks.'

'And I'm wrong about that kid being yours?'

Ard blew out a breath. 'No, you're not. I believe that it's true. Mary wrote me.'

'You can believe it, all right. He's only a wee tacker, but he's yours. If I hadn't seen that O'Rourke brand on him, I might have doubted it, I might not have believed Mary writing you're a da.'

Ard felt the two letters against his chest. 'When she wrote me … what she said. I had no doubt of it.'

'How long you known?'

Ard glanced over at Sam. 'Only when you told me.'

'What?' Sam's head came up. 'You just said she wrote to you.'

'The first I knew of it you told me in the pub that time. You said that Mary gave him to Linley. Before that, I thought they both died when Mary was birthing.' Ard rubbed his head, keeping his hands away from his scars.

Sam stared at him. 'Was that the first you knew he was alive?'

'Swear.' Ard held Sam's gaze.

'Shit.' Sam took a swig of water, wiped his mouth. He frowned a moment. 'So, what happened to your shoulder? Linley didn't stab you herself, did she?' He snorted. 'Mind you, if she did, she'd have done a proper job of it. Maybe she should have. She's loved you forever.'

Ard slid his leg down and crossed his ankles. 'Toby—my boy— had money coming to him. Mary's husband thought it would go to him on her death, but he had to be guardian of the baby and he wasn't.' Ard shook his head. 'He came after Linley and Toby, here in Echuca. And Miss CeeCee, he grabbed her by the throat. Nearly killed her. Got me in the end.' Ard waved a hand at his side. 'It's a long story. Over now. The man's dead. Accident, they reckon.'

Sam shot him a look. 'You didn't do it?'

'No.'

'Was a nasty little bugger,' he said. 'Your ma and pa know about the baby?'

'No. Only Linley's aunt and that Mr Anderson.'

Sam sat quiet a moment.

'What?' Ard asked, swatting flies.

'You gonna marry Linley?'

Ard inhaled loudly and exhaled long. 'I want to. God knows I want to. I've been thinking up ways to get her to talk to me. At least, meet me to talk and …'

'If that's what you want,' Sam said, hammering one hand into the palm of his other, 'then you don't give up, laddie.'

Ard gave Sam a sideways glance. 'And you're a good one to talk.'

'I haven't given up. I'm thinking up ways to get to talk to your sister, don't you worry about that. Just need time. The trick's never giving up.'

'I won't,' said Ard. 'But I don't reckon she'll have me, no matter what I do.'

Sam nodded. 'I know that feeling well.'

Fifty-Four

Linley, with Toby in her arms, perched herself on the edge of CeeCee's hospital bed. Toby had been fed just before she left the house and though he'd gurgled up some of his lunch, he seemed content to gaze quietly at his surroundings. He had a good strong set of lungs on him, as Annie had said more than once. She had good reason. Linley hoped he wouldn't take it upon himself to bring the hospital ward down on their heads today.

CeeCee was again propped up on some thin pillows. Her eyes were open and it appeared she focused on Linley. However, there didn't seem to be any reaction.

Linley talked anyway, rocking Toby in her arms. The pram was nearby and if he fell asleep she could put him in it and stay a bit longer with her beloved aunt.

'... Of course, Annie wouldn't have it, but Millie insisted and so there was almost a fight in the kitchen. So now, a fence is built, but only a low one so we can see over it. Miss Agnes Blackwell is coming soon, and James is in a hurry to build extra accommodation. Oh, he's probably told you that himself.'

A nurse heading in their direction caught Linley's eye. 'All that chatter, miss. You must know she can't hear you,' she said, a pitying little smile on her face. 'There's no response, you see.' She worked around the bed, straightening linen, fluffing pillows, sniffing close to CeeCee's person. Satisfied, she stood up, then felt CeeCee's forehead. 'She seems comfortable. Not in need of changing. You'll have to think of placing her somewhere soon.'

Linley started. 'What did you say?'

'She can't stay here, miss.' She turned smartly on her heels and walked to the next bed.

Linley sat up straight and frowned. 'My aunt will stay here until something changes.'

The nurse turned, and smiled a sad, condescending smile. 'Is that right, miss?' She turned back again, straightening up around the poor patient in the next bed.

'And I will go on speaking to her until she wakes up. You don't know that she's deaf.'

'Of course, miss. Whatever you prefer to do.' More tucking and pulling and slapping of linen.

Linley felt the heat under her blouse thread into her cheeks. 'And another thing, nurse.' She waited until the woman stopped. 'Sometimes I talk to her for my sake because I miss her that much. I can't see why anyone would think both of us are imbeciles.'

The nurse's features changed instantly. 'Well, I ...' But nothing else was forthcoming. She turned smartly back to the other bed. Her brisk businesslike efforts of before were now more moderate, considered, until she clearly sought to remove herself from her own embarrassment. She marched off down the ward and out the door.

Toby grumbled and Linley tried to calm herself. How would anyone know what her aunt heard or didn't hear? She looked back at CeeCee. Was that a tiny frown on her brow? 'Don't you worry, Aunty. I will keep chattering until you tell me not to.'

Placing her somewhere soon. How ludicrous. She would report to James. And if it did mean CeeCee had to be moved out of the hospital, Linley would look after her aunt. Why, perhaps Annie, or Millie once she was well, would help, too.

Another deep breath. 'I have been writing to, and receiving letters from the Goldstein ladies, and Mrs Lawson, who all wish you speedy recovery. And they report they are happy to continue writing to me. They are very interested in our houses for the ladies, and our work, and I've told James as much. He seems happy for me to continue. I know you would be happy.' She jiggled the baby.

'And Toby is very fine, as you can see,' Linley continued. 'He's growing and growing and soon will be on solid food. He's three months now and very active. Sometimes it looks like he can nearly sit up by himself. I haven't seen any sign of teeth yet, but Annie said we'd know the moment one was going to appear.'

CeeCee's gaze hadn't left Linley's face. Was that a questioning look?

Ard. It seemed for some reason his name hung in the air between them.

Linley took a breath. 'And did you know that Ard and his family are on a block here? Yes, by the river. A wonderful place I've heard. James has been there. He tells me all about it. It has two houses on it, Ard is in one, and they've planted all manner of fruit and vegetables. Ard is apparently building stables. He has his friend with him. I don't know if you remember Sam Taylor. He was a bit of a lad, you know, but he seems to have grown up now. Oh yes, and Ard is well now too, James says. Oh, James might already have told you all that too.' Linley fiddled with Toby's shawl.

Ard, the father of this baby.

She bounced Toby a little.

Ard who saved CeeCee's life.

'And of course, I am happy as well.' She felt the tears sting her eyes. 'I am, Aunty,' she said and looked down at Toby.

Ard.

Fifty-Five

The midafternoon sun beat down and the dusty main street baked in the early summer heat. Flies buzzed around the horses and carts. Shopkeepers swept their verandahs, futile but busily. The clanging of the smithy's hammer on his anvil echoed and swooped along the street.

Nary a breeze moved among the great gums. The smell of the river hung in the air, faint, dank with drying tree roots and vegetation as the water level receded a little more. Now and again the blast of a steam whistle rent the air.

Ard and Sam were ready to head home, waiting for Eleanor, who'd come with them for her haberdashery, when Ard spotted Linley on the footpath.

Sam was untying the reins outside the bank, ready to turn the cart for home, when he shot a look across at Ard. 'Not that it will bite me on the arse, boyo, but if your ma takes one look at the occupant of Miss Linley's baby cart, your life won't be worth spit.' He nodded to where Eleanor was approaching.

Ard had spotted Linley before Sam, but not his mother nor the path she was taking. It looked to be directly towards Linley, who was by now out the front of the grocer's shop. She was wearing a pale dress, the colour of weak tea, and a plain white hat, soft and wide-brimmed, sat atop her coppery head.

Eleanor O'Rourke was heading along the footpath in Linley's direction. Ard held his breath. Linley stopped and waved at Eleanor, then looked to be packing and tucking something into the pram. His life would indeed be worth dust if his mother saw the baby and made the not-so-unbelievable leap. For sure, she would stop and talk to Linley. He hadn't told his parents; there hadn't been the right moment.

Only last week, four days ago, Linley had shunned him. Ard hadn't had time to regroup and plan. So much work to do and—

Too late. He squinted for an agonised few seconds, and then couldn't help but stare. Linley straightened up and smiled at Eleanor, who didn't even take a peek into the pram. It looked as if they exchanged happy greetings. But when Linley reached in and picked up a bundle to show her and laugh, Ard thought he would fall over dead.

'Time you found your mettle, mate,' Sam said, a chuckle in his voice. 'It's a cauliflower she's holding.'

Ard side-glanced his friend and said nothing. Sure enough, it was a cauliflower. So where was his son?

'If it were me, and it's not, I know it,' Sam began, scratching his head. 'But if it *were* me, I would go up and ask to walk her to the river bank.'

'With my ma there?' Ard blustered.

'No, you daft bugger. But it's time to do something. Can't be gutless forever.' Sam leaned on the cart.

'You can talk.' Ard snorted.

'Aye, I can. It's not my son, the cauliflower.'

Ard looked at the sky. Getting on for late afternoon. His mother would want to be on her way home soon, to get the evening meal on the table, do her chores.

'I'll walk home later. Take ma home without me, tell her … something.'

'You're leaving me alone with your ma?' Sam's eyes popped. 'She hates me.'

'She doesn't hate you.' Ard glanced over at Sam, then back to the women. 'She hates that Maggie's hurting and you're the stupid knucklehead my sister blames.'

'That must be why I'm sleeping in the woodshed.'

'Could be why. But I'd reckon more because my house has no floor and no roof yet.'

Sam kicked the dirt at his feet. 'Don't matter this time of year, anyway. No rain. Woodshed's getting crowded with you in it, though. We best get on with finishing your place.'

'Aye.' Ard's stare hadn't left Linley and her interaction with his mother. They looked like they'd made their goodbyes and his mother entered the grocer's shop. Linley fiddled with something in the pram. Ard stood tall a moment and then strode over the road. In the time he took to get to her, she'd turned the pram and was heading away from the grocer's.

He stepped alongside her. 'Afternoon, Linley.' He tipped his hat.

'Afternoon, Ard,' she said, pleasantly enough.

But he couldn't read her. He continued alongside her a few paces in silence, craning to see into the pram. 'Is my son under those vegetables?'

Linley burst out a laugh. 'No. Toby is at home.' She pushed the pram a little faster. 'It's the only thing I have to pack our stores into. I don't have a horse and cart.'

He pointed to the next cross road. 'Linley, if we take this corner we can go to the river bank.'

She looked at him blankly. 'And why would I do that, Ard O'Rourke?'

He kept up with her. 'Because I want to talk to you. Properly.'

'I have nothing to say.' Linley moved a little faster still and the pram rattled along. She eased it off the footpath.

'I do.' Ard bent to catch her eye. 'I have something to say, Linley.'

'Then you may as well say it now, while we're walking.' The pram bounced over the ruts and stones in the road as her stride lengthened.

He sighed, trotting along with her. 'We can sit in the shade on the bank a while.' He pointed to the river then rubbed his forehead. 'I still can't walk as fast as I'd like—'

'Oh. Of course.' She stopped and turned to him. 'But you'll have to be quick with your talk. The light is going.'

'There's plenty of daylight.' He glanced briefly at the sky. 'Besides, I'll walk you home after.'

She eyed him, hesitant. He couldn't read her expression, but he was encouraged that she hadn't said 'no' again. Indicating they should turn left, he followed as she marched across the road with the baby-less perambulator.

His pulse pounded. His brow furrowed. His shoulder ached. But he was walking with Linley.

———

Linley settled the pram full of vegetables and other groceries against a solid rock jutting out next to where they would sit. She was reasonably sure the thing wouldn't take flight and end up in the river. The old brakes hadn't been fixed so they weren't at all trustworthy.

'I haven't got anything for you to sit on,' Ard said and stood by, waiting until she'd organised the pram.

'I didn't expect you would.' She promptly sat on the sparse patch of grass, the tips of which had browned off. Her dress would hardly be affected by a little dust and dried grass.

He sat beside her. She was sure he would hear her heart thumping. It beat so loud her ears hurt. She knew her face was flaming, but she couldn't decide whether she was angry or nervous or flustered …

'And how is Miss CeeCee?' Hat in his hand, his arm draped over a knee.

'She's opened her eyes, but apart from that, no change.' Linley stared out over the river. Boats were tied to moorings, another chugged quietly in a turn back past the wharf. The cranes were now still. Only a few men could be seen atop, readying for the night.

'And Toby?'

Linley nodded, felt the glimmer of a smile. 'He is well.'

Ard scratched his head, flicked at the dirt at his feet. 'I want to see him, Linley.'

'You can see him.' She tried to smile but her heart thudded so hard, it felt a bit wobbly. 'Though because he has such the look of you, it will be difficult to hide—'

'I don't want to hide him, Linley. Or how he came to be.' Ard slapped his hat on his leg. 'But it is no one else's business.'

Linley's face burned. She glared across the river.

'I found out about him from Sam,' he said.

Ard's leg was close to hers. She brushed down her skirt, tucked it loosely around her, and stared at the far bank. 'How would Sam have known?'

'Not that he was mine, but that he was alive. Mary sent me this.' Two rumpled envelopes came out from his top pocket. He held one out to her, handling it as if it were fragile. 'This came, and then not four days after, or only just, I got your letter.' He looked at the envelopes. 'In hers, she says he's mine and about giving Toby to you if something happened to her.'

Linley swallowed down a catch in her throat. She pressed her hands into her lap, closed her fingers around the fabric of her skirt.

She couldn't look at Ard. She couldn't. She'd break, say something stupid, ridiculous. Something bad.

Ard went on, a jag in his voice. 'I thought both Mary and the baby had died. I didn't know he was alive until Sam told me you had him. Your letter said—'

'I know,' she burst out. Linley still watched the small ripples land on to the banks. 'I know what I said. I remember every word.'

'Had I known then, I—'

'You'd what, Ard O'Rourke?' She spun around to face him. 'You'd what? It was already too late. She was dead.'

'I know, I know.' He held his hands palm up. 'And I'm sorry that happ—'

'You … you'd been *with* her!' Her face screwed up but the dam of emotion burst. She shot to her feet. 'You were with *her* and made a baby, and left,' she rasped between her teeth.

'But I didn't know there was a baby. Look—read what she says to me. Read it, Linley.' He held the letter up to her.

She smacked his hand away. 'I don't want to read it. She was nothing to me! But you were, Ard O'Rourke. You were.' Tears threatened. *No. I. Will. Not. Cry.*

'I know. I'm sorry. I'm sorry.' His eyes squeezed shut a moment.

'*Sorry* for what? You don't even know—'

'I'm sorry I hurt you,' he said, quickly. 'I'm sorry for that.' Staring at his hands, he turned them over and looked at his palms as if there were answers there. 'I am, Linley.' He looked back at her. 'But if she was nothing to you, why is it she wanted you to be the baby's guardian?'

Linley almost stamped her foot. 'Because she knew how I felt about you.' Her voice was too loud. *Too loud, Linley.* She glanced around.

He seemed bewildered, shook his head, the dark hair brushing his collar. 'But that's strange. Odd. Look at what it's doing now, it's making it worse. Is that what she wanted?'

'Don't turn this around, Ard O'Rourke.' Her voice shook, rumbled. 'This is about you.'

Colour shot to his face and his eyes reddened. He clambered to his feet. 'This is about a mistake I made,' he ground out.

'Yes, who is now *three months old*.' Linley felt herself breathless, out of control. She needed to stop shouting, needed to slow her heart rate down. But his face. Looking at that face she loved, wanting to reach out and make it all good, and right and … She couldn't stop a sob of frustration.

He scowled. 'I know how old he is.'

'Oh *really?*' she snapped. And cursed herself. *This is not going to plan, Linley.*

'Stop. Stop.' Ard took a breath. 'Linley. Please. Listen.'

'I don't have to listen. I loved you, Ard O'Rourke and you knew it. But you laid with her and then went away.' She felt the snivel leave her before she could stop it. She thrashed at his hands in front of her. 'You were with her!'

'Linley, it's not what you think,' Ard pressed. 'It was a … a thing, I didn't love her, it was just a thing that just happened and I—'

'A thing? How can it be a *thing?* You made a baby,' she shouted. Aghast, she checked her surroundings. No one was nearby. She had to calm herself. She had to.

Ard put his hands to his head. 'I can't explain … it … to you.'

'That's as lame as an old donkey!' She still shouted. Couldn't seem not to.

Ard let his hands drop. 'If I'd known … Had she come to me and said about the baby, I would have married her.' He met her angry glare. Spoke deliberately. 'I would have, Linley. I would have married Mary.'

She blinked as the tears dribbled down her face.

'I would have married Mary.'

Linley stopped cold. Abruptly, as decisive as the swift cut of a sharp blade, something deep inside, a piece of her, suddenly flew off, and burned to a wisp in the light of day.

Then he'd have been lost to me forever.

She heard the words again in her empty, addled head. *Forever.*

Ard stood taller and turned to face the river. The late-afternoon sun highlighted the stubble on his cheeks, the muscle moving in his jaw. 'But she didn't tell me until after she'd married Wilkin. It's here, in the letter.' He waved it at her. 'Until after she needed help. By the time she let me know that, well, it was too late. A few days later I got your letter.'

And Mary was already dead.

Linley didn't know what she wanted to say. To shout. To berate …
He would have married Mary. She still looked at him blankly.

He blew out a breath. 'It was that time after the picnic—'

'I don't want to know that,' she said brusquely.

'And I'd left you there because I couldn't stand to be with you and not touch you. I know there were no promises between us.' He let out a breath as if he'd been holding on too long. 'I knew I had nothing to offer you. Nothing to make a life with you. And yet I …'

Linley waited.

He let out another long breath, a hand raked through his hair. 'I got back to the orchard and tried to get back to work. But the orchard wasn't making us a living, any of us. I knew I was going to Renmark, didn't know for how long, or where I'd go from there.' He stared at his feet. Shuffled. 'And then, no excuse, but along came another quart of rum—'

'A quart?'

'I didn't *drink* a quart. God knows if I had, I wouldn't have been able to—' He stopped then and looked away.

Linley had no clue what he was about to say.

'Mary was without a care in the world, it seemed. And I—'

'Ard, don't.' She held up her hands.

His jaw firmed up. 'If there wasn't a baby from Mary and me, if there wasn't Toby here and now, we wouldn't be having this conversation.'

Linley shook her head, bewildered. 'What?'

'I wasn't a goddamned virgin, Linley,' he exploded. 'Mary wasn't the only woman I'd had in my life. If it wasn't for Toby, you wouldn't have known about it.'

Burning heat flared in Linley's face. She stepped away, confusion rattling through her. 'Oh. Well, I—'

'Don't even try to make a comment about that,' he ordered gruffly. 'You have no clue about any of that sort of business.' He rubbed a hand over his face. 'If you won't marry me, then I will find other ways to see my son—'

'Marry?' she burst.

'And to help support him.' He threw out a hand.

She spoke softly. 'Ard.'

But he carried on. 'Watch him grow up, have him know my ma and my pa, teach him how to sow a paddock, and ride a horse, steer a riverboat, go fishing and ...' He waved up and down the river.

'Ard.' She held her hand out.

He spun back to her, took a breath. 'Marry me.' He scowled. 'My uncle is finally marrying a woman he's loved for thirty years. I don't want to wait that long. I don't want to go through what he did just because people would talk. I don't.' He glared at her. 'When he told me his story I could see just by looking at him what it had done to him. I don't want that, Linley.'

She cast about for something to grasp. Something she could hold on to, to keep herself together. 'What if I don't want to marry?' she blurted. 'CeeCee never married James. What if I don't want to marry?'

'*What?*'

'I'm going to carry on with the work CeeCee was doing. I am.' She knew her eyes were squinting at him. 'The unmarried women with a child or children, or the deserted ones, the beaten ones, homeless, cast out.' She flung out a pointed finger. 'James and CeeCee have houses, they support … I can't do that with a husband.' She saw her life so clearly in that one moment, all the good she could do. But something else cracked inside her, gave way.

He shook his head to clear it. 'Why can't you do that with a husband?' He still glared at her. 'Why not?'

She glared in return, hands on hips. 'Because you'd want your dinner on the table, or your trousers fixed, or your tea made, or the laundry done, or the fruit preserved—'

'Or my children cared for, fed, bathed. Happy. Exactly what you're doing with Toby, now,' he stormed.

'And I want so much to continue CeeCee's work. I've only scratched the surface of this work, never before fully realised how important it is to me, to be of use.' She clamped a hand on her hat, holding tight. 'To write the letters to champion the causes. To battle with government for education and nurture.' Fists bunched at her hips. 'For CeeCee, as much as me. She gave me so much. And because I don't think she can do it anymore. I can't do both,' she finally shouted.

'You can,' he shouted back at her. 'Because I will be there, too.' He threw his hands in the air. 'Like James is with CeeCee.'

Facing him, shouting at him, believing him, Linley felt her fear fall away. She stood stock still, the light slipping away. She could see the anger slip from him, too.

He reached out and his callused hands closed over hers. She heard him swallow, saw his Adam's apple bob in his neck. 'I have a son, Linley, and you are his guardian. I want to know him, and him to know me, and my family. I want nothing more than for him to have brothers and sisters that are yours and mine.' He looked down at their hands. 'I never wanted a life without you, Linley. Never.' He licked his lips. 'I never had much to offer. I don't know that I have anything much more to offer now, but I will have.'

She looked down at the grip he had on her hands. Felt the caress of the roughened, dense skin. Watched as his large hands engulfed hers.

'And I know,' he said softly, 'if I have you, and everything you are, I will get what we want. For you, for me, for our family. Ours.'

Numb, she withdrew her hands. She backed up the bank, tears falling. It was too much. Too much feeling, too much uncertainty, too much. She turned to walk the rest of the way up the hill. She needed to think.

'Linley?' Ard called.

She had to keep going. She couldn't work out all the things she'd said to him. Where they'd come from, what she had even tried to say. All the things he'd said to her—

'Linley,' he called again, softly this time.

She shouldn't resist this. Why did she want to? She didn't want to. She wanted Ard. Wanted to be with him. She'd go back to him, talk some more. Work something out.

She turned.

'Do I have to walk your cauliflower home alone?' he asked, holding the pram with one hand, and the cauliflower, the huge white floret sitting inside its leafy greens, in his other.

Holding her hat on her head, she hurried the few steps back and stopped a whisker from him. Carefully, he placed the huge vegetable back into the pram.

He slid a hand down her arm, and squeezed her fingers. His other hand came up to her cheeks and a crooked finger stroked the contours of her face.

'It's always been you, Linley.'

Fifty-Six

James nodded at the sister in the ward. 'Just a few more minutes and then I'll be off.'

'It is dinner time, Mr Anderson, and we do need to finish up with our patients so they can get to their sleep.' She waited a moment.

'I heard you.'

She clamped her mouth shut and left him to it.

He remained holding CeeCee's limp hand. Her stare followed him. He was sure she could hear him, could understand him. He squeezed her fingers.

'We will take you home, my darling girl, early next week,' he said and pressed his lips to her fingers. They were warm, pliant. 'I think we will settle here in Echuca, don't you? Linley is here, of course, and we have two staunch allies in Millie and Annie. A couple of new houses to build. What do you say?'

Why couldn't she speak, or at least engage? Nothing but the soft stare, her beautiful dark eyes on his.

'Well, for now, the nurse is ordering me off the premises. I'll go back to Millie's house. I've been staying there until their nerves settle.' He nodded and smiled as if he could imagine her surprise. 'Oh, yes, I sleep in the laundry room. Annie sleeps in Millie's room to tend her in the night, and the little children are in the other room. Linley and Toby sleep in the parlour.' He gave a small laugh. 'It is a very noisy household. So we might have to purchase another house sooner than later. Linley is not in a hurry to return to where you were living.'

He brushed a long tendril of dark hair from her face, tucking it back behind her ear. Cupping her chin, he planted a light kiss on warm but unresponsive lips.

'I'll take you home next week, Cecilia Celeste. And I'll continue to love you and care for you until my dying day, and beyond.' He looked into her eyes and he knew, he just knew she was there.

He clasped her hand in both of his, bent and kissed it, pressed it to his cheek. Felt his tears fall and wet his fingers. Over twenty years he'd known her. Loved her. Had done whatever it took to be with her, on her terms, her way. He loved her. What else would he have done? And in return he got a life of sheer joy and happiness and warmth.

Honour. It was his honour to be with CeeCee, and with her, he had honour. He would never let her down. Ever.

I promise you, CeeCee.

———

Weary, James rode home, not looking forward to the chaos of young children at their mealtime. Perhaps he would move Millie and Annie into the other house so he and CeeCee and Linley could reside in this one. He shook his head at that. Mrs Bailey's house was opposite. Too close a reminder.

He cantered a little way, and turned into their street. Since putting up the fence he had to ride around the back and enter from the gate he'd made. At least the horse had some shelter under the lean-to, with a food bag and a water trough. It was close to the laundry, James' own temporary sleeping quarters. Dismounting, he grunted, then stretched. He was getting too old for this. Time he set about a proper house for him and his lady. The doctor had said it would be a slow recovery for CeeCee, but he was hopeful for a good one. James wanted to be ready.

At the back door, he spied a pair of large boots—a man's boots—alongside a daintier pair. He called out before he entered the house. The children greeted him with happy yells, their pudgy hands clutching bread sopped in dripping, waving at him. Little faces were sodden with mashed food. Millie was scraping bits into open mouths, and wiping faces down, her movements slow but determined. Her face was no longer puffed, and around her eye the bruise was fading to a pale yellow. Annie had just laid her youngest in his crib.

And there was Linley in her house slippers. And Ard in his socks, holding Toby. The expression on the lad's face nearly brought more tears to James' eyes. It was a look of sheer joy. Ard held the bundle of Toby up to greet him, and the smile on Linley's face said more than words ever could.

James felt his chest constrict. This was his family. These people. And they were waiting for him to bring CeeCee home.

'Evening, James,' Ard said, a broad grin across his face. He held out a free hand.

'Evening.' James clasped his hand in a quick grip. 'I see you've found someone who belongs to you.'

'I have indeed. And a bright boy he is, too.'

Toby had a smile on his face, gummy and moving, and his alert little eyes hadn't left Ard's face.

Annie straightened up and adjusted her smock a little. 'Well, the bright boy has to have his dinner now, if you please, Mr O'Rourke.' She held out her hands.

Ard reluctantly handed Toby over, and Linley took his arm. 'Let's go into the parlour. Would you take your dinner with us there, James? You look tired.'

'Thank you, I would. I am.'

Millie spooned cold mutton and hot vegetables and gravy into three bowls for them. They took their leave of the kitchen and sat in the parlour.

James felt old all of a sudden. Worn down. He looked across at these two people who would be lovers, if they were not already, and felt loss, grief. They should be lovers. They should marry and have a long life together. He'd wished to marry CeeCee long before she had finally agreed. By delaying, it meant they'd never lived together. He desperately wanted that, before it was too late. Before he got too much older. Before she died.

He sat his bowl aside, food untouched, and leaned forward, choosing his words carefully. 'I might be too unsteady of late to think clearly,' he began, noticing the look that passed between Linley and Ard. 'But I must take my own course of action now.' He clasped his hands. 'CeeCee will come home soon, to which-ever house we decide—I decide—will be the best for her.'

Ard and Linley nodded.

'So you need to decide, Linley, where you and Toby will live.'

Linley looked as if she had a moment of complete shock. 'Where—?'

'You see,' James continued, his face now lined and hollowed, 'CeeCee will need care as if she were in hospital. Perhaps night and day until she recovers some more.'

'I can be there for her, James,' Linley said.

He sighed. 'You have Toby. And you are to carry on with CeeCee's work, build a stronger foundation for us. You can do it. I know you can. But you can't be looking after your aunt as well.'

'James, I—'

'I will take either Millie, or Annie, or both, and they can nurse her. You can visit, bring her the news, the letters. Be the extra sunshine in an otherwise ...' He paused, seeking the right words. '... lonely day.'

———•———

A tremor of fear skittered up Linley's spine. 'She's not going to die, James.'

He shrugged. He was tired and he looked it. 'I don't know.' He reached into his pocket and withdrew a crinkled paper. 'I nearly forgot. I got this when I registered Toby's birth. It's a marriage licence paper.'

Linley's eyes widened.

'CeeCee agreed we should be married, which is why I have it.' He held the paper as if it were a gold leaf.

'You won't be able to marry unless she can—'

'I know that, Linley. And it is my one other great fear that perhaps we will never be able to marry now,' he said, sadly. 'She has carried my name for a long time, but I would like to protect her lawfully if something were to happen to me. As it stands now, I can't do that unless we are married.'

Linley set her meal down. She knew what he was saying but CeeCee was in no state to agree to marry.

'So until I can work out how to make it so, take this paper. Don't waste it.' He stood up. 'Apparently, there's a pastor here, McNeill. He needs that paper, and a good donation, which I will provide, but he doesn't need a church.' He pressed the paper into her hands. 'In hindsight, I should have made sure CeeCee knew that no matter what she wanted to do, our marriage would protect her, not stifle her. That I would support her to her dying day ...' He inhaled deeply. 'And now I will take my leave for the laundry house before I need my handkerchief.' He looked at Ard. 'You can borrow my horse to go home, lad. I'll leave the saddle out. Bring him back in the morning, early. Goodnight.'

Fifty-Seven

Ard watched as James left. He stooped as he turned away from them and walked through the open door.

Ard picked up his bowl and ate. Mindful of the silence in the room, he thought of two men he knew, grown men—his uncle, and James—worn down by decisions they believed they had no control over.

I do not want to be one of them.

He thought fleetingly of his parents. They seemed happy enough, though he recalled feisty arguments. His mother had always stood her ground. Sometimes she won, sometimes she didn't. It was all about the talking, she'd say.

Linley toyed with her food. Ard glanced around. Toby's crib was opposite the fireplace, a small tallboy chest close by. Next to that, a pallet had been laid on the floor, linens and blankets and pillows strewn upon it. That must be where Linley slept.

'The sort of violence we work against follows a family, Ard.' She drew in a deep breath, pushing the food around with her spoon. 'My own father, for instance. And Gareth Wilkin had a horrible life as a child, so Millie found out. He visited it upon others, upon Mary for one. That's how it works, they say.' Her head was still bowed. 'These women we look after.'

'It's good work you do,' Ard offered.

'I won't leave it now.'

'I don't ask that of you,' he said quietly.

She kept her eyes averted and nodded. He didn't know what else he could do to state his case. It was best to leave it to her own mind, whatever decision she came to when he learned of it.

His heart hammered anew. He needed to feel as if he'd won her over. Had he done enough? He didn't think so, and feared he didn't know what else to do.

Standing, bowl in hand, he said, 'I'm going, Linley. I'll say goodbye to Toby and your friends.' She nodded again. 'Don't want to leave Sam on his own around my mother too long.'

She smiled a little. She stood up and left her bowl on the sideboard.

'Don't be sad.' He took her hand. 'I love you, Linley. I love my wee boy. I want us to be a family, but only when you're ready.'

He kissed her forehead, her nose. He dipped to kiss her mouth. Her lips were soft and warm and open for him, but the moment was lost when she pulled away, shaking her head.

He sighed inwardly. 'I'll see you tomorrow when I bring the horse back.' He hoped for something then, any indication ... Nothing. He shut his eyes briefly then said, 'Goodnight, Linley.'

'Goodnight.' She trailed a hand over the edge of the tallboy.

So he went to the doorway, heart heavy, but tomorrow was another day—

'Ard.' Whisper soft.

His ears rang with her words. He turned back. His brain wasn't working. He just stood there. His feet were lumps of clay in his socks.

'Thank you for saving my aunt's life.'

She stood so close he could see the golden tips of her eye-lashes, the slight crease in her brow. 'Linley, I would have done anything—'

'I know.' She reached up and drew his head down to hers, pressed her lips once more to his.

'Linley,' he breathed, and smoothed his hand down her side. 'You haven't told me,' he said, releasing her, his eyes searching hers.

'Told you what?' Her gaze roved over his face. She slid her hand across his chest, hesitating over the hair there at his collar.

'That you'll marry me,' he answered in a hoarse whisper, close to her ear.

She inhaled, whispered in return. 'No. I haven't.'

———

Ard went into the kitchen. Millie held her hand out for his bowl, but he took it to the pail of warm water still on the stove and dunked it.

He scrubbed at it fiercely with the dishrag; any excuse not to leave. He looked around for other plates and bowls. With no more in sight, he shook his hands free of dishwater and dried them on a towel hanging on the stove rail.

'No more to do here, Mr O'Rourke,' Millie said, eyes wide. 'Though I have to say, 'tis a rare sight to see a man with a dishrag. P'raps we should find more dishes, some pots and pans just to see it again.'

He laughed, and hoped the happiness, the pure joy of being with Linley, wasn't somehow written all over his face.

Annie had Toby over her shoulder. She turned so Ard could see the baby's face. 'He's ready for his bed, Mr O'Rourke.'

'So am I, Mrs Rutherford.' He held out a finger to the snuffly baby, who gave him a wide-eyed stare. 'Thank you for looking after him.' His chest felt like it would burst.

'Pleasure's all mine while it's lasted. He's a fine little lad. Won't need me much more now, if Mrs O'Rourke can manage with cow's milk.' Annie bobbed Toby up and down.

'Of course.' Ard had no clue about the feeding of babies. He tipped his forehead and said, 'Goodnight'. Didn't miss the exchange of looks between the two women as he left the kitchen. *Yes, indeed. Why aren't I staying with 'Mrs O'Rourke'?*

True to his word, James' saddle sat outside the laundry door. Ard buckled it on the horse, a muscular Waler by the look of him, mounted and rode away. He'd take a keener look at him tomorrow in the daylight. He needed to learn more about the horse-breeding business. All very well to fall back on the family's traditional trade of fruit and vegetables. But there were many opportunities to establish another line of income before the drought and another depression sunk its vulture-like talons into the place.

Home was two miles or thereabouts out of town so he wouldn't be in the saddle long. His shoulder ached a little, but he barely noticed. He smiled.

Linley. His beautiful Linley. Passionate, fiery … She'd told him to leave. And he'd done as she asked. He'd sleep on what to do next. How to approach her, court her. No doubt about it. Give it time and court her. Make her see he was right for her.

Work hard. Learn fast. Keep—

See his boy grow.

That was all-important. Toby O'Rourke needed his family, too.

Dusk lengthened the shadows, but there was still plenty of light to see the road. Ard rode home a little faster than he should have. At the first cottage, he slid out of the saddle, undid the girth buckle and hoisted it off the horse. He felt his injury snag again. If he wasn't smart, he'd be taking longer to recover than he was warned about. He had to be smart from now on.

He led the horse to the trough, tethered the reins to a post, grabbed a cloth that hung nearby and gave him a quick rub down. A pail of oats would do until morning, before he returned the horse to James Anderson. Perhaps he'd see Linley again then.

He turned to the house in which his parents now resided. A light flickered up the hallway. They'd be in the kitchen at dinner, perhaps just finished. Laughter, two male voices. Sam must be in there, still. He smiled to himself. His friend might yet win over his mother after the falling out with his sister.

Ard took a big breath and opened the door. His footsteps clomped down the newly floored hallway. He swallowed and let the breath go.

Eleanor's eyes lit up when she saw him. Lorcan lifted his pannikin of tea in his direction, a smile splitting his much-loved face. Sam nodded, a flicker of mirth in his eye.

'You're home, lad. Heard a damned cauliflower got the better of you,' his father boomed and stuck the pipe into his mouth.

Ard looked at his mother and she instantly stilled. He looked at Sam, who nodded at him. Encouragement.

Dry mouthed, he licked his lips. 'I have a son, and he's with Linley Seymour.'

Fifty-Eight

Linley jiggled an active Toby while she sat at CeeCee's hospital bed. Though he was happy enough, cackling and gurgling and squeaking, he wouldn't keep still.

'Sorry, Aunty, he's a handful today.' She jiggled him a bit more. 'Like I said, Ard O'Rourke asked me to marry him the other day.' Her heart did a little jump and she felt herself burn up. She looked for a response from her aunt but there was none. CeeCee's eyes were on her, and though she looked as if she'd heard, there was no indication.

'But of course, there's a lot to think about ahead of that and I certainly didn't give him an answer. For one thing, we have to get you and James into the new house and get you settled and everything.'

Toby wriggled and gurgled some more. Perhaps he was hot? The weather was certainly getting warmer, full summer not far off.

'James has found something to buy. He's also put *that* house up for sale and the agent says he has a buyer already. Especially when James reduced the price so much to get rid of it.' She waggled Toby high in the air above her head and he oohed happily. She brought him down again and bumped him up and down on her knee.

'James says Mr Campbell is coming in the next weeks, so we can sign the papers for Toby. That saves all of us going to him.

He's such a good advocate for us,' she said. 'And I will be heartily glad to get that over and done with.'

Toby squirmed around and reached for CeeCee. He waved a little fist at her and made some noises. He leaned right over and Linley struggled to hold him up. Instead, she checked for a safe place to rest him and then put him on the bed. On his stomach, he gurgled happily, his head lifted in CeeCee's direction.

And that was when CeeCee turned her gaze on him.

Linley held her breath.

CeeCee's eyes focused on Toby and narrowed, just the merest of a squint but it was there. Toby cooed at her, wobbling, with a grin and a gurgle simultaneously. He plopped his head down then, the effort clearly all too much. He gurgled some more, but the noises were fading off. Then he shut his eyes and was asleep.

Linley turned him on his side and covered him with her shawl. She looked at her aunt again. Those wide-open eyes were back on her.

'Aunty.' She absently patted Toby's back. 'I think you're getting better.'

Her eyes only blinked as they normally would. But Linley had seen the squint. Her aunt was still in there, and she had focused on Toby.

Dr Wilson had said hers was most likely an injury still healing. He said there was new information in the medical journals now, a school of thought regarding injuries to the brain. Perhaps CeeCee had hit her head harder than anyone imagined. Or perhaps it was in her mind. Some were beginning to note that this could be a type of injury, too, the doctor said. He also said that strangulation patients sometimes presented with very different and unusual symptoms.

She stared at her aunt. CeeCee stared back. The flicker of whatever Linley thought she had seen was gone. She squeezed her aunt's hand and carried on.

'I have decided to take in Mrs Bailey when we have the other house for more ladies. It appears she has not fully recovered her wits. She's not decrepit, the doctor says, just in some sort of shock.' Linley glanced at CeeCee but there was no discernible response. 'Mrs Bailey is Gareth Wilkin's sister.' Still nothing. 'Anyway, if Millie can forgive her for her nastiness, I think we can give her a safe place to recover. After all, she can't fully look after herself yet. She has nowhere else to go.'

She doubted Mrs Bailey would want to go back into her own house after her brother's shocking death in it. Linley shuddered, and continued to pat Toby on the back, a rhythmic pulse that lulled both of them.

'And I've heard again from Mrs Lawson and her suffragists. She's going to visit South Australia and be with the ladies when they cast their first vote.' She shifted in her seat, laughing a little. 'I think she's very brave, don't you? I'd be full of nerves at that. There might be trouble at the polls. People can be so stupid, can't they?' Linley took CeeCee's hands in hers and massaged her fingers. 'But I know it's one place you'd *love* to be.'

She glanced down at the warm fingers in hers, at CeeCee's left hand. She frowned, touching the knuckle of her aunt's ring finger. 'Would you marry now, Aunt? Would you marry James?' She pondered aloud, and kept rubbing the finger. 'Would you have waited this long if you had your time over again?' Linley felt tears gathering. 'I don't know if I can wait, Aunty, or if I even want to.' She bit her lip. 'But I'd feel as if I was letting you down by marrying, somehow.' She glanced at Toby sleeping, his mouth open and a little snore emanating. 'I look at Toby and I see Ard. I look at Ard and I believe I so want a baby of my own. Of Ard's.'

There. She'd said it. She sat back a little, gazing at CeeCee's face. The dark eyes were clear, watching, but there was no facial expression except the resting one.

Then, there, on her fingers—a slight pressure.

Linley stilled, looking at CeeCee's face. No expression. Was that tiny pressure real or had she imagined it?

She took a breath. 'Would you marry James, Aunt?' she asked again.

Pressure, like a little tremor on her fingers.

It *was* real. *It was real.*

How would she know if it meant anything, much less a 'yes' or a 'no'? Her mind cast about.

'You would marry James?' Again the tremor. Her aunt's eyes were steady on hers.

Linley searched for a question, the answer to which would give her something definitive. 'Is your name Cecilia Celeste?' A tremor. 'Is Toby a girl?' Nothing. 'Is Toby a boy?'

Pressure.

'Is my name Tommy Tucker?'

Nothing.

'Is my name Linley Seymour?'

Pressure.

Tears spurted out of Linley's eyes. She backtracked a bit, her heart in a pitter-patter with relief, excitement. 'I so want a baby of my own, with Ard,' she said again. And there was the pressure, a tremor. Linley bent to kiss her aunt's hand, her breath short, her voice ragged. 'Oh, welcome back, Aunty.'

Toby awoke with a squawk and his face screwed up and reddened. Then something else occurred.

'Oh dear,' she said and crinkled her nose, swiping away happy tears at the same time. 'We have to take you away and change you, Toby.'

And the ever-so-light pressure on her fingers made her laugh aloud.

Fifty-Nine

Ard stood back and watched as Sam hammered the last of the iron onto the roof of his cottage.

'How's it look?' Sam yelled.

'Looks good.' Ard yelled back.

Sam shinnied down the ladder. Then he stood back and surveyed his work. 'If I do say so myself.' He dusted down his trousers and grabbed the water bucket, pouring it over himself, head to toe.

'Just in time, too,' Ard commented.

Sam snorted. 'If you hadn't been so tardy with the extra trusses we'd have been done by now.'

Ard looked down the paddock to where the frontage met the river. The bank didn't drop away much, the summer water level not a great depth below. Last week they'd finished putting in a makeshift landing until they could build something sturdier. Ard had decided to use his first round of roof trusses to build the landing's frame. 'Just lucky we built it up over the high-water mark.'

Sam barked a laugh. 'River comes up, mate, it'll take out a few miles or more around here. Your paddle-steamers will sail past the houses.' He took off his shirt and wrung it out. 'That won't be for a while, though, by all accounts.'

Along with the landing, Ard and Sam had put all their energy into rebuilding. When it wasn't work on the cottage, it was ploughing up the block, and planting his season's stock and vegetables. They marked out the trenches for irrigation then secured a team to help dig them. Plenty of men were available to work.

Lorc had taken Ard and Sam to Mr Lenne's property to inspect his centrifugal pump. Over the river on the New South Wales side, they visited a Mr McLaren who had a Tangye pump—a steam engine with eight horse power. Both properties were long established and flourishing. Irrigation would suit Ard well, and the sooner the better.

Sam had done the harder work in the early days of Ard's recovery, but slowly, carefully, and looking after himself, Ard had been able to pull his weight. The landing had been his idea. His uncle's son, Dane MacHenry, was still running boats and Ard wanted a place for him to tie up for when they'd eventually meet. Liam was bringing Dane's mother Jemimah with him from Swan Hill the next week, and all being well, theirs would be the first boat to tie up at O'Rourke's Landing.

Mr Egge had said he'd tie up for a visit with the *Murrumbidgee,* once he'd off-loaded. Maybe take Ard downriver a time or two before he finally retired. Ard had caught up with Mr Egge when he'd bought stock for his mother off his boat at the main wharf last week.

A week and a half had gone by since Ard had told his parents about his son. Eleanor, stunned at first by the news of Toby, as he fully expected, had made it her business to go to Linley immediately she could—the following day—to meet her grandson. Lorc had gone along, just as her driver, mind you, he'd said, but he wasn't fooling anyone.

Though there had been no formal request to visit, Linley must have expected them at some point because she met them with open arms. Eleanor couldn't keep the smile off her face. Lorc had been smitten. By all accounts, it was a happy, joyous meeting.

A roaring, unrelenting summer was biting at their heels, but the family was moving on schedule. Their block was taking shape.

'Ard.' Eleanor was walking across from her house. The fifty or so yards between the houses was becoming a worn path. 'You have about an hour before they arrive. See that you get washed up. And you too, Mr Taylor.'

'We finished the roof, Ma.' Ard pointed above.

'It's a fine thing.' She stood and surveyed Ard's cottage, hand on hips. 'Very fine.' She flashed them a wide smile and headed back to her house.

Sam threw his shirt back on. 'You say Mr Anderson is bringing a solicitor from Bendigo?'

'Mr Campbell. He's come to visit Linley and CeeCee with papers he needs signing off. James is bringing them for the day.'

It would give CeeCee an outing, too, James had said. She'd recovered well enough to be driven in the buggy and sit for an afternoon's social occasion. And James would clearly welcome the diversion and the business of Mr Campbell's.

Not to mention that the visit would allow Eleanor and Lorcan a chance to dither about over their grandson again. At least they hadn't the worry of local society bothering itself with the baby's origins. Ard had made it clear that Linley already carried his surname. If they married, it could be quietly and with no fuss to embarrass anyone.

Ard couldn't wait to see his boy again. Or Linley. His heartbeat banged a moment or two. He sucked in a breath. *Calm down, calm down.*

He and Linley hadn't had time together since the night at her place. Every day since, it seemed his plans were thwarted no matter what tack he took, and the days stretched. It made him nervous. What if she would reject him? What if she wouldn't consent to being his lawful wife? His hands became clammy. He rubbed them down his pants. *Steady yourself, man.*

He needed her to see his progress. He needed her to see he was serious and intent on his family being together. Ard was sure the house would impress her. He'd take her on a tour of the place, point out the new roof, show her the marked-out trenches, the landing … He and Sam had done so much, yet there was so much more to do, to complete—

'You've got those stars in your eyes again, laddie.' Sam slapped a hand on his shoulder.

'I'm not giving up hope.' Though Ard heard the creep of doubt in his voice.

———

Ard watched Mr Campbell adjust his glasses. 'Excellent lunch, thank you, Mrs O'Rourke,' he said to Eleanor. 'And a fine shady spot it is here on the verandah.'

Ard and Sam had lugged Eleanor's prized table out from the kitchen to under her new verandah for the lunch occasion. There were no trees old enough or big enough nearby for shade. The table was then laden with a fare of river cod and potatoes, cooked on the open fire, pumpkin and carrot and onion, boiled eggs, and Eleanor's apricot preserve over bread baked that morning.

'It's a pleasure, Mr Campbell.' She smiled at him. Smiled at everyone.

In fact, Ard thought that she'd never stop smiling.

James sat beside CeeCee. He held her hand and guided a cup of water to her mouth. 'Mr Campbell has something to present for us,' he began. 'Actually, for Linley and Toby.'

Linley was beside Ard, and Toby sat on her knee. Lorc had carved him a toy tree, and it became a favourite to be thrown on the ground for any nearby adult to retrieve.

Eleanor had been busy sewing little trousers and shirts for him.

'Please go ahead, Mr Campbell,' James said.

The lawyer withdrew a slim packet of papers from his coat that hung on his chair. Such was the temperature of the day. It was far too hot to wear full coat and waistcoat for an outdoor picnic-style lunch.

'As you know, Mary Bonner—as she was to all of us—was bequeathed a sum of money from her aunt, Edith Bending.' He opened the packet and took out a large paper, folded in three. 'And as we all know, she never lived to receive it.'

Numerous pairs of feet shuffled, and Ard sat back in his seat.

'It was believed at one point, by someone who shall remain nameless, that it was a sum of two hundred pounds.' He glanced at everyone over his spectacles.

Sam's eyes widened. Lorc nodded appreciatively.

'I have to say that person was very wrong.' Mr Campbell opened the paper.

No one made a sound. Ard frowned, puzzled, because Mr Campbell was smiling benignly at them all.

'Also,' he went on, 'as someone else had the great foresight to register young Toby with both his correct mother's name *and* correct father's name, my job was made much easier in the long run. As things transpired, it didn't make much difference to the outcome.' Mr Campbell looked first at Linley beside him and nodded, then looked at Ard, to whom he smiled.

Ard felt a lump in his throat. Things could have gone a lot worse than they did. He glanced at his little lad, who sucked on the piece of tree. He only got a fleeting glance from his son, but the grey eyes twinkled. Ard's breath whooshed out.

'So without going over all that old and sad history, it is my great pleasure to hand Miss Linley Toby's inheritance from his mother, via of course, her maternal aunt Edith, to be held in trust for use in his safe upbringing.' Mr Campbell stood and held a banker's cheque out to Linley.

She shifted Toby to Ard. As she stood up and took the cheque, she read the amount. Colour flared in her cheeks. 'Two thousand pounds,' she announced breathlessly.

'There are of course, a number of papers to sign ...'

Mr Campbell's words were lost in the uproar over the huge amount of money the baby boy, who chewed on his wooden tree, would inherit.

Stunned, Ard stood for all the congratulations and the slaps on the back and the kisses on cheeks. Toby waved his slimy tree at everyone.

The amount of money was enormous. Ard turned to Linley. She smiled up at him. He didn't return her smile. She frowned a little, took Toby from him and jiggled him on her hip over to Eleanor. His grandmother happily distracted Toby from his piece of timber with some mashed fruit.

Ard stepped off the verandah with an excuse to get more cool drink from the kitchen. His chest was tight. He found the lemonade jug, wrapped his hands around it. He barely heard the revelry behind him outside. His head fell forward.

Two thousand pounds. He never imagined ...

'Ard.' Linley had followed him inside. 'I can tell you are not thrilled by Toby's news, but I don't know why.'

He turned to her. Her reddy-copper hair, swept up in a soft wavy pile atop her head, looked darker somehow. Those green eyes looked perplexed, and something else ... Was that a nervousness? Was she readying herself to tell him the thing he feared most? She had a large folded paper crushed in one hand. He could see her breathing quicken.

She'd dropped her chin to look at her hands. The rumpled paper crackled. 'I was going—'

'You don't have to say no.' He glared at her, thumped the lemonade jug back on the stool under the window. 'I wanted to marry you. I still want that. But now, all I ask,' he said, and he gritted his teeth, 'is that you allow me to see my son. Allow me to have him spend time here, with me.' His voice rose as his hands came up in a surrender. 'I make no claim on it. None. I don't want the money. I never wanted any of the money.'

He watched the colour rise in her cheeks. 'You *can't* make a claim on it,' she asserted.

It boiled his blood. As if he was an idiot who couldn't understand what was said to him.

'Because the—' she began.

He held up a hand. 'Oh, I understand, now. It was never going to be marriage for us, was it? Because of what happened with Mary, and now this two thousand pounds.'

She shook her head, her mouth trying to form words.

He carried on. 'Just promise me this one thing. That I *will* be able to see my son.' Oh yes, he could see the dawning on her features. She knew he'd worked out what was happening.

'Ard.' She clamped her hands on her hips.

'Promise me!' His heartbeat pounded at his temples, his frown so deep it hurt.

Her cheeks reddened, then paled, as if she'd lost all blood to her face, and all in a few moments. Then those usually cool eyes snapped into a fierce glare, and those soft warm, full lips firmed into a line. He couldn't work out what her facial expressions meant at first.

Then he took a big step back.

She slapped her hands down on her dress then stabbed a forefinger at him. 'You, Ard O'Rourke, are likely to remain a dolt forever because *stupid* can't be cured.'

She flung the crushed paper at him, turned on her heels and marched down the short hallway. He glared after her. She stepped out of house, still marching, and sailed past James coming in.

Ard jolted out of the white mist swirling around his head.

James looked at him, eyes wide. He held up his hands. 'All I heard was something like "stupid can't be cured". Then a copper-haired bolt of lightning shot past me.'

Ard stared at James then back at the paper he'd caught on his chest, still crushed in his hand. He let out a long breath. 'With money like this for Toby,' he said, shaking the paper, 'no woman in her right mind would marry and have to hand it over.'

James snorted. 'One thing about these Seymour women you need to know.' He held up a finger. 'They know the law where it pertains to their rights. So even if that money wasn't in trust for Toby's upbringing, even if it was meant for Linley herself, you wouldn't be able to touch it unless she wanted you to.'

Ard frowned. 'What?'

'Marriage no longer means you get to own all her possessions once you're wed.'

Ard straightened up. 'Is this new?'

'No, it's not. A few years old now.' James folded his arms. 'I'll offer some advice to you about that money for Toby. Unsolicited advice, I know,' he went on. He leaned in the doorway of the kitchen. 'If I were you and Linley, I'd get married, cash that cheque and put it into property as soon as possible.' He waved a hand around. 'Like this property, for instance, ensure the boy's future. Pay it off, if it's not already, and transfer a portion of your portion to his name.'

'*Transfer* it to his name? I don't understand.'

'In trust for him for when he's of age. The law hasn't changed with regard to a child born out of wedlock. He can't inherit.'

Ard's gut clenched.

'And do it quickly,' James added. 'With a depression on its way, you might not be able to realise the cash in the very near future.' He looked over his shoulder back out the door. 'I'd tell Linley that myself but it seems she hurried off somewhere.'

Ard rubbed his forehead, felt the tingle over the scar on his scalp. 'Christ almighty.'

James pushed himself off the doorjamb. 'So, can stupid be cured?'

Ard hung his head, then flicked a glance at James. 'I doubt she'll marry me now. I may as well have accused her of money-grubbing.'

'Linley's forgiven you for worse.' James gave a wry smile.

Ard felt bleak. 'I don't think she's forgiven anything.'

'Think again, and have a look at that.' James pointed to the paper in Ard's hand.

Shaking his head, Ard held it out to James. 'Take it. I know what it says. I don't need to look at it.'

James laughed. 'Mr Campbell still has that paper. This paper is a different one. Look at it.' He pointed again. 'I'll see you outside.'

Ard opened his fist, smoothed the crumpled paper. It was the marriage declaration. And Linley had filled it in. All except for the date.

His heart banged and thudded. *What an idiot!*

He loped outside but couldn't see her. He spun around and caught his father's eye. 'Linley?' he asked, and swivelled, searching. His father shook his head, palms up, and went back to his conversation with Mr Campbell.

Ard ran across to Eleanor, who still jigged and danced with Toby on her hip. 'Ma, you seen Linley?'

'No, lad.' His mother barely lifted her glance from Toby.

Ard planted a quick kiss on his son's head and ran back to the verandah where James and CeeCee had their heads together. CeeCee was smiling and nodding, her hands resting in his.

James looked up as Ard approached. 'If you're looking for our lightning, she went around the back way, with Sam.' He pointed back to Ard's cottage.

Ard sprinted. He was through the front entrance, down the hallway and out the back before he saw either of them. He pulled up sharply.

There was Sam, hands on hips, looking at the roof. 'Really good job on the roof,' he was saying.

Linley was looking blankly at the roof. She finally turned her attention to Ard. Her foot began to tap.

He waved the paper at her. It shook in his fist. 'I need a date.'

Sixty

Linley narrowed her gaze at Ard as he shook the crumpled paper.

Sam stopped admiring the roof, and scratched his head. 'A date?' he asked Ard. 'Well, any time you want. Only needs the furniture moved in now, so it's ready to occupy.' He turned to the outhouse behind him. 'That thing's all ready to go, too.'

Ard still held the paper. 'Linley?' He shook it at her.

In the silence Sam glanced from one to the other. 'Right. I'll just go check on my horses.' He tipped his head at Linley and nudged Ard as he passed him.

Linley felt her nostrils pinch. 'Have you stopped feeling quite so ... stupid?'

He nodded once. 'Yes.'

'I'm sure it won't be the last time.'

'Probably not.' He looked at the paper in his hand. 'I thought you'd want to live your own life, now you have that amount of money.'

'I will be living my own life, Ard O'Rourke. And it's not my money.' She walked to him. 'It's your son's money.'

He nodded, looking resigned, accepting. 'Linley, I've done enough stupid things in my life to date. I want to do the one clever thing I could ever do, and that is to ask you, again, to marry me. To have you marry me. Make us a family.' He shook the paper again. 'You came this far. Put a date here.'

She spread her hands. '*I* can't.' She watched as his fight came up, as his mouth tightened into a flat line. The blaze in those black eyes flared, and frustration and despair crowded in at the same time. She shook her head. 'That's the job for the pastor or the registrar to do,' she said, and exasperation tinged her voice. 'Once *we* decide to finally get the job done, Ard.'

She looped her arm through his and tugged against his hesitancy. 'And as much as Sam's explanation about his roof was riveting—and I'm so glad there *is* a roof—for heaven's sake, I'm much more interested to see the inside of my house.' She smiled.

He gaped at her and for a moment it seemed speech wouldn't come to him. Then he grabbed her, kissed her, hugged her, and kissed her again.

'We need to be married quite soon, I think,' she whispered, her breath in his ear as his warm hard body pressed against hers.

'Very soon.' He let her go. 'But first, let me show you what I have for you.'

Arm in arm, he took her to where he'd built a garden bed, ready for anything she wished to have planted there. They passed the orchard taking shape, admired the vegetable patch that was already green-tipped with rows of seedlings pushing up through the topsoil.

Linley smiled at Ard smiling at her. The dimple in his cheek had deepened, the furrow between his brows had gone, and suddenly he dipped, and his generous mouth brushed softly on hers again.

They ambled their way down to the landing. At the river, the scent of eucalyptus and dusty baked earth wafted across the water. The only sounds they heard were the musical warbles of magpies and the faint rustle of a breeze high up in the red gum leaves.

'We will sit here and picnic often, Linley, with our family.' His big hand squeezed hers. 'I'll teach our children to swim.'

Her heart swelled. This was the Ard she had waited for. This was her Ard O'Rourke, all hers. Hers, and Toby's of course. And if they were lucky, the other children he spoke of. Oh, how she loved the promise of this future with him.

For fear her emotion would give way to uncontrollable weeping, she leaned on him, her head on his shoulder. Instead of jagged sobs, she felt her eyes glisten and her smile widen.

They wandered back to the house, through the refurbished cottage, the cool air inside a welcome relief from the afternoon's heat. Ard told her in which room he thought they should sleep, where Toby's room would be for the moment, and where the other children, still to come, would reside. Linley felt a red hot blush tinge her cheeks again, but in happy anticipation.

He'd build a fine table for the family out of a massive gum he'd fell. 'I know just the one,' he said, pointing through the window and across the yard back to the river.

'An O'Rourke tradition?' she asked.

'Nothing like a big family table.'

They wandered along the hallway. Linley's hand trailed the timbers of the walls, still smelling raw, waiting for more treatment. Out the front and onto the new verandah. The vista before her was the very earth on which she would build a new life with Ard. 'This is wonderful, Ard. Toby will so love his life here. And I will, too.' She looked across at the small forge hut. 'What are those timbers for?'

'They're posts to hold up the grape vines.' He pointed in an arc. 'And there is where we'll build the stables, and the other buildings we'll need for a fledgling horse stud.'

'Such a big task ahead, Ard.'

'A lifetime's worth.'

They waved to the others at his parents' cottage. Eleanor held Toby up and waved him bodily at them.

'I have something else to show you,' Ard said and took her hand to tug her back into the hallway. 'The kitchen.'

Linley slowed up. Time to confess her shortcoming. At least, one of many. 'Ard, I'm not very good in the kitchen. CeeCee and I just plodded along. I hope you have no grand expectations ...'

'Not the kitchen itself, but this space over here.'

Linley followed his pointing finger to a nook with a window. And under the sill was a smooth wide plank of timber, beautifully grained and deep red in colour. It fitted the nook wall to wall then turned on the adjoining wall, held up by solid L-shaped brackets underneath. It was a benchtop. Under the bench was a fine-looking chair, simple and practical, a cushion in plain calico on the seat.

'The plank is temporary until I can build something more permanent.' Ard had his hands on her shoulders and guided her closer to the spot. 'It's specially for when you're writing your letters.' He opened the shuttered window. 'Cool in the summer. Close to the stove in the winter.'

She stared at it, unable to speak for the moment, a tightness in her throat. She bit her lip. A space just for her, built into this house ... Their home.

When you can't resist him ...

'A fine inclusion,' she managed. Her own space from which to carry on with her work, the work CeeCee had to relinquish. Tears threatened again, but she was already thinking that the ink-well would sit *there*, and how a tiny chest of drawers would fit under there.

Ard seemed hesitant again. 'I don't know what else you'd do at it, but I know you need a quiet space, and a bit of room. I understand there's lots of letters, and things to organise.' His voice trailed off.

He had no clue, she knew, but he'd done it for her. She turned to look at him. 'Ard,' she said softly.

He forged on. 'James said CeeCee always had a lot of letter-writing to do. A lot of planning and … things.'

'James was always very involved.' Linley tilted her head a little.

Ard looked at his hands. 'I'll do whatever I can do. As well as keep this place going, I'll do whatever you need help with.' He closed his hands to fists, and opened them again. 'But I need to get this place up and running for us, with the others, keep it all going so the family survives.'

His ideals, his honour …

She nodded. 'The orchard, the vineyard, the horse stud.'

He stepped closer. 'I'll learn your work, too. We'll be able to do it from here. You could still manage the houses in town for James and CeeCee.' He looked up, his black eyes depthless, tense. 'We could even go to Melbourne on occasion, if we had to.'

She flattened her hands on his chest. 'In that case, it sounds like we'll be very busy.'

'Very busy.' He bent and touched his lips to hers, her face framed in his hands.

Her heart seemed to miss a beat. Here he was, this man she had loved all her life, offering to share his life, to give her children, to care for her needs. To support her work.

When you go there of your own free will …

Linley broke away and turned back to the nook. Her finger glided along the timber bench, the glossy smooth finish polished with great care. 'I love this plank, Ard. Don't change it. I want to write many letters here, and do great things.'

She traced her hands over the back of the chair. Her gaze fell on the cushion, noticed its meticulous, decorative stitches, and she knew that Eleanor must have been aware of Ard's intention.

A little sound escaped her. If hope and joy could be a sound, it was that tiny lyrical note that bubbled up. She spun around to him. 'Ard. It's perfect. It's all perfect.'

… there is no point of return.

She heard his laugh, his relief, his happiness. Felt his solid warmth, and his strong arms wrap around her.

Acknowledgements

What a year it's been. Once again, my heartfelt gratitude to:

My readers. You've made this journey a wonderful thing.

Susi Parslow. Your ongoing staunch support and encouragement keeps me on the right track. Your red pen is invaluable, though I did notice your book-boyfriend Ard was hardly ever red penned.

Amy Andrews of WordWitchery.com.au, whose eye for right and wrong in a storyline is infallible.

Melody Berden. Your love of all things 19th-century Australian means we time travel constantly, and for hours and hours—researching, of course.

Trove. What would we do without Trove?

The Swan Hill Genealogical & Historical Society, the Swan Hill Pioneer Settlement, the Echuca Historical Society, and the Echuca Discovery Centre.

The Swan Hill Library and the Kerang Library for your warm reception.

Those members of the Romance Writers of Australia who have shown great comradeship.

My home community on Kangaroo Island—all those who supported me unconditionally, along with the booksellers and the library.

My friends who bear with a writing hermit for most of the year and still ask me to dinner.

My Harlequin Mira team, for great patience and guidance—Jo Mackay, Laurie Ormond, editors Dianne Blacklock and Kate James. To the book's cover designer, Michelle Zaiter, who found the perfect Linley.

Cristina Lee for her input on the titles for both *Daughter of the Murray* and *Where The Murray River Runs*.

Hamish the Wonder-dog, for ensuring he walks me every day.

Not least, my sister and my brother and their families. It's been a year of firsts without Mum, and she would be proud.

The mighty River Murray whose many stories are yet to be told.

Turn over for a sneak peek.

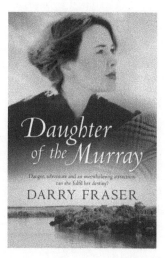

Daughter
of the Murray

by

DARRY FRASER

OUT NOW

One

1890—*River Murray, Victoria*

There was no escaping this day, no matter what she did.

A vibrant sun dawned over Mallee country and the bedroom lit up. 'For goodness' sake, Ruth. Keep the curtains shut.' Georgie buried her face under the threadbare bedsheet.

'Now, come along, Miss Georgie. You love the early morning.' Plump Ruth bustled about. She drew back the other heavy curtain one-handed before she thumped a breakfast plate of bread and jam on the dresser beside Georgie's bed.

Eucalyptus scented the shimmering heat and it drifted to Georgie even under the bedclothes. 'If you're going to tell me one more time that Mr Dane is coming home today, so help me, I'll—'

'You know Mr Dane comes home today.'

'I know it, Ruth. You've told me a dozen times.' Georgie pushed the sheet away. 'I can't stand the man and yet I've never met him. All I ever hear is Mr Dane this, Mr Dane that. Mr Dane, so handsome. Mr Dane—' She sat up, yawned and flexed her back, flinging her arms above her head. Her fingers splayed then she relaxed bonelessly onto the pillow with a long exhale. She'd heard it all before. 'The poor man has no clue he's coming home to this.'

'Oh, he's not a poor man, miss. He's a rich young gentleman now. And I remember him well when we was in the schoolyard; I was only a year younger. He was fine to look at an' all, even back in them days.'

Georgie pulled a face. 'If he looks anything like his father, I certainly can't imagine you'd call him fine to look at.'

Ruth cast her a quick glance and swiped a hand over her untidy mousey brown hair. 'No, miss. He *doesn't* look like Mr Tom—'

A screech outside the room interrupted her: Elspeth wanting her hairbrush.

'Oh God. My cousin intends to wake the dead this morning.' Georgie swung her legs to the floor.

'Miss Georgina, blaspheming. And where's your nightdress?' Ruth fussed about the bed like some hen pecking at corn kernels. Her backside wobbled under her dress as she bent to rummage through a pile of linen under the wash-stand.

'It's too hot for a nightdress, Ruth.'

'Hardly, and you shouldn't sleep like it.' Ruth found the discarded nightdress on the floor and held it out.

Georgie tugged the worn shift from her and wriggled into it. She padded barefoot to sit on the stool in front of a plain timber table with a small mirror on it. A fresh bowl of hot water and a hard scrap of soap waited for her. 'And why are you here, anyway? God knows we can't pay you.' Georgie rubbed her face with bare hands. 'Bloody depression coming, says Uncle Tom.'

'You shouldn't speak of that either, Miss Georgie. Mr Tom will pay—'

'Don't talk foolishly, Ruth. The whole district knows he'll drink it away before any bloody depression gets here.'

'The devil will come get you with talk like that, that's a fact.' Ruth huffed and puffed as she blew hair out of her eyes. 'And what if Miss Jem was to hear you say that?'

'The devil is welcome,' Georgie said and Ruth crossed herself. 'And my Aunt Jemimah won't hear of it. All she cares about is her son coming home.'

'He is your cousin, Miss Georgie, he's family and—'

'He's not my family, Ruth. He's my *step*-cousin.' Georgie pulled her hair back from her face. 'Now, would you please do my hair for me?' Her thick dark hair was only ever plaited, and that was how she preferred it. 'You do it so well.'

'Miss, I'm not to dilly-dally here. With Mr Dane coming, Miss Jem and Miss Elspeth want their hair attended to, and yours being so simple you can do it yourself, they said that I—'

'Bloody Mr Dane has been coming for nigh on the four years I've been here and I haven't seen hide nor hair of him yet. What makes today so bloody different?'

'Oh, and gutter talk. The devil *will* come, missy, right here, to the good Queen's colony of Victoria. You make no mistake.' Ruth shook her forefinger and bustled out.

Georgie smiled into the mirror. *The devil will come ... To our River Murray landing, no less. What rubbish. I'm sure the devil has better work to do.* Some said God had forgotten the Australian colonies years ago, the devil even earlier. She dragged the brush through her hair in long strokes, bringing back the gleam after its tousling on the pillow.

Bloody Mr Dane will get a shock when he arrives.

From the furtive whispers and heated arguments in the dead of night when no one thought she could hear, Georgie would wager bloody Mr Dane, the mighty son and heir, knew little of what had befallen Jacaranda since he'd been gone.

Even Georgie's stepfather, her Papa Rupert in England, hadn't believed her. She'd confided her suspicions by letter but he'd not answered them. To the contrary, he'd chided her for her lack of charity, implied her imagination was still quite rich and that she should try to be more tolerant of the family's ways.

There'd been nothing but silence from England since, and that had been well over a year ago.

She was nearing twenty-two ... so old and unmarried *still*. And with no prospects of a good life ahead of her if she remained with the MacHenrys, she reasoned it was her right to fend for herself. When Uncle Tom slurred and slurped his way into rum-addled unconsciousness, she'd ease a few coins from his pockets and secrete them away to a cache under a floorboard in her room. She hadn't scraped together nearly enough to pursue her chance at life, though.

If only Uncle Tom had taken her up on her offer to handle the books for him. At least that would be something she could do. She was good at sums; she preferred them to needle work and cooking. But he remained adamant to the point of belligerence that she would not attempt such a thing, 'being a woman and all'. Tom's books were under lock and key. A key he never left around.

However, there was Conor Foley. Her Conor Foley.

She smiled as she thought of him. Only three weeks ago, his riverboat, the *Lady Mitchell*, had docked at the landing on the MacHenrys' property to deliver the goods Jemimah had ordered from the city. Conor brought the much anticipated newspapers from Swan Hill that Georgie read line by line, hungry for the world outside.

Conor Foley.

His soft Irish brogue, the gleam in his eyes, the deep auburn hair, the broad shoulders. A man who towered over most men, weighty and solid. He was much older than the tiresome boys of the neighbouring homesteads, well past his thirties; he had been to war in South Africa.

Conor Foley offered her a new life with just a glance of mystery and intrigue.

Ruth burst back into the room. She grabbed the hairbrush in Georgie's hand, apologising as she did so.

'What are you doing?' Georgie held fast to the brush.

'Please, Miss Georgina. There's such a commotion today. Miss Elspeth's misplaced her brush. Please let me have the brush. What with Mr Dane returning … He's been away far too long, wouldn't you say?' Ruth had her firm grip over Georgie's hand on the brush.

Georgie wrenched the hairbrush free. 'Since I have never met him,' she said sternly, 'his absence has hardly bothered me. But his homecoming is sorely testing my very good manners.' She thrust the brush into Ruth's hand, sending the woman back a pace or two.

Clutching the brush to her chest, Ruth disappeared as loudly as she had arrived, muttering something that sounded distinctly like 'Good manners, my arse. You'll get yours, my girl.'

Georgie sighed long and hard, then set about plaiting her hair.

Impatient with having to be modest, especially now she was alone, she hoisted the nightgown off. Once naked again, she washed in a hurry, and dried with the threadbare towel. The drought meant deep, long baths were rare, so a quick but thorough wash with a flannel and basin had to do.

She stood in front of her wardrobe, an open box built of river gum. It contained hand-me-downs from neighbouring ladies. Georgie hadn't received new clothes for years, even though she had requested some in her last two letters to England. She'd grown out of the last set of clothes her stepfather had sent from England and they'd been altered long ago for the much smaller Elspeth.

Hands on hips, Georgie stared at the four dresses. A bleached day dress, one light blue dress, one dark blue and a faded pink one. None of them suited her today. No, today was a good day for a long ride along the banks of her beloved river. She needed to escape the madness of today.

She knelt by her bed, flipped up the thin, lumpy mattress and dragged out a pair of men's trousers, an old shirt and a checked piece of cloth. She took the cloth, a piece of wide fabric torn from an old bed sheet destined for the horses for rubdowns, and wound it around her chest to flatten her breasts. The shirt went on over the top, the trousers pulled up over bare legs and arse, drawn around her waist by a slim leather rope she had borrowed from the tack room. She faced the little mirror again, coiled her long, black plait atop her head and stabbed some pins into it to hold it there.

Then she reached for her flat-heeled riding boots, the only thing she had left from England. They were the colour of burnt caramel, laced to mid-calf, the leather supple and soft after years of loving care. She pulled them on, tied each lace firmly, let the pants drape over them and stood tall.

She grabbed the thick slice of bread left by Ruth, shoved it into a small calico bag then picked up a hat lying under her bed. She sidled out the door to the veranda. A quick look to the left, then the right, and she marched across the dusty yard to the stables. Nobody would be bothering her this morning, all too busy awaiting his lordship's arrival.

Joe, the stocky, barrel-chested contract stableman, and Watti, an Aboriginal man with a shock of wiry grey hair, were in the stall with the black stallion, MacNamara. Joe crooned as he swept the brush powerfully over the horse's flank and back. The horse swung his head to stare at Georgie, but waited patiently as his groomsman prepared him for the day. Watti polished the big saddle as it hung over the rail.

Georgie leaned on the stable doorway. She watched Joe as he whispered in MacNamara's ear, rubbed his nose and plied him with soft Irish compliments, the lilting murmur music to her ears. Joe ran his hands over a glossy flank, down to a fetlock and back, and the horse stood nodding his proud head. Joe would camp in the stalls on the days he spent at Jacaranda, for MacNamara was a prized possession, and Tom MacHenry dared not neglect him.

MacNamara stood sixteen hands. Georgie could just see over his withers. He was eight years old now, past the silly stage, and he had responded well to her training. She'd fed him and groomed him as a younger horse, cleaned and oiled his saddle, looked after his teeth and, when he got too big for her to look after his hooves, Joe had been called in to keep the horse in top condition. She loved the horse. Joe knew it, the horse knew it.

Joe was also the one who made sure Dane MacHenry himself would foot the bill for MacNamara's upkeep, and for the other two horses: Douglas, a gentle roan, and Brandy, a chestnut. Left to Tom, the horses wouldn't survive. Georgie knew that well enough.

She pushed off the doorway and walked into Joe's line of sight, reaching up to scratch MacNamara's forelock. 'Morning, Joe. Morning, Watti.'

Watti mumbled something as he nodded, his dusty black face sombre, eyes averted.

Joe lifted his chin at her. 'Morning, Miss Georgina. In your ridin' clobber today, I see.'

'I thought to take myself away from all the gormless softheads for a while.'

Joe snorted a laugh.

'Is Mac ready?' Her hands ran down the horse's neck and slid across the muscled chest. How she loved that sleek, hard body and its power. Mac was a dream to ride, obedient to her lightest command. They would tear through the paddocks together, whatever the weather, and end up exhausted and exhilarated.

'Mr Dane's coming home and Mr Tom wants the horse ready for him. Sorry, miss. Not MacNamara today.' Joe kept his gaze on the horse. 'Mr Dane comes straight to the stables when he comes home. Wouldn't be too good if Mac were gone with you.'

'That would be your opinion, Joseph O'Grady.'

Joe inclined his head. 'It would be that.'

Georgie inhaled with a low hiss. That blasted Dane MacHenry again. 'Comes straight to the stables, does he? Since when, in the last four years?'

Joe studied her. 'Believe me, Miss Georgie, it wouldn't be worth the trouble.' He returned to his brush work. 'Besides, miss, I doubt you'd want to see Mrs Jemimah out of sorts over it.'

Georgie shot a glance at Joe. 'No, of course I wouldn't. I know Aunt Jem is looking forward to his return.' She tapped her foot. 'Then it looks like I'll have to take Brandy.'

Joe dipped his head and kicked the dirt with his boot. 'Miss Elspeth wants to ride Brandy today.' Georgie lovingly looked after Brandy, Elspeth's mount, too.

Georgie's eyes widened. 'Elspeth? How extraordinary. That poor horse.' She paused. 'Do you think the donkey would be available, Joe, or is he also engaged to ride with the rest of his kin?'

'If we had a donkey.' Joe gave her a smile. 'Douglas here is rarin' for a good run, miss. He's in good form and no one to ride him. Take Douglas. He's a good boy.' Joe tethered MacNamara and unlatched the next stall door. He stepped inside and ran his hand over the muzzle of the roan. 'He's a good boy,' he repeated to the horse.

'He is at that.' She loved Douglas too, he just wasn't MacNamara. But her mood lifted. 'All right. I'll saddle him up, but not with one of those stupid women's things.'

Joe threw a blanket over Douglas's back. He knew better than to assist further, so he watched Georgie heft the saddle onto Douglas. As she tightened the girth, she muttered.

He cupped a hand to his ear. 'What's that? Did I miss some of your colourful language?'

She stepped into the stirrup and threw herself astride the horse, then beamed at him. 'I said, let the blasted devil come for his horse. But not a word of that to anyone, Joseph O'Grady.'

''Pon my Celtic soul, as usual, miss.'

She gee-upped Douglas into the yard, stooped gracefully to unlatch the gate and swung it open. Joe would latch it behind her.